BLACK DAWN

Black Dawn

CHRISTOPHER NICOLE

ST. MARTIN'S PRESS   NEW YORK

Library of Congress Cataloging in Publication Data

Nicole, Christopher.
    Black dawn.

    I. Title.
PZ4.N6425Bk3   [PR9320.9.N5]   813   77-76648
ISBN 0-312-08307-6

Contents

THE HILTON FAMILY

Tegramond (d. 1625)

(*) Yarico (1609-1702)

Thomas (Indian Warner) (1626-1685)

Thomas Warner (1577-1649) = (1) Sarah (d. 1603) = (2) Rebecca Payne (1592-1626) = (3) Anne (1606-1660)

Sarah (1619-1632)

Anthony Hilton (1600-1657) = Susan Deardon (1606-1668) = (*) Edward (1609-1663) = Aline Galante (1613-1670)

Philip (1614-1689)

= (*) name unknown = (2) Celestine

MAIN WARNER LINE

Edward (father uncertain) (1631-1657)

Joachim   Joan

Lillan Christianssen (2) = Christopher (Kit) (1651-1722) = (1)(2) Marguerite (Meg) (1652-1690) = (1) Harry Templeton (d. 1672)
(1659-1727)

Rebecca (1680-1782)

Carl (1692-1746)

Anthony (1675-1737)

Thomas (1703-1760) = (1) Joanna (d. 1753) = (2) Penelope (1744-1762)

Edward (Ned) (1732-1777)

ROBERT (1740-1810)

Georgiana (1761-1792) = Louis Corbeau (1751-1792)

Francis (1787-1792)   Oriole (1789-1792)   Louis (1792)

MATTHEW (MATT) (b. 1760) = (2) SUZANNE (SUE) (b. 1759) = (1) Dirk Huys (1741-1803)

RICHARD (b. 1785) = CARTARETTE D'ESTAING (b. 1800)

ELLEN TAGGART = ANTHONY (1783-1831)
(b. 1793)

RICHARD (b. 1822)   ANNE (b. 1824)   THOMAS (b. 1826)

=(1) First Marriage
=(2) Second Marriage
=(*) No Legal Marriage
Italics—Appeared in previous novels
Capitals—Appear in BLACK DAWN

1

Prelude to Disaster

A roll of drums reverberated across the still of the afternoon. It rumbled up the hillside behind Charleston, climbing the single great mountain that dominates the island of Nevis; it seeped across the calm Caribbean Sea, perhaps heard in neighbouring St Kitts; it shrouded the weatherbeaten houses of Charleston itself, sending a rotting wooden shutter banging, seeming to accentuate the peeling paint, the crumbling shingles of the sloping roofs. If the Americans' successful war for their independence had left all of the West Indies in straitened circumstances, nowhere was poverty quite so evident as in the smaller islands, and nowhere in the smaller islands so much as in tiny Nevis.

And the drum roll stirred the crowd. It was a recent crowd, gathered by the waterfront. Its members had come here, panting, swinging bottles of rum, in haste from inside the courthouse, if privileged; from the street outside, if black and therefore unprivileged. They had been hot, and sweaty, and excited. In the past hour their enthusiasm had somewhat cooled along with their skins. But now it was awakened again, by the rolling of the drums.

It was a decrepit crowd, in keeping with its decrepit surroundings. The white people, men and women, who formed the first ranks, were sallow and emaciated; their linen was soiled, their hair lank. They shaded their heads beneath wide and tattered straw hats, indulged in no frills such as stockings or cravats; the setting sun silhouetted the legs of their women through the thin muslin gowns and chemises which were all any of them wore.

The black people formed a much vaster gathering, behind and to either side of the whites, and revealed a proportionate poverty; not one possessed more than a single garment, a pair of drawers for the men, a shift for the women, and none wore shoes. Their bodies were half-starved, bones seeming more prominent than muscles, faces hardly more than skulls. And like the whites they gazed, in almost silent wonder, at the gallows standing immediately before the worm-eaten wooden dock which thrust its ancient timbers into the pale green of the sea. They could not believe they were witnessing this scene. They knew, indeed, that they would *not* be witnessing this scene, but for the line of red-coated marines which stood between the crowd and the dock, but for the frigate which rode to anchor beyond, her guns trained on the town. And but, too, for the sloop which also lay at anchor, close to the frigate.

'Hiltons,' muttered one of the white men.

'Nigger lovers,' said a woman.

'Scum,' said another.

'Traitors,' shouted another.

Heads turned to look along the street at the balcony of Government House, only slightly less decrepit than the buildings which surrounded it, above which the Union Jack floated lazily in the gentle breeze. But the crowd's enmity was directed against the three men who had appeared on the balcony. It was composed of jealousy, certainly; each of the three was well dressed, if scarcely more elegantly than anyone else, with open coats, and an absence of vests or cravats—but there was no emaciation in *their* faces. And it was composed of fear, equally certainly; Hugh Elliott was Governor of all the Leewards, and he had declared a state of emergency this day, which gave him power of life and death over everyone present. But even the Governor had no such power, no such ability to reach out and seize what he wanted, and tear it down or build it up, as the two men who stood, one on each side of him. Obviously they were related; they possessed the high forehead, the thrusting chin, the grey eyes and the surprisingly small, exquisitely shaped nose which dominated the big features surrounding it. Only in size were they clearly differentiated: Robert Hilton was of average height and heavily built in shoulder and thigh—he was some years the elder. His cousin Matthew was tall and slim. But their appearances counted for nothing. It was the name which mattered, the history which illuminated the Hilton family like a beacon, the wealth which surrounded it like a suit of armour. And the power created by that wealth, a power

2

which could bring about a scene such as this.

For the drum roll was again increasing its tempo, and from the courthouse there now marched another squad of marines, muskets at the slope, confident in the protection afforded them by their fellows. In their midst walked two men. The priest read from his Bible, finger tracing the lines; his voice was low, intended to be heard only by his companion. But James Hodge was not listening. He turned his head from side to side, seeking his compatriots, seeking his enemies, looking up at the balcony as he passed beneath. Perhaps he too would have shaken his fist had his hands been free.

A sigh rose from the watching whites, while the very last sound ceased from the Negroes. One or two of the older men and women amongst them had actually seen a white man hang; but he had been a pirate. James Hodge was a planter, and his crime was neither piracy nor treason.

The procession reached the foot of the scaffold, and halted. The drum roll faded, and the afternoon was for a moment utterly quiet. Hodge's shoes could be heard on the wooden steps as he climbed them, assisted by the priest. And now the hangman and the bailiff also appeared on the platform; hitherto they had sheltered behind the soldiers.

The boards creaked as Hodge turned to face the crowd. Slowly he filled his lungs with air. 'Scum,' he bawled, his face red. 'You stand there, while I hang. But when I drop, you all drop with me. You . . .'

'No speechifying, Mr Hodge,' said the bailiff, and held his arm.

'Scum,' Hodge bawled again. 'Filthy wretches. Lousy . . .'

The words gagged in his throat as the hangman dropped the noose over his head and tightened the knot. The bailiff nodded, and stepped back, beside the priest, who had forgotten to pray in horror at what he was watching. The drum roll started again, and the trapdoor was released. Hodge's body shot through the gap, and jerked there at the end of its rope, legs flailing for a moment to suggest that the knot had not been accurately placed.

A great moan arose from the slaves; but it was of amazement rather than pity, and it was immediately overtaken by the shriek of anger from the whites as they surged forward, were met by the bayonets of the marines, and turned to vent their rage on Government House.

3

But the balcony was empty. The watchers had returned inside.

'It's done, then.' Hugh Elliott poured three glasses of wine. 'You must be a proud man, Matt.'

'Aye.' Matt Hilton looked into his glass for some seconds before he drank. 'If I knew what I *had* done.'

'Doubts?'

'And well he should have doubts,' Robert Hilton remarked. 'Do you think any of those niggers will forget what they have just seen? Do you think the West Indies will ever forget it? If a white man can be hanged for killing a slave, then there is not a man of us does not deserve to change places with that blackguard. You know that, Hugh, as well as Matt does.'

'Yet was Hodge a bigger scoundrel in his sleep than you ever were when awake, Robert,' Elliott insisted. 'He was not hanged for murder, and you know that. He was hanged for the systematic ill-treatment of his people. If his death encourages but the slightest spark of humanity in the plantocracy, then it was well done.'

'And the woman?' Robert asked.

'She is pregnant, and cannot be executed, at least not for a long time. Thus I have not even charged her. I do not think those people would have stood for it, anyway.'

'She is more of a rascal than was her husband,' Matt said, softly.

'Oh, indeed,' Elliott agreed. 'But we'll hear no more of her. The plantation is up for sale. She'll go back to England, I have no doubt. Would you see her?'

'Not I,' Matt said. 'I saw Hodge, and that was enough.'

'I would like to see her,' Robert said.

His cousin and the Governor looked at him in surprise.

'She'll get naught for the plantation,' Robert said.

'And you feel that her well-being is your concern?' Elliott demanded.

Robert Hilton flushed, a sufficiently rare sight. 'I wish to be sure we performed justice here today, and not merely satisfied a personal vendetta.'

Elliott hesitated, glanced at Matt, and then shrugged. 'You'd best come along then.' He led them down the stairs and through a covered passageway towards the courthouse. Here the noise of the still shouting crowd was muted, and even the heat of the afternoon was dwindling amidst the cool, damp stone.

The gaoler threw open the doors, and they walked between the

4

cells, stared at by the white man imprisoned for assaulting his wife, by the two free blacks awaiting trial for smuggling, and reached the end, to gaze at the woman, short and thin and sallow-skinned, fair hair straggling in rat-tails on her shoulders, bare feet soiled with dust, white gown a mass of rents and dirty stains. She sat on her cot bed, only glanced up as the men arrived, and then scrambled to her feet and backed against the wall as she recognized them.

'I am with child,' she gasped. 'I have not been condemned.'

'Nor will you be,' the Governor said. 'Mr Hilton would speak with you.'

Robert looked through the bars. ''Tis done, Janet.'

She met his gaze; her tongue slowly came out and circled her lips. 'I heard the shouts. And you are avenged, Mr Hilton.'

Robert sighed. 'It was an act of justice, not vengeance.'

Janet Hodge crossed the floor, to stand close to him. 'You are a hypocrite, Robert Hilton, You and your Bible-thumping cousin. You wanted that little nigger girl, and when you couldn't have her, you went for Jamie. You're no better than any of us, Robert Hilton, for all your money. For all your fine clothes.'

'You'll believe what you will, Janet.' Robert hesitated, then reached into his pocket. 'You'll need money. I'll give you an order on my agent.'

Janet Hodge frowned, for just a moment. 'Money? From you? I'd not use it to wipe my arse.'

'Janet . . .'

'Hiltons! The wealthiest people in the world, they say, and the most powerful, who can have a man hanged at their whim. But also the stupidest, Master Robert. You think you have hanged my Jamie? You have hanged us all, every white man in the West Indies, aye, and their women, and their children. The Hiltons too.' She flung out her arm, finger pointed at Matt. 'He lives with your sister. There's morality. He has two little boys, too, eh? Lucky little bastards, because they'll be called Hilton. But they'll all go down, the same way Jamie did.' Her face broke into a ghastly smile, and she rubbed her belly. 'And by God, there will be a Hodge there to see it.'

The Opportunity

'Seventy-five thousand, eight hundred and seventeen pounds, twelve shillings, and eleven pence.' Richard Hilton underlined the figures with great care, using a pen dipped into red ink.

'At last,' Maurice Beden said.

Richard slipped off his stool, rubbed the somewhat shiny seat of his trousers, ran his fingers into his straight fair hair. 'Seventeen minutes past five. Not as bad as I thought.' He was a tall young man, just twenty-five years old. A West Indian would have recognized his face immediately; the long, rather large features, the grey eyes, the delicious little nose, were all too clearly those of the family which had dominated the plantocracy for a hundred years. But a West Indian would have puzzled over the absence of a brogue, just as he would have frowned at the threadbare cuffs, on both shirt and coat, at the well-worn pants and boots, at the absence of the slightest suggestion of a tan from the pale flesh. In the high vaulted office of Bridle's Bank in Lombard Street, Richard Hilton was no more than another of the score of clerks who spent their entire days shut away from the sun, however famous his forbears.

'You be off then,' Beden agreed. 'I'll lock up.'

'Will you, Maurice? Oh, splendid fellow.' Richard punched his friend on the arm, seized his tall hat from the peg, and ran for the door.

'In a hurry, Mr Hilton?' Perkins, peering over his pince-nez from behind the big desk in the accountants' room.

Richard paused, and panted. 'No, Mr Perkins.'

'But the ledger is balanced?'

'Oh, yes, Mr Perkins. And Mr Beden will lock up, whenever you are ready.'

'How good of him,' Perkins remarked drily. 'I attended your father's meeting, last night.'

Richard sighed. 'Yes, Mr Perkins?'

'The man is a fool. No offence, Mr Hilton, but slavery was ordained by God Himself. No man can go against God. And for a West Indian, why, it smacks of madness.'

'Yes, sir, Mr Perkins. Father knows he is not the most popular of men.'

'Save with the mob, Mr Hilton. Save with the mob. You tell him from me, he and his friends are trouble makers. He's not the worst. I blame Wilberforce.'

'Yes, sir, Mr Perkins. I'll tell Father. Good night, Mr Perkins. Good night.'

He closed the door behind him, stood on the stone steps, inhaled the crisp spring air. To enter the bank in the early morning was to be sealed in a vast cavern, a place of studied quiet and neatly inked figures, a place, indeed, of ink itself, and a place populated by Perkins, and all the other, more senior Perkinses, reaching up to Jonas Bridle. Young men like himself, or Maurice Beden, were merely in transit, neither free nor forever lost, in the process of being converted into suitable Perkinses. He supposed that another couple of years would do the trick, where he was concerned.

He ran down the steps, hurried along the pavement. It was late, although on a May afternoon there were still another two hours of daylight. But Ellen would not wait forever. And it was quiet; most of the traffic had already left the city, and he could hear his own heels drumming on the cobbles. And wondered why he hurried. He approached Ellen Taggart in the guise of a beggar, seeking a smile, a touch of her hand. Not Ellen's fault. She would give him much more. She offered more, continually. But a gentleman, retired from Company service in Bombay—with all that *that* suggested—and with the rank of colonel, would never consider permitting his only daughter to marry a bank clerk, even if the fellow's father was an MP. The wrong sort of MP was worse than not being one at all.

He rounded a corner, nearly stumbled into two red-coated officers, hastily apologized and hurried on. But paused at the next corner to look back. How splendid they were. How confident, no, how arrogant. With reason, no doubt. He studied the military, their manners, their morals, and their uniforms, could identify these two as members of the 16th Foot, the Bedfordshire regiment, from their badges as well as from the yellow facings to their tunics and the silver lace. The 16th were under orders to sail for Lisbon, there to join General Wellesley. No wonder they were arrogant; they were now part of the only English army ever to face the French with success.

He hurried on, his belly rumbling with excitement. Whenever he saw a uniform, his instincts screamed at him to find the nearest colour-sergeant, and surrender his liberty even more definitely; he had neither the money nor the backing to purchase a commission. But he would rise, he had no doubt at all. The Hiltons had always been men of ability, and men of action, too. His earliest remembered ancestor had been an associate of Tom Warner and his son, Edward, who had defended St Kitts against the Indians and the Spaniards, and founded the British West Indian Empire; one of his great-grandfathers had marched with Morgan on Panama; why, Father himself had fought with Rodney at the Saintes. But there was the problem. Father had found himself in the Navy by accident, as a pressed man, and his experiences, both there and elsewhere, had raised within him a seething distaste for all things military, for any possible event where blood could be shed. It was treason, in this spring of 1810, even to hint that Great Britain should not pursue the war against Napoleon, but Father suggested peace whenever it was his turn to speak in the House.

Another bend, and the trees of the Park came in sight. He could pause, to catch his breath and straighten his cravat. She would be there.

To join the army would mean a quarrel. And yet, it was not one he would avoid. But for Mama. He often wondered what she thought of it all. Certainly she supported her husband with total loyalty. But in the privacy of her bedchamber, must she not often count the cost? To live with Matt Hilton, her own cousin, she had abandoned her lawful husband and prosperity and respectability; to marry him, in defiance of her brother, had lost her the chance of inheriting the greatest plantations in the West Indies; to follow his point of view had cost her the friendship of every planter, and every planter's wife, and even forced her to watch her own sister being torn to pieces by the very slaves Matt sought to free; and to bring up her two sons she had been obliged to deprive herself of almost everything that a woman could wish from life.

Now to deprive her of one of those sons would surely be a crime. Besides, to leave Mama? There was an incredible thought. She remained the most magnificent woman he had ever seen, could ever envisage.

Saving perhaps Ellen Taggart. He paused, and took off his hat, at once to wave it and wipe his brow. Because there she was.

The gig approached at no more than a walk. On a fine afternoon the park was crowded with ladies and gentlemen strolling, ladies and gentlemen riding, ladies and gentlemen taking the air in their phaetons. And with uniformed nursemaids, wheeling their charges, gossiping and prattling. They could not have asked for a better setting. The huge trees were in leaf, the grass was brilliantly green, and the flowers were coming into bloom, dominated by the stiff rows of tulips, all yellows and reds, almost like a guard of honour drawn up for inspection. Dick Hilton supposed that nowhere more than in Hyde Park of an evening was the prosperity, the confidence, the bursting energy of this nation so amply displayed. Why, old Boney might spend his time rushing about Europe, from Madrid to Vienna to Berlin to Tilsit and thence back to Paris, defeating armies here, executing opponents there, pausing whenever he passed a Channel port to wave his fists at the sea, and the rulers of the sea; the fact was that Great Britain did rule the sea—the men Nelson had led had imbibed the master's beliefs and plans too well to fear any alteration in the strategy and the tactics which had won Trafalgar.

And behind the Navy, the trade, ballooning year after year. Even old Bridle nowadays smiled, from time to time. But he took care to see that little of his wealth filtered down to his clerks in the forms of an adequate salary.

'Why, Mr Hilton.' Aunt Julia Taggart had the long face of her family, in her case accompanied by the pop eyes and prominent teeth of her brother, as well as the somewhat braying voice. She was the only senior Taggart who had the least time for Dick, but even she allowed her gaze to sweep over his pants and coat and hat, perhaps estimating their age, before permitting herself to smile at him. He suspected she was less partial to him than to the concept of romance. 'What a pleasant surprise.'

'Miss Taggart. Ellen.'

'I had given you up,' Ellen Taggart held the reins, her gloved fingers tight on the leather. The pony waited docilely enough. The fingers, the hand, were no more than an extension of the determination in her expression. So no doubt, Dick thought, should I ever be able to marry this girl, I will be exchanging one imprisonment for another. But what a delightful gaoler she would make. She was tall, and slim, but her deep green pelisse was suitably full at both breast and thigh; her chestnut hair was almost lost beneath the pale green silk bonnet, leaving her face exposed, but on her the long oval, the straight nose, the wide-set grey eyes and no less wide mouth, the firm lips and the pointed chin, were boldly handsome. And her voice, at least when greeting him, was soft.

'I was delayed. Our business seems to double every day.'

'I suppose it is for the good of the country,' Julia Taggart agreed. 'But money . . . it is such a dirty thing. Well, Mr Hilton, it has been our pleasure. But we are already late. We must take our leave of you.'

'Oh, I . . .' Dick flushed, and glanced at Ellen, who laughed. She had an unusual laugh, surprisingly low, and somehow conspiratorial, although he had always felt that the secret which amused her was private to her alone.

'You are a tease, Auntie,' she said. 'We have at least half an hour. And look, is that not Lady Beamish, peering out from the window of her carriage like a goldfish?'

'Oh, really, Ellen. You are too disrespectful.'

'So will you be, Auntie, if you do not at least pass a moment with her. Dick, will you help Aunt Julia down?'

Dick offered his arm, and Julia Taggart descended to the turf, somewhat heavily. 'Thank you, young man. I shall not be long.' She made her way across the grass, skirts swinging, prodding the ground with her stick as if suspecting a sudden ravine.

'Wretched man,' Ellen said. 'Do you place your figures above me?'

He leaned on the step, his elbow on the door itself; this way his hand could drop inside and find her fingers. 'Do you really believe that?'

'No.' She sighed. 'But I suspect I am the most unfortunate of women, to love a man who must earn his living. And at what an occupation.' She frowned at him. 'Tony doesn't earn his living.'

10

'And sometimes barely lives,' Dick pointed out. 'Besides, he has not marriage in mind. To anyone, much less you.'

'I have never met two brothers less alike,' she agreed. 'As for your fine words, Master Dick, I wonder I still believe them.'

Clearly she was in one of her moods. From being kept waiting, no doubt.

'Can you imagine your father's comments were I to ask for your hand?'

She gave another of her secret laughs. 'Can you imagine his comments were you to climb up here beside me, whip this horse into a gallop, and not stop before Gretna?'

'He'd have the runners after me.'

'Oh, indeed he would. But as you would have me securely bedded before they caught up with us . . .'

'Ellen!'

'You are a prig and a hypocrite, Dick. Or perhaps you do not *want* to bed me?'

'Why, of course I do. I . . .' He felt his cheeks burning.

'You feel it is not a subject for discussion, until we are wed? By then I suspect it will no longer be practical, for either of us.' Her fingers tightened on his, and she leaned slightly forward. 'Listen. You know my inheritance?'

'Now, Ellen, we have discussed this . . .'

'Listen,' she said. 'I have discovered what it is going to be. Four thousand pounds. Can you believe it? Oh, that darling old grandpapa. I used to hate him when he was alive. But four thousand pounds. Mama says I can expect an income of four hundred a year. More than enough to live on.'

'Ellen,' Dick protested patiently. 'What sort of a man would I be if I agreed to live off your income?'

'Oh, bah,' she said. 'What absolute nonsense.'

'Anyway, you are seventeen. We have four years to negotiate.'

She withdrew her hand. 'And you propose to wait four years. You cannot be certain I am as patient.'

'Ellen . . .'

'Why, Mr Hilton. You'll be inside the carriage next.' Julia Taggart's tone suggested there was no worse crime conceivable. 'Lady Beamish sends her best regards, Ellen. And now we really must be getting home. You'll excuse us, I'm sure.'

Dick handed her up, trying to catch Ellen's eye. But she merely flicked the reins. 'Indeed, Auntie, it is extremely late. I cannot imagine why we linger so long. Good day to you, Mr Hilton.'

He stepped back to avoid having a wheel run over his toe, watched the gig proceeding slowly down the Row. Perhaps she would look back. But the bonnet never moved. Of course she was not seriously angry. She was punishing him for not being as enthusiastic as she wished. And was she not right? Four thousand pounds. Four hundred a year. His wage was fifty-two. On four hundred a year he could leave the bank, perhaps do something worthwhile with his life. Supposing he could decide what was worthwhile. And supposing too he could reconcile himself to being supported by his wife.

He thrust his hands into his pockets, began his walk down to Chelsea Village. And of course she was right in another direction, as well. She was now an heiress. Suitors would no doubt go flocking to her door, once this news got about. Why *should* she wait for a bank clerk? But to challenge the law, to challenge Colonel Taggart, even with Ellen behind him. Why, it was Matt and Robert Hilton all over again, with Ellen playing the part of Mama. Was he then going to admit he lacked the courage of his own father?

But things had been different, thirty years ago. Life had been less ordered, more exciting. And Father and Mother had been living in the West Indies, not in London, in sunshine rather than endless cloud. But the sun was still shining, this evening.

'There you are.'

Dick's head jerked. He had strolled down the little street of terraced houses without really being aware of it.

'Been exercising the horse, have you?' Tony Hilton lounged on the step.

'I ought to punch you on the nose for that,' Dick said.

'Ah-ah.' Tony raised his finger. 'Be sure I'd punch you back. And she does look like a horse, you have to agree. A very lovely horse, to be sure. But none the less, a horse.' He laughed as he spoke, and made it difficult to take offence. Tony laughed at everything. He seemed to regard life as a long and endless joke, perpetrated by some omnipotent force—it could hardly be God—on cowering mankind. A joke he somehow managed to turn to his own advantage. He certainly possessed no visible means of support, and yet his trousers were pressed, his jacket neat, his

12

cravat new. And his silk hat gleamed to match the gold head to his cane. His features were perhaps a little coarse, for a Hilton, although the small nose left no doubt that he *was* a Hilton, and his cheeks were flushed — there was wine on his breath.

'And are you waiting to sober up before going in?' Dick inquired.

'Indeed no. I was waiting to have a word with you.' Tony Hilton linked arms with his brother. 'I have had a disastrous day.'

'Oh, yes.'

'Not a card would turn for me, at the right time. I could not believe it. Quite incredible.'

'And so you played on. Expecting your luck to change.'

'A gentleman can do no less. I even gave a note. Trouble is, old boy, I gave a note a week ago. You wouldn't happen to have five guineas on you?'

'You must be joking.'

'I only wish I were. For God's sake, Dick, you handle thousands every day. Some of it must stick. Or should. It would, I can tell you, were I behind that desk.'

'You'd go to gaol.'

Tony gave one of his winning smiles. 'I shall, in any event, should they decide so. Ah, well, I will have to touch Mama. She usually has a penny or two to spare.' He opened the door.

Dick caught his arm. 'You are a swine. She has enough to worry about without your debts.'

Tony looked down at him. 'And you are a sanctimonious little prig. You're not even a gentleman by instinct. You're a clerk to the very backbone.' He shrugged himself free, went into the house. Dick hesitated for a moment before following. It was the second time in the space of an hour that he had been called a prig. And by the two people he held most dear in all the world, after Mama. Was it then being a prig to prefer not to worry his father and mother about money he knew they did not have, to prefer not to accept charity from Ellen when he knew it would cause an estrangement between her and her family? There was a topsy-turvy world.

He went inside, hung his hat beside Tony's, knocked and entered the little parlour, discovered his brother standing in the room, gaping at his parents. 'Dick,' he shouted. 'There is some mystery here.'

'Dick.' Suzanne Hilton got up, seized her younger son by the hand. 'Thank God you are here.' He kissed her on the cheek. Incredible to suppose she was fifty-one years old. Incredible to suppose she had also been present at the Saintes, had, if legend could be believed, actually served a gun there. Incredible to suppose she had once spent a month as prisoner of Henry Christophe's Negro army in the hinterland of St Domingue. There were lines on her neck, and reaching away from her eyes. But the complexion itself was smooth, the sun tan of her youth faded to a rich cream; the grey eyes were as clear as ever, the Hilton beauty as untarnished, and what streaks of white there were seemed no more than an enhancing pattern against the yellow of her hair.

'I'm sorry to be late. I met Ellen in the park.'

She kissed him in turn. 'As you should. But poor old Tony has been hopping about like a wild man. I have a secret.' She smiled, archly, and doubled her beauty.

'Concerning me? Father.' He reached for Matt Hilton's hand, and frowned. His father looked even more ill than usual, his cheeks grey, his mouth turned down. And his hair was as grey as his cheeks. He could still fire himself with enthusiasm, when he would speak on his favourite subject. But too much of the time, as he watched English opinion hardening against all liberalism in the pursuit of victory over the French, he seemed to sink into a trough of depression.

'Dick. Ill news, boy. Ill news.'

'Oh, what rubbish,' Suzanne cried. 'We have received a letter from Robert.'

'Uncle Robert?' Dick asked, stupidly. 'From Jamaica?' They had not heard from Suzanne's brother in ten years; Robert Hilton did not exactly approve of his cousin's continual preaching in favour of Abolition.

'And that is your secret, Mama?' Tony demanded. 'He is visiting London, no doubt. And expects us to pay homage.'

She shook her head, sat down again, opening the creased paper. 'He considers himself too old to stand an Atlantic crossing. Indeed, age is all he speaks of. Thus he worries about the future. For the first time, that I can remember.' She raised her head, gazed at her sons. 'He wishes to be sure Hilltop and Green Grove descend to the proper hands. And he wishes those hands to understand planting, and the problems of planting. He would

14

train his nephew.'

There was a sudden silence, then Tony gave a bellow of joy. 'Good old Uncle Bob. You said he'd never forget us. A planter, by God. Slave girls. All the horses I desire. All the clothes I desire. All the money I desire. Gad, I can scarce believe it.'

Dick was watching his mother. Some of the animation had left her face.

As Tony had noticed. 'Well?' he asked. 'Or are there conditions attached?'

'No conditions,' Suzanne said, very quietly.

'Well, then . . .'

'Save as regards the nephew he wishes,' she said, even more quietly. 'He asks for Dick.'

Dick sat down. He was aware of something having happened, but for the moment it was impossible to place it in his mind.

'It's a mistake, of course,' Tony declared. 'Uncle Robert has got the names mixed up.'

Suzanne Hilton's face had assumed that frozen expression both her sons, and her husband, knew very well. 'I'm afraid not, Tony. Robert refers to you by name in another part of his letter, and refers to you also as my elder child.'

'But . . .' Tony's cheeks slowly began to fill with blood.

'There is always the possibility that your uncle has gone mad, at last,' Matt Hilton remarked. 'He consumes more alcohol than food, rides to the fields in the midday sun, and lives in a state of total omnipotence. And has done all of these things for the past forty years, to my certain knowledge.'

'Robert is not mad,' Suzanne said, still speaking very quietly. 'At least, there is no indication of it in this letter. And quarrelling about what is a remarkable stroke of fortune seems to me to be the height of absurdity. Dick?'

Dick slowly focussed on his mother. Jamaica. The West Indies. He had been born in Jamaica, but he could remember nothing of it. Save dark faces. But that had not been in Jamaica. That had been in St Domingue, after the revolt. The faces had leered at him, and grinned at him, and threatened him, and he had clung to his mother, and hid his face in her skirts.

'He's speechless,' Tony said, contemptuously. 'Try to imagine, Dickie boy, what you will feel like when you flog your first

15

Negress. They strip them, you know, and then they . . .'

'Be quiet,' Suzanne commanded.

'Yet it is something that has to be considered,' Matt Hilton said. 'I had supposed I had brought up my sons to regard all human beings as God's creation. No West Indian planter can hold that point of view.'

It will mean leaving England, Richard thought. Why, he had always dreamed of leaving England, of going out into the world, of earning himself fame and fortune.

But it would also mean leaving Ellen. And Mother. That was quite impossible. Except that Mother clearly wished him to go.

'Whenever he eventually wakes up,' Tony said, 'be sure to let me know. In the meanwhile, Mama, can you possibly lend me five guineas? I'm terribly short, and now that Richard is to be heir to a fortune . . .'

Suzanne sighed. 'You shall have the money, Tony. But Richard is not necessarily heir to a fortune. No doubt your uncle has some such idea at the back of his mind, but obviously he wishes to see Richard, to have him on the plantation, to discover if he is the right sort of person to own a sugar estate . . .'

'In other words, to corrupt him,' Matt remarked.

A fortune, Richard thought. Four thousand pounds. There was a fortune, to Ellen. And to Ellen's parents. But Robert Hilton was worth four hundred thousand pounds. No, four million pounds would probably be nearer the mark. That figure would make old Taggart's eyes bulge. He'd be happy to have Richard Hilton as a son-in-law then. Even if it meant a brief separation.

He suddenly realized that it was probably the only way in which he would ever be acceptable to the Taggarts.

He raised his head, met his mother's gaze. She was staring at him, willing him to accept, obviously, but not to hurt his father at the same time.

He crossed the room, knelt beside Matt Hilton's chair. 'But don't you see, Father, that this could be the chance we have all waited for. I don't speak of the money, although heaven knows we can do with it . . .'

'Blood money,' Matt growled.

'That can be changed,' Dick insisted. 'That is what I mean. Supposing I do inherit, well then, can we not practise all the beliefs you have ever held?'

'Oh, yes,' Tony said. 'Free the slaves. Go bankrupt. Get stoned in the street. And don't suppose the blacks will ever thank you. They'll be throwing stones as hard as anyone. You remember St Domingue. I can remember St Domingue. I remember Aunt Georgiana screaming. I . . .'

'That will do,' Suzanne said. 'We can all remember Georgiana screaming. But that was St Domingue, and it happened because of the revolution in France. It could never happen in a British colony. And certainly never on Hilltop. I think Dick is quite right. It is entirely possible to be both a planter and a Christian. Why, you were a planter, and a Christian, Matt, before you quarrelled with Robert.'

'It'll all turn out for the best, Father. You'll see.' Dick scrambled to his feet. 'Now, Mama, will you excuse me?'

Suzanne frowned at him. 'It will be time for dinner in an hour. Where are you off to?'

Dick smiled at her. 'To the Taggarts, Mama. I'm going to ask Ellen to marry me.'

The butler regarded him as if he were a beetle. 'I am sorry, sir,' he said. 'But Colonel and Mrs Taggart do not receive, unless a card has been presented beforehand. *Do* you have a card, sir?'

'I do not have a card,' Dick said. All the way here he had been repeating to himself, over and over again, I am going to the West Indies, I am going to inherit Hilltop, and Green Grove, I am going to be one of the wealthiest men in the British Empire. Perhaps in the world. But how his resolution and his courage were draining away, now he was actually here. He took a long breath. 'But I shall speak with the colonel, none the less. Tell him Hilton, of Hilltop in Jamaica, is calling.'

The butler hesitated; in the dim light the shabbiness of Dick's coat, the tarnish on his beaver, were not clearly discernible. 'You had best come in, sir.'

'Thank you.' Dick entered the hallway. The door closed behind him, and the butler relieved him of his hat. He was inside the Taggart house. For the first time in his life. He gazed at the walnut panelling, the acanthus motif, the paintings, no doubt of previous Taggarts, staring disapprovingly down from the wall. He watched the butler walking ahead of him, to open the double doors to the parlour.

17

'I do beg your pardon, colonel, but there is a gentleman insists on seeing you.'

'Eh? Eh?'

'What's that, Varley?' asked a woman. 'A gentleman? Give me his card.'

'The gentleman does not have a card, madam,' Varley explained. 'He says he is Hilton, of Hilltop in Jamaica.'

'Eh? Eh?' Varley was pushed aside, to allow the colonel into the hall. 'Hilltop? Jamaica, you say. Why . . .' Colonel Taggart paused, and frowned. He was surprisingly short, for Ellen's father, and had big, rather vacant features. His head was quite bald save for a fringe of hair over the ears, but he attempted to compensate by wearing an enormous pair of moustaches, which drooped on either side of his lips. Now the moustaches, and the eyebrows, seemed to come together as he peered at his visitor. 'I know you, sir. Why . . .'

'Richard Hilton, Colonel Taggart.' Dick stepped past him, entered the room. 'Mistress Taggart.' His heart was pounding fit to burst.

'Richard Hilton?' There could never be any argument that this was Ellen's mother. Indeed, it was a rather startling thought that Ellen herself would look like this in twenty years' time, the long face, the prominent nose and chin, and even more prominent teeth, the high, rather strained voice, the towering coiffure of fading brown hair.

'Why, Mr Hilton,' cried Aunt Julia Taggart. 'Mr *Hilton*?'

'Dick.' Ellen put down her needlework and hastily got up. 'Oh, my Lord, Dick?'

'Gad, sir,' Taggart shouted, following him into the room. 'You are the young lout who has been pestering my daughter. Gad, sir. Varley, fetch my whip.'

'The bank clerk?' Mrs Taggart asked, her tone suggesting she was at the very least blaspheming.

'Dick?' Ellen asked again, watching the colour rise in his cheeks and then fade again. She could tell how nervous he was.

'The whip, Varley. The whip,' Taggart was shouting. 'Breaking in here, sir, under false pretences. Why . . .'

Dick had got his breathing back under control. 'If you will permit me, sir,' he said, 'I meant exactly what I said. I leave for Jamaica on the first available ship, to assume the management of

18

my Uncle Robert's plantations. Hilltop, as you may be aware, is only one of the Hilton estates in the West Indies.'

'Jamaica,' cried Mrs Taggart.

'Jamaica? You, Dick?' Ellen sat down again as if her knees had suddenly lost their strength.

'Aaaaah,' said Aunt Julia, and fainted.

'Jamaica?' Taggart bellowed. 'Oh, my God, she's gone. Varley, the salts. Quickly, man.'

Ellen regained her strength, hurried across the room to kneel beside her aunt and pat her hands and face. 'Aunt Julia, Aunt Julia, Dick meant no harm.'

'I'm terribly sorry, truly I am,' Dick gabbled, all his courage having finally fled. 'I wished Ellen, I wished you all to know. My uncle has sent for me. I am to be his heir.'

'The salts, sir,' Varley said from the doorway. He also carried a riding whip, in his left hand, but did not offer it.

'Here. Wake her up.' Taggart gave the bottle to his daughter. 'Varley, bring out the brandy. You'd best sit down, lad, and tell us about it. And you'd better be speaking the truth.'

Dick perched on the edge of a straight chair, watched Ellen moving the bottle slowly to and fro beneath her aunt's nose. 'Will she be all right?'

'Of course she'll be all right. She only does it for effect. Now come on, lad, speak up. Jamaica?'

'Yes, sir.'

'By the first available ship?'

'Yes, sir.'

'Jamaica,' Ellen muttered. 'Oh, aunt, you are all right?'

'It's so terrible,' Aunt Julia complained, opening her eyes and sitting up. 'Breaking in here. Really, Mr Hilton, you deserve to be whipped. Really you do.'

'Oh, do be quiet, Julia,' her brother suggested. 'Mr Hilton is going to Jamaica. To be a planter. Aye, here . . .' He seized the two glasses from the tray presented by the butler, handed one to Dick. 'Drink up, lad. Jamaica. There's the life for a young fellow. Planting with Robert Hilton. Gad, sir, the Empire could do with more like him. Your uncle, eh? You, young lady,' he shouted at Ellen. 'Why did you never tell me this lad was Robert Hilton's nephew?'

'I did, Papa,' Ellen said, standing in front of them. 'Are you really leaving England, Dick?'

Dick sipped his brandy, felt his chest explode into flame, and confidence. 'I came straight round to tell you. I must, Ellen. It is my entire future, opening before me. Will you wait for me?'

'Eh? Eh? What's this?' Taggart bellowed.

'Wait for you, Dick? Oh, of course I'll wait for you.'

'Ellen,' boomed her mother. 'Whatever are you saying? Colonel Taggart, these young people are mad.'

'Wait? What's this? Wait?' Taggart bawled.

Dick stood up, finished his brandy, set down the glass. How simple life was suddenly become. It was merely a matter of declaring one's intentions. 'I have the honour to ask for Ellen's hand in marriage, sir.'

'Good God,' cried Colonel Taggart.

'Dick,' Ellen cried. 'Oh, you darling.'

'Marriage?' said Mrs Taggart. 'Good heavens.'

'Aaaah,' said Aunt Julia, once more subsiding.

'Ellen is only seventeen,' Colonel Taggart pointed out.

'Now, really, Papa,' she protested.

'Jamaica?' Mrs Taggart said. 'All those black people?'

'She will be mistress of the finest plantation in the world, Mrs Taggart,' Dick explained. 'And of course, sir, I realize that we cannot be married immediately.'

'Dick!'

'No, no, Ellen,' he said. 'Your father is quite right about that. I must go, and see what it is like, and make my mark with my uncle, and then I can send for you. I but came tonight to ask you to wait for me, as I said.'

'Bless my soul.' Colonel Taggart gazed at his wife. 'Robert Hilton's nephew. Why wasn't I told? Why wasn't I told?'

'Jamaica,' Mrs Taggart said. 'It is across the ocean. Oh, my God, Ellen, you cannot travel across the ocean.'

'Why not?'

'Well, there are storms. And privateers. There is a war on. Have you forgotten that?'

'There are few privateers any more, Mrs Taggart,' Dick said. 'The Navy has seen to that. Anyway, it will be at least a year before Ellen comes out, so . . .'

'A year?' Ellen cried.

'Well, I . . . there will be a great deal to be done. To be

prepared. But when the time is ready, I will come back for her, Mrs Taggart. For you, Ellen. We shall be married here in London, and honeymoon our way across the ocean.'

'Robert Hilton's nephew,' Colonel Taggart said. 'Well, well. We must discuss this, Charlotte. Oh, indeed. Come with me, and we'll have a talk. Julia. Julia, for God's sake wake up. We must have a chat.'

Mrs Taggart got up. 'Ellen?'

'I think Ellen should stay here, and entertain Mr Hilton, while we discuss this,' Colonel Taggart said.

'Then had not Julia better stay as well?' Mrs Taggart inquired.

Colonel Taggart seized his wife by one arm, his sister by the other, half carried them to the door. 'I am sure Mr Hilton would prefer to be alone with Ellen, my dears. After all, they are betrothed. There can be no impropriety. You'll stay to supper, Mr Hilton. Simple fare, I'm afraid, but good company, sir. Good company. And the best port. Oh, yes, indeed.' The doors closed behind them.

'My God,' Dick said. 'I am shaking like a jelly.'

Ellen gazed at him for some seconds. 'It is all true?' she asked at last. 'I think I am dreaming.'

'So do I. Constantly. But it is all true. I am to take the first ship.'

'And Papa has said yes. Oh, Dick.'

He reached for her hands, checked. He had once kissed her cheek, quickly and surreptitiously.

'You *are* just a jelly,' she said, softly, and freed her hands, to slide them up his arms, round his neck. Her body was against him, and his own fingers were closing on her shoulders. He felt a terrific pressure building up inside himself, as if he would burst. 'I love you, Dick,' she said, in hardly more than a whisper. 'I am so happy.' She kissed him on the mouth, lightly, waited for a moment, their lips pressed together, then allowed her tongue to come out and stroke across his, and then suddenly held him close and seemed to fill his mouth. She tasted faintly sweet, and he realized she must be tasting his brandy. He had never touched a woman's tongue before. He had never been able to afford to buy, and had been too shy to attempt to pursue and possess. Saving Ellen, and theirs had been a clandestine romance, beginning that autumn day last year when he had raised his hat, and been rewarded with a smile, progressing through hasty snatches of conversation to holding hands, and the one immortal moment when Aunt Julia had left her gig to talk to a friend and he had kissed Ellen on the cheek, and discovered then that they loved each other.

'Dick,' she whispered in his ear. 'Oh, Dick. Hold me close, Dick. Dick . . .' She drew him down on to the couch, seized his hands, and guided them round her waist to slide up the hardness of her stays to the sudden softness above.

'Ellen,' he begged. 'No. We must wait.'

'Wait?' she demanded. 'With you about to leave England, for a year, you say.'

'Only a year, sweetheart,' he said. 'Only a year. And then . . .'

'Then why not now?' she asked fiercely.

'I . . .' How to say, I scarce know how to go about it? Indeed I do not know how to go about it. How to say, I am so excited, by the event, so terrified of my own boldness in being here at all that I would never manage the necessary erection? 'Ellen, just a year. It is not so long to wait. And then, my darling, then, we shall have our entire lives together, with no risk of interruption, no risk of impropriety . . .'

'Impropriety,' she said, and released him, moving to the far end of the settee. 'And will you wait for a year also, Dick?'

'Of course,' he said. 'I swear it, Ellen. Just say you'll marry me.' He attempted a smile. 'You have not said so, yet.'

'Tell me about Hilltop,' she said. 'Is it really the finest plantation in the West Indies?'

'In the world.'

'Oh . . .' she panted. 'How big is it?'

Dick did a hasty calculation. 'About ten thousand acres.'

'Ten thousand . . . I don't believe you.'

'Twenty square miles, Mother always said. That's more than ten thousand acres. And the Great House is a palace, Mother says. An army of servants, a drawing room the size of this house, a piano . . . you'll be mistress of all that, Ellen.'

'Mistress Hilton,' she murmured, 'of Hilltop in Jamaica. Angela Coleman will be *green*. Oh, I'll marry you, Dick. Only a year. Be sure it *is* only a year.'

He sang as he walked back through the Park, flicking at the flowers with his cane, disturbing more than one courting couple with his boisterous passage, enjoying the soft spring air on his face, the loom of the rising moon peeping through the trees, the distant rumble of the traffic on the Lane and down Grosvenor Street. Colonel Taggart's port bubbled in his veins, the scent of Ellen filled his nostrils, the touch of her hand, of her lips as they had been allowed another brief moment alone together before parting, seemed imprinted on his flesh. It was the most glorious evening of his life, he decided. There was nothing which had ever happened which could possibly stand comparison. He could not, indeed, envisage anything ever happening in the future to compare. Except of course the night they were wed.

And even that could have been his, this night, had he wished. The song disappeared with the smile, and he sloped his cane across his shoulder as he walked into the darkness. She would have surrendered everything a woman should most hold dear, on the spot. And indeed, had become angry when he would not accept her surrender.

Of course, in retrospect, she would be grateful for his forbearance. And himself? Now, he felt like it. Now his breeches were full. Now he would seek out the lowest whore to spend his desire as rapidly as possible. And now he had given his word, to remain chaste for a year.

It had been the correct, the only thing to do, in the circumstances. His instincts had not played him false. Yet the fact was, he had known nothing but cold fright at the prospect of Ellen; Ellen, with all that her body, her mind, her personality, her very name, meant to him, surrendering to his passion. He had been afraid that she would be disappointed, that he would be disappointed, that they would not have the time to survive the slightest setback, that they might be interrupted to compound a catastrophe, that . . . it would all be different when they were married. Once that was accomplished, all difficulties would melt away, because they would be tied to each other, unable to escape, forced to love each other, or hate each other. What a remarkable thought.

And what a vast gulp of the future he was attempting to digest at a single swallow. Marriage to Ellen, possession of Ellen, with all the joy and all the passion that that would entail, was better than a year in the future. Perhaps longer than that. Suppose Uncle Robert did not like him? Suppose he did not like Uncle Robert?

Oh, he would like Uncle Robert. No question about that. But suppose Uncle Robert dismissed him as incompetent, or as a milksop? The West Indies. Sugar cane. He knew nothing of sugar cane. He must get some books from the library, for a start.

And then slaves. What had Tony said? They strip them, to whip them. His step slowed. Men as well as women. Black people. He would supervise. Would he have to use the whip himself? He doubted that he could. Well, then, when commanded to do so, what then? And after his promise to Father.

Another gulp of the future. He was anticipating, too far and too fast. Suppose he did not survive the voyage itself? Mrs Taggart had been right about the dangers of·an Atlantic crossing. He had not properly considered the matter. He had supposed himself snapping his fingers, and finding himself in Jamaica, safe and sound. He knew nothing of the sea, either, save the tales Father had told him of life in the Navy, and those had been grim enough.

He found himself hesitating upon his own doorstep, his hand on the latch. Another anticipation. There was decision, crisis, closer at hand than even that. Tomorrow he must resign from Bridle's Bank. What would Perkins say? What would Maurice say? Oh, Maurice would throw his hat in the air for joy. No doubts for Maurice. So, then, why doubts for Dick Hilton?

But suppose . . .

'Dick. Come in here, will you?'

He checked his tiptoe, turned to the parlour door. The fire had burned low, and so had the candles. In the dim light he could just make out the loom of his mother's hair.

'You should not have waited up.'

'Should I not? To welcome you home on the most fateful evening of your life?'

He closed the door behind him. 'I was just considering that very fact.'

'And you are exhaling port,' Suzanne said. 'Am I to take it that I can congratulate you?'

'Oh, Mama.' He crossed the floor, knelt beside her chair. 'It had quite slipped my mind. The Taggarts were overwhelmed.'

'And when is the great day?'

'Well, I explained that I must make my mark with Uncle Robert first. We agreed to wait for a year, when I would hope to return to England. To see you all. And to be married.'

24

'Sensible,' she said. 'Sober. You are very like your father.' She smiled, sadly. 'He once assaulted a young lady's house in just that fashion.'

'Yours?'

She shook her head. 'Not mine. And it led to tragedy. Pray God your venture shall be different. You have had no second thoughts?'

'Second, third, and fourth. I am trembling like a jelly.'

Her smile widened, and she thrust her fingers into his hair. 'But you'll not change your mind.'

'No, Mama. This is our chance. All of our chance.'

'To be rich, to be famous.'

'You almost sound disapproving. I had thought . . .'

'Quite correctly, Dick. Planting, money, power is in my blood. I have found it uncommonly hard these last twenty years. But I would have you understand what you do. Here, in London, not even Boney has been able to trouble us, to trouble you. You are blessed with some size, with splendid health, with a very level head, as you have just illustrated. You have naught to fear, from life.'

'And as Master of Hilltop, I will have something to fear?'

Her other hand joined the first, to hold his head. 'Something,' she said. 'Your past, to begin with. Hush. Listen. The Hiltons, the Warners, were not given their sugar plantations, their islands; they took them.'

'You could say the same of every family, did you reach back far enough into their past.'

'I am reaching back not two hundred years, Dick. And in that taking, they committed horrible crimes. Tom Warner, Tony Hilton the first, they once massacred an entire Indian nation, to obtain St Kitts. Your great-great-grandfather, Christopher Hilton, marched with Morgan on Panama. Your Uncle Robert, this man you go to live with, my own brother, once mutilated and hanged a Negro for uncovering himself before my sister.'

'Uncovering himself?'

'You know what I mean, Dick. And the affair was Georgiana's fault. Robert hoisted the boy with his own hands.'

'Thirty years ago.'

'Is that so very long? But even that, even everything else, done individually, is as nothing beside the greater crime, that of populating the islands with slaves themselves. The Warners, the

25

Hiltons, played their part in that.'

'You sound like Father.'

'Should I not? We have stood shoulder to shoulder, these twenty years.'

'I had always supposed you supported him from love, and not conviction.'

'I supported him. There is all that matters.'

He kissed her fingers. 'And I support you both. I meant what I said, this evening. And slavery will soon be a thing of the past. Father says so, and he is winning his fight. The trade is already outlawed.'

'The trade,' Suzanne said. 'What rubbish. There is a nation of Negroes in the West Indies now, Dick. They need no increments from Africa to grow. As for being over, do you think the planters will agree to emancipation? There is their wealth, this wealth you look forward to inheriting, gone at a stroke. And can you imagine, for one moment, what will happen when two million black people are presented with their freedom, suddenly, in the presence of twenty thousand whites? Do you remember St Domingue?'

'Vaguely. As a nightmare. Mama, I know how you must feel about it, about Aunt Georgiana's death, but . . .'

'I feel nothing about it, now. I am merely trying to be sure you understand that this is no sinecure you undertake. Nor will you even be able to stand to one side and watch events shape themselves. As Richard Hilton, as the Hilton of Hilltop, you will be expected to lead, not follow.'

'And I will lead as my conscience directs me. I promise, Mama.'

She withdrew her hands, leaned back in her chair. 'I have no doubt of that, Dick. Yet will even that not be easy. The whites will hate you as much as the blacks.'

'As their leader?'

'As their superior, certainly. Jealousy is always a cause for hate. But there is more. You will understand that almost every white man in the West Indies is violently opposed to any interference in his affairs, in the institution of slavery. As I said, it is the foundation of their wealth, if they are wealthy, of their claims to superiority over the blacks if they are poor. You are Matt Hilton's son. And Matt once had one of them hanged, for murdering a black.'

26

'James Hodge,' Dick said. 'Father has told me.'

'Aye. But not the whole truth, perhaps. You will have to know it. There was a great scandal. That house your father assaulted, was here in London. The young woman seemed to be white. But she had Negro blood. Worse, she was an absconded slave.'

Dick stared at her in horror. 'But . . .'

'Your father loved her, Dick. And Robert found out about it and had her returned to the West Indies. To her rightful owner, James Hodge.'

'My God. But . . . Father says Uncle Robert assisted him in bringing the case against Hodge. In having him hanged.'

'Aye. Perhaps Robert regretted his crime. I do not know for certain. I do know that Matt had no idea Gislane's arrest was due to Robert, at that time. It was after he found out the truth that they quarrelled.'

'What happened to the woman? Gislane?'

Suzanne Hilton shrugged. 'She was sold again. And again. Eventually to Louis Corbeau in St Domingue. She practised *obeah*, the Negro withcraft, became a leader in the revolt there. Perhaps she still rattles her bones, I do not know. She saved my life and yours, at the end. Because by then Matt had fallen in love with me.'

'Yet you hate her.'

'Should I not? In any event, I have always felt that she saved us out of contempt, not pity. I'm sorry. I did not mean to cause you distress. But the events were well known, and could be thrown in your face.'

'They happened a long time ago,' Dick said. 'Even Hodge was a long time ago.'

'There was a widow.'

'Will she spit in my face?'

'I doubt that. She is probably dead. Anyway, she has disappeared. Robert offered her money, and she spat in *his* face.'

Dick smiled. 'And this is the tyrant?'

Suzanne sighed, and got up. 'He is a strange man. Circumstances made him strange. He inherited Hilltop when he was scarce older than you. He had that fall from a horse. You have heard of that.'

'You have told me.'

'So I have. It left him unable to have children.'

'Thus I am in the position I now find myself.'

'But you must try to understand, Dick, the feelings of a man, left solitary and alone, with omnipotent power as far as his eye could see, and yet without the power inside himself, of commanding a decent woman into his bed, for fear of ridicule.'

'I see what you mean.'

'And then, one sister murdered by a mob, the other deserting husband and friends to marry her own cousin, who was an Abolitionist into the bargain . . .'

'Do you regret your life, Mama?'

'Not for an instant. I am attempting to think with Robert's brain. The wonder would be if he were not strange. And now . . .' She turned, violently, stood above him. 'He has made his feelings clear, Dick. He wishes you to inherit, presuming you show a tithe of the ability, the character, I know you possess, and he hopes of you. He has selected you, and not Tony. He is a cunning man. It seems he has had his agents here in England carry out a secret investigation, into the pair of you. And Tony is dismissed for his apparent weaknesses. The weaknesses of trying to be a gentleman. It is hard.'

'Mama . . .'

'Listen a moment. I have told you enough of my brother for you to know that while he is a man of strong hates, he is a man of utter generosity as well, given the reason.'

'Of course, Mama, but . . .'

Suzanne dropped to her knees beside her son. 'And you'd not deny that Tony deserves his chance in the world. Listen to me. I would not interfere with your chance at wealth, your chance to inherit Hilltop. I am only asking you to give your brother at least half of your chance. He is bitterly disappointed. Well, who would not be. But his disappointment may take him into strange paths, drink, gambling. Oh, I know he already treads those paths. Here is our opportunity to free him from those vices. Take him with you, Dick.'

'Tony? What will Uncle Robert say?'

'I will give you a letter. I ask nothing for Tony save that he be employed as an overseer. But give him the opportunity, to prove what he can do.'

'Well, I . . . anyway, he'd never agree.'

'He has already agreed.'

'Eh?'

'I have put it to him very straight.'

'And he agrees? He understands that . . . well, in view of the investigation you have just related, he must mend his ways.'

'He understands. He has agreed to follow your wishes in everything.'

'Tony?'

'Tony.' She got up again, went to the door, opened it. 'Come in here.'

Tony Hilton came in, slowly. 'We adventure together, then, Dick.'

Dick hesitated, then rose to his feet. 'Aye, well, I was wondering how I should survive the crossing, without company.' He held out his hand. Together then, Tony. With but one objective; to prove ourselves worthy of owning Hilltop.'

Tony's fingers squeezed his. 'I'll say amen to that.'

He was smiling. Even his eyes were smiling. When Tony Hilton smiled he was one of the handsomest men Dick could think of. Here was company, the best of company, to stand at your shoulder.

But what had Mama just said of her brother? A man is what he is, and cannot change?

My God, he thought; what have I done?

3

The Coward

'"It is convenient to divide the types of sugars into two main groups." ' Richard Hilton spoke the words slowly and carefully, and loudly, as the gusting wind whipped each syllable from his mouth before it was properly pronounced. ' "They are monosaccharoses, formerly called glucoses, and disaccharoses, formerly called saccharoses." Eh?'

Anthony Hilton yawned, and pulled his coat tighter. They sat on the poop deck, and faced aft, for the brig was beating into a stiff southwesterly; spray clouded over the bows with every dip into the rolling green of the waters, and often enough came flying the length of the deck, while astern of the ship, merging with the flowing white of the wake, the whitecaps pranced and broke, churned by the breeze which scattered the young men's hair, flapped their coats, ruffled the pages of Dick's book.

' "The first term," ' Dick continued, ' "includes the simple sugars, bearing the formula $Ca(H_2 0)$." We must remember that.'

'Oh, indeed,' Tony agreed. 'I am to plant $Ca(H_2 0)$. That sounds uncommonly like water to me.'

'Well,' Dick said thoughtfully. 'As in all plants, there must be a great deal of water in the average sugar stalk.'

'Oh, quite,' Tony agreed. 'But not half so much as there was in that gale the other day. Did you watch it coming over the bow? I thought we were for the bottom.'

'I was hanging on to Mistress Marjoribanks,' Dick said. 'I thought she was for it, certainly. She puked green, at the end. I expected to see her gut, at any moment.'

'Ugh,' Tony said. 'Do remember we don't all have a stomach like yours. Still, I suppose it pays to have a digestion like a carthorse, if one is going to marry a mare.'

'Now, look here . . .'

Tony smiled, and stretched. 'A very handsome mare, let us not forget. Do you dream of her?'

'Every night.'

'Ah, but you have only been separated three weeks,' Tony said. 'When it is three months, you will have forgotten what she looks like.'

'Never. She has promised to send me a likeness. She is having it commissioned.'

'How sweet. You'll want more than just a face, to keep you constant amidst all those brown-skinned wenches.'

'Tony!'

'Oh, I promised. To be a Hilton's Hilton. But so far as I can make out, they rather went for the brown. Don't frown so, I am only joking. Actually . . .' He sat up, his elbows on his knees. 'I have used this fortnight for thinking.'

'About brown bellies.'

'No.' Tony's face was quite unusually serious. 'About being a Hilton.'

'You are a Hilton.'

'And you are being deliberately dense. Mama gave me Uncle Robert's letter to read, you know. No, listen. Stuff that damnably boring tome. Listen. He decided on you, instead of me. Now why? Because I drink more than I ought, because I gamble more than I can afford, because I am flitting from whore to whore rather than attaching myself to some unworthy female. I am not thinking of Ellen, believe me. Any female I accumulated would be unworthy. But think on this. Robert Hilton has spent his life doing all of those things, at least according to Father.'

'Which no doubt, now that he is growing old, is why he doesn't wish his heir to follow his example.'

'Hm. You know, old boy, you are the priggiest prig I ever came across. Oh, you'll do well. But not while you are looking over your shoulder at your conscience. You want to let go a little, live a little, especially if you are going to spend the better part of your life married to Ellen Taggart. She'll have you hog-tied to the bed-post in seconds.'

'You do talk the most utter rubbish,' Dick said, without anger. 'Now, let us get back to it. Uncle Robert will certainly want us to know something about our crop. Where were we? "The formula of

31

the second group is $C_{18}H_{32}O_{16}$." Say it now.'

'Just what I was thinking of,' Tony said. 'Here they come.'

'Eh?' Dick marked his place with his finger, looked back along the poop deck where Captain Morrison, all red cheeks and unshaven chin, was welcoming the rest of the passengers for their afternoon constitutional. 'Oh, Lord.'

Mistress Marjoribanks came first. She was a large lady, although she had lost weight during their fortnight at sea; the weather had been unfailingly bad and she was a poor sailor. Then the Collies, Mistress Collie clutching her babe in her arms, while it wailed and gnawed at her pelisse, Dr Collie holding the older child by the hand, half dragging it across the deck; having made the appalling mistake of marrying before completing his medical studies, he had been forced to seek a livelihood in the colonies. Then Master Rowland, who sported yellow braces under his vest, and pretended to smoke a cheroot, for all that his cheeks were tinged permanently green — his father was a plantation manager, and he felt it necessary to act the part. And then Captain and Mistress Lanken. Captain Lanken was a very military gentleman, with square shoulders and a jutting chin, who seemed almost naked without his red jacket. He was in fact, like them, on his way to a post as manager of a plantation in Jamaica, having recently been invalided from the army as a result of a wound which had left him with an almost useless left leg. Thus he walked with the aid of a stick, and with the assistance of his wife.

Who was currently the object of Tony's admiration. Joan Lanken was less than half the age of her husband, Dick estimated, and was an extraordinarily pleasant young woman, not especially pretty because of her somewhat flattened features, but with an agreeably plump figure and a delightful little tinkle of laughter. Her hair was pale brown, and a positive mass of curls, although these were presently concealed beneath the edgings to her fur bonnet, for the breeze remained chill. Dick, indeed, was fast coming to regard her as almost a sister, as it was impossible not to regard all the cabin passengers as close relatives, in view of the intimacy in which they were forced to exist, sleeping, eating, dressing and undressing, quarrelling and laughing, grumbling and dreaming, all together in a cabin hardly twelve feet square.

Tony was on his feet. 'Ladies. A better day.'

'Oooh, this roll. Oooh, this pitch.' Mistress Marjoribanks sank to the blanket he had spread on the deck. 'I shall never travel again, Mr Hilton. Never. I should not be travelling now. It is cruel, cruel, to send for me like this. James has existed without me these four years. He could have done so for four more.'

'But think of it,' Dick said. 'The Caribbean. Why, save for the occasional hurricane, it never blows there. Endless months of calm seas, warm sun, blue skies . . . you will be wondering why you did not accompany your husband in the first place.'

'Ugh. All those cannibals?'

'I think the Caribs are just about extinct,' Dick said. 'Except perhaps for a few settlements in the smaller islands. In any event, they have learned to respect our strength.' His gaze drifted to the rail, where Joan Lanken and Tony were leaning, shoulders touching, apparently contemplating the sea.

'Reading, sir? Reading?' Humphrey Lanken barked rather than spoke.

'*The Essentials of Cane Growing*, sir,' Dick explained. 'By Dr James MacLaren.'

'Essentials? Why, sir, there is nothing to it. In those islands, sir, why, cane grows like grass. Oh, indeed, sir, it is a simple matter.'

'I'm sure you are right,' Dick agreed. 'Good afternoon, Captain Morrison. A fine day.'

'Good day to you, Mr Hilton. Oh, aye. The weather is on the mend. For the time.' He winked. 'We don't want to forget 'tis the storm season.'

'Oooh,' screamed Mistress Marjoribanks. 'Not a storm.'

'Ah, 'tis early yet,' Morrison declared. 'The first hurricane seldom sprouts before August; we've a week in hand. Soon enough we'll pick up a trade wind, and then, why, it'll be coasting along with the wind abaft the beam, and not a whitecap in sight. You'll like that, Mistress Marjoribanks.'

'Oooh,' remarked that lady. 'Will she still roll?'

'Oh, aye, well, ships do roll, madam. Ships do roll. But none of this pitching. Ah, no. There'll be no pitching once we find the trades. Now ladies, gentlemen, I'm unpacking my cheese today. Real Stilton, ladies, gentlemen. You'll want to be in the cabin at four, eh? Good stuff, no mildew, well, none you can't stomach, and going cheap. Oh, aye, four o'clock.'

He bustled forward, and the Collie children, momentarily silenced by his bellow, began to wail once more.

'Damned scoundrel,' Lanken said. 'Why did he not uncover his cheese last week, eh, while it was still fresh?'

'Because then we all had cheeses of our own, captain,' Tony said, having turned back from the rail. His cheeks were flushed, and to his consternation, Dick saw that Joan Lanken's were also pink. And they had been looking over the lee rail, backing the wind.

'And now he can charge us what he likes, knowing that our own stocks are low,' Collie grumbled. 'Truly they say that all seafaring men are pirates at heart.'

'Aye, well, we are in the rascal's power, and must make the best of it,' Lanken declared. 'Mistress Lanken, I'm for a stroll. You'll take my arm, if you please.'

'Of course, sir.' Joan Lanken gave Tony a quick smile, and seized her husband's left arm to propel him over the quarterdeck. Dick found that his own arm had been seized, and by his brother.

'Do you fancy her?' Tony whispered, pulling him to the taffrail.

'Eh? Good Lord, no.'

'Then you're a fool. She let me touch her titties just now, and right through the cloth. Big.'

'For heaven's sake, Tony, with her husband right there?'

'He is a total fool. And quite incapable, she says.' He grinned. 'His leg keeps getting in the way, and she says it is the stiffest part of him. Listen, she is absolutely begging for a little service.'

'Then are you the total fool. In our circumstances?'

'Ah, well, there's the difficulty. I suggested she and the captain shift their berths to our side of the cabin, but she feels he would suspect something. On the other hand, it is going to get much warmer in a day or two. No one could be blamed for waking in the middle of the night, and needing air.'

'What about the watch? What about when the captain also wakes up and needs air?'

'I have thought of that. We must act together. That way we can share the profits, and also the watch-keeping requirements. A very military matter.'

'You must be mad.'

'I am going mad, if that is what you mean, with sheer desire. To know all of that is just a few feet away from me, has been there for a fortnight, and will be there at least a fortnight more, my God. Listen, she really is a delicious little thing, under all that cloth. If you like, I'll arrange with her for you to stand at the rail tomorrow. Then you can discover for yourself.'

'I have no intention of discovering for myself. You gave me your word . . .'

'To act like a Hilton, now and always. You are the one behaving like a changeling.'

'I happen to be engaged.'

'And do you think Ellen would thank you for letting your weapon rust away from lack of use?'

'For God's sake, Ellen is well aware that it has never been used, in that sense.'

Tony stared at his brother with his mouth open. 'You're not serious?'

Dick flushed.

'Good Lord.' Tony seemed genuinely amazed. 'And you'd wed, without discovering what it is all about? You really are the most disorganized chap. I'll have no argument, young fellow. You'll pitch in.'

'I will not.'

'Well, then, you'll help me, or I'll have her right there in the cabin. Think of the foul-up that will cause.'

'Psst.'

Dick opened his eyes. He seemed to have been asleep only five minutes. The last thing he remembered was Captain Lanken snoring, and now again he listened to Captain Lanken's snores, rumbling through the cabin, keeping time to the sway of the lantern, just visible above his head, and thus to the creak of the ship's timbers.

Tony shook him again. 'Wake up,' he whispered. 'It's far too hot to sleep, wouldn't you say?'

Dick blinked, and began to focus. And watched a figure on the far side of the cabin wrapping her blanket around herself before tiptoeing to the door, stepping carefully across her husband and Master Rowland.

'You must be out of your mind,' he whispered. But Tony had already followed the woman to the companion, there to pause as Lanken gave another series of trumpets, and rolled over, his arm flying out to strike the mattress where his wife had been lying but a moment previously.

Joan Lanken's hand was already on the ladder; she froze, and looked over her shoulder. But Lanken merely snuffled and went back to sleep.

Joan climbed the ladder, silently; her feet were bare. Tony followed, and paused once again at the top, to give Dick a jerk of the head.

Dick sat up, folding back his blanket. Of all the crazy adventures. And yet, the blood was suddenly pumping in his own veins, and his own weapon was hard enough. The excitement had been building over the previous two days, as Tony had spoken to Joan again, and about them both, and she had taken to giving each of them a long and appraising stare, no doubt anticipating. As they had, equally, anticipated.

Slowly, carefully, he got to his feet, holding on to the bulkhead as the ship lurched. But it was a very gentle lurch. Captain Morrison had been right about the trade wind; they had picked it up the previous morning, quite without warning. The endless plunging and beating had ceased, the wind had shifted to the stern quarter, and in doing so seemed to lose all of its bite, and the ship had commenced a slow and regular roll as she careered on her way, downhill as the sailors called it.

The couple were gone from the top of the ladder. Dick buttoned his shirt and climbed behind them, squeezed into the narrow space at the top, where the door led to the deck, and found himself in the midst of human bodies.

'Good lad,' Tony whispered. 'Oh, give him a cuddle, Joan. He's as cold as ice.'

The woman's arm went round Dick's waist, and he felt her softness against his body; she wore only her shift. 'You're a right pair, you are,' she whispered. 'What's this?' Her hand stroked the front of his breeches.

'For God's sake,' he protested, and she giggled, and kissed him on the chin. 'You'll wake everyone else.'

'Aye,' Tony agreed. 'Don't get him overexcited, sweetheart. 'Tis the longboat. I unfastened the canvas this evening. Follow me.'

He wriggled past the woman, cautiously opened the door. Instantly the breeze plucked at them, sent a strand of Joan's hair across Dick's face.

'I'm all a goosebump,' she whispered. 'Feel these, Dickie lad.'

His hand was seized and inserted under the blanket; he caressed

36

the linen of her nightdress, and the point of the nipple, scraping across the palm like a finger, sent a tingle of anticipation all the way from his hand up his arm and into his chest.

She sighed. 'Christ, how I have waited, these weeks, looking at you two strong lads . . .'

'Come on,' Tony whispered, having checked the deck. The door swung open, and they emerged into the waist of the ship. With the breeze astern, here it was sheltered; immediately above them was the quarterdeck and the helm; they could hear the slow tread of the mate, the murmur of the pulleys as the helmsman twisted the wheel to and fro. The remainder of the watch were forward, sitting round the foremast, smoking and gossiping.

'Evening to you, Mr Ratchet,' Tony called. 'Ain't it a splendid one.'

'Better than before,' the mate grunted. He paused at the rail for a moment, squinting into the darkness. He would be able to make out three figures, and perhaps even to decide one was a woman, and from that, make his own deductions. But he could not be sure.

'This way,' Tony whispered, and led them across the deck, beyond the shelter of the mainmast, and round the far side of the longboat, resting on its chocks amidships. 'Here.'

Joan placed her elbows on the gunwale, to look at the phosphorescence streaming away from the ship's side. 'It's chill,' she said. 'Will no kind gentleman put his arm round my waist?'

Tony obeyed.

'I can stand the pair,' she said.

Dick hesitated. Now he was fully awake, where in the companionway he had not been sure he was not dreaming. He had promised Ellen. But oh how he wanted, this moment. But this was madness, had to be madness. And yet, why? If the mate, and the crew, would have little doubt about their purpose, it was none of their business to become involved in the passengers' affairs.

And besides, to have a woman, suddenly available, suddenly willing, suddenly, indeed, anxious . . . he realized with a sense of shock how many years he had waited for this, dreamed of this, how many things he wished to do.

And could do, now. His arm moved, slowly, but not round her waist. His fingers slid the blanket aside to caress her buttocks, and she gave a little murmur of pleasure, and squirmed beneath his hand.

'Long enough,' Tony decided. 'Now then, Dick boy, do you remain here, looking out. And should anyone come too close to that boat, you give a loud cough, eh?'

'Is that all he's for?' Joan demanded. 'To keep watch?'

'Keep your voice down, for God's sake,' Tony begged. 'You'll have him after.'

'I can manage you both together,' she said.

'After,' Tony insisted. 'It was my idea. I have first. Then I'll keep watch.'

'*Your* idea,' she remarked. 'May God save me from arrogant men.' She turned, under Dick's hand, kissed him on the chin, then seemed to change her mind, held his face between her hands, and kissed him on the mouth. The quest of her tongue took him by surprise; he had grown to expect it from Ellen, but from a comparative stranger . . .

'You stay hard,' she whispered. 'He'll not be long.'

Tony had already rolled back the canvas of the boat cover, and waited to give her a leg up. Dick watched her nightdress fly in the breeze, the white of her leg shine even in the darkness, and then she was gone, and Tony was gone behind her, pulling the flap across the boat to conceal them. Dick glanced aft. The mate continued his slow perambulation, up and down the quarterdeck. There was a snatch of laughter from forward. The timbers creaked, and the waves hissed, and the rigging thrummed, as the ship proceeded on her way. They were better than two thousand miles from land, Captain Morrison had estimated yesterday. A little world, all of their own. In the midst of which this microcosm was committing adultery. What madness. But what a delicious sport, too. Desire, and excitement, rippled through his system, and he found himself straining his ears to discover what was happening inside the boat, and hearing a faint gurgle of laughter.

He thought he would burst, turned back to the gunwale, gazed at the sea, tried to remember some of the things he had read in his book. And found himelf, instead, thinking of Jamaica. Thinking about Uncle Robert. Mama had a likeness of him in her bedroom, a somewhat short, heavily built man, although with undoubtedly Hilton features, leaning on a stick and looking as if he were about to start bellowing commands. Well, no doubt that summed him up, at least by reputation. But the man himself. Father thought him a total brute. Mama remembered, or affected to remember, how he could be amazingly generous, when the mood took him. But his moods were utterly capricious. As their presence on this ship at all testified.

'Psst.'

He turned, heart pounding, supposing them discovered, and saw Tony, climbing out of the boat. Which but set his heart pounding the more.

'Everything all right?'

'Oh, aye. Quiet as a grave. And with you?'

Tony dropped to the deck beside him. 'Christ, how we managed to wait this long. Up you go, boy. She'll make a man of you.'

Dick hesitated. 'No doubt she is sated, for one evening. Perhaps I should wait for another.'

'She is waiting for you, now,' Tony pointed out. 'You'd best not disappoint her, or there will not *be* another evening.'

Dick peered over the gunwale of the boat. He could not see in the darkness, but he could smell woman, combined with the faint scent she normally exuded.

'Would you run away?' she whispered. 'You are a faint-hearted fellow, Master Dick.'

He got his leg over, slid into the bottom of the boat, encountered a thwart, inserted himself beneath it, or had himself inserted, he could not be sure which. Her hands were on his thighs, seeking his belt.

'You are gorgeous,' she whispered. 'You are both gorgeous. But Tony, now, why he did no more than whet my appetite.'

He lay on the boards, and she was in his arms. He put his hand down to assist her fingers and discovered that her nightdress was pulled to her waist. His hand withdrew as if burned, and she gave the chuckle of amusement he had heard from the deck.

'You are a treasure,' she whispered, and once again seized his head to smother his mouth with her kiss, before suddenly appearing to freeze, fingers, mouth, tongue, and even toes, which had just previously been scraping his shin.

Now he also heard the slow, dragging movement on the deck, coming closer every moment. But not a sound from Tony.

'A nice night, Captain Lanken,' remarked the mate.

Lanken grunted. Dick felt Joan's fingers slowly leave his face;

her breath rushed against him.

'Seems it's hot in the cabin,' the mate said.

'Oh, aye.' Lanken's voice was very close. 'Where are they, then?'

'Gone below, I reckon,' the mate said.

'Oh, aye.'

Joan's fingers were locked in Dick's; her head rested on his chin. 'Oh, God,' she breathed. 'Oh, God.'

'We'll wait,' he said. 'Just lie there. We'll wait.'

After some seconds she seemed more reassured, even released his fingers. But her passion, like his, was fled, drained away in fear sweat.

'Do you think he's gone?' she whispered at last.

'Aye,' he said. 'Now listen. He'll know you came on deck. You'll have to tell him you had a privy urge.'

'Yes,' she said. 'Yes, I'll tell him.'

'So I'll just be sure he's away,' Dick said, 'and then I'll go forward, and stay there until you're back in bed, eh?'

'Yes,' she said, and gave a little giggle of laughter. 'We'll all have had belly ache. It was that cheese, I'll wager.'

Slowly Dick pushed himself up, and found her hand once again on his arm.

'I'll not cheat you,' she said. 'We'll have to be careful for a while, but I'll get to you, before Kingston. I promise.'

He kissed her on the forehead. 'Don't,' he said. 'It was a mad idea, anyway. But thanks, all the same.' He lifted the edge of the canvas cover, stared at Captain Lanken.

Dick's immediate reaction was to duck back into the relative safety of the boat. But Lanken was already seizing the cover to jerk it off.

'Gad, sir,' he bellowed. 'Gad.' Further speech seemed beyond him, for the moment.

'Oh, God,' Joan muttered. She realized her skirt was still around her waist, and endeavoured to straighten it.

Dick found his mouth opening, and then shutting again. There really was nothing to say. Where the devil was Tony?

'Gad, sir,' shouted Lanken, regaining his breath. 'I'll cut your balls, sir, indeed I will. Just let me fetch my sword, sir. Just let me . . .' He was shaking the entire boat, hanging on to the gunwale and rocking back and forth.

'I do assure you, Captain . . .' Joan began.

'As for you,' roared the captain. 'I'll have your arse raw, by Gad. I'll have your arse raw.'

'Captain, Captain,' remonstrated the mate, holding his shoulder. 'You'll have a seizure.' He peered into the boat. 'Mr Hilton? Oh, my God. Fetch the captain,' he shouted. 'Fetch the captain.'

Dick sat up. He wondered the sky did not fall and send the entire ship, and her company, to the bottom.

'My sword,' bawled Lanken. 'Hold him there, bo'sun. Hold him there. By God, I'll have at him.'

'Now really, sir,' said the boatswain, grinning at Dick and winking. 'It's a matter for the captain. He'll not have violence on board his ship.'

'Violence,' bellowed Lanken. 'Violence. I'll show you violence.'

'Dick?' Tony peered over Lanken's shoulder. 'Whatever are you at?' He waggled his eyebrows and pulled a face, and Dick decided that he was suggesting only one should shoulder the blame.

'Now, then, what's all this?' demanded Captain Morrison. Mr Hilton? My God. What have you to say for yourself?'

'Why, I . . .'

'We were on deck,' Joan Lanken explained. 'Answering a call of nature . . .'

'Together?' inquired the mate, and raised a roar of laughter from the crew, who by now had accumulated to see the fun.

'Well,' she said, 'it was cold . . .'

'Cold, madam?' bawled her husband. 'Cold? And you in your shift?'

'You come out of there, Mr Hilton,' Morrison decided. 'Captain Lanken, you'd best see to your wife.'

'See to her? Why, I'll see to her. After I've settled this young fellow.'

He made a grab at Dick, as Dick attempted to get out of the boat.

'Aaaagh,' screamed Mistress Marjoribanks, having joined the throng. 'Murder.'

'Murder,' yelled Tony. 'Stop him.'

Dick had already pushed his assailant in the chest, and sent him reeling across the deck, where he came to rest against Dr Collie.

'You'd best to my cabin, Mr Hilton,' Captain Morrison decided. 'He'll not follow you there. But really, young fellow, this is bad.

Very bad.'

'You'll not shelter him,' bawled Lanken. 'I'm entitled to an accounting. Yes, sir.'

Morrison hesitated, biting his lip.

'The man's right,' muttered one of the crew. 'To be cuckolded, in public.'

'I do assure you,' Dick began.

'Murder,' screamed Mistress Marjoribanks.

'It will be murder,' Joan cried. 'The young man can have no such knowledge of weapons as my husband.'

'Never handled a sword in his life,' Tony declared.

'Weapons?' Captain Morrison asked at large. 'My God.'

'A duel,' Lanken shouted. 'Aye, there's the answer. Let him stand up like a man, as he is so anxious to prove himself one.'

'Aye,' chorused the crew, seeking entertainment. 'A duel. 'Tis fitting, Captain.'

Morrison glanced from one to the other of the passengers. ''Tis illegal,' he said.

'By England's laws, Captain,' remarked Master Rowland. 'At sea, there's a different matter.'

'Bloodshed,' muttered Captain Morrison. 'On board my ship?'

'There'll be little blood,' Lanken promised. 'I'll just tickle him a little.'

'Oh, God,' Joan whispered, kneeling in the bottom of the boat, her shoulder pressed against Dick's. 'He'll slit your nose. That's what he'll do.'

Dick felt his stomach rolling over and rising into his throat. I didn't do anything, he wanted to wail. We had no more than a cuddle. But they wouldn't believe him, and he could not bring himself to beg.

'Well, Captain, well?' demanded Lanken.

'Give the man his right,' called the crew. 'He has his right.'

'Mr Hilton?'

Dick licked his lips. 'If the captain insists.'

'Insists?' Lanken bellowed. 'Insists? Let me at him, Captain. Let me at him.'

'Swords,' decided the mate. 'There's less risk of a fatality. And he will have his blood. He deserves his blood.'

'Swords?' Tony cried. 'We have no swords.'

'We have,' said the mate.

42

Captain Morrison sighed. 'Sorry, I am, Mr Hilton. But it'll be the only way to have peace, and we've another fortnight at sea, at best. You've brought it on yourself.'

'Swords?' Dick muttered. Sweat broke out on his neck. He had never even touched a sword, much less handled one.

'But it'll be done proper,' the captain decided. 'Daybreak. Aye, there's an hour or two, for tempers to cool. Daybreak. Back to your bunks. Everyone settle. Daybreak. Captain Lanken, you'll practise no violence, upon either this young man or your wife. You'll have your satisfaction at dawn. Understood?'

Lanken glared at Dick. 'Oh, aye. I can wait. But you'll accompany me, madam.'

Joan hesitated, then crawled out of the boat. 'You heard the captain.'

'I'll not lay a finger on your flesh, in anger,' he promised. 'Not until we're to land, anyway.'

'Here's a problem.' Tony leaned against the boat.

'A problem?' Dick cried. 'Where the devil were you?'

'Well, I slipped off for a pee, to say truth,' Tony confessed. 'And when I turned round, there the rascal was.'

'And you could not engage him in conversation? Anything?'

'He'd not have moved. He was already sure where you were, and what you were up to.'

'I wasn't up to anything,' Dick said.

'True? There's ill luck. You'll not even have the memory. But what's to be done, eh? Mama didn't send me along to have you killed.'

'Killed?' Dick looked at his hands. They were dripping wet. And his heart had stopped pounding, seemed to have sunk down to rest on his belly. My God, he thought. I am frightened. It had never occurred to him before. He had never been frightened before. Even the time he had been set upon by footpads, he had not been afraid. He had reacted instinctively, swung his stick and his fists, defended himself so well that they had taken to their heels.

'There's always the possibility,' Tony said. 'On a ship, especially. A lurch of the deck, and zing, you've a blade in your gut.'

'Do you think he's any good?'

'He's a soldier. He'll have been trained.'

'Oh, my God,' Dick said.

'Aye,' Tony said, thoughtfully. 'But He helps those that help themselves, they say. Listen. You sit down quietly for the next hour. It only wants that for daylight. And you may need all your strength.'

Dick blinked at him. He could not stop his mind repeating, over and over again: I'm going to be killed. My God. I'm going to be killed.

Tony had turned away. Now he checked. 'Oh, by the way, do you have any money?'

'Money?'

'Mama gave you sufficient coin to see us the voyage,' Tony said patiently. 'Any left?'

'Of course. But what . . .'

'Don't argue. Give me a guinea of it.'

'A guinea? Whatever for?'

'Mind your own business. It's in a very good cause.'

'It will leave us short.' Dick unbuckled his belt; the coin was carried in a pouch on the inside, next to his skin.

'We'll be shorter yet if you're chucked over the side in a hammock,' Tony pointed out. He held the coin to the light, nodded. 'Now do as I say. Sit there, and rest.'

Dick watched him disappear into the companionway, then sat down on the deck, his back against the gunwale. Oh, my God, he thought. But clearly he was suffering immediate and absolute punishment from that very source, for breaking his word to Ellen. Well, for attempting to break his word. If they hadn't been interrupted, he would certainly . . . he could still feel the touch of her, the hardness of her nipples. God Almighty, how he had wanted. He had been closing his eyes and imagining it was Ellen. And now . . .

'Well, young fellow. Ready?'

His head jerked. Captain Morrison stood above him, and it was already growing light. He must have dozed. Certainly some of his desire, as well as his fear, had receded. Although he could feel the fear at least, bubbling away in his belly. Would his hand tremble when he held the sword?

He got up. 'As ready as I'll ever be, Mr Morrison.'

The captain nodded. 'Aye, well, 'tis an unfortunate affair, I'll swear to that. Having a woman on board, at least when she's young and pretty, and willing, always leads to trouble. But a duel, now . . . why the old devil couldn't just have thrashed you . . . now mind, Mr Hilton, if he nicks you, go down, sir. Go down. If you lose your head, you're done.'

Dick nodded, wearily. 'Aye, Captain. I'll remember.'

'Come along then.' Morrison led him aft, to the space between the mainmast and the poop, where there was most room. The watch was already assembled, and now the watch below also arrived, whispering and grinning to each other. The passengers were gathered above, at the rail; but where was Tony?

'There's the scoundrel,' Lanken shouted. 'Let us to it, sir.'

'We'll do the thing properly, Mr Lanken,' Morrison insisted.

'And you, madam,' Lanken bawled at Mistress Marjoribanks, who stood next to Joan Lanken. 'Keep her there. Keep her watching. The lesson is as much for her as for this villain.'

Oh, how I wish you had attempted to thrash me, Dick thought. By God . . . but he was getting angry, and that was the one thing Captain Morrison had told him not to do.

Where was Tony?

'Now gentlemen,' Morrison said. 'Mr Ratchet?'

The mate stepped forward, with two cutlasses.

'What's this?' demanded Lanken. 'Cutlasses? I'm no sailor. I've a sword of my own.'

'Do you have a sword, Mr Hilton?' Morrison inquired.

'Why, no,' Dick said. 'I've never owned such a thing.'

'Ha,' Lanken announced.

'You must both have the same weapons, Captain Lanken,' Ratchet explained.

'Ha,' Lanken said again. He took one of the cutlasses, swished it to and fro, extended his arm, the weapon held lightly in his fingers. 'It will do.'

'Mr Hilton?'

Dick tried to copy the movements, watched Lanken smile. 'It seems to be all right.'

'Well, then, gentlemen,' Captain Morrison said. 'First blood. No more than that. Mr Ratchet?'

The mate presented a pistol.

'I'll drop the man who continues when I have .called stop,' Morrison said. 'Now, gentlemen . . .'

'You'll wait a moment, Captain Morrison.'

'Eh?' They turned to face the companionway, and Collie, now

emerging from the hatchway, with Tony Hilton at his heels. 'Wait for what, doctor?'

'You'll not permit a duel without a medical examination,' Collie said.

'Medical examination? Why, sir . . .'

'Never heard of such a thing,' Lanken declared.

'Then, sir,' Collie remarked, with quite unusual aggressiveness, 'you are clearly unused to fighting gentlemen. I'll begin with you, sir.'

'Eh? Eh?'

'Mouth wide.' Collie peered inside, blinked. 'Hm. Your wrist, sir.' He held Lanken's pulse, consulted his watch. 'Hm.' He placed two fingers on Lanken's chest, commenced tapping. 'Hm. You'll bend, sir, forward from the waist.'

'Of all the damned nonsense,' Lanken grumbled, but he did as he was told.

'Hm,' Collie said. 'I've known men in better condition, Mr Lanken, but you'll do.'

'Gad, sir,' shouted the captain. 'Of course I'll do.'

'Now, you, Mr Hilton,' Collie said, his face severely composed. 'Mouth wide.'

Dick obeyed, feeling the fear starting to rise. Five minutes ago he had been prepared to have at his opponent, vigorously, and take his chance. But this delay . . . whatever was Tony playing at? Because that Tony was behind this he could not doubt.

'Hm,' Collie said. 'Hm.' He was frowning. 'Your wrist, sir.'

The fingers closed on Dick's wrist, and Collie peered at his watch. 'Hm. Lower your head, sir.'

Dick bowed, and Collie felt behind his ears.

'Hm. Dear me. Oh, dear, dear me. I am afraid this duel cannot take place, Captain Morrison.'

'Eh?'

'What? What?' Lanken cried, swishing his cutlass.

'Mr Hilton has a fever,' Collie pronounced.

'A fever?' bawled Lanken. 'Fright, doctor. Fright.'

'Indeed, sir,' Collie said, 'the same thought occurred to me when I first observed the symptoms. They are similar to your own.'

'What, sir? What?'

'So I investigated further. Indeed, Captain Morrison, I

46

recommend that this young man be placed in a blanket, and separated from the other passengers. He has malaria.'

'Malaria?' the captain cried. 'Here? How did he get malaria on my ship?'

'Who can say, sir? Who can say? First we must be sure what causes the dread disease. But informed medical opinion, sir, suggests it arises from noxious airs, filling the lungs and thence impregnating the system. Oh, it is highly dangerous.'

'And contagious?'

'That is certainly possible. Rest, and cool, and isolation, that is the ticket.'

'Balderdash,' Lanken declared.

Dick felt like sitting down. He certainly felt very weak, and quite cold, on a sudden.

'There,' Collie said. 'He is shivering. A blanket, Mistress Marjoribanks. And quickly.'

'I am here to fight a duel,' Lanken insisted. 'Not to receive a lecture on medicine.'

'You cannot fight a sick man, Captain Lanken,' Morrison pointed out. 'Perhaps, indeed, it was the onset of the fever drove him to his act of madness. No doubt he will apologize.'

'Oh, willingly,' Dick said. He wanted to shout for joy. And sheer relief.

'And I do not accept your apology, sir,' Lanken said. 'Malaria, by God. You'll be well again, sir, and be sure I'll be waiting.'

'But . . .' Collie wrapped the blanket around Dick's shoulders.

'Well, then, sir, it would be a shame to disappoint your ardour,' Tony said. 'Will you not accept a substitute? I am a Hilton, sir. I am a man, sir. And if you will have it, I have also sampled your wife's charms, sir.'

There was a moment of utterly scandalized silence.

'Wretch,' cried Joan Lanken from the poop.

'My dear lady,' Tony said, smiling at them all, 'your husband is determined to have his duel. Why should we disappoint him?'

'Gad, sir,' shrieked Lanken, catching his breath. 'I'll have you, sir. I'll . . .' He waved his cutlass, and they all had to leap back to avoid injury.

'Captain Lanken, sir,' Morrison protested. 'You cannot behave so.'

'Give me that,' Tony snapped, and wrenched the cutlass from

47

Dick's fingers. 'Ha, sir,' he called, facing Lanken.

'Gad, sir, Gad,' Lanken bellowed, charging across the deck, blade carving the air in front of him. And to Dick's horror, Tony scarce moved, remained directly in front of the whistling cutlass, brought up his own weapon. There was a clash of steel which sent sparks arcing through the air and raised a scream from Mistress Marjoribanks, then the rasp seemed to become a scream itself, and Tony jumped back, his own weapon still presented, while Lanken's clattered to the deck at Morrison's feet, leaving the captain staring at his empty fingers in consternation.

'Gad, sir,' he muttered.

'Will you continue, sir?' Tony inquired. 'Pick it up, man. Pick it up.'

'Gad, sir.' Lanken gazed at Morrison, then up at the poop, where his wife looked down, a peculiar expression on her face.

'Enough,' Morrison declared. 'I am sure honour has been satisfied. You have crossed swords, and there is all that is needed. Mr Ratchet, stow these weapons.'

'And now, sir, bed,' Collie said, putting his arm around Dick's shoulders.

'Aye,' said one of the crew, standing close enough to be overheard. 'Best place for him.'

'But the other one had some guts, though, eh?' remarked another.

Dick looked up at Joan Lanken; her expression had now definitely settled into a sneer.

'I think the poor chap can get up now,' Tony said, leaning on the bulkhead and looking down at his brother. 'Don't you, doctor?'

'Oh, indeed,' Collie agreed. 'He is looking much better. A total recovery, I would say. Besides, Jamaica is in sight.' He smiled at Dick. 'That'll complete the cure, eh?' He left the tiny cabin originally occupied by Mr Ratchet, but utilized as a sickroom for the past week.

'Jamaica?' Dick sat up.

'We sighted it last evening,' Tony said. 'But I did not wish to excite you. We are entering Port Royal at this moment.'

Dick threw back the covers, peered through the port; the cabin looked aft, and he could see nothing but water. Yet the sea itself had changed, the great rolling waves had disappeared, and this ocean was so quiet it might almost have been painted into place.

'And I'll be right glad to get off this tub, I'll tell you that,' Tony said. 'And to get you off it in one piece.'

'I don't see how I'll dare leave.' Dick sat down again. He had been confined to the cabin since the duel, and had been happy to stay here, for all that it had been at once hot and boring, with only Tony and the doctor, and occasionally Mrs Collie, for company. At least he had finished his book on sugar. Not that he understood a great deal of it.

'Ah, bah. The whole thing was a nine days' wonder,' Tony declared. 'Why, I'd wager even Joan has forgiven you by now. She'd be ready for another tumble, if you'd take the risk.'

'I'd need my head examined for bumps,' Dick said. 'If only you'd told me what you planned.'

Tony sighed patiently. They had been through this almost every day. 'Then you wouldn't have acted so surprised. And you were obviously totally surprised. Everyone could see that.'

'But to bribe Collie. . . . Do you not think he will put it about?'

'He'll not, if he has any sense. I've told him he'll answer to me. Do get on with it.'

Dick pulled on his clothes. 'Yet will they all know that I was afraid to face him.'

Tony smiled at his brother. 'And weren't you?'

'Well . . .' Dick sighed. 'I was more afraid of making a total fool of myself, by sheer ineptitude. Would you believe that?'

'*I* would,' Tony said, gently. 'But then, I know you.'

'And you,' Dick said miserably. 'I was afraid for you. I never had any idea you could handle a sword like that.'

Tony winked. 'You think I spend *all* my time gambling and whoring? I practise with the best, Dickie boy. But how was I to tell the old lady? Or even more the old man?'

'But if you intended to fight Lanken anyway, and admit to bedding Mistress Lanken anyway,' Dick said in bewilderment, 'why did you not just do it from the start?'

'Ah, but it was necessary to gain the sympathy of Morrison first, and of the crew. Don't you see?'

'I suppose so,' Dick said. But he didn't.

'And it worked like a charm,' Tony said. 'And you think I'm good with a sword? You should see me with a pistol.'

'Aye,' Dick said. 'Maybe you should teach me. Although what

Uncle Robert will say . . .'

'From what I've heard of that devil, he'll approve. I'll teach you, Dickie lad. And we'll keep quiet about the voyage, eh?' He cocked his head. 'There's the anchor.'

Jamaica. The very name sent Dick's blood pounding through his veins. He had heard so much about this island, differing opinions, from both Mama and Father. He had read so much about it. And it was his birthplace, on top of everything else. He ran into the main cabin, and up the ladder, for the moment forgetting his circumstances, clung to the rail, and stared at the low curve of beach which half enclosed the magnificent natural harbour; this was lined with bending coconut trees, but the mainland which formed the northern arm of the bay rose very rapidly from a house-fringed shore into splendid mountains, higher than any he had seen, save for the glimpse of the peaks of the Negro-held island of Haiti they had passed a few days before.

But the scenery, at once green and lush and brown and dramatic, suggestive of a wet heat—which already had his shirt sticking to his chest, for all that the sun was drooping towards the western horizon—was not half so exciting as the myriad ships which rode to their anchors in the translucent green water, or as the bumboats, manned by black men, which were already swarming around the *Green Knight,* or indeed as their clothing, which was scanty in the extreme, scarcely more than drawers for the blacks, while the whites who came on board, if they added a shirt and occasionally a handkerchief knotted around the neck to absorb the sweat, wore the same calico, and were in the main unarmed, although several carried heavy whips dangling from their equally formidable leather belts. And above all there rose into the still afternoon air a babble of what was mainly English, but spoken with such a variety of accents, such a failure of punctuation, and such a delightful brogue, it was impossible to catch more than a word or two.

'Ah, it's a place, Jamaica,' remarked Captain Morrison, at his elbow. 'You'll want to be ashore, Mr Hilton.'

Dick turned in surprise. 'The other passengers . . .'

'Can wait. I'm to apologize. Until your brother spoke up yesterday none of us had any idea who you really were. Robert Hilton's nephews. God, sir, there's a compliment to my ship. I'm right sorry about that set-to the other day, Mr Hilton. But between you, you and your brother emerged with credit. Oh, indeed.'

'You mean Tony emerged with credit,' Dick said.

Morrison flushed. 'Ah, well, Mr Hilton, 'tis a fact that not any of us knows how he'll react to a given situation. Your brother tells me you'd no knowledge of weapons. You'd have been a fool not to be scared. And he acted the right part in stepping in, even if he had to practise a subterfuge. Now sir, here's your gear, and the boat is waiting.'

Dick hesitated, glanced at Tony, who had returned to the deck, carrying their bags. Then he thrust out his hand. 'You're a friend, Captain. If I can ever assist you . . .'

Morrison winked. 'I'll call, Mr Hilton. Indeed I will.'

Dick went down the ladder into the waist, gazed at the assembled passengers, who flushed, and averted their eyes. Except for Joan Lanken, who stuck out her tongue at him, and moved it round and round, in a most suggestive fashion, before hastily tucking it away again as her husband noticed her.

'He should beat her more often,' Tony said, and joined him in the boat, where the sailors waited to thread their way through the bumboats towards the wooden dock. 'Quite a place, eh? Christ, what heat. I'd forgotten the heat.'

'And 'tis cooling now, Mr Hilton,' said the coxswain. 'Come noon, why, a man can't hardly breathe.'

The boat nosed into the dock, and Tony jumped ashore, turned to assist his brother. They stood on the somewhat shaky timber, waved to the boat as it returned to the ship, and then gazed up a dusty street, lined on either side by what appeared to be shops of various descriptions, all fronted by wide verandahs beyond which doors and windows stood open. The noise and the bustle was intensified here, as they were surrounded by a crowd of men, white and black, offering them assistance.

'Park Hotel, massa, best in town.'

'You come with me, sir: I have girls. Good clean blacks, fresh from Africa. Make your hair curl.'

'You going up country, massa? Me massa got mules, easy for ride.'

'You'll want to spend the night, gentlemen. Mistress Easy's is the place for you. Good food. Hot water. No bugs. You come with me.'

'Man, you ain't want to listen to he. You got for . . .'

'Hold on,' Tony bellowed, waving them back, for their breaths were as acrid as their bodies. 'We seek Mr Robert Hilton. Of Hilltop.'

His words acted like a pistol shot.

'Hilton?' asked one of the white men. 'Of Hilltop?'

'We are his nephews,' Tony said, importantly. 'And would acquaint him of our arrival.'

'Hilton?' cried a fresh voice, and the crowd parted to admit a sallow young man, dressed in a caricature of a London clerk, although sweat had sadly soiled his cravat, and his trousers were thick with dust. 'Not Mr Richard Hilton?'

'I am Richard Hilton,' Dick said.

'Ah, thank God, sir. Thank God. I have met every arrival this past month, hoping to find you, sir. You'll come with me, Mr Hilton. Oh, bring your friend. You, there . . .' He snapped his fingers at one of the Negroes. 'Fetch that bag. Quickly now.'

'Are you my uncle's man?' Dick fell into place beside the young man, already hurrying up the street.

'Oh, no,' he replied. 'I am Reynolds' clerk. Reynolds the lawyer, you know. Oh, no, no. We act for Mr Robert Hilton. Or I should say, we did.'

'Eh?' Tony demanded.

'Why, sir, didn't you know? How silly of me. How could you know, being at sea these last weeks. Why, sir, Mr Hilton, Mr Hilton died, but ten days ago.'

4

The Inheritance

Dick stopped as if he had walked into a brick wall. 'Dead? Oh, my God.'

'There's a problem,' Tony said. 'We are stony broke.'

The clerk smiled. 'Ah, you have nothing to worry about on that score, sir, if you are travelling with Mr Hilton.'

'Travelling with him?' Tony demanded. 'I *am* Mr Hilton.'

'Eh?'

'Mr Anthony Hilton,' Dick explained. 'My older brother.'

'Good heavens,' remarked the clerk. 'What a to-do. Oh, indeed, what a to-do. This is Reynolds and Son, gentlemen.'

The house appeared no different from any of the others lining the street; verandahs on both floors, sun-peeled warm paint, swing doors to some sort of an emporium at ground level. But the clerk was leading them up a flight of wooden steps at the side of the building.

'Oh, indeed,' he muttered. 'There will be a to-do. What Mr Reynolds will say . . .' He opened a jalousied door at the top. 'Mr Reynolds, sir. Mr Hilton, and why, Mr Hilton.'

The lawyer was not very much older than themselves, Dick decided, a tall, thin fellow with sandy hair and sandy moustaches to go with his complexion; he wore an enormous gold watch-chain, and a worried frown. 'Mr Hilton.' He came round his desk, glancing from one to the other, hand outstretched. 'And Mr Hilton?'

'I am Richard Hilton,' Dick explained. 'This is my brother, Anthony.'

'Good heavens. Welcome, gentlemen, welcome. You have heard the sad news?'

'Your man just broke it to us,' Tony said. 'Uncle Robert dead?

Why, it seems impossible.'

'Believe me, sir, all Jamaica is still holding its breath. But sit down, gentlemen, please. Charles, chairs. Look smart, man.'

The clerk hastily provided straight chairs for the two brothers, and Mr Reynolds resumed his seat behind his desk. 'You'll take a glass?'

'At five in the afternoon?' Dick asked.

'It might be an idea,' Tony said.

'Best madeira, I do assure you.' Reynolds nodded to Charles, and then placed his fingertips together, elbows on his desk, and gazed at the two men in front of him. 'Well, well, well. It was my father, you know, in this very office, who negotiated the sale of land to your mother and father, on which they built their church. The one Mr Robert Hilton burned down.'

'How did he die?' Dick asked.

'A fit. Oh, very sudden it was.' Reynolds filled three glasses, raised his own. 'I'm assured he felt no pain. Just collapsed and died. He was old. Old.' He peered into the liquid, then raised the glass again. 'We may drink to his soul. A fine man, Mr Hilton, a fine man. We could do with more of him.'

'Oh, indeed.' Tony sipped, glanced at his brother. 'He had invited us, that is, my brother, to join him on Hilltop.'

'Of course, of course. You were to learn the planting business, Mr Hilton. Ah, well, now is not the time to worry about that. Laidlaw is a good man. He'll show you the ropes.'

'Laidlaw?'

'Your late uncle's manager. You'll want to continue with the same staff, I imagine.'

'Continue with the same staff?' Dick asked. 'I don't understand.'

Reynolds frowned at him. 'You'll not sell the place?'

'You mean we could, if we wished?' Tony asked.

'Well . . . your brother could. Did your uncle not make it plain that you were his heir, Mr Hilton?'

'Why, no, not in so many words,' Dick said. 'His heir? Good Lord.'

'It is all here, in the will. Charles. Charles.'

'Here it is, Mr Reynolds.' Charles placed the folder in front of his employer.

'Ah.' Reynolds turned back the cardboard. 'Yes, indeed, a most straightforward document. But then, Mr Robert was like that. He knew what he wanted, ‍and he never wasted time on words. Everything he owned, Hilltop, Green Grove, and every article on them, is bequeathed to Mr Richard Hilton.'

'Eh?' Tony cried.

Dick stared at the lawyer in consternation.

'That is all?' Tony demanded. 'He had other relatives.'

'Oh, indeed, sir,' Reynolds agreed. 'And some, ah . . . very good friends. But not one of them has been left a thing. Mr Robert had strong views on keeping wealth all in one hand. And then, no doubt he felt that Mr Richard Hilton would wish to make his own arrangements.'

Dick continued to stare at the lawyer. His brain seemed frozen. The owning of the plantations, the position of being *the* Hilton, had been a magnificent dream, something to linger over, a promise of the future. To have it happen, without any warning, was more than he had been prepared for.

'But that is outrageous,' Tony shouted. 'The will must be contested. Obviously Uncle Robert was not in his right mind.'

Reynolds' face became cold. 'I do assure you, sir, Mr Hilton was in full possession of all his faculties, up to the moment of his death.'

'Yet is it an act of insanity,' Tony insisted. 'Oh, we shall contest it.'

'You may do as you choose, sir,' Reynolds said. 'It will make no difference. This is Jamaica, sir, not England. A man can do what he likes with his possessions, sir, here. And no one could argue that both Hilltop and Green Grove were Mr Robert Hilton's possessions.'

'Why . . .' Tony's face was suffused with blood.

Dick had at last gathered his wits. Here was something he could cope with. 'Easy, Tony,' he said. 'We knew already that Uncle Robert was an odd fellow. But it can make no difference now that he is dead. We shall split the inheritance down the middle.'

'Well . . .' Tony seemed to recover some of his composure. 'I had really not supposed I would ever have to accept your charity, Dick. But of course it is the most equitable arrangement.'

'No doubt you can draw up a suitable document, Mr Reynolds,' Dick said.

'Ah, well, sir,' Reynolds said, looking distinctly disapproving. 'I'm afraid that will not be possible. I have told you that Mr

Robert Hilton was against any tendency to split the estates. And indeed it is specifically stated in the will that the Hilton estates are not to be divided . . .'

'But we are brothers,' Dick protested. 'The property will remain Hilton.'

'Even between brothers, sir. It goes back a long time, but was the decision of Captain Christopher Hilton, who founded the Hilton wealth, you may remember, sir. Captain Hilton married twice, and had a son by each marriage, but yet left the plantations entirely to his son by his first wife, Marguerite, although with instructions that that son, whose name, as I recall, was also Anthony, was to employ and take care of his half-brother. That tradition has existed to this day, and you may recall, Mr Hilton, that your father, Mr Matthew Hilton, was employed as a manager by Mr Robert before their quarrel, but, belonging as he did to the junior branch of the family, he had no share in the plantations themselves.'

'Are you trying to say that while the plantations are mine, they are not mine to dispose of, should I wish?'

'Let me see the will,' Tony said.

Reynolds handed over the document, and smiled at Dick. They are yours, sir. And you may dispose of them. But by the provisions of Mr Robert Hilton's will, should you decide to sell them, you must discover a purchaser who will take the entire estate; i.e. both plantations together. Similarly, you may bequeath them to whomsoever you choose, on your death, but they must be passed on in their entirety, as well.'

That is what it says,' Tony agreed. 'Well, I seem to be destitute.' His voice was quiet enough, but there could be no doubting his anger.

'Oh, fiddlesticks,' Dick declared. 'So legally I cannot make you my equal partner. Be sure that you will be my equal partner. You cannot prevent that, Mr Reynolds.'

'Indeed not, sir. You and your brother can come to whatever private arrangement you choose, providing you remember that any business transactions made with regard to the plantations must be conducted in your name and yours alone.'

'Which is mere legal fiddle-faddle, eh, Tony?'

Tony gazed at his brother for some seconds. 'So, it comes down to charity, after all.'

56

'Oh, really . . .'

'But beggars cannot be choosers. I shall be your assistant, then.'
He gave a short laugh. 'Why, Mama will be delighted.'

'Well, then,' Dick said. 'There is everything solved. Now, all we
wish to do is get out to Hilltop.'

'This evening?' Reynolds inquired. 'Why, sir, Mr Hilton, it is
already gone six. And Hilltop is some distance.'

'That decides it then,' Tony said. 'We'll find a bed in town. If
you can assist us with some money, Mr Reynolds.'

'Of course, sir. If Mr Richard Hilton will sign a note . . .'

'Ye gods,' Tony said.

Dick sighed. 'Of course I will sign a note for you. But I really
would like to get out there tonight, Mr Reynolds. If you could
assist me, with a horse, and perhaps a guide?'

'I shall attend to it immediately.'

'Thank you very much. Will you not accompany me, Tony?'

His brother shook his head. 'I'm for an early bed, here in
Kingston.' He 'got up, grinned at the expression on Dick's face,
slapped him on the shoulder. 'I will be out in the morning. You
have my promise. Anyway, I'd not interfere with your pleasure at
seeing your plantation for the first time.'

Having climbed the hill, the horse stopped of its own accord. But
Dick was glad of the opportunity to relax his knees, pull out his
kerchief and wipe sweat from his brow. It was several hours past
dusk, and the sun had disappeared, huge and round and glowing,
into the Caribbean Sea. Now the mountains which loomed on
either side were nothing more than vast shadows. Yet it remained
still and almost stifling; he had discarded his coat, and carried it
across the saddle in front of him. Apart from the climate, he was
not very used to lengthy rides; the occasional Sunday outing to
Hammersmith with Mama, on hired nags, was the limit of his
previous experience.

But this was a well-chosen, quiet mount. He twisted in the
saddle to look back at the steep incline; at the top of the last rise
he had looked down on the twinkling lights of the houses in
Kingston, the ships riding to their anchors in Port Royal Bay.
Now there was nothing but the darkness, black where the trees
gathered in the dips between the hills. It was a strange blackness,
fragrant as he had never suspected the night could be, the scent of

oleander, of jasmine, of the very grass, rising sweetly to his nostrils; and it was a noisy darkness as well, for from every bush there came the disturbing grunt of the bull-frogs, the slither of the crickets, the buzz of mosquitoes, while amidst it all there flitted the glowing fireflies.

He wondered he was not afraid at this world he had only previously read of, or experienced in his mother's stories. He wondered he was not afraid of his companion, who waited, patiently, on the mule immediately in front of him. His name was Joshua Merriman, Reynolds had said, and he was one of the lawyer's slaves. A huge black man, with a ready smile and a soft voice, to be sure, but none the less, the operative thought in connection with his presence was the word black, combined with the word slave. And here he was, some fifteen miles from civilization, alone with one of the hated white people. That was how Mama would have put it, anyway. And from his belt there hung one of those very long, very sharp, and very dangerous-looking knives known as machetes, while Dick did not even possess a pistol.

'We best be getting on,' Merriman said. 'There's another three hours to Hilltop.'

Dick kicked his horse, got the animal moving again. 'You have been there before?'

'A couple of times, Mr Hilton. I did carry documents for Mr Robert Hilton to sign.'

'With Mr Reynolds?'

The black man allowed his mule to pick its way down the next incline; it was too dark to see where the animals were placing their hooves.

'By myself, Mr Hilton. I is Mr Reynolds' best boy. I can read, man, and write.' He glanced at his companion. 'Maybe you ain't believing me, sir.'

'Oh, I believe you,' Dick said, hastily. 'I was merely surprised, that a . . . well, that a Negro should . . . well . . .'

'That I should be trusted, Mr Hilton? I ain't no Negro.'

'Eh? But . . .'

'They's Congo people. Is the name what the masters give us all, no matter what. I's Ibo.'

'That is your real name, you mean?'

'No, sir, Mr Hilton. I am of the Ibo people. It is a nation, sir, like the Negroes. To call me a Negro is like if I was to call all white men English, whether they is French or Spanish or Dutch, or what.'

Dick removed his hat to scratch his head. 'Oh,' he said. 'Then I apologize. I never knew that before.'

But what a remarkable thing, for a white man to be apologizing to a Negro, Oh, dear, he thought: A black man. On the other hand, Merriman also seemed surprised, as he lapsed into silence.

They proceeded up and down, along tracks cut into the side of cliffs, with empty darkness to their left, through wooded copses, loud with rustling sound. Dick could not help but begin to wonder, eventually, if he was *not* being led astray, to his murder.

He urged his horse forward, beside the mule. 'But even Ibos do not all read and write,' he said conversationally.

'No, sir, Mr Hilton. But I's even more Jamaican than Ibo.'

'Would you explain that?'

'Is me great grandpappy what made the middle passage, Mr Hilton. That is back a hundred year.'

'Ah. Are there many slaves in Jamaica who were born here?'

'The most. All, from now, with the slave trade finish.'

'And are *they* all as well educated as yourself?'

'They ain't got no well educated field slave, Mr Hilton. It is all depending on what you train for. I did be a field slave, one time. Man, I did be a driver. But then they see how's I got brains like them, and they sell me too good. Now, I am a clerk, so I got for be educated.'

'I see. And are you happy, to be educated?'

At last the big man's head turned. 'Slave can be happy, Mr Hilton?'

'Ah. No, I suppose it is difficult. Yet there is not much trouble in Jamaica, I have been told.'

'Trouble, sir?'

'Well, when you think of what has happened in St Domingue . . .'

'Them boys had more cause, maybe,' Merriman said thoughtfully. 'And there weren't no government, that time, what with the revolution in France. Jamaica got plenty government. And anyway, where would they go? The Cockpit Country ain't no good now.'

'The Cockpit Country?'

'Well, sir, Mr Hilton, is a bad place in the north, all hill and ravine and bog and river. And is where all the runaway slaves did go, oh, since the Spaniards held Jamaica. So they become a nation, like, and the white folk call them Maroons. And they fighting, fighting, with the white folk all them years, but they getting push back, and back. And you know what, when they know what is happening in St Domingue, they start fighting again. That is only fifteen years gone. But they get beat again, and they sign treaty with the Governor. He ain't going trouble them no more, providing there ain't no murder up there, and they ain't going trouble the white folk no more. And they going send back any runaways what join them. That is the thing.' He urged his mule a little faster, came to the top of a rise, and pointed. 'Hilltop, Mr Hilton.'

And as if he had given a magic signal, the moon, enormous and round and yellow, and so low it might have been a lantern held by a giant, topped the mountains to send cold yellow light across the valley beneath them. Less a valley, Dick thought, than a large amphitheatre, almost oval in shape, mainly an endless series of canefields, but cleared in the centre, perhaps three miles away; there the moonlight showed up the sloping roofs and white walls of a little town, dominated by its chapel, silent in the darkness; farther off he could make out the bulk of the boiling house, also suggestive of a church because of its enormous chimney pointing skywards — and was it not a church, he thought, the religion of an entire economy — and then the equally orderly rows of logies in the slave village. He swung his gaze round, Mama's descriptions returning to him, and found the stables and the kitchens and the slight, man-made rise on which stood the Great House, four-square and two-storied, the white-painted verandahs shimmering in the half light, the rest of the house in darkness save for a slight glow from one of the downstairs rooms. Hilltop! The name, given to a protected valley, somehow epitomized all the Hilton philosophy. Or was it the Hilton arrogance?

'I can ask, sir?' Merriman suggested.

'Anything you like.'

'Is what it is feeling like, Mr Hilton, sir, to own all this?'

Dick glanced at the man. 'Feel like. It is terrifying, if you really want to know, Joshua. Come on.'

He kicked his horse, sent it galloping down the slope, dust flying from its heels. Up the beaten earth road he raced, the tall cane stalks waving gently beside him, hooves setting up an echo. Past the white village, where a dog commenced to bark, and was soon joined by another, and up the slope to the house, head spinning now, breath panting to match that of his horse, aware only of a consuming excitement, which made him feel almost sick, bubbling up from his belly.

'Hold there.'

He dragged on his rein, and the horse gasped to a halt before the steps of the Great House.

'You got business here, mister?'

Two black men, carrying sticks and knives, and whips.

'And who may you be?' Suddenly he was utterly grateful for the presence of Joshua.

'We is watchman, mister. And we ain't told to expect nobody this night.'

'Man, you stupid?' Joshua dismounted, held Dick's bridle. 'This is Mr Richard Hilton. This your new massa, and you had best watch out.'

'Eh? Eh?' The black men moved closer together.

'A natural mistake,' Dick assured them. 'I only landed this evening. Is the house open?'

'Oh, yes, massa. Oh, yes,' said the spokesman for the two watchmen. 'Jeremiah, you had best hustle down to town and wake up Mr Laidlaw.'

'Oh, I am sure that can wait.' Dick was already mounting the steps, hearing his boots clumping on the wood. His wood. He looked up at the bulk of the house, towering above him. His house.

'Man, massa, Mr Laidlaw would take the skin from we back if we didn't tell him you here,' said the spokesman. 'I is Absolom, massa.'

'Oh, indeed? How are you, Absolom?' He found that he had stuck out his hand without meaning to, and Absolom was regarding it with a perplexed expression. But clearly he couldn't continue apologizing every time he made a *faux pas*. 'Well,' he said. 'Shake it, Absolom. It won't contaminate you.'

Absolom glanced at Joshua, then took the fingers, very carefully.

'Thank you,' Dick said, and continued up the steps. From the verandah he looked through opened jalousies, which in turn rested against huge, thick mahogany doors, ready to be closed in the event that trouble, which Joshua said could not occur, did ever occur; and into an enormous hallway, with parquet floor and high ceiling, dominated by a great wide right-angled staircase which led to the gallery surrounding the upper floor, and by a series of portraits, both up the stairs and along the opposite wall. The whole was illuminated by a gigantic chandelier in which the candles still burned brightly.

He decided this must have been the glow he had seen from the hillside, for the light in the room to his right where the door also stood wide, had burned to nothing more than a glimmer. He stepped inside, gazed in amazement at the apparently endless sweep of parquet flooring reaching into the darkness at the back, at the upholstered chairs, at the occasional tables, laden with beaten brass trays filled with ornaments representing a variety of animals and birds, fabulous as well as actual, at the grand piano and the billiards table, and then in horror at the woman who lay, on her face, in the very centre of the floor, not six feet from where he stood.

'My God.' He ran forward, Joshua at his heels, turned her over, gazed at pale features, somewhat too big for beauty, but undeniably handsome in their regularity, and perfectly fitted to the mass of straight dark brown hair, which flowed over from his fingers to brush the floor. 'My God,' he said again. 'Is . . . is she dead?'

Joshua was kneeling beside him, peering at the woman. 'No, sir, Mr Hilton,' he said at last. 'She ain't dead. But she is dead drunk.'

Dick realized that there was, indeed, a strong smell of alcohol, and that in fact the woman was breathing, and most disturbingly; she wore an undressing robe, and nothing else that he could discover; the robe itself was flopping open, and it was easy to decide that her figure was a match to her face, at once large and well-shaped.

'That is Mistress Gale,' Absolom remarked.

'And who is she?' Dick asked.

'She does be Mr Hilton housekeeper. She is always this way.'

'Eh?'

'Drunk, Mr Hilton,' Joshua explained. 'It is well known in Kingston.'

'Good Lord. But we cannot just leave her here.'

'I going fetch Boscawen. Oh, there he is,' Absolom announced.

Dick raised his head, gaped at the black man, who wore a brilliant red jacket over black and white striped calico drawers, no stockings or shoes, but was hastily fitting a white peruke over his black curls. 'What is this?' he demanded.

'Man, hush up your mouth,' Absolom recommended. 'This is Mr Richard Hilton.'

'Eh-eh?' The butler hastened forward, ignoring the unconscious woman so far as to step over her. 'Man, Mr Hilton, sir, let me welcome you to Hilltop.'

'Glad to be here, Mr Boscawen,' Dick agreed, and straightened to shake hands. Boscawen looked at Absolom, received a quick nod, and seized Dick's fingers. 'Now, this lady, Mistress Gale? She must be put to bed.'

'Oh, you can leave she there, Mr Hilton,' Boscawen said. 'She going to wake up, soon enough.'

'She cannot stay there,' Dick decided. 'If you chaps would care to lift . . .' He frowned. She really was very scantily clad. 'No. I will lift her. If you would be good enough to show me her bedchamber, Mr Boscawen.'

Again it took some seconds for the butler to understand he was being addressed; no doubt, Dick decided, he was still half asleep. Dick stooped, got one hand under Harriet Gale's shoulders and the other under her knees, and struggled back to his feet, watching with complete dismay the front of her undressing robe once again flopping open to expose one absolutely perfect breast.

'Joshua,' he suggested.

Joshua folded the material back into place, and scratched his head. 'I going be back to town, then, Mr Hilton.'

'Of course not,' Dick said. 'You must be exhausted. Mr Boscawen will find you a bed, I have no doubt at all. As soon as we have taken care of Mistress Gale. Will you lead on, Mr Boscawen?'

The butler lit a candle and climbed the stairs, and Dick followed, the woman in his arms. Her breathing was less stertorous by now, but she was still unconscious. At the gallery he paused for breath, and also because he had become aware of noise below him; in the doorway to the left of the hall there had suddenly accumulated at least a dozen black people, women as well as men, peering at their new master.

'Good day to you,' he said. 'I will see you all in a moment.'

They stared at him, and Boscawen was waiting farther along the gallery. He now opened a bedroom door, and Dick entered, to find himself in a chamber on a scale similar to the rest of the house, some twenty-five feet square, he reckoned, containing a large tent bed as well as a variety of dressing tables. The bed had not been slept in, and he laid Harriet Gale on top of the coverlet; the night remained warm.

'Thank you, Mr Boscawen,' he said. 'Poor woman, she must be grieving for my uncle.'

'Oh, she doing that, Mr Hilton,' Boscawen agreed.

'Well, we'd best let her sleep it off, I suppose.' He backed to the door; Boscawen continued to hold the candle. She made a quite entrancing sight, he thought, and tried to estimate her age. Certainly she was not a girl, but equally certainly she was nowhere as old as Mama. And she was his housekeeper, now, presumably. What a delightful thought.

He closed the door, followed Boscawen back along the gallery, and discovered yet another two additions downstairs, a tall, spare white man, and an equally tall, thin white woman, both with red hair, and freckled rather than sunburned complexions, and both fully dressed, despite the hour; it was just beginning to grow light outside.

'Mr Hilton?' The woman stood at the foot of the stairs; she spoke with a pronounced brogue. 'I'm Clarissa Laidlaw. Charlie is your manager.'

'Mistress Laidlaw,' Dick said, and hurried down the stairs. 'I really am sorry to have awakened you at this hour, but the watchman insisted.'

'Hoots, man,' Laidlaw said, squeezing his hand. ' 'Tis dawn, and time we were adoing.'

'Oh. Yes, of course.' He glanced around the suddenly empty hallway. 'But where is everyone?'

'The house servants, you mean?' Clarissa Laidlaw inquired. 'I have sent them packing. They are the laziest swine, who only wish to stand and stare. Your coffee is being prepared.'

'At this hour?'

' 'Tis the normal time, man. The normal time,' Laidlaw said. 'Well, Boscawen, you black devil, get on with it. And send that other scoundrel back to town.'

'Yes sir, Mr Laidlaw,' Boscawen said.

'Wait a moment,' Dick said. 'That other, ah, person, is Mr Merriman. Am I correct?'

'Mr Merriman?' Laidlaw looked at him in amazement.

'Reynolds' clerk,' Dick explained. 'A very good fellow, who accompanied me out here despite the inconvenience. He certainly needs a good rest and a square meal before he can return, and I would like to thank him personally. Will you attend to that, Mr Boscawen?'

'Oh, yes, sir, Mr Hilton,' Boscawen agreed, and hurried off.

'*Mr* Boscawen?' Laidlaw remarked at large.

Clarissa Laidlaw cleared her throat. 'I'm sure you are also very tired, Mr Hilton.'

'And quite overwhelmed by my circumstances, Mrs Laidlaw,' Dick agreed. 'I had no idea my uncle had died, or that I had inherited, until yesterday afternoon.'

'Oh, good Lord, you poor boy,' she cried. 'We just did not realize.' She hesitated, her hand on his arm, frowning at him. 'I am told you have already encountered the Gale woman.'

'Mistress Gale? Oh, yes. She seemed a little unwell, so I put her to bed. 'Tis not correct, I know, but hardly so incorrect as leaving her on the floor.'

'Unwell?' Laidlaw demanded. 'The woman was drunk.'

'Well, yes, I suppose she was.'

'Incorrect? You'd not find it easy to be incorrect with that woman, Mr Hilton,' Clarissa Laidlaw said. 'But now you've arrived, we'll be seeing the last of her, and thanking the Lord for that.'

'Seeing the last . . .' Dick scratched his head. 'I'm told she was my uncle's housekeeper. Will she not perform the same duty for me?'

'Land's sakes,' cried Mrs Laidlaw.

'The lad does not understand,' her husband said. 'Housekeeper, Mr Hilton, why, 'tis just a word used in Jamaica, for . . . well . . .'

'The wretched girl was Mr Robert's mistress,' Clarissa Laidlaw declared. 'Why, she is nothing more than a prostitute. But you'll be sending her packing this morning, Mr Hilton. Oh, yes.'

'His mistress?' Dick exclaimed. 'Good Lord. But you mean, she has been living here . . .'

'As openly as you could wish,' Clarissa Laidlaw said. 'Disgusting. And then, when Mr Robert died, she just refused to move out, if you please. Said she'd wait to discover what the new owner would be like.'

'Good heavens,' Dick said. 'No wonder she was nervous.'

'But now you are here, why, you will see to it.'

'Oh, of course,' Dick agreed. 'I mean, she can't possibly stay. I could settle some sort of an income on her, I suppose . . .'

'On that woman?'

'Well, I rather feel this is what Uncle Robert had in mind,' Dick said. 'You may leave it to me, Mrs Laidlaw. Now . . .'

'Coffee,' she said.

'The bookkeepers are waiting,' said Laidlaw, who had stepped outside for a moment.

'Bookkeepers?' Dick asked. 'I'm sure that can wait until I have seen something of the plantation.'

'Bookkeepers are overseers, really,' Mrs Laidlaw explained. 'It is a local terminology. They assemble every morning for their orders.'

'We, that is, you and I, Mr Hilton, must decide which fields need the most weeding, and where we shall employ our work gangs,' Laidlaw explained. 'When we are grinding, of course, it is simpler, in a sense. But we are still some weeks away from that, thank the Lord.'

'Coffee,' Mrs Laidlaw decided, very firmly. 'Mr Hilton has been up all night.' She smiled at Dick. 'I'm sure you'll permit Mr Laidlaw to give the necessary orders, Mr Hilton. He has been doing it for years.'

'Why, yes, if you would,' Dick said. 'I wish to meet my overseers . . . I mean, my bookkeepers, as soon as possible. Perhaps later on this morning.'

Laidlaw gave a brief smile. 'These men are going four, five miles aback, Mr Hilton. They'll not return before eleven, and then it will be time for siesta.'

'Aback?' Dick asked. 'Siesta? I can see I have a great deal to learn. When would you suggest?'

'Perhaps this evening,' Laidlaw suggested. 'You'll have had a rest by then. Will you excuse me?'

Dick allowed himself to be led into the archway to the left of the stairs, found himself in a dining room hardly smaller than the

66

huge withdrawing room, containing a mahogany table which would seat sixty without discomfort, he estimated, and lined with equally large mahogany sideboards, laden with silver and crystal, while the walls were once again covered with the paintings of previous Hiltons. In the midst of this splendour the single cover looked distinctly lonely.

'But are you not going to eat with me, Mrs Laidlaw?'

'I have already had my coffee,' she explained. 'We rise early on Hilltop. Do sit down, Mr Hilton.' She rang a brass bell from the sideboard, and immediately a parade of black girls entered, each dressed in white and with a white cap on her head, each bearing a large silver dish from which arose a most delicious aroma of fried eggs and bacon and bread.

Dick sat down, had his plate loaded, and suddenly remembered Joshua. 'The man, Merriman,' he said.

Clarissa Laidlaw's smile was a trifle less warm. 'He will be fed in the kitchen, Mr Hilton. You did not really expect him to sit with you?'

'Well, no, I suppose not.' He chewed. How good it tasted.

Mrs Laidlaw poured coffee. 'You were born in Jamaica, I understand?'

'Oh, yes.'

'But left as a child. I wonder . . . do you mind if I call you Richard, Mr Hilton? It would be so much simpler. And of course I would be most obliged if you would call me Clarissa.'

'Well, of course, Mrs Laidlaw. I mean, Clarissa.'

She sat next to him, placed the mug of steaming black liquid beside his plate. 'Because the sooner you learn something of the manners and, er, morals, of the country the better.' She gave him one of her bright, paper-thin smiles. 'Not all of our morals are as loose as, well, one hates to speak ill of the dead, and Mr Robert Hilton was a good friend, oh a very good friend, but of course towards the end of his life, he had troubles, you know, oh yes, he had troubles.' She stopped, perhaps because she needed breath, perhaps because of the clipclop of hooves outside the window. 'We are busy today.'

She got up, walked to the door, and was almost bowled over by Tony. 'Eggs,' he shouted. 'By God, there's a meal. Eggs.' He sat at the table. 'Shove some over, there's a good lad. Christ, what a place. Have you seen it, Dickie lad? Have you taken a good look?

Christ what a place.'

'Who is this person?' demanded Clarissa Laidlaw.

'My brother. Mrs Laidlaw, Tony Hilton.'

'Pleased to make your acquaintance, ma'am,' Tony said, through a mouthful of egg.

'Your brother?' Clarissa Laidlaw frowned at Tony. 'Of course, he has the Hilton nose. Bu. I would have supposed he was the elder.'

'He is,' Dick said.

'But . . .'

Tony swallowed, drank some coffee, hastily placed at his elbow by one of the servants. 'It's a rum world, Mrs Laidlaw. Yes, indeed. Now, Dickie boy, you'll not credit it, but at the hotel I put up for the night there was a school of cards. And my luck was simply abominable.'

Dick sighed, also drank some coffee. 'How much?'

'I suspect they were sharpers. Before I knew what hit me, it was up to fifteen guineas. That is why I did not stay. Galloped all the way, I did, with an old nigger to guide me.'

'Where is he?'

'Oh, I sent him packing when we reached the valley. But the point is, my friends were reluctant to let me go until I signed a note. They were happy when I told them I was Robert Hilton's nephew.'

'I can imagine,' Dick said.

'Trouble is, I told them to fetch out here today and it would be settled. So if you'd be so kind, old son . . .'

'Fifteen guineas?' Dick cried. 'I have not fifteen shillings in the world in cash. Mrs Laidlaw, Clarissa, what am I to do?'

'Send *them* packing,' she said. 'Give them an order on your agent, and tell them to clear off or you'll set the dogs on them. We don't have any dogs now, more's the pity; Robert had them put down when he found he was dying. But you can have Absolom chase them with his stick.'

'Good Lord,' Dick said. 'Won't they have the law on me?'

'You are the law on Hilltop, Richard,' she said severely.

'Good Lord,' he said again.

'Sounds good, eh?' Tony said.

'But if I am the law, then I can't break it, can I?' Dick asked. 'This order on my agent, will he pay it?'

68

'From the proceeds of the crop, when it is ground,' Clarissa explained.

'But your husband says that is some weeks off.'

'So they'll have to wait. They'll be glad to, for an order on the Hilton crop. Now, then, if you are finished . . . oh, what is it, Boscawen?'

The butler cleared his throat. 'Is Mistress Gale, Mistress Laidlaw. She has woke up, and is calling for Mr Hilton.'

'Calling for him, indeed,' remarked Mrs Laidlaw.

'Ah,' Dick said. 'I suppose . . .'

'Who is Mistress Gale?' Tony asked, helping himself to more eggs.

'A lady,' Dick began.

'A lady, indeed,' snorted Mrs Laidlaw.

'I suppose we'd better see her,' Dick said, getting up.

'We'd?'

'Well, I . . .'

' 'Tis a time to show your authority, Richard,' Clarissa declared. 'A time to be a Hilton. A time to be *the* Hilton.'

'But . . .'

'Besides, she has a most foul tongue. She'd likely slander herself if she saw me. But you, now, she'll listen to *the* Hilton.'

Dick glanced at Tony, who winked; his mouth was too full to speak.

'Well,' he decided, 'I'm sure Uncle Robert intended to see her all right.'

'Friend of Uncle Robert's, was she?' Tony inquired, having swallowed.

'His kept woman,' Clarissa explained, in a huge whisper.

'I say, what fun. Good luck, Dickie old boy. Better hope she's not like him, eh?'

Dick sighed, and followed Boscawen into the hall. 'Where is she?'

'Oh, she in bed, Mr Hilton. Where you put she last night.'

Dick hesitated, then climbed the stairs, knocked on the door. After all, it was simply a matter of being firm. Courteous, but firm. And anyway, she would be so pleased to receive money she'd go without argument. The question was, how much should he give her?

He found himself staring at a young girl, and being stared at in

69

turn. The child was definitely a relation of Harriet Gale's, with the same bold features, the same potential breadth of shoulder and therefore voluptuousness of figure; he estimated she was not more than ten.

'Who're you?' she inquired.

'My name is Richard Hilton,' he said. 'I believe Mistress Gale wishes to have a word.'

The girl stared at him for some seconds longer, her mouth forming a disturbing O. Then she turned and ran into the room. ' 'Tis Mr Hilton, Mama. Oooh, but he's young.'

'Mr Hilton. Oh, please come in, Mr Hilton.' Her voice was low, and had a delightful brogue. Dick stepped round the door and realized his worst fears; Harriet Gale had undressed and got beneath the covers, and was now sitting up, naked from the waist up, and, he could not doubt, from the waist down as well; her left hand held the sheet imperfectly across her chest, her right hand held a handkerchief obviously containing ice, which she was pressing to her temple.

'Are you all right, Mistress Gale?' he asked.

'Save for me head,' she said. 'Christ, it bangs.'

'Ain't he young, Mama,' screamed the child. 'Ain't he young.'

'Ah, shut up,' bawled her mother. 'And get out. Close the door.'

The girl pouted, then gave Dick a quick smile as she sidled past. The door closed.

'Her name is Judith, Mr Hilton, and she's naught but a pack of trouble. You'll sit down?'

There was a chair in the room, but the legs beneath the sheet had moved to one side. Cautiously he lowered himself on to the bed, and inhaled her scent, which was a compelling mixture of woman and musk and stale gin.

'Perhaps you'd rather rest a little while longer.' His resolution was oozing away.

'Ah.' She tossed the handkerchief over her shoulder, and it settled on the floor. 'It does me no good at all. But I'm to apologize, Mr Hilton, indeed I am.' She peered at him; she had splendid eyes, in keeping with the rest of her, large and dark and fathomless. 'I've had that difficult a time since your dear uncle died. You *are* young.'

'I'm sorry,' he said. 'I hadn't expected to be in charge quite so

soon, you know. As for apologizing, please don't. I do understand.
Mrs Laidlaw has explained . . .'

'That bitch? She's been here already?'

'Well . . .'

'Demanding me departure, I reckon.'

'Well . . .' Dick got up, walked around the bed. The legs
promptly moved again, to allow a space on the other side. But he
remained standing. 'I mean, I doubt you'd want to stay,' he said.
'In view of your, ah, relationship with my uncle. Not now I'm
here. Oh, please, I understand about the money. I'm prepared to
make you an offer. I mean, a settlement.' He could feel his cheeks
burning. 'What do you think would be right?'

Little creases appeared on that high forehead. Then she patted
the bed, with the hand which had been holding the sheet; a pink
nipple peeped at him. 'Sit down, Mr Hilton.'

'Oh, I . . .' But he obeyed, waited for the hand to return to its
duty. It didn't.

'She'll have told you all she thinks you need know,' Harriet Gale
said. 'Bitch. They're all bitches. Jealous bitches, while my Bob
lived. Vengeful bitches, now. There's nothing worse.'

'Well, of course, I suppose it was reasonable of them to be
jealous . . .'

'Do you remember your uncle?'

He shook his head. 'I suppose he may have patted me on the
head as a child, but I don't remember him at all.'

'He was a fine man, Mr Hilton. A fine man. But he had that
accident. You've heard of that.'

'My mother has mentioned it.'

'Aye,' she said. 'But think of it, man. He'd just inherited the
plantation. Why, just like you, Mr Hilton, and no older I'll
swear.' She smiled at him. 'Not that I was born then, you'll
understand. But he told me himself. His horse threw him, and
then kicked him. You'll know where?'

'Well . . .'

'If it'd been his worst enemy it couldn't have aimed better. They
say he nearly died, from the pain of it. One ball was gone
altogether, and his tool was bent like a branch.'

'Oh. I say, do . . .'

'So you'll understand what it did to him. The most eligible
bachelor in all the West Indies, and he was afraid to lower his

breeches for fear of being laughed at. So first of all they rumoured about him, and then, when the truth was out, they laughed behind their fans. Women can be a cruel lot, Mr Hilton. I should know. Christ, how me head hurts. You'd not pour me some of that water?'

Hastily he filled a glass from the earthenware pitcher on the window sill, and held it to her lips.

'So he turned in on himself,' she said. 'He couldn't even take a nigger girl, because they laugh louder than anyone, and a white man must have authority. He was just shrivelling away.'

'I can understand how bitter he was,' Dick said. 'But I don't see . . .'

'Harry was a bookkeeper, right here on Hilltop. Oh, he was a miserable little lout. If me father hadn't left me destitute I'd never have looked at him twice. But it was Harry Gale or starve. And do you know what he did? He filled me belly with that terror out there, and then died of a colic.'

'Oh, dear,' Dick said. 'I am sorry to hear that.'

'Well, I had to go. So I came up here to say goodbye, all swollen belly, and there was me Bob staring through the window of the study, and you know, Mr Hilton, we didn't hardly say a word? Maybe he'd been looking at me during the year I'd lived here. And I had to be looking at him, because he was the master. And we looked at each other for five minutes, then he said, why not stay a while, Mistress Gale. Oh, he was nervous. I'd never have believed it, in a man like Robert Hilton. And would *you* believe it, Mr Hilton, all he wanted was the company, then. He figured with me belly full there couldn't be anything else. But I knew what he really wanted.'

Dick scratched his head. He was interested, despite his embarrassment. 'I don't quite understand, if he was as crippled as you say . . .'

'I used me hands, Mr Hilton. He could still feel.'

'Oh. I . . .' Hastily he got up again.

'I made him happy, Mr Hilton. His last nine years were the happiest he'd ever known.'

'I'm sure they were.'

'But of course, you can imagine the gossip,' she said. 'They used to make up lampoons about what we did in bed. And they'd whisper behind me back. But with Mr Robert Hilton protecting me, there wasn't anyone dare say nothing to me face. And then he died. Would you believe it, Mr Hilton, he wasn't buried, wasn't even cold, when those bitches from down the hill, led by that Laidlaw, came marching up here demanding that I leave, immediately.'

'But you refused?'

'I locked Judith and meself in here and told them to break down the door. Well, they've no belly for it, have they? We'll not soil our hands with her, they said, loud enough for me to hear. When the new owner arrives, he'll see to her. Mr Hilton . . .' She rose out of the bed rather like Venus rising from the waves, and as the sheet fell down to her thighs it occurred to Dick that she was indeed Venus. He had never actually seen a naked woman before, and these were the most flawless breasts he had ever imagined, large and firm, white-skinned and blue-veined, with hardened pink nipples and a wondrous damp valley between.

'Mistress Gale,' he gasped. 'For heaven's sake.'

She subsided, and regained the sheet. 'Mr Hilton, if you turn me out of here, they'll have tar and feathers to me arse before I reach the end of the drive. And what they'd do in town . . .'

'Surely you're exaggerating.'

'I'm not, Mr Hilton. Truly, I'm not. It's not the money, Mr Hilton. I'm in fear of me life. I made him happy, Mr Hilton. I swear I made him happy.'

Dick scratched his head some more. How he wanted just to lie down and go to sleep. But how the idea of lying down and going to sleep, or not as the case might be, was associated with that magnificent sight of a moment ago, and the even more magnificent sight he had just avoided. 'Well, of course,' he said. 'We'll have to make arrangements for your safety. Perhaps if you were to leave Jamaica . . .'

'Leave Jamaica?' she cried. 'I was born here, Mr Hilton. I've never been nowhere else.'

'Ah. Well . . .'

'Just let me stay a while, Mr Hilton. I'll not be in your way. Just 'til the gossip dies down. It won't be long.'

'Hm. Yes, I suppose that would be the simplest thing. All right, Mistress Gale, you can stay, until you think it is safe to leave.'

'Oh, thank God. And thank you, Mr Hilton.' She started to move again, and he hastily backed to the door.

'I think you want to have a good rest,' he said. 'But perhaps you'd join my brother and me for lunch.'

'Your brother? Well, land's sakes. But it'll be a pleasure, Mr Hilton. I don't know how to thank you, Mr Hilton, really I don't.'

He gave her a smile, backed through the door, closed it behind him, and found himself sweating. And more than sweating. The sight of her, the sound of her, the smell of her, the very *idea* of her, and Uncle Robert, had him remembering Joan Lanken, and quite forgetting poor Ellen.

'Well, Mr Hilton? Does she leave now?'

He looked down the stairs. Clarissa Laidlaw waited there, and she had been joined by half a dozen other white women, some giving him a nervous smile, others attempting to look suitably severe.

'Ah,' he said, and began his descent. He could hear the clatter of a knife and fork from the dining room to suggest that Tony was still eating. 'Well, you see, Mrs Laidlaw, Clarissa, ladies, she has explained her circumstances, and I am inclined to agree that it would be heartless of me to set her in the street so to speak . . .'

'She's not going?' Clarissa Laidlaw's voice rose an octave.

'Well, not immediately. When she has got over her grief, and . . .'

'She's flashed her tits at you,' Clarissa Laidlaw shouted. 'That's what she's done.'

'Please, Clarissa.' He reached the bottom step. 'Well, of course . . .'

'I'll not stand for it,' Clarissa declared. 'We'll not stand for it. You must make up your mind, Mr Hilton. It's us or her. If she stays, we go. All of us. And we'll take our husbands with us.'

5

The Planter

Dick scratched his head. 'Now, really, ladies, please do not take on so. It will only be a short while, and then Mistress Gale will be gone.'

'A short while?' cried Clarissa Laidlaw.

'She'll be here forever,' said another voice.

'We know her like, Mr Hilton,' said a third.

'We'll get rid of her for you, Mr Hilton,' said a fourth. 'But tell us to do so.'

'Ah,' Dick said. 'That is exactly what she is afraid of. No, no, ladies. I have told her that she may stay for a while, and given her my promise that she will not be molested.'

Clarissa Laidlaw glared at him. 'And that is your last word on the matter?'

'Why, yes, I suppose it is, for the time being. Now, Clarissa, if you'd be good enough to introduce me . . .'

'That's it, then,' she declared. 'We leave. The moment our men come in from aback.'

'Leave?' Dick cried. 'You're not serious.'

'They say they're going,' Tony observed, from the dining room archway. 'Well, then, Mrs Laidlaw, I suggest you get on with it.'

She glanced at him, and flushed. 'There's the notice . . .'

'Just clear out,' Tony said. 'We'll forget the notice.'

'You can't speak to me like that,' she declared. 'You're not Mr Hilton.'

'What they are trying to do, Dickie boy,' Tony explained continuing to smile at the women, 'is to establish who really is the master here. You surrender to them now, and they'll have you waiting on table.'

'Really,' said one of the other women. Mrs Laidlaw appeared to have lost the power of speech.

It occurred to Dick that Tony, as usual, was absolutely right, that in fact Clarissa Laidlaw had been treating him like a slightly backward younger brother all morning.

Tony could read his expression. 'And it is always better to dismiss people than have them dismiss you,' he said. 'Ladies, as of this moment, you are under twenty-four hours' notice to quit Hilltop. Oh, and take your husbands with you.'

'You . . . you . . . you'll not permit this, Richard,' Clarissa shouted.

'I'm afraid you have brought it on yourself,' Dick said. 'Of course, I'm perfectly willing to forget the whole business . . .'

'Never,' she cried. 'Not while that woman stays.'

She was looking up the stairs, and Dick turned his head; Harriet Gale, wearing the same crimson undressing robe as when he had first seen her and with her feet bare, was standing on the gallery above him.

'Christalmighty,' Tony remarked. 'Well, then, ladies, you'd best be off.'

'Mr Hilton,' began one of the other women.

'Out,' Tony commanded, advancing on them. 'What are the magic words, Mrs Laidlaw? I'll set the dogs on you. Or is it Absolom?'

The other women were already backing towards the door. But still Clarissa hesitated. 'You won't get away with this,' she said. 'You think you'll find other overseers? None like my Charlie. Your cane will rot. You'll go bankrupt. Hiltons. You think . . .'

'Boscawen,' Tony said, for the butler, and the other domestics, were hovering behind him in the pantry, listening to the row. 'Would you find this chap Absolom. Tell him to bring his stick.'

'Oh, you . . .' Clarissa Laidlaw turned and fled behind her companions.

'You were magnificent. Magnificent.' Harriet Gale descended the stairs, her undressing robe threatening to disintegrate at every movement.

'I wonder if we weren't a little hard,' Dick mused.

'Strength, boy, that's all any of these people understand,' Tony declared. 'Aren't you going to introduce us?'

'I do apologize. Harriet Gale, Anthony Hilton. Mr Hilton is my brother, Mistress Gale.'

'Me pleasure, Mr Hilton.' She gave Tony her hand, but withdrew it immediately to grasp Dick's arm. 'But your brother is right, you know. You must be strong. With those people no less than with the blacks.'

'Oh, no doubt,' he agreed. 'But supposing they carry out their threat . . .'

'Carry out *their* threat?' Tony demanded. 'You have dismissed them, Dickie boy. You can't change your mind now.'

'Oh, indeed, your brother is right, Mr Hilton,' Harriet said.

'Aye, well, when they have gone, who is going to manage the plantation?'

Harriet gave his arm a squeeze. 'Why, you are, Mr Hilton. It'll be in your blood. And besides, I'll show you.'

Laidlaw looked uncomfortable, shifted from foot to foot. 'I'm right sorry it had to come to this. That woman is a trouble-maker. Oh, indeed, yes.'

'I'm afraid I don't agree with you at all,' Dick said. 'She is an extremely unfortunate woman. It would be betraying my inheritance were I to turn her into the street.' He spoke as evenly as he could, for all the churning misery that had been swelling in his belly throughout the day. What a beginning to his career as a planter. Whatever would Mama say? Or Ellen? He had a terrible suspicion that Ellen might well take the side of Clarissa Laidlaw. He couldn't be sure about Mama.

And even that became quite irrelevant beside the question of how the plantation was to be operated.

'Aye, well, if that's your attitude, there's naught more to be said.' Laidlaw looked down the drive at the town. The scene reminded Dick of a Biblical exodus. Although he had not intended to press the matter, the white staff were leaving this very evening. The men had been informed of the situation when they had returned from the fields at eleven o'clock, and the packing had commenced immediately. Now each house was faced by a wagon, into which the domestic slaves were piling furniture and clothes, while children wailed and dogs barked and dust eddied. Laidlaw sighed. ' 'Tis not a sight I'd ever expected to see on Hilltop. Man, this place was our home.'

'There is really no need to leave in such haste,' Dick pointed out. 'You're welcome to stay until you find accommodation, or new posts, elsewhere in the island.'

'Aye, well, 'tis the women, you understand, Mr Hilton. When they get their tails up, if you'll pardon the expression. Maybe if we could delay their departure, give them time to cool off . . .' He turned back, and checked, and Dick also turned to look at the stairs. Harriet Gale had rested, and was now dressed. She wore a pink riding habit and carried a pink tricorne in her hand; her cravat was white lace, bubbling under her throat, and her long dark hair lay straight down her back. She looked absolutely magnificent, and save for the shadows under her eyes there was no trace of discomfort from her drinking. Laidlaw sighed. 'They'll not, if she goes out like that.'

'I am going to show Mr Hilton his plantation,' she announced. 'Boscawen. Boscawen. Are the horses ready?'

'They's waiting, Mistress Gale.'

'I'll take my leave, Mr Hilton,' Laidlaw said. He glanced at Harriet. 'Your day, Mistress Gale. Your day. But wheels turn. Indeed they do.'

He clumped down the steps to his waiting mule. Dick took a step forward, and had his arm seized. 'You'll not weaken now, Mr Hilton,' she whispered. 'Then 'tis you would have to leave.'

He was shrouded in the scent of musk. He dared not look at her. 'I'm shivering like a jelly.'

'Ah, but no one would know it.'

'So they're off then.' Tony had also donned riding gear, and slapped his boots with his crop. 'Damned good riddance. Now then . . .'

'Aye,' Dick said. 'Now then. What do we do?'

'Well, as the heat is leaving the sun,' Harriet said, 'the gangs would normally be resuming work.'

'Supervised by bookkeepers.'

'Oh, indeed. They are lazy scoundrels, and will not work unless driven to it.'

'I'm sure you are too hard on them,' Dick said. 'And anyway, we have no bookkeepers *to* drive them.'

'But you have the drivers,' Tony said. 'I have been talking to that chap Merriman.'

'Merriman,' Dick exclaimed. 'By God. Joshua, are you there?'

'Well, here I am, Mr Hilton.' Merriman wore his hat and also carried a crop. 'I's best be getting back to town, or Mr Reynolds going have the Custos out after me.' He grinned at Dick. 'You's the master now, Mr Hilton. You's just got to show them boys, and they going obey you all right.' His right hand started to move, and then hastily dropped back to his side.

But Dick was gazing at him in delight, an idea forming in his mind. 'Joshua. You'll stay.'

'Eh? Mr Reynolds . . .'

'I'll send to Mr Reynolds. Make him an offer. Stay and be my overseer.'

'Me, Mr Hilton?'

'A black man?' Harriet demanded. 'That is not possible.'

'Why not?'

'Well . . . I'm sure it's not legal.'

'Mistress Laidlaw told me I am the law, on Hilltop. You know planting, Joshua. You told me so.'

'Well, that is a fact, Mr Hilton.'

'You'll head the drivers,' Dick decided.

'I wonder if you are not being a little premature,' Tony said. 'Will the niggers follow one of their own people?'

'Or will they follow him too well?' Harriet suggested.

'They will follow us,' Dick said. 'Joshua will act for us. Now, Joshua, go down the hill and tell them I will address them in half an hour.'

'Yes, sir, Mr Hilton.' Joshua ran for his mule.

'Address them?' Tony inquired.

'You do not speak with those creatures, Mr Hilton,' Harriet said. 'They understand the whip, and nothing less.'

'Couldn't that be because they have never known anything different?' Dick asked. 'And in any event, surely they are entitled at least to see their new owner.'

'There's a point,' Tony agreed. 'Whips. We'll need whips. You have whips, Boscawen?'

'There's Mr Robert's big whip, sir.'

'Fetch it.'

'I'm not going to whip anyone,' Dick said. 'I'm going to speak with them.'

'Can't be too careful, old boy,' Tony said. 'Besides, the whip is the symbol of authority in these parts, eh? I've read all about it.'

'Your brother is right,' Harriet said. 'No white man should go amidst the blacks without a whip.'

'Oh, very well,' Dick said. 'You can carry the whip, Tony. Shall we go?'

He led them down the stairs, climbed into the saddle; the waiting grooms held the stirrup and made a back for Harriet, and she settled herself side saddle, right knee high, pulling gloves over her fingers. It occurred to Dick that she was the loveliest sight he had ever seen. But what an amazing thought. He had only left Ellen and Mama five weeks before. And yet, it was a thought quite in keeping with his surroundings, the heat and the dust and the glaring sun, and his position, sitting on a horse in front of a magnificent house, also his, having dismissed with a wave of his hand some thirty employees, and now about to face up to . . . he had no idea how many more. Surely he was dreaming all of this. Or he had dreamed all of his previous existence. But there was the truth of the matter. The old cliché that the West Indies were a different world was absolutely true.

'Well?' Tony was also mounted, the huge bull whip resting in front of him on his horse's neck.

Dick kicked his mount, moved slowly down the hill. First the town had to be passed, and the bookkeepers stopped in their work to watch him. He expected more than just looks, but they offered no comments. Again, this was not England, where one man was as good as the next, at least in physical matters. As Clarissa Laidlaw had truly said, he was the master, the law itself, within the valley of Hilltop, and no one would risk his anger. He felt almost sick with excitement.

The town was behind him, and he faced the village, and the largest crowd he had ever seen, or so it seemed. He drew rein, and watched Joshua spurring up the rise towards him.

'They's waiting, Mr Hilton.'

'Good man. How many are there?'

Joshua rolled his eyes. 'A good number, sir. A good number.'

'There are one thousand and fifty-three slaves on Hilltop, at the last count,' Harriet said.

'Good Lord. How do you know?'

'Your uncle kept a very careful tally,' she said. 'Now, there were three women due to deliver, last week. But I do not know if they have, and if the piccaninnies were born alive.'

Dick frowned at her; she might have been speaking of a herd of cattle.

80

She returned a smile. 'That is something you have to deal with as well. But I will help you. I love watching the births.'

'Eh? Oh. Good Lord.' Watch a birth? He walked his horse down the hill, Joshua falling in at his rear, and checked again. 'What on earth are they guilty of?'

He pointed at the four triangles, each filled with a naked black man, suspended by the wrists, feet dragging in the dust.

'Well, I ain't knowing that, Mr Hilton,' Joshua confessed. 'You got for ask Absolom.'

The drivers waited in a group in front of the slaves, dominated by the bulk of Absolom. Dick turned his horse towards them.

'Why are those fellows suspended?'

'They're waiting for the lash, Mr Hilton, sir,' Absolom said. 'I does beat them, but a bookkeeper got for be present.'

'And their crime?'

'Well, sir, they does be insolent and lazy fellows. Mr Laidlaw done say so.'

'Ah. Well, cut them down.'

'Sir?'

'Cut them down. This is my first day on Hilltop, and there'll be no whipping today. Haste, man.'

'They should be whipped,' Harriet said. 'A flogging does them good.'

'Let's call it an amnesty,' he said. 'My aim is to win the affection, the hearts, if you like, of these people.'

'My God,' Tony said, apparently to himself.

Harriet was frowning. 'They have no hearts, no affection,' she declared. 'They are ruled by fear. I quote your uncle, Mr Hilton. The sentiments are not me own.'

'We shall see.' Dick watched the four naked men, having been released from the triangles, coming towards him. 'Cover them up,' he bawled, flushing with embarrassment, wondering if being tied up to await a whipping would have the same effect on him.

Absolom hastily marched the men round the back of the crowd, and Dick moved closer. He regarded, by Harriet's figures, a thousand and more people, men and women and children, gathered in a huge dark group, black faces remarkably contrasting with the white cotton drawers and chemises which were all any of them wore; while the children were naked. But as he approached he realized that they were not all of the same colour, while their faces were noticeably varied, from the broad, friendly features of the darker Congolese Negroes to the aquiline reservedness of the Mandingoes.

'Will they all understand English?' he asked Joshua.

'I think so, Mr Hilton. They all must be living in Jamaica these two years at the least.'

He drew a long breath. The crowd seemed absolutely still, save for the restless movements of the children. But they gazed at him, expectantly. And with what in their hearts, he wondered. Hatred? Respect? Fear? Or merely apathy?

'I am Richard Hilton,' he shouted. 'I shall live here from now on. I shall take the place of my uncle, Robert Hilton. But I am not Robert Hilton. You will discover who I am, as the days go by. I am here to grow sugar, to make this plantation prosperous. You will help me to do that. You will work hard, and please me, and none of you will be punished. And I will work beside you, as hard as any of you. So will my brother here, and in all things you will regard him as me. With mine, his word is law on Hilltop. Should you not work hard, be sure that you will be punished. But why be punished? See, I have taken down your four comrades who were to be whipped, because I will have no man suffer for a crime committed before I came to Hilltop. And I have dismissed my bookkeepers, because they would rule by the whip. Now then, this afternoon there will be no more work. Tomorrow morning you will go aback as usual, and recommence your labour. You will be commanded by Absolom here, and his drivers, and the inspection will be carried out by this gentleman, Joshua Merriman, who you will regard as my deputy in all things. Very good. You are dismissed to your houses.' He turned to Joshua. 'Go amongst them, and make sure they understand me.'

'Oh, I going do that, Mr Hilton. They going follow you, sir. They going follow you.'

He rode down the hill towards the silent crowd.

'What do you think?'

'A very good speech,' Harriet said. 'I doubt they'll know what to make of it. Let's get back to the house. The stench of their bodies afflicts me nostrils.'

'You said something about an inspection.'

'Tomorrow will do,' she said. 'Christ, how me throat is dry.'

'Me too,' Tony said. 'When I saw all those black faces, why, I doubted not our last moment had come.'

'Rubbish,' Dick declared. 'They are but people, who require to be treated as people, and we shall have no trouble.' He wheeled his horse, saw Laidlaw seated on his mount only a few feet away; the first of the wagons had already begun its journey down the drive.

'You speak well, Mr Hilton,' the manager said. 'You should be a politician, like your father. But those people need the whip, not words.'

'They'll work, Mr Laidlaw. They'll work.'

'Aye,' Laidlaw said. 'We'll see how they work, when it comes to grinding.'

'A toast.' Tony Hilton stood, and raised his glass. 'To the Hiltons of Hilltop. Long may they prosper.'

He slurred, very slightly, and swayed. At the opposite side of the table Harriet Gale gave a giggle of tipsy laughter. They had both drunk far too much.

But then, Dick wondered, had he not also drunk far too much? Without achieving the blessings of inebriation. He kept thinking how absurd they looked, the three of them, he and Tony in their black jackets and white stocks, Harriet in a splendid evening gown in dark blue taffeta which seemed to hang from her breasts as if attached there, leaving shoulders and arms exposed; they were milky-white shoulders and arms, with a dusting of freckles, and plumper than he had first observed.

Now she tossed her head, scattering that long, straight dark mane, so that some fell behind and odd strands descended most entrancingly in front, trickling across the white swell of flesh, and raised her own glass, to squint through it at the light. 'Empty, by God. Vernon, you black devil, fill it up. Fill it up.'

Dick sighed, and watched the footman hastily reaching for the decanter. It apparently had been his uncle's humour to name all of his house servants after British admirals. But he also felt like another drink. It was a form of hysterical release, he decided. The bookkeepers, and their wives, and their children, and their dogs, had gone. The town stood derelict. No doubt it would soon fill again, as Reynolds advertised, as they obtained the right people. But what a remarkable day it had been. No, indeed, what a remarkable two days; he had not slept a wink last night. Now he could hardly keep his eyes open, and his head swung, at once with exhaustion and alcohol, and his brain seemed filled with nothing but the presence of Harriet Gale. He thought he could sit here the entire night, just staring at the freckled flesh, just dreaming.

The decanter crashed past his ear, struck the parquet, and shattered into a hundred pieces of crystal.

'Ow me God,' cried Vernon, staring at the liquid spreading across the floor.

'Oh, Christ,' Harriet screamed, sitting up.

'God damn you for a bastard,' Tony bawled.

Dick rubbed his ears, watched Boscawen pounding in from the pantry.

'What is this?' cried the butler.

'It slip, man, it slip.' Vernon was on his knees, his napkin turning red as he swabbed at the wine.

'Ah, well, fetch another,' Tony commanded.

'Crystal,' Dick said. 'My God. What did that thing cost? Mistress Gale?'

'Ah, what does it matter. 'Tis a waste of good wine,' she said. 'There's the problem. They are crazy swine, these people, careless as devils from hell. 'Tis break this and smash that, all the while.'

'Crystal,' he muttered. 'There's pounds and pounds. My God.' His money. Supposing he had any. He hadn't seen a single entry in a book, so far, to prove he wasn't bankrupt. If they threw crystal around like snowballs . . . he sat upright at the sound of hooves. 'What's that?'

'See to it, Boscawen,' Tony commanded. 'And for God's sake bring on the meat, man.'

'Yes, sir, Mr Hilton, sir.' Boscawen took the commands in order, daintily stepped round the kneeling figure of Vernon, crunched some glass beneath his bare feet and paused, with a pained expression on his face, then continued towards the door, without even a limp. 'Absolom? But what you doing up here this time?'

The driver wore only his drawers; his huge chest heaved and dripped sweat. 'Is that Mary Nine. She screaming fit to raise Damballah.'

'Eh?' Dick raised his head. 'Screaming?'

'Well, is the child, see, Mr Hilton, sir? He pushing he head out and causing she too much pain. And is a fact Mr Roche done gone

84

with them others.'

'Roche?' Dick asked, stupidly.

'The white dispenser,' Harriet said. 'This girl, Mary Nine, is too young to have a child, really. She will probably die.'

'Die?' Dick scrambled to his feet. 'We must do something, Harriet. Mistress Gale, you must help me.' He inhaled. 'I mean help her.'

'Me? Help a nigger girl give birth?'

'You must. You said you like to watch. Now you can do more. Horses, Mr Boscawen. Quick, now.'

Boscawen glared at Absolom. 'You seeing what you done, you stupid black man? You upset the master.'

'Well, she screaming . . .'

'Horses,' Dick said firmly. He seized Harriet's wrist and half dragged her from her chair. 'Please. Tony . . .?'

Tony was regarding the enormous side of beef being brought into the dining room by two other of the footmen. 'I'll just stay here and mind the house,' he said.

'For God's sake.' Dick pulled Harriet from the room. 'Horses.'

'You can use mine, Mr Hilton, sir,' Absolom said.

'Oh, thanks.' Dick gasped, and swung into the saddle.

'I will come whenever mine is saddled,' Harriet decided.

'Now,' he insisted, leaned down, grasped her under the armpits, and tried to lift her.

'Aaaagh,' she screamed.

'Help me,' he shouted at Absolom.

The driver hesitated for a moment, then ran forward, seized Harriet's ankles, and pumped them upwards. A moment later she was sitting in the saddle in front of Dick, squirming to make herself comfortable, her hair flowing back to fill his mouth, while she gasped for breath.

He was already kicking the horse forward, sending it galloping down the hill, towards the hubbub which marked the slave village.

'Really, Mr Hilton,' she said, having got her breathing under control. ' 'Tis no way to treat a lady, indeed it is not. I'd not remained on Hilltop to be midwife to a black.'

'I'd not know what to do without you,' he said, and rode into the street of the village, to find himself in the midst of the slaves, all clamouring at him, setting up a tremendous din, but mostly, he realized, in wonderment at his presence.

'Is the master, man.'

'Eh-eh, but you seeing that?'

'And Mistress Gale.'

'Man, but what is this?'

Harriet slid from the saddle, struck the ground rather heavily, and hastily adjusted her skirts. Dick jumped down beside her. 'Where is the hospital?'

'Hospital, massa? Hospital?'

'The dispensary,' Harriet shouted, possibly at him.

'Ah, yes, the dispensary.'

The unearthly scream which cut through the night was a better directive than any of the gabbled instructions. He thrust them aside and ducked his head to enter the building, slightly larger than the average hut, to recoil in horror at the foetid stench which swept across his nostrils. The dispensary was hardly less crowded than the street, and the flickering torches seemed to be licking at the very beams of the rafters. In the centre of the floor a space had been left clear, and here Joshua Merriman knelt.

'Joshua,' Dick gasped in relief, ran to his side, and again recoiled as he watched the blood trickling across the beaten earth floor, issuing from between the legs of the young Negress, she really was only a girl, who lay there, her head on Joshua's knees.

'Oh, my Christ.' Harriet stood beside him. 'She's gone.'

'Joshua?'

Joshua raised his head. He looked tired. But he held in his hands a tiny scrap of black humanity. 'It jammed up,' he said. 'I had to take it, hard.'

'Godalmighty!' Dick had to shake his head to clear his senses. 'And the child?'

Joshua sighed. 'That too, Mr Hilton, sir. That too. I done make a messup of this one.'

'And you needn't have called us at all,' Harriet said severely. 'Ugh. Me dress has blood on it. Really, Mr Hilton . . .'

'You can have another dress,' he promised. Wasn't that the attitude around here, and with lives no less than possessions? 'What do we do?'

Joshua laid the babe beside its mother. 'Well, we got for bury them, Mr Hilton. You there, take them out.'

Two of the men came forward, one to seize the wrists and the other the ankles of the dead woman, as if she had been a sack of coal. Another picked up the child by the ankles.

'My God,' Dick said. 'It can't be done now. There is no coffin, no priest . . .'

'Coffin? For a black girl?' Joshua was amazed.

'Well, at least let us wait until morning.'

'It warm, Mr Hilton, sir,' Joshua pointed out. 'Morning time she going be smelling high, and causing sickness.'

Dick scratched his head. The bodies had already been removed. 'But . . . a priest . . .'

'Mr Hilton, sir, that girl ain't no Christian. If you can pray like Damballah, now, then maybe you got cause.'

'Damballah?'

'He speaks of the voodoo gods,' Harriet whispered. 'These people are heathens, snake worshippers, most of them. For Christ's sake, Mr Hilton, let us be away.'

'Is a fact, Mr Hilton,' Joshua said. 'I am too sorry to interrupt your dinner, for nothing.'

'For heaven's sake,' Dick said, 'you did the right thing, Joshua. I should be present whenever any one of them is born. Or dies. They are my people.'

'Christ,' Harriet remarked. 'You'd be down here all the time.' She ducked her head and gained the open air. The slaves stared at her.

Dick followed, gave her a leg into the saddle, mounted behind her. 'I am sorry, good people,' he called. 'It was an act of God.' Or should he have said, an act of Damballah? Clearly he must learn about this snake god. Mama had mentioned it, but in the warmth of an English parlour it had seemed a fairy tale.

The horse picked its way out of the compound, back up the hill. Harriet Gale lay against his chest with a sigh. 'You must alter the list,' she said. 'One thousand and fifty-two.'

'Eh? Just like that?'

'You must keep track of them, Mr Hilton.'

Like cattle, he thought. Count heads, every morning. 'Why was she called Mary Nine?'

'Well, think of it,' Harriet said. 'Better than a thousand. How are you to keep a tally? Your uncle decided it. Half a dozen names, male and female, and after that, numbers. Each field gang has a name, you see.'

'Absolom has no number.'

'Ah,' she said. 'When they get to be drivers, they get proper names, like the house slaves.' She nestled her shoulders against his chest. 'You've a lot to learn, Mr Hilton. But the sooner you start the better. Like the way to carry a lady on a horse is to hold her round the waist.'

'I am holding you round the waist,' he said, 'as my arms are on either side of you.'

'Pfft,' she said. ' 'Tis not what I meant at all.'

'Now really, Mistress Gale,' he said. 'You were my uncle's . . .'

'Housekeeper.'

'Yes, but you have yourself told me . . .'

'That I administered to his needs. But if you think a bit you'll understand I have not been penetrated by a man these nine years. 'Tis a long time.'

'For heaven's sake, a girl has just died.'

'Ah, you'd not confuse a nigger with a human being, now would you? That Merriman himself told you they're not Christian.'

He sighed. 'Anyway, I'm betrothed.'

'Are you now.' Her head half turned, her musk and her hair seemed to balloon around his face. 'To a girl in England?'

'Of course. She'll be joining me whenever I am settled. My God, I am settled.'

'You think so? You want to be sure,' she said. ' 'Tis a mighty big business bringing a young lady all the way from England to Jamaica. Why think on tonight. She'd be fainting by now.'

He frowned into the darkness. Ellen? Somehow he did not think she would have fainted tonight. She'd be far more likely to have replaced Joshua on the floor, holding the dead child.

'Nine years,' Harriet said. 'Ah, 'tis a long time. I doubt not I'll have forgotten what it's like.'

The horse stopped in front of the steps, and Dick hastily dismounted. She fell from the saddle into his arms. 'Anyway,' he said, 'there is the matter of, well . . .'

'So I'm a year or two the elder. A young man always wants to begin with an older woman. 'Tis a well known fact.'

He escorted her to the steps. What an incredible conversation to be having, with an incredible woman, on an incredible day. 'I'm starving,' he said, and stopped in the archway to the dining room, to gaze at Tony, asleep with his hair trailing in an overturned glass of port. 'For heaven's sake. Mr Boscawen,' he called. 'Where is that side of beef?'

'Eh-eh, but you back quick, Mr Hilton.' The butler came in from the pantry, minus his wig, and wiping his lips with a linen napkin. 'The beef, master? We — we just done finish it.'

'Eh? A whole side of beef?'

'Well, sir, Mr Hilton, there does be fourteen of us out there, what with the maid and thing.'

'My God.' Dick sat down.

'But no matter, sir, I going fetch another side of beef. It only a matter of cooking it quick. One hour, on the spit. Meantime you and Mistress Gale can drink some wine, eh?'

'One hour? More wine?' Dick got up again. 'I'm for bed. I'll say good night, Mistress Gale. Maybe you'd try waking up my brother.'

'They're waiting, Mr Hilton.' Joshua stood in the door to the dining room, his straw hat in his hands. In the half light of the dawn he looked even bigger than he was.

Dick finished his mug of steaming black coffee, handed it to the serving girl — he still could not remember their names — and got up. 'No sign of Mr Hilton?'

'No, sir. Mr Boscawen saying his bed ain't been slept in.'

Dick nodded, and sighed. All week Tony had been growing more and more restless, more and more bored with life on Hilltop. And it had seemed a good idea to send someone into Kingston, to see how Reynolds was getting on with raising some new bookkeepers . . . but then there had been the quarrel over money. Tony just had not been able to understand the need for economy. He had discovered that in the good old days Robert Hilton had kept his own string of race horses, had matched them, here on Hilltop, against the best in the island on magnificent social occasions which were still the talk of Kingston. But that had been twenty years ago, and the race course was now overgrown, the grandstand rotting. It would cost a fortune to clear and repair. Money they did not have, and would never have, so far as Dick could see. The waste on this plantation was on a scale he had not suspected possible. By reasonable accounting techniques they were quite literally tearing their wealth up. Nor had his day spent in studying the books in the office brought him much happiness.

The turnover was in figures not even his banking background allowed him properly to grasp, and yet there was no profit that he could see. The plantation was worth five million pounds, on paper; there was the question as to whom they could ever sell it to. Their last crop had fetched nearly five hundred thousand pounds on the London market, but by the time all the notes had been settled, all the provisions, the wines and the cheeses and the sweetmeats, the clothes and the furniture, the staves and the barrels, the replacement machinery for the factory, the powder and the ammunition for the firearm store, the perfumes for Mistress Gale, the ice for the cold cellars, brought all the way from Newfoundland by specially equipped ships, had been accounted for, they had been left with a debit balance of two thousand, which had had to be added to the debit balances accumulated over the previous twenty years to make a total outstanding of thirty-one thousand pounds. The London agent was not apparently concerned. It was the war, the closure of the European markets, the high freight and insurance costs. Once the war ended, why, the debt would rapidly be reduced. At one time in the middle of the last century, a Hilltop crop had fetched a million pounds on the London market. Another year like that and the debt would be liquidated. Supposing sugar ever regained quite that place in the nation's favour. Because now the American market was closed as well.

But Tony, for all his huffing and puffing, had promised to return by dawn.

Dick put on his hat and went outside. The drivers were assembled in front of the steps. Even after a week they still grinned with embarrassment, and shifted their feet, to be standing where the white bookkeepers had assembled in the past. But they chorused their 'good morning master' with enthusiasm.

'Well, Josh, what's the programme for today?' Dick asked.

'I thinking the north west corner, Mr Richard, sir.' Joshua had spread the map of the plantation on the table Boscawen had placed in the centre of the verandah. 'There is too much weed up there. So I thinking we making a concentrated effort there, and working our way down. Is only two months to grinding.'

'Aye.' And what then, Dick wondered. Joshua was an excellent field manager, to be sure; as good as any white man. But who would be sure all the machinery worked properly, or indeed that

90

the sugar was properly boiled, the molasses properly separated? 'See to it then. I'll follow in a few moments.'

'Yes, sir, Mr Richard, sir. Come on. Come on,' Joshua bawled. 'Mount up. Get those black people moving.'

He mounted his horse, his whip slapping his thigh. He wore a white shirt tucked into his brown corduroy breeches, and a wide-brimmed straw hat, and black boots. He was the most enthusiastic man on the plantation. This was his chance of a lifetime, and he did not intend to waste a moment of it.

Boscawen held Dick's stirrup, and he swung himself into the saddle, carefully. He really was not used to spending half of every day sitting on hard leather which happened to be situated on an even harder horse; his backside was raw. 'Thank you, Mr Boscawen,' he said. 'Whenever Mistress Gale arises, invite her to join me for breakfast, will you?'

The meal was taken at eleven, when the sun grew too hot to remain longer in the fields. And of course she always joined him; but he was determined to maintain the formality of their relationship. When sober she was the soul of propriety, but she did not believe in staying sober a moment longer than was absolutely necessary. Presumably he should do something about that, such as refusing her all alcohol. Presumably . . . there was so much that he should do something about. Whoever had given the English public the idea that West Indian planters were a bunch of arrogant megalomaniacs who whipped their slaves and gambled and fornicated and drank themselves into early graves?

Although he could believe the early grave aspect of the situation. He drew rein at the foot of the hill. 'For God's sake, Judith, whatever are you at?'

The girl had been playing at tag with several black children, and had apparently fallen, or been rolled, in the dust. Her hair was matted and her face might have been coated with a brown powder.

'Just playing, Mr Hilton. Just playing.' She straightened her skirt, which had wrapped itself around her legs. She had very long legs, a trifle thin. But they would fill out. As the matchstick which formed the upper part of her body would also no doubt fill out. There was a problem, for the future. As if she was the only one.

He walked his horse into the little cemetery, dismounted, took off his hat. He came here every day. It was a peculiarly solemn place. The graves seemed to frown at him, each headstone a piece of West Indian history.

'Christopher Hilton, born 1651, died 1722, Rest in Peace.'

He wondered if old buccaneers ever rested in peace. But Kit Hilton had been the most successful of the breed, however many men, or women, he had had to kill to reach his prosperous heights. Which had been responsible for all this.

'Marguerite Hilton, born 1652, died 1690, Rest in Peace.'

There was nothing under that stone, neither bones nor peace. Marguerite Hilton had died of leprosy, had mouldered away on the leper island off Green Grove in Antigua. My God, Green Grove. He owned the place and had never visited it. Something to be done. But Reynolds said John Tickwell was a good man, and the Green Grove bookkeepers had not elected to quit. Now there was an idea; perhaps one or two of them could be persuaded to come to Jamaica for the grinding.

'Lillan Hilton, born 1659, died 1727, Rest in Peace.'

His own great-great-grandmother, Kit Hilton's second wife, the Quaker who had brought some goodness into that turbulent family, whose influence had perhaps made Matthew Hilton what he was. And thus his son? Or at least one of them.

An unmarked grave. But the stone was now being carved, and would read, 'Robert Hilton, born 1740, died 1810, Rest in Peace.' His decision, to follow the fashion of the severely limited wording, the blessing at the end. But of them all, Robert Hilton would perhaps lie the least peacefully. If all the tales were to be believed. He was Marguerite's great-grandson, not Lillan's, and had acted the part.

And in time, perhaps, Richard Hilton, born 1785, died —? And would there be a Rest in Peace on that? Dick climbed into his saddle, walked his horse away from the cemetery and into the avenue of canes, tall now, reaching above even a mounted man to shut him away from human sight, from even the dawn breeze. A lonely, quiet place, and the pleasanter for that. And yet, an evocative place, as well. The towering green stalks to either side symbolized his wealth, and his power, and his responsibility, and the labour which was rushing on him like a runaway horse.

He rounded a bend, came upon a gang of women, presumably weeding; they squatted, most of them to either side of the path, their chemises drawn up to their thighs in a most indecent manner, and flicked at the stones with their knives. At the sound of his hooves perhaps half a dozen increased their rhythm; the rest merely glanced up, and giggled at him, tilting the wide-brimmed straw hats back on their heads the better to look at him.

'Come on,' he said. 'Come on. Get on with it.' He slapped the whip which Boscawen always attached to his saddle, and tried to look, and sound, like Joshua, or Absolom, or indeed, Tony. But like animals, they could sense where they were in danger of a beating and where they were not. Their giggles increased, and one called out.

'Man, Mr Hilton, sir, but it hot. Why we ain't resting like?'

'There's the weeds,' he said. 'It'll choke the cane. Get on with it.'

'Not this cane, Mr Hilton, sir, it all but ready for cut.'

'Hey, Mr Hilton,' cried another, standing up. 'Why you ain't getting off that horse and having a little sweetness?' She raised her skirt to her waist and wagged her mount at him, at once bushy and dusty and provocative. He cursed the colour rising into his cheeks, and wrenched his horse round, and sighed with relief at the sound of hooves.

'Mr Boscawen? Has something happened at the house?'

The butler drew rein, adjusted his wig. 'You got a caller, Mr Richard, sir. Mr Kendrick, from Rivermouth.'

'Indeed. I'd best get back. Speak to these women, will you, Mr Boscawen. They don't seem very energetic.'

'Ah, get on with your work, you worthless whores,' shouted the butler, riding his horse into their midst, and laying about him with his crop. 'Get to it. You ain't hear what the master done say?'

They cackled with a mixture of amusement if they had avoided the blows, or anger if their flesh happened to be stinging. But the sound of the machetes quickened. Dick sighed, and trotted out of sight. Presumably it was easy enough to do, to charge into the middle of a mob of women and lay about him as hard as he could. All one had to do was do it. All.

He came in sight of the house, and the horse standing before the steps. By now Boscawen had caught him up again, and was waiting to take his bridle. He ran up the steps, faced the short, heavy man, dressed in planting clothes but with a sweat-stained blue coat over his open shirt, and carrying an old tricorne, who was seated at the top, in one of the cane chairs which lined the wall. Harriet Gale was beside him, looking her cool best in a green morning gown.

'Mr Hilton,' she cried. 'Mr Kendrick has come to call.'

Dick took off his hat, held out his hand. 'Richard Hilton, sir. Welcome.'

Kendrick was on his feet. 'Tobias Kendrick, sir. My pleasure. Mistress Gale has been making me most welcome.' He glanced at Harriet, his cheeks pink. 'Your servant, ma'am.'

'Oh, indeed.' She smiled at Dick, archly. 'He wishes to discuss business. You'll excuse me, gentlemen. There is a menu to be planned.'

She swept from the verandah with a rustle of skirts, leaving the scent of her musk on the still air.

'A remarkable woman,' Kendrick observed, shifting from one foot to the other.

'Indeed she is,' Dick agreed. 'Mr Boscawen, coffee. Do be seated, Mr Kendrick. Let me see, Rivermouth. You are my nearest neighbour.'

Kendrick sat down, carefully. 'That is so. Do you call all your people mister?'

'Those in a position of authority, certainly. Should I not? It is common politeness.'

'Politeness?' Kendrick scratched his head. ' 'Tis true, then.'

'What?'

'Well . . .' Kendrick flushed still darker, accepted a mug of coffee from Boscawen's tray. 'That you call your slaves mister, that you intend to maintain your uncle's domestic arrangements . . . 'tis what Laidlaw told me.'

'Oh, yes?'

Kendrick held up his hand. 'Please, Mr Hilton, no offence. A man does what he chooses. And by God, sir, in my belly I envy you Mistress Gale. Indeed I do. But it is difficult, sir, difficult. Your uncle, may God rest his soul, pursued his own path, enjoyed the ostracism he courted. We had hoped, my wife and I, that new blood, so to speak, would change things. Why, Mistress Kendrick would ask you for dinner, sir, to meet the other planters in Middlesex county, but to say truth, she was disturbed, disturbed, sir, to learn that you had immediately assumed, well, your uncle's prerogatives towards Mistress Gale. Well, sir, you must know, she is forty, if she is a day. And besides, why, the whole thing smacks

94

of incest.' He frowned. 'I am trying to explain a serious matter, sir.'

Dick continued to smile. 'And I was thinking how short you people must be of true conversation to engage in so much gossip. Mistress Gale is the one in a difficult position, sir. She is my housekeeper, in the most strict sense of the word. You may believe me.'

Kendrick stared at him. 'True? Good God. Well, I . . . Mrs Kendrick will never believe it. No one will ever believe it. Especially in view of what that Laidlaw woman is spreading all over Kingston.'

Dick got up. 'Your wife may believe whatever she wishes, Mr Kendrick. I understood this to be a social call. If you have come here merely to criticize my domestic arrangements I suggest you take your leave, now.' He wondered if his anger was induced by his own guilt, at his thoughts, his desires, his certainty that Harriet planned nothing less, at some future date.

'Oh, permit me to apologize, Mr Hilton. I do, indeed, and abjectly.' Kendrick remained seated. 'I am here on a far more important matter. Your seat.'

'Eh?' Dick sat down again.

'The Hilton seat in the House. It is yours, as owner of Hilltop. Here again, I must say, your uncle cared little for politics in his later years. The seat has gathered dust these last twelve sessions. But we have hopes that you, sir . . . well, these are dangerous times. The English Parliament, God damn them, is out to get us, sir. There is no doubt about that. This abolishing of the slave trade, and done by a relative of yours too, I believe . . .'

'You are referring to my father, sir,' Dick said. 'And he would hate to take the credit for that accomplishment. He merely supported Mr Wilberforce and Mr Fox.'

'Your father? God damn. Matthew Hilton is your father?' Kendrick looked thunderstruck. 'I remember Matt Hilton. Building churches he was, when any young man of sense would have been turning a card or raising a skirt. And running off with his . . . good God.'

'My mother, sir.'

'Oh, I say, my day for disaster. Of course, he had two sons. Do you know, I had not linked the matter? Well, well. Once again, Mr Hilton, I apologize.' He frowned at his empty coffee cup, then set it down, seemed to be drawing himself together. 'Yet, sir, I must speak plain. How do you stand?'

'On what, sir?'

'Slavery, sir. You have undertaken the ownership of this plantation. You are aware of the scurrilous methods they are employing in England? They know the nation would never stand for Abolition, so they are preaching Amelioration, sir.'

'You had best explain.'

'Well, sir, if they are forced to agree that slavery is decreed by God, and more important, is an economic necessity, they are concerned that it should be as polite as possible. Why, sir, there is a contradiction in terms. Will a slave ever work unless driven to it?'

'No doubt you are right, Mr Kendrick. But cannot even the driving be divided into the vicious and the necessary?'

'You'd withdraw the whip?'

'I understand it is mainly intended to be withdrawn from the women. But in fact, I have withdrawn it altogether, or at least, not found sufficient cause for its use in my week on Hilltop. And the plantation appears to prosper.'

'A week? By God. You've not had to plant. And from the women? You've not sampled their tongues.'

Dick thought of the gang he had just left. Indeed he had no idea how else to bring them to heel. But his spirit rebelled at being ordered to brutality by his neighbour.

'Anyway,' Kendrick continued. 'You'll learn the facts soon enough. 'Tis your seat we are concerned with. You'll take it?'

But now Dick was very angry indeed. He wondered if it had not been bubbling within him all this time, ever since that ill-fated duel, perhaps, but certainly since the bookkeepers had abandoned him. And all for the wrong reason. He got up again. 'And will I be welcome, sir, if I bring Mistress Gale to sit in the gallery to oversee me, and if I stand up and support Amelioration or, indeed, Abolition?'

Kendrick had also risen. His cheeks were so purple he might have been about to have a fit. 'Indeed, sir, you would not, on either score.'

'Well, then,' Dick said, 'as I perceive that Jamaica has managed to survive without a Hilton in the House these twelve years, it had best continue to do so, and allow me to get on with my own problems. And my housekeeper, sir.'

'Gad, sir,' Kendrick snorted. 'Gad. I had hoped we could be friends. Gad, sir. You're nothing but old Robert, come back to life.' He stamped down the stairs, vaulted into the saddle, and rode off.

Dick sat down and wiped his brow. Christ, what a stupid way to act, he thought. It must be the heat, affecting my senses.

'You were magnificent, Mr Hilton. Magnificent.' Harriet Gale carried two goblets filled with sangaree, iced red wine to which brandy and fruits had been added. She held one out for him to take, sat beside him. 'He spoke nothing better than the truth. You *are* a reincarnation of Robert Hilton.'

'Me? He was having his little joke. As you are, no doubt. Me? There can be no man in all the world more confused. More miserable, perhaps. I know not where to start, to be a Hilton, to be a planter. To be a man, even.'

Harriet Gale gazed at him, over the top of her glass as she sipped.

'Then there is the matter of you. If you were listening, you must have heard what he said. What everyone is saying, perhaps. Oh, don't be alarmed. I would not have you leave, Mistress Gale. I would protect your reputation. And mine, no doubt. Perhaps if we could obtain another white woman, to live here with you. Aye, that is the ticket.'

Harriet Gale put down her glass beside Kendrick's coffee cup.

'I do not wish, or need, another woman to live with me. Are you afraid of people's talk?'

'Why, I suppose not. But . . .'

'Well, then,' she said. 'The best way to answer gossip is to make it the truth, then the wagging tongues lose interest.' She leaned forward, held his face between her hands, and kissed him very deliberately on the mouth.

6

The Betrothed

Where Ellen Taggart had thrust, and Joan Lanken had ballooned, Harriet Gale licked. The sensation was so delicious, the assault was so sudden, the feel of her body against his was so much what he had wanted throughout the previous week, that Dick was for a few moments unable to move. Then he remembered where they were, and seized her wrists.

'Mistress Gale. Harriet . . .'

'Don't you like me even a little?' Her face was only inches away, her enormous deep brown eyes looming at him. And her body still rested on his.

'Of course I like you. But on this verandah . . .'

'There is nobody here. Save slaves.'

'Yes, but . . .'

She laughed, deep in her throat. 'I forgot. You regard them as important. Will you come upstairs?'

'But . . . they will know.' There was no question of refusing her. As a quick exploration now assured her.

She gave his breeches a squeeze, smiled at him. 'Of course. But does it matter?' She rose away from him, holding his hand. And God, how he wanted. How he had wanted, it seemed, since that evening with Ellen. Ellen. And all his promises.

But Harriet was already at the stairs, and starting up, and he was still holding her hand.

Boscawen was standing in the archway to the dining room. 'You want me put away the horse, Mr Richard?'

'Ah . . .' Colour flamed into his cheeks. 'If you would be so kind, Mr Boscawen.'

'Right away, Mr Richard.' Boscawen looked up at the gallery. 'You there,' he bawled. 'Come down here.'

Two of the maids hastily appeared, armed with dusters and brooms and pans. They scurried down the stairs, averting their eyes from Harriet, who had released him and reached the top, and smiled at him. He almost ran after her. 'My God. They know.'

'And are anxious that you should enjoy me.'

'My God,' he said again. 'I doubt I will be able.'

Again the low laugh, and she went into her bedchamber. 'Out.'

Judith had been lying on the bed, peering at one of the books from the library; she could not read but enjoyed the illustrations. Now she scrambled to her feet, gazed at Dick.

'Oh, my God,' he said. 'This is impossible.'

The child sidled past him, and as she reached him, gave a little moue with her lips and tossed her head, almost suggestively.

'She'll be a right whore, one of these days.' Harriet closed the door. 'I'll have to watch her.'

'Mistress Gale,' he gabbled. 'Really . . . we must be mad.'

'I am mad,' she agreed, and held his arm to escort him across the room. 'Mad with desire for you, Dick. God, even to think of you inside me reduces me to a jelly. And you want me as well. I can see it in your eyes, Dick.'

He found himself sitting on the bed, and realized what had been bothering him for the previous ten minutes; she was absolutely sober. She released her gown, stepped out of it — she wore nothing underneath — and knelt to pull off his boots, her breasts sagging towards him in a most entrancing fashion, and below the breasts the fold of flesh at her waist, the pout of her belly, the sudden rise of silky brown hair. He reached for her, closing his hands on the soft mounds of flesh, to hold them and use them to bring her against him, while she smiled, and busied herself with his breeches, and lay on top of him as he fell back across the bed, kissing his mouth and eyes and nose and chin, sighing as he caressed, her hair drooping on either side of her face to scatter across his.

But he wanted to possess, as she was willing enough to be possessed. He rolled her on her back, watched her eyes dilate with pleasure, and then without warning she uttered a scream of ecstasy, and dug her fingernails into his back and shoulders, scraping them across the flesh so that he too reached an orgasm in a frenzy of pain which left him lying panting, on the no less

99

exhausted woman.

'I did not mean to hurt you.' His lips were against her ear.

'You have not hurt me enough. Nine years? I think I was almost a virgin again. Dick. Dick. How I have longed for your coming. And yet, I feared it, too. I did not know what you would be like, whether you would like me . . . I cannot breathe.'

He rolled away from her, and she sat up, and knelt above him, straddling him, to remove the last of his shirt, play with his nipples in turn, while she worked her haunches to restore him once again to desire.

And this time she would be the mistress, her fingers digging into his chest, her tongue lolling, her hair scattering as she shook her head.

Her entire body sagged, and she slowly lowered herself, to lie on him, blood pumping through the arteries of her neck to fill her cheeks, while her flesh was sweat-wet to his touch. 'Christ,' she said. 'You must have wanted, as much as I.'

A time to think. As if thought were possible, except of the woman, except of desire, except of wanting to arouse again, except of feeling her legs lying on his, her groin pulsing on his, her nipples scraping on his, her mouth sucking at his. But yet, a time to think. The whole house would have heard her scream, would have known what they had accomplished. But the whole house would have known, anyway, once the bedroom door had shut behind them. How could he ever look any of them in the face?

And there were hooves, outside the opened window, and that so well remembered voice.

'Oh, my God,' he said. 'Tony.'

'Now perhaps he will leave me alone,' she said.

'Eh? Tony?'

'Ever since the first night. Oh, I permitted nothing. But he would persevere. Will he be jealous?'

'Of me? Very likely. I must get up.'

Because there were other voices, rising through the old wooden floors. Boscawen, certainly, protesting. Tony, laughing. And boots on the stairs.

Harriet rolled away from him, regained her robe in a single movement, and pulled it on, in the same instant draping his breeches across his thighs.

The door opened. 'Great God in Heaven,' Tony said. 'I did not credit my ears.'

'You are a rude fellow, Mr Hilton,' Harriet said. 'Breaking into a lady's bedchamber.'

Tony nodded. 'Oh, I am. Well, madam, I am to congratulate you. For at least knowing what you wanted. Are you alive, down there?'

Dick sat up. 'I'll not apologize, to you or to anyone.'

'Spoken like a Hilton, old boy. Why should you apologize, to me or anyone? But while you tossed your delightful grandmother, I have been working for Hilltop.'

'Grandmother?' Harriet cried. 'Why, you . . .'

She ran at him, and he caught her wrist. 'A jest, Harriet. Merely a jest.'

'How much did you lose, last night?' Dick asked, buttoning his shirt.

'A trifle, compared with what I won. James. James. Come up here and meet your employer.'

'Eh?' Dick stood up.

'James Hardy,' Tony said. 'Mr Richard Hilton, Hilltop's new owner. Oh, and Mistress Harriet Gale.' Tony beamed at them.

The man was at once short and thin, with a sallow, West Indian complexion and somewhat straggling brown hair. He wore a coat over his opened shirt, and carried his hat in his hand; he had not shaved this morning, and this combined with his thin, even pinched features, and his long nose, gave him a slightly villainous air. But he was by no means dull; Dick observed that a flicker of his green eyes took in the entire room, although he did not appear to look away. 'Mr Hilton,' he said. 'I am honoured, sir. I wish I had come at a more opportune moment.'

'Bah,' Tony said. 'They were finished. You were finished, Dickie, lad? And you could not have come at a more opportune moment, James. He plants, Dick. And has done so all his life.'

'Indeed?' Dick shook the young man's hand, and frowned. Because he was very young; in fact he would have estimated Hardy was the youngest of the three. 'That cannot have been so very long.'

'Eight years, sir,' Hardy said. 'I first rode aback when I was fifteen.'

'He was orphaned,' Tony explained. 'And had to earn his keep. But his people were planters before him. It is in his blood, as it is in ours. But *he* has the experience. And there is more.'

'Indeed,' Dick said. 'Well, of course you are welcome, Mr Hardy. We shall go down and have a glass and discuss the matter. Perhaps you will dress and join us, Harriet.' He glanced at her; now it was difficult to believe what had happened. But her smile was enough to reassure him that it had been no dream. Christ, what a future suddenly opened in front of him. Of Harriet, endless hours, endless days, endless months of nothing but Harriet. He wanted to scream with joy. Which made the pleasure of being *the* Hilton, of employing labour, of sitting over a glass of sangaree and discussing business matters, knowing always that she was there, twice as delightful. He escorted Hardy to the stairs. 'But what of your present employers?'

'I will be frank with you, sir,' Hardy said. 'When I heard how you had dismissed all your bookkeepers, I quit my post, sir, hoping for employment here. Then I discovered I lacked the courage to ride out and see you, and was utterly miserable, before I encountered Mr Anthony last night in town.'

'And approached him. Mr Boscawen, sangaree if you please.' It was all but eleven, and too late to return aback now, in any event. And surprisingly, he found no difficulty at all in meeting Boscawen's gaze.

'Yes, sir, Mr Richard. Right away.'

'But you have not heard the best of it,' Tony said, following them down the stairs. 'James is well experienced in field work, of course. But his principal business has always been concerned with the factory.'

'The factory?' Dick cried. 'And us within a month of grinding. But this is splendid news. Did you see the Reverend?'

'I did. A detestable fellow.'

'He'd not come?'

'He explained to me that he could see no purpose in attending Hilltop to conduct a service where there was no congregation left to hear him. He'd spoken with Laidlaw, of course.'

'But . . . how do we exist, without a service on Sunday?'

Tony smiled at him. 'He also said he doubted his services were really required by a planter determined to live in the most blatant immorality.'

'Why . . .' But the man was speaking nothing more than the truth, even if he could not have *known* it was the truth when he

102

uttered the words. And yet, strangely, Dick felt only anger, not shame.

As Tony saw. 'So I told him we really had no need of him. We have no need of anyone, Dick. We are Hiltons. And we have James.' He swept the first goblet from Boscawen's tray, held it high. 'I give you Hilltop, and its finest ever crop.'

Its finest ever crop. It was difficult to believe anything valuable could come out of this turmoil, this heat, this filth. Dick Hilton stood on the high catwalk, situated near the roof of his factory, and looked down on the huge vats, which seethed and bubbled immediately beneath him, sending both their heat—for beneath each enormous metal tub there was a glowing fire—and their aroma, the sickly sweet smell of evaporating molasses, to shroud him, to paste his shirt to his chest like a second skin, to have sweat rolling from his hair to cloud his eyes.

He watched the slaves, standing on the catwalk immediately beneath him, most of them naked, poking the thick liquid with long poles, making sure it kept moving, while others watched the huge gutters off which the molten sugar drained, to fill the cooling vats on the other side of the factory, where it would evaporate, the molasses to drip through the perforated bottoms into yet more vats, to be used as a basis for the plantation's other main product, rum, while the crystalline sugar would remain in the hogsheads and gradually fill them, until they were ready for shipping. The slaves were watched in turn by Absolom, also naked, marching up and down behind them with his whip, slicing the air, and a streaming back from time to time, shouting at them, but all unheard by Dick ten feet above.

The noise was quite remarkable. He had not supposed it possible. It seemed to fill the entire plantation, from the slash of the machetes as the cane was cut in the fields, through the creaking axles of the carts as they were trundled behind the mules up the ramp to the great shoot above the factory, increasing in the power mill, where the biggest and strongest of his slaves marched round and round the treadmill, chased by Tony's whip, to propel the huge, squealing rollers which gave the cane its first crushing, before it was pulled and prodded by another army of slaves, who added water to the partially crushed stalks, a carefully calculated twelve per cent dilution, based on Hardy's assertion that even pulped cane will retain, for some moments, a given percentage of water, which will mix with the unextracted juice to increase the volume by as much as twenty-five per cent on a second crushing. He had even spoken of repeating the operation a third time, but Dick had argued against this, as it was apparently an experiment not yet carried out with success on any other plantation.

But the refreshed cane was continuing on its way, to the next set of rollers, which completed its destruction, squeezing the very last drop of liquid into the great vats, while the shattered stalks, now hardly more than straw, and called bagasse, dropped from the shoots into the pits beneath, to be turned with pitchforks by another army of slaves, and then shunted along in man-drawn carts to feed the great fires. A sugar estate wasted nothing, when grinding. It was a self-perpetuating hell, producing the sweetest substance in the world.

His wealth. Just a seething liquid, a few crushed stalks, a few gallons of water, an endless procession of sweating flesh, male and female, adult and child, and all driven by the ceaselessly flailing whips of the drivers. Even he had been forced to accept this, at least during grinding. He did not see how Father could have managed any other way, had he been here. To maintain this level of effort, this level of labour, this level of unceasing brutality, to humans and cane alike, the whip was an essential adjunct.

Not that he would have been able to use it. He would not have been able to produce a tenth of this liquid gold. He watched James Hardy climbing the ladders. The little man was stripped to the waist, and his skin glistened. His hair was matted and he had not shaved in ten days, so that his beard sprouted, pale brown and bristly.

'Mr Richard,' he bawled. 'Twenty-five thousand tons, at the last count. And that to come.'

He looked down at the vats.

'Twenty-five thousand tons?' Dick could not grasp the immensity of the figure.

'Aye. The books say Laidlaw cleared seventeen thousand a year gone. We'll improve on that by twenty per cent and more.'

'By dilution?'

'In the main. It will make no difference to the quality of the sugar, believe me. And do you know what a ton of Jamaica sugar was fetching on the London market last year? Thirty-five pounds, sterling.'

Eight hundred and seventy-five thousand pounds. Plus what was still crystallizing. There was a fortune. Why, that figure of a million might not be so far off. 'We must celebrate.'

Hardy grinned, and shook his head. 'We've a way to go yet, Mr Hilton. You've five thousand acres under cultivation. 'Tis less than half your property. We are getting fifty tons of sugar per acre. That should be sixty, at least. And we have managed, with dilution, to get ten per cent sugar from the crop. So Laidlaw only managed seven. I've my mind set on eleven. We'll celebrate, Mr Richard, when this crop is shipped, and the next crop is ratooned and planted.' He closed one eye. 'But you can tell Mistress Gale.'

He played the father, in every way, and he was by two years the younger. Richard felt he should be ashamed. Or suspicious. Why should a man work this hard, this willingly, this enthusiastically, for a wage? But perhaps Hardy represented the true West Indies, the spirit of planting. And anyway, how could James Hardy, itinerant orphan, harm Richard Hilton, of Hilltop and Green Grove, *the* Hilton?

He laughed, and clapped his manager on the shoulder. 'I'll do that, James.' He clambered down the ladder, hands slipping on the sweat-wet iron. Because that was all he wanted to do. To bring news of the day to Harriet, to watch her smile, and then to hear her give that delicious laugh, and to know her arms, her body, were there for his embrace. Why, she had transformed him. No doubt he had been no more than a prig. But life was there to be enjoyed, if one was a Hilton, with prosperity stretching in every direction as far as the eye could see. So Tony had himself been right, when he had claimed his misfortunes arose from nothing more than attempting to be a Hilton without the means. He had the means now. So he gambled every Saturday night, and invariably lost what to other men would have been a fortune, and undoubtedly he also saw Joan Lanken every Saturday night as well. But Lanken would not dare recognize it. He knew Tony Hilton's ability with a sword and, rumour had it, with a pistol. So he could play the Hilton the length and breadth of Middlesex county.

And Richard Hilton? Sheltering behind the ability of his manager, the prowess of his brother, the aura of his name? Contradicting every social or moral tenet, living with his uncle's

105

mistress, who was also old enough to be his own mother, and loving every moment of it? He must be mad. There would be time to take stock, when the grinding was over, and the replanting was completed, as Hardy had said. Oh, indeed, then there would be time to take stock. He galloped his horse up the drive, Harriet already clearly in sight, seated on the verandah in her crimson robe. He threw himself from the saddle, doubts disappeared in the knowledge that in a few moments she would be in his arms.

'Twenty-five thousand,' he shouted. 'We have topped twenty-five thousand tons, with another couple of thousand to go, for sure.'

She smiled at him. Her face was unusually serious this morning. 'Then you are to be congratulated, Dick. Your bath is ready. But first, there is a letter.'

She held out the envelope, and he seized it, and checked, heart pounding. 'From Mama?'

'Open it and see.'

How joy could drain away in the threat of responsibility. Mama must have heard . . . he slit the envelope with his thumb, turned over the sheet of paper, looked at the signature. Ellen. He had not seen her writing before. Then why did not his heart jump for joy? He scanned the lines. Commonplaces, about England. Declarations of love, and passion. Inquiries as to what the death of his uncle would mean, whether it would shorten or lengthen the time between their reunion. Please to let it shorten the time, no matter what.

'Your betrothed?' Harriet asked.

He flushed. 'Aye.'

'And now you are master of Hilltop, with a successful crop on its way, there is naught to stand in the way of your marriage.'

He looked down at her, and she met his gaze. Her fingers played with the sash of her robe, and he knew she would be wearing nothing underneath. 'I'm for my bath,' he said. 'Will you not scrub my back?'

'The fact is, I tread a difficult path.' Dick formed the letters slowly and carefully. 'As I have explained before, as I am sure you understand. Believe me, dearest, when I landed, or at least, when I had recovered from the shock, not only of Uncle Robert's death, but of my own inheritance, I was resolved to send for you on

106

the instant. Fortunately, other counsel, wiser and more experienced than my own, prevailed. This is still a wild and dangerous country, where we live in daily fear of a Negro revolt which will bring fire and sword, and bloodshed, the length and breadth of the colony. Now, how could I expose you to such a peril, and for a woman you may suspect it is far worse.'

He leaned back in his chair, sucked the stem of his pen. He'd be writing novels, next. There could be no more accomplished literary liar in the world. But a lie, to be palatable, and to be convincing, must be spiced with more than a segment of truth. He dipped his nib once again into the ink.

'In such conditions, in such surroundings, as I stated above, my path is difficult. I will, in so far as I am able, follow my father's precepts and attempt to deal with the blacks as if they were Christians, which indeed they are not, in the main. But this has naturally diminished my popularity with my fellow planters, who consider me at best a weakling, and at worst a positive incendiary. So to the dangers of our position, is added a total social ostracism by the white folk. I am indeed fortunate in having Tony with me, and in having procured the services of a most remarkable man, by name James Hardy, whose entire life seems to be bound up in the business of growing and grinding sugar. Thanks entirely to him, both my crops so far have been exceptional, and we may hope, as this dreadful war draws to a close, to see our prices also regain their former level, and thus embark upon a new period of prosperity which will serve to grace the beauty and the company of the future Mistress of Hilltop. And in this regard I tell you frankly, my dearest Ellen, that I am inclined *to* wait for affairs in Europe to settle down, as there can be no doubt that French privateers do abound, and truly I shudder to think of the dangers to which I might be exposing you during the long weeks of an Atlantic crossing. But now that Bonaparte seems to have failed in his Russian design, why surely even he will seek peace, or France will seek peace without him.'

He leaned back again, and laid down his pen. Truly, a novelist. And yet, a labour of love, as well. He could envisage her, sitting opposite him. This was not the least difficult, as her portrait smiled at him from the wall over his desk. And it was certainly Ellen. The artist indeed had captured less of her true likeness than her essential expression. It was an utterly entrancing thought, that one day, one day soon, in fact, that look of conscious superiority, that promising body, which could only have grown in the last few years, that so firm mouth and those so steady eyes, would have to surrender to him. To all that he now knew, of woman, and of love.

Just as it was a nightmare occasionally, that she might not surrender, or might do so only once. But these were his earliest fears, looming out of the recesses of his mind only to be dismissed again. How could she not surrender, here on Hilltop, alone with him and his belongings. He was master here. And the Ellen he remembered had not been backward in offering to surrender. As if she had known, as if she could possibly have known, what indeed she was offering to give into his keeping. Certainly he had not suspected.

He inhaled musk, and waited. What would happen when Ellen discovered about Harriet? But then, why should she ever discover about Harriet? Oh, in Jamaica she certainly would. There would be tears, perhaps. But the marriage would already have been consummated, and she would learn that he was no different from any other planter, by repute at least. It was the character of Harriet herself which offended the Jamaican society. Well, then . . . but it would also offend Ellen. And yet, to give up Harriet, to order her from the plantation . . . he really did not see himself doing that. The very thought of her, even after two years in her bed, brought him up hard and anxious. She seemed to have accumulated all the experience possible within her one eager body, and still retained the ability to project it forth as a wondrous introduction. Nor did she appear to possess any other interest. Save perhaps drink. Indeed, she drank with a determined enjoyment he had not supposed possible, and often remained sitting up in bed, intent on finishing her bottle, long after he was asleep. And yet, she kept herself so clean and sweet-smelling, it was impossible to take offence, expecially as the drunker she became the happier she became. But for the rest, she neither read nor sewed, and her supervision of the house was of the briefest description. Even as regards her daughter she seemed perfectly uninterested. Judith's education, or lack of it, was a source of considerable worry to him, as the girl appeared visibly to grow, day by day. But his instincts warned him not to interfere, and indeed, not even to make a friend of the child, who seemed

108

contented enough in pursuing solitary habits, turning the pages of the books in the library, occasionally romping with Boscawen's children, or sitting on the verandah staring into space with an expression of deep concentration in her eyes.

He felt fingers on his shoulders, leaned back to rest his head against her breast, look down on the hand, long and strong. It was her fingers, the thought of her fingers, in connection with Uncle Robert, that had first created the desire for her within him. And now he knew Uncle Robert had died happy. And guilty? Not Uncle Robert, by all accounts. Then why Richard? He was *the* Hilton. He repeated this to himself, constantly, to remind himself of his position. Hiltons took. Then, guilty about Ellen? That was stupid. Ellen had herself indicated that she would prefer a man to a boy. When he was ready for her, she would have a man.

'They have returned,' Harriet said.

'Ah.' His belly filled with lead. His first runaways, after two years. The fingers left his shoulders, and he stood up. 'Will you come out?'

She shook her head. 'I will watch from the house. But Dick . . .' the fingers were back, closing on his arm. 'They must be punished. You know that.'

'Aye.' He sighed. 'I had supposed we had put that behind us, on Hilltop. If only I knew why.'

She glanced at him, frowning. 'There is talk, in the servants . . .'

'Talk? About what?'

Her frown faded into that marvellous smile. 'It is no matter. Certainly not beside the fact of their absconding. You'd best go out.'

He went down the hallway, past the staircase. Talk, amongst the servants? He must find out about that.

He stood on the verandah, watched the procession coming slowly up the hill. Hardy came first, followed by Absolom and two other drivers. These were mounted and Absolom held the leashes of the two giant mastiffs. They had been Hardy's first purchases, and were called Robinson and Crusoe. Dick did not like them; he suspected they were Hardy's pets, not his. But apparently a plantation had to have dogs, and this day at the least they had proved their worth. The runaways walked behind, or occasionally fell, and were dragged; they were secured by their wrists to the saddles of two of the horses, but the ropes were sufficiently long to allow them to lag by some ten feet.

And perhaps they had been punished enough, he thought. Their flesh was torn and bleeding, and they were clearly in the last stages of exhaustion, while presumably they had had little enough food or drink during the past two days.

He glanced to the left, at the drive leading past the town, and frowned again. Here came another horseman, swaying in the saddle, hatless, although he had certainly worn one last night when he had set out. Here was the lie to his letters to Mama, which repeated constantly what a tower of strength Tony was, how well he was behaving. The fact was, Tony enjoyed planting, there was no doubt about that. It was in the Hilton blood no less than in the Hardy. But this apart, his promises had been as worthless as any other promise he had ever made. He drank, and he gambled, losing a fortune on every occasion, and he continued to see Joan Lanken. Their affair, indeed, was the scandal of Kingston, only overshadowed by the far greater scandal of his brother and Harriet Gale. So how could he criticize? Well, he did not criticize.

'What do you think, Josh?'

Merriman sighed. 'Well, sir, Mr Richard, they got for be flogged. I ain't seeing no other way.'

The procession stopped at the foot of the steps, and Hardy dismounted. 'Making for the Cockpit Country, Mr Richard. They're not the most intelligent of niggers.'

Dick walked down the steps, heart pounding. Both the runaways were naked, both were young, both were well-formed, the girl especially so. He found them remarkably attractive people, as a whole, in the grace of their movements, the humour which seemed their principal characteristic, even the dishonesty which marred their attitudes to life. And he had often wondered what sort of a lover one would make, and then rejected the thought immediately, and been the more grateful to Harriet for making such rejection a possibility.

'Do you know why they ran away, James?'

Hardy shifted from foot to foot. 'Well, sir, Mr Richard . . .'

'It ain't mattering, Mr Richard,' Merriman said. 'They just got to be punished.'

Dick glanced at him with a surprise almost equal to Hardy's.

110

Josh had never advocated flogging before. If Dick had so far given in to Hardy's demands as to allow him, and the drivers, to carry whips in the field, and use them wherever necessary, Josh had been his most staunch support that the plantation would work and prosper without descending to a formal flogging, but rather in punishments such as confinement on slave holidays, or curtailment of the rum ration.

'Why, Merriman is right, Mr Richard,' Hardy said. 'An example must be made. It is possible that the slaves have been waiting to take advantage of you. Your generosity of spirit is well known.'

Dick frowned at him; Hardy was given to sarcasm.

'So it were best to nip their tendencies in the bud by an example. A severe example.'

'Such as?'

'Well, sir, on most plantations the penalty for running away would be two hundred lashes.'

'Two hundred . . . they'd not survive.'

'Well, sir, Mr Richard, down to a few years ago they'd have been hanged without argument. And a few years before that they'd have been burned alive.'

'This is 1813, Mr Hardy. Not 1713. I am happy to say.' Dick walked closer to the two prisoners. The man saw his boots, and attempted to rise, but could only reach his knees. 'What have you to say for yourself?'

The Negro's tongue came out and slowly circled his lips. 'Water, massa. Water.'

'You'd best . . .'

'After they've been flogged, Mr Richard,' Hardy said.

'It would be best, sir,' Merriman agreed.

Once again Dick glanced at them. Never before had he known them in such total agreement; indeed Merriman usually and obviously disliked Hardy as much as the white man objected to having a black colleague.

'Hullo, hullo, hullo.' Tony fell from his saddle, kept his feet by hanging on to his horse's bridle. 'Court day?'

'Where on earth have you been?' Dick demanded.

'Aye, well, it was a long game. There are notes . . .'

'Give them to me later. 'Tis a crisis.'

'Runaways?' Tony blinked at the prisoners, and the girl raised her head to stare at him. 'Good God.'

'Aye,' Dick said. ' 'Tis bad. They will have to be flogged. Twenty lashes apiece.'

'Twenty lashes?' Hardy cried. ' 'Tis no punishment at all. Their skin is like leather.'

'Twenty lashes,' Dick insisted. 'I'll not murder them. And they have been punished already.'

'Mercy,' screamed the girl. 'Mercy, massa. Massa Tony . . .'

Dick's head swung, and Tony flushed.

'Aye, well, I'm for a bath. Christ, it's hot work.'

Dick caught his sleeve. 'What is hot work?'

Tony looked down at the hand. 'Why, riding from town. And let go my coat, little brother, or I'll break your head.'

Dick let go before he really intended to. But when Tony spoke in that very low and even tone he generally meant what he said, and they could not afford to fight in front of the slaves. But my God, what had Harriet said? There is talk, amongst the servants. So perhaps he did not waste his time in visiting Joan Lanken, having known her for two years. Or perhaps a white skin alone was not enough for him.

He looked at Merriman, who kept his expression blank, and then at Hardy.

' 'Tis not a crime, Mr Richard. Not compared with running away.'

'And suppose it was the cause of the runaway? This girl and this boy, maybe they love each other. Was she forced? I must get to the bottom of this.'

'Oh, come now, sir,' Hardy remonstrated. 'How can a nigger girl be forced? And indeed, sir, how can she know love? They are animals, sir, and copulate as the urge takes them. Let us compromise, sir, on twenty-five lashes apiece. I will see to it personally. But they must be punished, sir, and in your name. You must rule, sir, and you must be seen to rule. You are *the* Hilton, Mr Richard. You are the master here.'

The master here. How the phrase haunted him, where once it had rolled around his head like a euphoric cloud. He walked his horse between the rows of cane, and received the nods of the bookkeepers, the obeisances of the weeding gangs. His cane, tall and proud and filled with sugar, approaching his fourth grinding,

112

and every one a record. His drivers. His slaves. His bookkeepers every one recruited by Hardy, by the promise of the revival of Hilltop into the bubbling work cauldron of fifty years before, and the salaries commensurate with such success.

But did they obey him, or James Hardy? And yet, he could not manage this plantation without Hardy. Planting might be in his blood, but it was only a microcosm. He did not react to it instinctively, did not know at a glance where needed the most work, could not look at a field of cane and tell whether it was healthy or whether it desperately needed water. Hardy could.

On the other hand, he could manage the accounting side of the business. Hilltop was probably more financially sound than ever before in its history. So was Green Grove. He had taken ship there, and sat down and discussed affairs with Tickwell, and impressed him with his knowledge of money and markets, and convinced him that the best thing for the two plantations was to amalgamate the bookkeeping side of it, with Green Grove sending all its returns and accounts to Hilltop, where he could enter them up in the great ledger, and have them under his hand.

But why had he had to convince Tickwell, instead of just telling him, I have decided? I am *the* Hilton. So then, he was, after all, nothing more than a bookkeeper. A bank clerk. And for the time being, Hardy went along with his economies, supported his decisions, however much Tony might criticize.

But there was the crux of the matter. For the time being. Hilltop, and Green Grove, prospered as long as James Hardy so elected. By God, he thought, you are becoming jealous of your own employee.

He took off his hat to wipe sweat from his brow, hastily restored it again; the sun seemed to hang immediately above his head, intent on scorching his brain. It was clearly time to return to the house, and Harriet. It was the only part of the day he enjoyed. He disliked the early morning assembly of the drivers, because although everyone looked to him for the final decision, he knew they expected it to come from Hardy. He loathed and feared the punishment sessions. But what was he to do? Hardy had convinced him it was the only way to maintain discipline, after all. But the sound of the cartwhip, the sight of that steel tip biting into the brown flesh and then snatching slivers of it away, to leave red flecks on the dark skins, made him wish to vomit, just as the sight of the bodies, male or female, twisting in agony, made him feel ashamed of himself. He found the obligatory rides through the canefields embarrassing, because he was sure they smiled behind his back, no matter how they bowed to his face. He dreaded the arrival of messengers from town, with news, with mail. He did not want to know what went on in Kingston; he had almost forgotten what the town looked like, and he knew he would never be able to face any other planter, much less any government official, much less the Governor himself. There had been one invitation, to dinner at Government House, and he had declined, through pressure of work. That had been two years ago.

Why, he had even forgotten there was a world outside this valley.

Except for the mail, which constantly reminded him. News, of Father, and his ill health. Of Mama, worrying. But at least she felt easy about her sons, felt that they were prospering, proving themselves Hiltons, making the plantations more successful than ever before, and in a way their father would approve. And at least she was benefiting from that prosperity, as he had been able to make an income on his parents which had removed their financial problems. But if ever she were to learn the truth? Oh yes. They were proving themselves Hiltons.

And then, Ellen. Apparently resigned to waiting, until the passage became safer, the endless Negro revolts of which he wrote became pacified. Every letter a lie, because it replied to a lie. But Ellen . . . it was four years since their betrothal. He had all but forgotten what she looked like, even. Which did not make her any the less attractive. On a sudden. Ellen. But then, what of Harriet? Could he be that much of a swine? The fact was, he was even less of a master in his own house than he was in his own fields or in his own factory. Harriet totally ignored him, except in bed. So perhaps she was worth it, in bed. Had been worth it, four years ago. Three years ago. Two years ago. Last night.

But was she worth it? Now? Oh, she enjoyed sex as much as ever before, and her appetite embraced enough variety to keep most men happy. But it was *her* appetite. He was young enough and strong enough to satisfy her. He was also her bread and butter. Otherwise no doubt she would find him boring. Oh, no doubt at all.

But did not the satisfying of her satisfy him as well? Or was he

114

the one becoming bored? He knew her too well. They shared nothing, except sex. They had no conversation, no other interest. She did not seem to require any. And there was the nagging desire to reveal his education, his ability at love, to a younger woman, someone who would be overwhelmed by his prowess. Oh, he was studying to be a villain, sure enough. Or a Hilton.

So then, today he was merely out of sorts, and proving himself a bigger blackguard than he had supposed. Harriet might be incapable of providing true company, but she was utterly faithful. She was well aware that without his support she was nothing. Less than nothing. And the same went for Hardy, and even for Tony. No doubt they all took every possible advantage of his . . . what was the word? Weakness? Good Lord, no. He would bring them all to heel with a snap of his fingers, if he really found cause. Indolence was a far better word.

On the other hand, for all her effort, her careful diet and her daily exercise, Harriet was certainly past forty. Ellen was just twenty-one, and as healthy and high-spirited as a young mare. As Tony would say. Why, she would even have come into her inheritance.

By God, what a scoundrel are you become. But once the war was ended, and it could not be long now surely, he would return to England, for his bride. No risk to his lie in England, and Harriet could have that large settlement he had promised her. Tony would enjoy playing the planter for a season. There would be a great occasion. There would . . . he rounded the last bend in the fields, came in sight of the village and the Great House beyond, and of Joshua Merriman, spurring his horse towards him. And smiled. Josh was his only true friend, the only man on the plantation who clearly sought to serve him and no other. For all that he was just as knowledgeable as James Hardy, and therefore just as indispensable.

'Mr Richard,' he bawled, waving his hat. 'Mr Richard. Man, there is news. That Boney done abdicate.'

'Eh?'

'Yes, sir, man. The ship drop anchor in Kingston this last night and it flying all it flag and bunting and thing. The man done give up the throne and surrender. The war is done.'

'Good Lord.' He could scarce remember a time when there had not been a war, save for that abortive truce in 1802. He had been eight years old when it had started, and now . . . 'By God,' he shouted, 'we must celebrate. Ring the bell, Josh. Ring the bell. We'll declare a holiday. Why, the end of the war . . .' He galloped up to the house, leapt from the saddle, throwing his reins to the groom who hurried round from the stables, ran up the steps on to the verandah, and stopped at the squeal, it could hardly be called a cry, of mingled laughter and fear which came from the drawing room to his right. He turned into the archway, and was nearly bowled over by the fleeing figure of Judith Gale, tumbling into his arms, her gown disordered, her hair flying. And gazed over the girl's head at his brother.

Judith scraped hair from her eyes, stared at Dick. 'Oh, Lord,' she said. 'I didn't know you were home, Uncle Richard.'

'What's been going on?'

Tony was pulling up his pants. 'I came home early . . .'

'And assaulted Judith? You must be out of your mind.'

'Assaulted her?' Tony cried. 'That little whore.'

Judith wriggled against Dick. 'Do let me go, Uncle Dick. You're hurting me.'

Dick released the girl, slowly, looking at her for the first time. And perhaps the first time in his life; certainly in the past couple of years. The long legs, bare beneath the thin muslin housegown, and she wore but a single shift, the long arms, delightfully muscular, were still there, but now almost perfect in their shape and strength. The body too, had not changed its proportion, but there was a fullness to her bodice which had previously escaped his notice.

'You'll apologize to Judith, Tony,' he said, a sudden anger bubbling through his system, as it had threatened to do all day. 'And swear to me you have not harmed her.'

'Apologize? Harmed her?' Tony gave a bellow of laughter. 'What a hypocrite you are, little brother. If you mean have I raped the bitch, the answer is no. I'm saving it for a while. She services me, Dickie boy, with her hands. Learned it from watching her Mum, she tells me. And likes it a treat. Well, it is a treat.'

Dick gazed at his brother in consternation, then turned to Judith.

'Oh, Lord,' she muttered again, ducked under his arm and ran for the stairs, only to encounter her mother. 'Oh, Lord.'

'Did you hear that?' Dick asked.

'I should think every servant in the house heard that,' Harriet declared. 'Go to your room, Judith. I'll attend to you in a moment.'

'Attend to her?' Tony shouted. 'Why, you pair of hypocrites. You spend your entire time feeling each other, and you object to Judith and me? By God . . .' He came forward, and Dick seized his arm. He turned, swung a careless blow, and Dick ducked and pushed at the same time. Tony lost his balance, fell over a chair, struck the floor heavily. 'By God,' he said, 'I'll . . .'

Dick was aware of a sensation he had never known before, a tearing anger which seemed to be racing through his system, a culmination of resentment which had been building ever since the duel. 'You'll get out,' he said, keeping his voice even. 'You'll collect your things and get on your horse and clear off. Find yourself a passage back to England. I'll pay. But get out and stay out. There's no place for you on Hilltop. No place for you in Jamaica.'

Slowly Tony pushed himself up. His eyes were grey flints, and colour was filling his cheeks.

Harriet had remained in the doorway. Now she stepped back into the hall. 'Josh,' she called. 'Boscawen.'

The two big black men appeared immediately.

Tony looked at them, then at his brother. Then he turned and left the room.

'Very good, Josh,' Harriet said. 'Very good, Boscawen. But stay near until Mr Hilton leaves the plantation. Perhaps you could escort him to the boundary.'

'Mr Richard?' Joshua asked.

Dick seemed to awake from a deep sleep. 'Aye,' he said. ' 'Tis best, Josh.'

The black men nodded, and went back on to the verandah.

Dick gazed at Harriet. 'Did you suppose I was afraid of him?'

She blew him a kiss. 'He boasts of his prowess. You do not pretend to be a fighting man.'

'He has told you of the duel?'

A faint flush. 'I told you, he boasts.'

Was I afraid of him? Again, I was too angry, then. Now? He looked down at his hands, which trembled. In a fist fight? They were the same size. But did he possess the confidence, the resolution? And if it came to weapons?

Harriet took his arm. 'But you did the right thing, Dick. I am

117

surprised you put up with Tony that long. How I have longed to hear you discipline him. If you knew the number of times he has made advances to me. He is insatiable.'

'And Judith?'

'Must be punished. Will you help me? She regards you as a father.'

'Well, I . . .'

'I think it would be best,' she decided. 'Perhaps she feels you are too soft. You must show her the iron in your soul, as you showed Tony.'

The iron in my soul, he thought, as he climbed the stairs. Christ, what a joke. He was trembling again, praying that they would not encounter Tony on the stairs; they could hear him thumping about his room as he packed.

Harriet opened her bedroom door, waited for Dick to enter. Judith stood by the window, but turned, sharply, as they entered. Her face was pale, but pink spots filled her cheeks. Fourteen, Dick thought. Christalmighty. She could be married.

'Well?' Harriet demanded.

Judith's tongue, long and pink, came out and circled her lips. 'It was his idea.'

'But you didn't object?'

Again the quick lick. 'He's a man. You like to play with men, Mama.'

'That will cost you another six stripes,' Harriet promised, and went to her bureau.

'She was trying to get away when I came in,' Dick said, desperately. But his desperation was about himself. He wanted it to happen.

'Indeed?' Harriet straightened, carrying a dried cane stalk, four feet long, with hardened ridges every six inches. Judith caught her breath. 'Why did you do that?'

Judith stared at the cane. 'I . . . he wanted . . .'

'To lay you?'

'No. To . . .'

'Ah. One good turn deserves another? Kneel, over the bed.'

Judith gazed at Dick.

'I think I had better be off,' Dick said.

'Of course not, Dick,' Harriet said. 'The child regards you as a father. Besides, you must hold her wrists. She'll never stay still,

118

otherwise. Come on, Judith. Every delay is another stroke.'

Judith came slowly across the room, allowed her groin to hit the bed, and fell forward.

'Put out your arms,' Harriet commanded.

Slowly Judith stretched her arms across the bed; her gaze never left Dick's face.

'Hold her, please, Dick,' Harriet said.

Dick gripped the slender wrists, looked into the girl's eyes. They were like her mother's, but perhaps still darker and still deeper.

Harriet seized her daughter's skirts and rolled them up to her waist. Dick felt his gaze drawn over the girl's glossy hair to the gently rounded buttocks, watched in fascinated horror as the cane swung through the air; Harriet was chewing her lower lip with concentration. And then was brought back to the girl's expression as the eyes widened with the shock of the blow, and the flat mouth flopped open. The second blow brought a similar reaction, the third a tear, and then a shout of agony, followed by sobbed screams.

'Louder,' Harriet gasped, her hair tumbling down, sweat soaking her neck. 'Let them all hear, you little slut.'

As no doubt they would, Dick thought. The wrists writhed and twisted in his grip, and once Judith attempted to get up, only to be forced down again by her mother. He lost count of the cracks, of the screams, of the sobs, before Harriet finally stopped, having run out of breath. 'There,' she panted. 'Let that be a lesson to you. You'll mind whose breeches you get inside, in the future.'

Dick released the wrists; the marks of his fingers remained on the suntanned flesh. Judith slowly subsided across the bed, trying to stop her sobs, eyes swollen, hair scattered.

'Get out,' Harriet commanded. 'Get out. Spend the rest of the day in your room.'

Judith pushed herself to her feet. Her skirts fell into place of their own accord. She stumbled rather than walked towards the door.

'And close it behind you,' Harriet said.

The door closed, and Harriet smiled at Dick. 'Christ, but whipping that child makes me want. You're home for the afternoon, Dick?'

He stared at her. 'Aye,' he said. 'Maybe . . . maybe after breakfast.' He pulled the door open, found himself on the gallery.

119

Now why had he refused her? His tool was as hard as ever in his life. But the desire was for the girl twisting under his hands, not the woman who had laid on the blows. Oh, Christ, he thought. What have you done? Who? Tony, by making her a woman? Harriet, by exposing all that woman? And by reaching into the deepest recesses of his own mind to bring out the ghastly desires that must dominate the dream world of every man?

He stumbled down the stairs, collapsed in a chair in the withdrawing room. The plantation was silent, save for the distant rumble of hooves. Tony? No doubt he had stayed to listen to the screams.

He held his head in his hands, tried to rid himself of that vision. But the girl would stay in his mind for the rest of his life.

And sat bolt upright as a terrible suspicion crossed his mind. Harriet's punishment had been quite unnaturally severe. Unnecessarily severe. And his presence had certainly *not* been necessary, as she had whipped Judith before, and not required his assistance. And Harriet, being Harriet, would certainly have noticed that he was not quite so fervent in his love making as a year back. Christalmighty.

The hooves had stopped, but at the steps to the verandah. Tony, come back again. Where was Josh?

But there was Josh's voice, greeting someone, and being summarily told to stand aside. Dick reached his feet in a long bound as the voice slowly penetrated his seething mind, and his jaw dropped in sheer horror as he gazed at the door, and Ellen Taggart.

7

The Fugitive

Ellen wore a brown pelisse over a cream gown, and a matching brown bonnet; as might be expected, she looked extremely hot. Coat and hat were smothered in dust, and there was dust on her face, slightly diminishing the pink in her cheeks.

But it was Ellen. An Ellen who had filled out, was a tall and buxom young woman, and an Ellen who had also developed an even firmer mouth and chin.

'Ellen,' he cried. 'I must be dreaming.'

'Indeed you are not, Richard.' She gave him her hand. 'We are arrived, Mama.'

Mrs Taggart was even more warmly clad, and thus even more hot and bothered than her daughter.

'I must have a chair,' she groaned and sat down. 'My God, these boots . . . I swear my feet are swollen.' She looked around her. 'But this is a palace.'

'Filled with revolting Negroes,' Ellen observed. 'And owned by a dumb planter.'

Dick endeavoured to gather his wits. 'You very nearly induced a seizure, I assure you.' He discovered he had let go of her glove, and hastily grasped them both again. 'Ellen. How absolutely marvellous. If I could but understand. But wait . . .' He released her once more, went to the archway. 'Mr Boscawen. Mr Boscawen,' he shouted, as loudly as he could. 'Sangaree, if you please. My fiancée has arrived. See to it, Mr Boscawen, and have the girls prepare the guest bedrooms. Quickly, man.'

Ellen sat beside her mother, pulled off her gloves, and released the bow securing her bonnet. 'We shall not be staying, at this moment, Richard. It would not be proper.'

'Proper? But your mother is here.'

She was inspecting the room with her gaze. 'This is a most palatial residence, Richard. You did not do it justice in your descriptions.'

'Ellen.' He formed a third on the settee. 'Would you please explain? If only you had given me some notice . . .'

'You would no doubt have formed some reason for delaying me,' she said. 'As you have done for four years.'

'Have you not read my letters?'

'Indeed I have. So has Mama. And so, last night, has Mistress Laidlaw.'

'Clarissa Laidlaw? My God.'

'You have not been my only Jamaica correspondent, Richard,' Ellen pointed out. 'Clarissa has been writing me for years, almost from the moment her inquiries discovered my existence.'

'Why, the bitch,' Dick said.

'Really, Mr Hilton, such language,' protested Mrs Taggart.

'Nothing less than I expected, Mama,' Ellen said. 'You may believe, Richard, that in the beginning I was almost of your opinion, regarded her tales as nothing more than scurrilous, and indeed refused to reply. Yet she persisted in informing me of exactly what you were up to. And I must confess, as the weeks became months and the months became even years, I began to wonder if there might not be at least some truth in her account. I preferred not to discuss the matter with either Mama or Papa, as I was afraid they might decide to terminate our engagement, and immediately. But I leave it to you to attempt to imagine the agonies I suffered alone in my room, comparing your letters with hers, wondering which I was to believe.'

'Cruel, cruel man,' remarked Mrs Taggart.

'Ellen,' Dick said, seizing her hands once more. 'If you'd let me explain . . .'

'I am expecting that you will, Richard,' she said. 'When I have finished. And so I waited, and languished, and suffered, until my twenty-first birthday, when I received my inheritance, and which happily took place only a few days before Bonaparte decided to end his career of crime. Then it was, my mind made up by these fortuitous circumstances, that I confided in Mama. And discovered that I had indeed been wise to wait.'

'Outrageous,' said Mrs Taggart. 'I would have had none of you, young man. None at all. As for Colonel Taggart . . . what is that?'

Boscawen had appeared with a tray of sangaree.

Dick handed them each a glass. 'Something cooling, after your journey. But you prevailed upon your mother to be merciful, Ellen.'

'My mind was already made up. I prevailed upon her to accompany me, to discover the truth for myself, to hold you to your engagement.'

'Hold me? Did you suppose . . .'

'And you may further imagine my shock and disgust,' Ellen continued, as if he had not spoken, 'when on arriving in Kingston yesterday, we repaired to the dwelling of Clarissa, as she had long invited me to do, and there learned that she had spoken not a word but the absolute truth these three years.' She paused, to sip sangaree.

'She deserves to be whipped for slander,' Dick protested, his brain whirring.

'Indeed? She invited us to stay the night, which we did, while considering our next manoeuvre. Having decided to come out today, whom should we meet on the road just now but your very own brother, who informed us that he had been dismissed his living for daring to come between you and your . . . your paramour.'

'Good God,' Dick said. 'Of all the liars.' He squeezed her free hand. 'Ellen, believe me, I have only your good, our good, at heart. If I could speak with you alone . . .'

'Never,' declared Mrs Taggart.

'What can you possibly say to me that Mama should not hear?' Ellen asked.

'Well . . .' He flushed. 'I might just possibly wish to take you in my arms and tell you how much I love you.'

'Good heavens,' declared Mrs Taggart.

Ellen's expression seemed a trifle softer. 'I am hoping you will do that, Dick, and soon.'

He decided to press home his advantage. 'Then there is the matter of our wedding, as you are here . . .'

'I am hoping that that also will soon be discussed,' she agreed. 'But I would prefer that both should wait until we have completed our consideration of your present position.'

'Present position, why . . .'

123

'This woman, Gale,' Ellen said. 'Where do you keep her hidden?'

'Why, I . . .'

'I am not hidden, Miss Taggart,' Harriet said, stepping through the archway from the hall, nor could Dick, knowing her, doubt that she had been there for some time. She wore her pink riding habit, which she was well aware was her most flattering garment.

'My God,' cried Mrs Taggart.

Ellen stood up. '*You* are Mistress Gale?'

Dick also got up. 'Allow me to introduce you.'

'I have no desire to meet this person,' Ellen declared. 'I merely wish her to pack her belongings and leave, this instant.'

'You've a big tongue in that horse face of yours,' Harriet declared. 'Anyone would suppose you owned the place.'

'I do own this place,' Ellen said. 'By virtue of my forthcoming marriage with Mr Hilton.'

Her cheeks were pink. But then, pink spots were also gathering in Harriet's cheeks.

'I'm sure we can all sit down and discuss this,' Dick said.

'You hold your miserable tongue, sir,' said Mrs Taggart.

'Are you going to let these people talk to you like this, Dick?' Harriet demanded. 'Why don't you call the servants and have them thrown out?'

'On the contrary, madam,' Ellen said, 'it is you who are about to be thrown out. You are nothing but a whore, by all accounts. Certainly you are a wicked woman who clearly has taken advantage of Mr Hilton's generosity to feather her own nest these four years. Well, madam, your little charade is over. I will give you ten minutes to be off Hilltop, or I will have my people carry you. And should you ever venture on to this property again, I will have you whipped.'

Harriet stared at her for a moment in utter consternation, her face glowing. Dick made a move forward, fearing the worst, but was too late.

'Why, you little wretch,' Harriet shouted, and swung her hand.

But now it appeared that Ellen, for all her self-control was equally angry. And she was much the younger, stronger, bigger woman. She stepped inside Harriet's hand, seized her antagonist by the hair, dislodging her hat, swung her round while Harriet gave a gasp of horror, and thrust her away again, with all her force. Off balance, Harriet staggered across the floor and fell to her hands and knees in the doorway, her back to her assailant. And to Dick's total amazement, Ellen followed her, raising her skirts as she did so to reveal that she was wearing boots, and kicked her rival in the buttocks.

Harriet gave a strangled scream and fell forward once more, landing on her face at the foot of the stairs, and virtually at the feet of Boscawen, who, accompanied by half a dozen of the maids and Vernon the footman, had come hurrying from the kitchen to discover what the noise was about.

'You,' Ellen shouted. 'Find her a horse, and set her on it. You can clear her room out later and send her belongings behind her.'

Boscawen gazed from the woman on the floor to his master in a mixture of bewilderment and dismay.

'Ellen,' begged Mrs Taggart. 'Now don't lose your temper. Behave like a lady.'

Dick supposed he must be dreaming.

Harriet slowly rose once again to her hands and knees, turning as she did so to present less of a target. To Dick's distress he saw that she was weeping, tears of pain and shame. 'Dick,' she begged. 'You can't let her treat me so.'

Oh God, he thought. Oh, my God.

'Well, Dick?' Ellen demanded.

Oh, my God, he thought. So Clarissa has her way after all. And her revenge. No doubt sweeter for the delay. And certainly rougher on Harriet.

'Have you lost your tongue, Mr Hilton?' Mrs Taggart inquired.

'Dick,' Harriet said.

Dick licked his lips. 'Perhaps . . . perhaps it would be better, Harriet, if . . .'

'If I was to go?' Her voice rose an octave, to a level he had not previously heard.

'Ah . . . well . . . just for the time. Until we can get things sorted out. Go to the Park Hotel. Yes, that is it. Tell them the charge is mine. I . . .' he glanced at Ellen, 'I will visit you shortly.'

Harriet had reached her feet. She looked at Dick, then at Ellen, and then, without a word, turned and limped out of the front door.

Ellen stooped and picked up the hat, handed it to Boscawen.

'She'll need this. We'd not have the creature catching sunstroke.'

'Yes'm,' Boscawen said. He glanced at Dick, rolled his eyes most expressively, and hurried behind Harriet.

'I'm sure you spoke for the best, Dick,' Ellen said, 'in order to avoid a scene . . .'

'A scene?' he said. 'My God.'

'But I must warn you that if you ever attempt to see that woman again I shall leave Jamaica. Mama, are you ready to return to town?'

'But . . . you are leaving now,' he protested.

'Of course. It would not be proper for me to stay until we are wed, and besides, that woman's presence, her scent, remains. As do her clothes. You will send them off, as you promised. I will expect you to call, Dick. Not today. I really am feeling quite faint after what has happened. But tomorrow. Mama and I are staying with the Laidlaws.'

'The Laidlaws? But . . .' he grasped her hand. 'You haven't given me a chance to explain.'

She allowed him a smile. 'There is nothing to explain, Dick. I feel I know enough about humanity to understand that a man, a young man especially, like yourself, and innocent of the ways of the world, readily succumbs to female charms when those charms are made available, and when, perhaps, he is already subject to temptation . . .' she glanced around her. 'In his surroundings, in his position. You have my word, I shall say no more about it. Unless of course you give me reason. You may kiss me goodbye.'

He hesitated. A wild urge came seeping up from some recess of his mind to shout, balderdash, to bellow, I am Hilton, of Hilltop, and you are nothing, save as my bride, to say that, unless you stay now, I shall terminate our engagement . . . but would all of those things not mean he was indeed trying to ape Robert Hilton, riding roughshod over manners and morals and people's feelings in the gratification of his own desires? He had behaved abominably, and everyone knew it. Why, it was exceedingly generous of Ellen still to wish to marry him.

He leaned forward, and touched her lips with his, and waited, for the sudden thrust of passion he still remembered. But her mouth remained closed.

'Until tomorrow, Richard.' She withdrew her hand. 'Shall we go, Mama?'

126

'Good day, Mr Hilton,' Mrs Taggart said. 'I trust you will think very deeply about your past life, and endeavour to mend your ways.'

She followed her daughter into the hall, leaving Dick standing in the drawing room. Presumably he should go to the verandah to wave them off, but he felt incapable of movement. He listened to the sound of the hooves, the rumble of the wheels, gazed at Boscawen.

'They gone, Mr Richard.'

'Oh, thanks, Mr Boscawen. Is Josh around?'

'Well, no, sir, it gone eleven. Josh back to the village.'

'And Mr Hardy?'

'He gone to he house, I should think, sir.'

Where he was looked after, in every possible sense, by a mulatto girl he had picked up in Kingston. How he would laugh, when he heard the story.

And they had been going to ring the bells, and celebrate Bonaparte's abdication.

'You going breakfast, Mr Richard?'

'Eh?' He doubted he could stomach a thing. If only Tony had been here. He'd have sorted them out. But *he* had just finished sorting Tony out, and been proud of it. For a moment. 'No, Mr Boscawen. I'll not breakfast today. But I wouldn't mind a drink.'

'Oh, yes, sir. I going mix some more sangaree.'

Dick shook his head. 'I think something a little stronger. A glass of rum. No, bring the bottle.' He sat down. He felt exhausted.

'Yes, sir, Mr Richard.' Boscawen was back in a moment, set the silver tray with the bottle and the glass in front of his master, straightened. 'Mr Richard, I can ask?'

'Of course. What?'

'That lady, Mr Richard. Is true she going marry you?'

Dick drank, felt the hot liquid scorch his mouth and burn its way down his chest. 'I'm afraid it is true, Mr Boscawen.' And wondered why he had used the word 'afraid'.

Boscawen rolled his eyes some more. 'Ayayay,' he remarked, and left the room.

Dick poured himself another glass. He supposed he should try to think. He had been humiliated. And Ellen was making sure he would be even more humiliated tomorrow, by forcing him to call upon the Laidlaws, who would this evening be regaled with the

127

story of how she had quite literally kicked Harriet Gale off the plantation.

But if he did not go tomorrow, she might well refuse to marry him. And was he not betrothed? Had he not dreadfully deceived her these four years? And was not Ellen born to be mistress of a house like this? He could imagine her, sweeping through these great rooms, hostessing vast receptions, playing the piano . . . why, in the four years he had been here the piano had never once been played. Harriet had no such accomplishments.

But, to be out here, alone with Ellen, and Mrs Taggart? Good God. He had not thought of that. But Mrs Taggart would hardly have sailed all the way across the Atlantic just to turn round and sail back again. She must be planning to stay some time.

He poured himself another glass of rum, discovered that while the day had undoubtedly grown hotter, which was reasonable at noon, it had also become somewhat lighter in atmosphere. The room had taken on a pleasant glow, again caused by the noonday sun, no doubt, and he found that he could think more clearly.

And objectively. If he was going to have to live in a perpetual confrontation with the Taggarts, then he had to have support. And if he was going to have to eat humble pie in any event, at the Laidlaws, he might as well eat humble pie to his own brother. There was the answer. Tony had behaved badly, but he was still the best support to be found anywhere. He could not imagine Tony putting up with Ellen's bullying and Mrs Taggart's snide remarks. And anyway, he had sent Tony packing because of Judith Gale. But if Judith and her mother were in any event leaving the plantation . . . Christalmighty, he thought. Judith Gale.

He raised his head. Because there she was.

'My God.' He attempted to stand, lost his balance, and sat down again.

'She deserved it,' Judith said. 'All of it. And then, riding off and forgetting about me.'

Harriet, forget her own daughter? That did not make sense. She had abandoned her deliberately. To be sure she retained a link with the plantation, a reason either for Dick to call on her, or for her to return.

'Uncle Dick,' Judith said, coming into the room. 'Are you really going to marry that woman?'

'Eh? Why, yes, I suppose I am. My God, if she learns about you . . . we must get you into town. I was going anyway.' Oh, indeed. Why should he wait until tomorrow, merely because Ellen had decided so? He had been taken by surprise. That was it. And he had been feeling at once exhilarated by the news of the peace, and excited by Judith's whipping. Judith's whipping. He regained his feet, peered at her. 'Can you ride?'

She rubbed her backside, carefully. 'I could put a blanket on the saddle. But Uncle Dick, it's the middle of the afternoon.'

'I'll show them,' Dick muttered. 'Middle of the afternoon? What does that matter?' He discovered himself in the hall, holding on to the bannisters. 'Mr Boscawen. Mr Boscawen. Saddle my horse. And one for Miss Gale.'

'You going now, Mr Richard?'

'Right now. Right this minute. Judith. Get yourself a coat and a hat. And put on boots, girl. You can't go into Kingston barefoot. Hurry, now.'

She hesitated. 'Are you sure you're all right, Uncle Dick?'

'All right? All right?'

'Don't you think you should have a nap, and then perhaps this evening . . .'

'Now,' he shouted. 'Hurry.'

She gazed at him for a moment, clearly uncertain. But he had held her wrists while her mother had flogged her. She ran up the stairs.

'Come on, come on,' Dick bawled, returning to the drawing room for another glass of rum, and discovering the bottle was empty. 'Mr Boscawen, another bottle. No, bring two.' He put one in each pocket. As the child had said, it was the middle of the afternoon. The sun would be at its hottest. He'd probably need a drink on the way. 'Come on, come on.' He went into the office, unlocked the safe, took out his bag of coin. He always kept at least twenty guineas in coin on the plantation, mainly for settling Tony's debts. This night they might serve to settle Harriet's anger. He put the bag in his coat pocket, beside a bottle of rum.

Judith hurried down the stairs, wearing boots and a hat, but no coat. 'What about my clothes?'

'We'll send them on later. If they are going on at all. We must see about this. Yes, indeed,' Dick decided, negotiating the front stairs by holding on to the bannisters. 'We shall see about this. Ordering me about in my own house, indeed. Where the devil is the stirrup, man?'

Two of the grooms assisted him into the saddle, and he watched Judith mount. She rode as if part of a horse. But then, she had been born to it. And did he not also ride as if he were part of a horse? Was he not a Hilton? By God, was he not *the* Hilton? He drew rein to take a drink and discovered that they were at the boundary. There was a quick ride. He could look back over the whole sweep of the valley. His valley. There was a sight to give a man confidence.

He wiped his mouth with the back of his hand, held out the bottle.

Judith shook her head. 'You will have a seizure, most like, Uncle Dick. Drinking in the sun is very bad for you.'

'Listen,' he said. 'I am done . . . done, do you hear, being told what I can do and what I can't do, what I must do and what I mustn't do. Done.'

He kicked his horse, and set it moving again, and she rode behind him. She really was a good child, and a brave one; sitting a horse must be agony in her condition. But they wouldn't be long now. And the sun was already drooping. On Hilltop he'd be going aback again, and he felt no discomfort. Siesta was all rubbish, when you came down to it. Perhaps he should make a change in the system. If the blacks worked all day instead of taking two hours off in the middle, surely they could produce more cane. Or could they? The cane grew, and there was an end to it. Standing there looking at it would not make it grow any faster. He must ask Hardy about that one.

Houses. Flags flying from every building. Bunting draped across Harbour Street. Masses of people, white and black, men and women, mostly drunk, filling the roadway, waving bottles and cheering, reaching up to stop their horses and squeeze their hands. Kingston, celebrating the end of the war.

'I doubt I'll ever sit again,' Judith remarked. 'I think I'm a big blister. What do we do now, Uncle Dick?'

'Hey,' Dick bawled. If only he wasn't so sleepy. And his head was banging away as if divided into two. But it would soon be cool. 'Where does Mr Laidlaw lodge?'

A black man stared at him. 'Eh-eh,' he said. 'But you is Mr

Hilton.'

'You are God damned right I am Mr Hilton,' Dick said. 'Laidlaw, where is he?'

'Well, he does be living down Union Street. Is that second corner.'

'Over there,' Dick said, and kicked his horse. People parted in front of him, reluctantly.

'Maybe I should stay here,' Judith suggested.

'Rubbish. Rubbish,' he shouted. 'You go where I go. That's an order. From me.' He turned his horse down a quiet tree-lined avenue, away from the bustle of the town centre. 'Laidlaw,' he bellowed at a white couple obviously on their way back from the celebrations. 'Laidlaw.'

'Why, 'tis Mr Hilton,' said the man. 'Melissa, 'tis Mr Hilton. Good day to you, sir.' He raised his hat, and his wife gave a nervous smile.

'Oh, good day to you, sir. Madam. I seek Laidlaw.'

'Why, Mr Hilton, sir, his house is straight across the street.'

'I thank you.' Dick dismounted, strode up the stairs. Judith leaned from her own saddle to take his bridle.

The house was small, and had verandahs on both floors, inevitably. Laidlaw had taken a post in the government, as agricultural adviser. The front door was shut, but in response to his banging was opened by a black butler. 'Sir?'

'You have a Miss Taggart staying here, I believe,' Dick said. 'I wish to see her.'

'Miss Taggart only just come in, sir,' the man said. 'She is weary, Mr Hilton, sir, and lying down.'

'I'll see her, by God,' Dick shouted. 'I'll see her.'

'You'll do no such thing, sir,' Charles Laidlaw said, coming into the hallway behind his servant. 'We saw you, sir, coming down the street, reeling in the saddle. What, did you stop to drink with that disgusting mob? Miss Taggart says if you do not leave on the instant, she will not speak with you again. And I am empowered to have you ejected, sir.'

'To have me . . .' Dick stared at him. But Laidlaw was at least his size, and the servant even bigger. 'By God,' he shouted. 'Had I a pistol . . .'

'You'd attempt murder?' Laidlaw inquired.

Dick turned and stamped down the steps. He should have

broken their heads. He should have taken the precaution of bringing Josh and Absolom with him. Then they'd have sung a different song. He had never been so angry in his life. Why . . .

'She'd not receive you?' Judith asked.

'Silly bitch,' he grumbled. 'Maybe it was seeing you. We'll to your mother first. Aye, I should have done that. Then I'll seek out Tony, by God. And then we'll see.'

Judith said nothing, but released his bridle and turned her horse.

'Drunk, am I?' Dick grumbled, following her. 'By God, I'll show her, drunk. I'll . . .' He discovered himself in front of the hotel, just round the corner from Harbour Street. The noise crashed and boomed in his ears. 'Come on,' he said, and dismounted. God, how his head hurt. He stamped into the reception hall, peered at the clerk. 'I am looking for Mistress Gale.'

The clerk looked from him to Judith. 'Ah . . . if you'd wait, sir, perhaps I could acquaint Mistress Gale with your arrival.'

'Acquaint?' Dick shouted. 'Give me her room number, dolt. I am Richard Hilton. I'll see myself up.'

'I know who you are, Mr Hilton.' The clerk looked at Judith again. 'The number is seven hundred and four. But really, sir . . .'

'Seven hundred and four?' Dick gaped at him. 'You have seven hundred rooms in this dump?'

'No, sir, we have seven. But Mr Mortlake decided to start the numbering at seven hundred and one. Gives the place a bit of class, you see.'

'Seven hundred and four. Good God Almighty.' Dick climbed the stairs, looked over his shoulder. 'Aren't you coming?'

Judith crammed her hat on her head, ran behind him. Dick was already in the uncarpeted corridor. By now it was growing dark, and the candles had not yet been lit. He peered at a door, found it was open; the room beyond was empty. The number read seven hundred and two.

'This one,' he decided, and tried the next handle. It was bolted. 'Open up,' he bawled, banging on the door. 'Open up, Harriet. It's me.'

'She's probably out celebrating,' Judith whispered.

'Celebrating? She'd have seen us.' He resumed banging on the door. 'Open up. Open up.'

The door swung in, and he found himself looking at a very large white man.

'Who the devil are you?' he demanded, peered past him into the candlelit room. 'Harriet?'

'Well, well,' she said, and got off the bed. 'Come to your senses?'

'Harriet?' She was naked. 'Good God. You only left Hilltop at eleven.'

She tossed her head. 'I have friends,' she said. 'I decided to look one up.'

Dick tried to enter the room, and found the large man's hand on his chest. 'What'll I do?' the man asked.

'Oh, throw him out,' Harriet said. 'And come back to bed.'

'You heard the lady,' said the large man.

'Now look here,' Dick declared. 'I am Richard Hilton. I intend to enter that room. Stand aside.' He once again tried to push in, and gained the sensation that a mule had kicked him under the chin.

Dick found himself lying against the wall opposite the door marked 704, which had again closed. He did not remember it closing, so presumably he had been unconscious. But only for seconds; he watched Judith Gale coming towards him, apparently, from the flutter of her skirt and her hair, moving quickly, but seeming to take an eternity actually to kneel beside him.

You shouldn't be here, he wanted to say. You should be inside with your mother. But when he attempted to move his chin nothing happened.

'Oh, God,' she said. She was kneeling now, and stretching out her hand to touch the corner of his mouth, then take it away again and look at the blood. 'Oh, God.'

He pushed himself up. The corridor appeared to be rising and falling, like a ship in a rough sea, and the wall against which he lay was also moving, back and forth.

There were noises from the stairs. Judith heard them as well. 'They mustn't see you like this, Uncle Dick,' she said, and grasped his arm. What a strong child she was. With only the minimum of help from him she dragged and pushed and propped him, first to his knees, and then to his feet, and then through the still opened door of seven hundred and two. Here, she released him, and he staggered across the room and fell over the bed.

133

Behind him the door closed, and the bolt was slipped. Dimly he heard feet in the corridor, and voices, but it was impossible to decide what they were saying. The entire hotel seemed shrouded in the racket from the next street. A board creaked, and then the mattress—the bed was not made up—depressed beside him. 'Shall I light a candle?' she whispered. 'There must be one.'

He rolled on his back. 'No,' he said. There. He could speak again. 'They might see it.'

She nodded; in the gloom he could see her head move, although he could not make out her face. Although perhaps he could make out the glow of her eyes.

'He took you unawares,' she said. 'Next time you'll kill him.'

He watched the glow. He felt sick, in his belly and in his heart, and in his mind. His last remembered thought before the fist had exploded against his chin had been shame, a certain knowledge that he was in a situation about which he could do nothing, and which would leave him even more bereft of self-respect than before.

But mingled with the shame, incessantly and increasingly, was the memory of this girl's wrists in his as she had knelt across the bed, and the tears issuing from her eyes. The very eyes which now gloomed at him. And of the pale-skinned buttocks, so contrasted with the suntan of her face and arms and feet, quivering and reddening beneath the blows.

The eyes came closer; and she was lying beside him, propped on her elbow. 'Uncle Dick,' she said, softly. 'Do you think Miss Taggart would object if I stayed on Hilltop? I could be her maid. You could tell her you employed me as a surprise, to be her maid. I can be a maid, Uncle Dick. I've brushed Mummy's hair, oh, often. And if you make me stay in town Mummy will beat me again, I know she will, Uncle Dick.' She seemed struck by an afterthought, and came closer yet; he could feel her breath on his face. 'I'd call you Mr Hilton, Uncle Dick.'

Oh, Christ, he thought. Oh, Christ. Because he had touched her before he had realized what he was doing. His hand seemed to leave his side as if impelled with some other force than his mind, and lay for a moment on her shoulder, before slipping down her back.

Foolishly, he thought he must make conversation. It was the only way. 'Are you sore?'

'I'm burning, Uncle Dick. Oh, Uncle Dick.' But it wasn't a protest. Her bottom gave a little wriggle under his hand, and she licked his face. Like a cat, he thought. Like a cat. He wanted to look at her, but not her face. He sat up to raise her skirts, and found he could see the slender slivers of white which were her legs, just as he could inhale the utter freshness of her youth. But not that young. When he buried his head in her groin, he found hair. And now she was sitting up as well, hugging his face between belly and thighs as she brought up her knees. 'Oh, Uncle Dick,' she said again.

How long, he wondered. How many nights, how many dreams, have you lurked there at the back of my mind? How many hours in bed with your mother have been dominated by the thought of you?

He was lying again, on his face, and she was reaching down his back to release his belt, and then drive her hands inside his breeches. So then, had *she* dreamed? Or had she just been awakened by Tony's assault, this morning? But had that been an assault, or had she not just been seeking, from any man? Her own mother called her a whore. *Was* she a whore? He had discovered her and Tony because this day he had returned to the house early, to celebrate the news of Bonaparte's abdication. He had supposed it had been a coincidence. But there was no such thing as coincidence. Suppose Tony and Judith had been frolicking together every day? The servants would have known. How they must have grinned and winked, behind his back. Why, even Harriet must have known. By God, Harriet. She had known, and done nothing about it until she could act the mother to her best advantage.

Only Dick Hilton had not known, would never have known, save for Bonaparte. Just as Ellen would not have discovered his guilt, but for Bonaparte. God damn Bonaparte. But *was* she a whore?

He pushed himself up, and her arm went round his neck. She had learned, from her mother, no doubt, and drew him to her, fingers busy. He had a wild, irrelevant thought that she might scream, as her mother did, when he entered. But instead she gave the longest sigh he had ever heard, seeming to expel all the air from her lungs and then go on exhaling even after that, so that her body appeared to deflate, and she lay absolutely still, her arms

135

tight on his neck, her cheek next to his, causing his bruise the most exquisite agony as his face surged against hers.

Then he lay as still as she, lips together, bodies together, feet together, his hair mingling with hers as it flopped from his forehead, passion disappeared in a gnawing, a growing despair. The sickness was back, eating at his belly, eating at his brain, eating at his heart. This girl was fourteen years old. She called him uncle. She had stayed with him after he had been beaten, rather than taking refuge with her mother. She had not fought him, because she trusted him. And his reply had been to rape her.

For merely attempting to molest her, he had quarrelled with Tony, and sent him from the plantation.

He wanted to vomit. He wanted to choke. He wished he could choke. He pushed himself away from her, pulled up his breeches, threaded his belt.

'We could stay the night, Uncle Dick,' she said. 'You could keep this room for the night. It is too late to ride back to Hilltop now.'

Too late, he thought. And she, in her innocence, would compound the crime, again and again.

He went to the door.

'Uncle Dick?' She raised herself on her elbow.

'Your mother,' he mumbled. 'You must go to your mother.' He stepped into the corridor, was for a moment dazzled by the flickering candles. The door closed behind him. He went down the stairs, and the clerk gazed at him in amazement. No doubt he remained untidy, his hair scattered.

He stood on the porch, inhaled the night air. It was quite dark, and the windows of the houses were dotted with light. It was also quieter; the revellers had returned home to eat. And talk. And laugh. They would have Richard Hilton to discuss, this night. Harriet Gale, laughing with her friend at the way he had been dismissed. Tony Hilton, laughing with his gambling friends over his brother's absurd attitudes. Ellen Taggart, laughing with the Laidlaws over the way they had brought him to heel. And Judith Gale, sobbing to herself, as the enormity of what had happened slowly overtook her.

He felt in his coat pocket, discovered a bottle of rum. Had he finished the other one? He pulled out the cork, took a long drink, and lost some of the sick feeling. But the street kept rising and falling.

136

His horse gave a faint whinny, but he ignored it, walked down the street, staggering a little, brain buzzing, head opening and shutting with gigantic bangs, stomach rolling. And came to a full stop at the beginnings of the dock. Before him the harbour was quiet, the water lapping at the piles, the ships riding to their anchors. He took another drink.

A noise, from behind him. He turned, stepping aside as he did so. Half a dozen men came down the street, laughing and chattering amongst themselves. They walked past him without a glance, began to drag a dinghy out from beneath the piles. Seamen. Returning to their ship, and thence, no doubt, to England. Theirs was a freedom which landsmen, and plantation owners, could never know. A freedom to leave their problems, and their women, and their detractors, and those who would give them orders, behind, and look to new horizons.

England. The boat was free of the wooden uprights, and one man was already on board, holding it close while the others got in. Mama was in England, and Father. To tell him where he had gone wrong. To be confessed to, where he had gone wrong, and to tell him what he must now do. Why, perhaps he could persuade Mama to return to Jamaica with him. It would not take very long.

The last man was in the boat. He must act now, or he would have lost the opportunity.

'Ahoy,' he said, stepping forward.

The coxswain had been about to cast off. 'Aye?'

'Where are you bound?' Dick asked.

'Plymouth, your honour.'

'Do you take passengers?' Dick dug his hand into his pocket, found a handful of guineas, brought them out to glint in the faint light.

The sailors exchanged glances.

'You'd have to ask the captain.'

'He's aboard?'

'Oh, aye, We're sailing at midnight.'

'Then give me a ride out to your ship. I'd talk with him.'

The coxswain peered at him. 'You're drunk, your honour, if you'll pardon the liberty. When you wakes up, we'll be at sea.'

'Aye,' Dick said. 'There's a happy thought.' He threw his empty bottle into the harbour.

8

The Brother

Anthony Hilton turned over his cards, one by one. 'Ah, bah,' he said. 'Twenty-three.' He threw them into the pile in the middle of the table.

' 'Tis that unlucky you are, Mr Hilton,' said the dealer, smiling at him. 'You'll sign another note?'

'I will not. 'Tis damn near dawn.' Tony stretched, leaning back in his chair. The other players waited, politely. Once he stopped, they had small reason to continue. 'One day, Lewis, my luck will turn. Or I'll discover how you cheat.'

'Why, Mr Hilton,' Lewis said. 'A man could take offence at that, indeed he could.'

'But you won't, Lewis,' Tony said. 'There's a pity.' He got up, draped his coat over his shoulder, stuck his hat on the back of his head. 'Good morning, gentlemen.'

He opened the door, inhaled the cleaner air of the corridor, closed it behind him, and listened to a cock crow. It was indeed all but dawn. And he had lost near a hundred guineas. Dick would not be pleased.

And then he remembered. Christalmighty, Dick would not be settling these notes. Or would he, because he was Dick? But he'd be expecting his brother to be on a ship to England. Christalmighty.

He lurched along the corridor, found the window at the end, and put his head out, once again breathing deeply to clear the tobacco fumes from his head. Of all the stupid quarrels, over a little cock teaser. But of course it went deeper than that. Dick had not been himself recently, had seemed to have something on his mind.

He smiled at the lightening darkness. And now he had more

than just something. Ellen had been at Hilltop yesterday, was probably still there now. That would have put the cat amongst the pigeons.

'Mr Hilton?'

He turned. Noble belied his name by actually owning this establishment. He was a nervous little man, who looked even more nervous this morning.

'I did not wish to disturb you, earlier. But there is a young woman wishing to see you.'

'Eh? I'm not in the mood, Noble.'

'Oh, no, sir, not one of mine.' Noble allowed himself a grin. 'Although she could be, sir, given time. 'Tis the Gale girl. Harriet's daughter.'

'Eh?'

'Downstairs, Mr Hilton.'

Tony brushed the man aside, ran down the stairs. Judith sat in a straight chair at the bottom. She wore no hat, and was indeed not dressed for town at all. He had never seen her face so solemn. But how good it was to see her. So perhaps she was no more than a tease. He knew now that she was what he wanted, in every way. It was not an admission he would dream of making to anyone — save himself — but women, Joan Lanken, the blacks, expected to be mastered by Tony Hilton. And became contemptuous when he would have them respond in kind.

After Joan's sly smile, Harriet Gale, the thought of Harriet Gale and Uncle Robert, had seemed the answer to a dream. But that bitch had been interested only in *the* Hilton, in a perpetuation of her position. She had forgotten she had a daughter, who knew no other way of love, as she knew no other man.

'Judith? What has happened?'

She stood up. 'I don't know, Uncle Tony. I'm so afraid.'

'Afraid?' He took her hand; it was as cold as ice. 'Sit down. Tell me.'

'Uncle Dick,' she said. 'He's disappeared.'

'Dick? Rubbish.'

'We came into town,' she said.

'You and Dick? Why?'

'Well, there was this quarrel, Uncle Tony. Between Uncle Dick and that lady. I don't remember her name.'

'Miss Taggart?'

'Aye. And Mummy left in a rage, and then Miss Taggart left, with her mother. And then Uncle Dick said, we'll go into town and see them. He'd been drinking, Uncle Tony.'

'Dick? You mean he was drunk? Good God.'

'So we came in, Uncle Tony, and he went to the Laidlaws' house, where Miss Taggart is staying, and they wouldn't let him in. So then he went to the Park Hotel, where Mummy is rooming. But . . .' She bit her lip.

'She wouldn't let him in, either?'

'She had a man with her, Uncle Tony. He . . . he hit Uncle Dick.'

'Hit him? Beat him up, you mean?'

Her chin flopped up and down, as she nodded.

'Christalmighty. So what happened then?'

Judith Gale inhaled, slowly. 'He left, Uncle Tony. He just walked out of the hotel. But he was very upset, and he had a bottle.'

'What time was this?'

She shrugged. 'About eight o'clock last night.'

Tony felt in his fob, took out his watch. The time was a quarter to six. 'He probably fell down and is sleeping in a ditch.'

'I've looked, Uncle Tony. Well, I waited at the hotel for him to come back. Then I started looking. I've walked all Kingston, Uncle Tony.'

Tony frowned at her. 'You have wandered the streets of Kingston all night. Unmolested?'

'Nobody bothered me, Uncle Tony.'

'Good God Almighty. You are an odd child. Don't you realize that he's gone back out to Hilltop?'

'His horse is still outside the Park Hotel, Uncle Tony.'

'Eh?' Tony seized another chair, pulled it next to hers, and sat down.

'And I met one man, Uncle Tony, last night, who remembers a drunken man leaving the Park Hotel. He can't be sure it was Uncle Dick, but the time would have been about right. And Uncle Tony, the man walked towards the docks. The harbour, Uncle Tony.'

Tony gazed at her. Dick, drunk and irresponsible? He would not have said that was possible, for such a level-headed prig. Although he had had a lot on his mind, and more building up all

140

the time. But not enough, perhaps. Unless . . .

'So what do you think has happened to him?'

She licked her lips. 'I think he may have fallen in. Or . . .'

'Or jumped? Because he was beaten up by some client of your mother's?'

'He was very upset,' she said.

It was quite light now; the clerk was snuffing the candles. And Judith thought Dick might have committed suicide. Now why should a girl like Judith Gale even think in terms like that?

And if she had cause, what unimaginable vistas were suddenly opening in front of him. Dick had run away from something. That seemed fairly obvious. From Ellen? Hardly likely. She still had every intention of marrying him. From Harriet's friend? That was nonsense. All he had to do was declare himself to the Custos and they'd have the fellow in gaol. From something on Hilltop? Of which he knew nothing? Or from someone.

And did it matter, alongside the plain fact that the owner of Jamaica's biggest plantation had apparently lost his senses, with a crop to be ground?

'Uncle Tony?' she asked. 'You will do something?'

Tony smiled at her. 'I will, Judith. When you tell me exactly what happened between you and my brother.'

'Seven hundred and four, Mr Hilton,' said the clerk. 'But Mr Hilton, there's a man in there.'

'Never,' Tony remarked.

The clerk looked at Judith.

'You sit down here,' Tony said. 'I'm going to have a word with your mother.'

The clerk licked his lips. 'This man . . . he had a fight with your brother, we think, Mr Hilton.'

'Oh, aye?' Tony said. 'Tell me about it.'

'Well, there was this noise, and a bump, and I went upstairs, with Harvey, the boy, you know? And there was no one there. But Mr Hilton had just gone up . . . and then, about an hour later, he came down, staggering, and went out of the door. And then, another half-hour later, that young lady came down . . .'

'They'd been in one of your empty rooms,' Tony said. 'Recovering. But you remember all of that. As a matter of fact, old son, I would write it out, just to be sure you have it straight.

141

I'll pick it up in a moment.'

'You be careful, Uncle Tony,' Judith said.

'I'm a careful man.' Because he did not want sex from Harriet Gale. Thus he could be the masterful man every woman who had never shared his bed supposed him to be. There was a paradox. One he found amusing, when he was in the mood to be amused.

He climbed the stairs, and at the top took off his coat and laid it on the floor; the bandanna he used when riding to keep dust from his mouth was in the pocket; he wrapped it several times around his right hand, to bring the fingers together and protect them. Then he knocked on the door of room seven hundred and four.

After a few minutes, it swung in; the time was still only eight-thirty. 'Christ,' said the large man. 'Another one?'

'Good morning to you,' Tony said, and hit him in the belly. The man wore only a pair of pants, and they were no protection. He gave a gasp and his face came forward. Tony put his left hand on his shoulder to stop him, and while he was momentarily checked, hit him exactly on the point of the jaw with his protected right fist. The man gave a sigh, and his knees lost all their strength. Tony caught him under the left arm as well, and gently laid him on the floor. 'And to you,' he said to Harriet.

She sat up in bed, naked, stared at him in total horror.

He dragged the large man into the corridor, sat him against the wall, re-entered the room, closed and locked the door.

Harriet licked her lips. 'What . . . what do you want?'

Tony crossed the room, sat on the bed. 'To talk with you. I believe Dick came here last night.'

Her head flopped up and down.

'And was ejected by your friend. I imagine you were pretty angry with Dickie boy.'

She gasped for breath. 'He just stood there, while that . . . that bitch kicked me out.'

'And she did, kick you out,' Tony said with great satisfaction. 'You must show me the mark, some time.'

'You . . . how did you know?'

'Judith told me. She told me a lot of things. Such as how, after leaving you last night, Dick raped her.'

'He did what? Oh, that little whore. Rape *her*? She's been dying to get him between her legs for months. Years, maybe.'

'Harriet,' Tony said, gently. 'You just do not seem to be paying attention. Judith was raped. She may not know it, yet, but you had better be sure she finds out. A fourteen-year-old girl? Of course she was raped.'

'But . . .' Harriet's brows drew together, slowly, in bewilderment. 'That's a criminal charge.'

'Indeed it is. And perpetrated by a man like Dick Hilton, why . . . imagination does not cope with the scandal. As he no doubt realizes. He has disappeared.'

'Disappeared?'

'He was last seen making for the waterfront. Certainly he is not to be found in Kingston. I have spent this last hour making inquiries.'

'But . . . oh, my God.'

'Suicide? Not Dick. On the other hand, he was drunk. He might have fallen in, and drowned. There's tragedy for you.'

'You can sit there? And say that, about your own brother?'

'An odd chap. Not really a Hilton. On the other hand, Harriet, a ship cleared last night about ten. The *Cormorant* for Bristol.'

'And you think he's on that? Oh, thank God.'

'It is a possibility. A guilty man, running, oh, yes, it is a possibility. But what a time to go, with a crop to be cut and ground.'

Harriet once more licked her lips. 'You . . . he ordered you from the plantation.'

'Ah. I was wondering, do you remember that, Harriet?'

She gazed at him.

'Because I was thinking, he has also ordered you from the plantation. In effect. Now, even were I to be allowed to act for him, and in the circumstances, with him gone, and us not knowing whether he is alive or dead, and being unable to know until the *Cormorant* makes Bristol and returns again — why, twelve weeks at the very least — I could not take you back out there.' He leaned forward, gently cupped her right breast in his hand, adjusting its sag. Her eyes widened. 'But at the same time, being a very generous fellow by nature, were I put in charge of Hilltop I certainly would not think of letting you starve, especially after what Dick did to your daughter. And there is another point. With you making a formal accusation of rape, and concerning your daughter, it is doubtful whether Dick will ever dare return to Jamaica, and if he did, he would very probably go to gaol. Twelve

143

weeks, was I saying? Twelve years more like.' He turned his attention to her left breast, stroked the nipple erect. 'I do not see, in the circumstances, how Reynolds could do anything different. Dick has made a will you know, leaving everything to me. Well, perhaps he isn't dead. But there it is. I am his appointed heir.'

Harriet gazed at him. 'How much?'

'Your own house, for a start. And shall we say, a thousand a year? There'll be no quarrelling with Judith, mind. She'll live with you, and you'll be the perfect mother, as regards her. What else you do with your time, and who else you do it with, is your business.'

'A thousand pounds?'

'A thousand guineas.'

'My God,' she whispered. Then her head jerked. 'Boscawen. Merriman. They were there when you left.'

Tony Hilton smiled. 'Boscawen and Merriman are slaves, Harriet. And Dick was an indulgent, an over-indulgent master. Why, those two, they'd perjure themselves to have him back. But I know how to deal with perjury. So do the Custos, I imagine. They're all planters.'

Harriet Gale licked her lips. 'You are a devil from hell, Mr Hilton.'

Tony Hilton stood up. 'I'm a Hilton, Mistress Gale. No doubt Reynolds will be in touch, for a statement.' He went to the door. 'I'll send Judith up. Be sure you treat her kindly.'

The sun was swinging low in the western sky when Anthony Hilton rode up the slope. The rain of yesterday had left the air clean. The rain and the wind. There had been a lot of wind, although it was too late in the year for a full hurricane. And indeed, the gale had already blown itself out. But it could not have sprung up at a better time. It occurred to Tony that he might be an unlucky gambler, but there was nothing wrong with his fortune in other directions.

He drew rein before the Great House. Instantly the yardboys surrounded the horse to take his bridle and give him a leg down. And instantly, too, Boscawen appeared on the verandah. 'Mr Hilton, sir? Man, I'm glad to see you, master. The master done gone to town, three days, and I ain't seen him.'

Tony climbed the steps, took off his hat to fan his face. 'Fetch

144

me something to drink. None of that damned sangaree. A bottle of good wine, from the cellar.'

'Man, Mr Tony, sir, Mr Richard done give instructions no wine to be taken from the good cellar unless he saying so.'

'Listen, old man,' Tony said. 'Fetch me a bottle, and jump to it. And then get the drivers and that Merriman up here, and send for Mr Hardy.'

Boscawen hesitated, looked down the steps as if hoping to see Dick materialize out of the dusk, then turned and went into his pantry. Tony entered the withdrawing room. The candles had just been lit, and burned brightly. The entire room glowed. It was a room meant to be crowded, with handsome, elegantly dressed men, and with beautiful, gayly dressed women. It had stood empty for too long.

And now it was his. His now, and, if he played his cards right, his forever. And he played cards well. There was no sharper sitting opposite him this time. All the high cards were tucked away in *his* sleeve.

Hardy hurried into the room. 'Mr Hilton? Thank God. If we only knew what was going on . . .'

'It seems my brother has fled the island, or committed suicide,' Tony explained.

'Good God. Because of that Taggart woman?'

'Have you met her?'

'Yesterday. She came out here, for the second time, I believe, looking for Mr Richard. It seems he had been meant to call on her in town.'

'Ah. Was she worried?'

'She was indeed, Mr Anthony. Well, she took the road in all that rain. Afraid for her safety, I was. But she would come. And then go again. What's to be done?'

'There is little can be done, about poor Dick. It is also a criminal matter, James. A business of rape, on Judith Gale.'

Hardy frowned. 'Judith? I would hardly call that . . .'

'Rape is rape, James. The innocent must be protected. A complaint has been laid, and the Custos would certainly have to take Dick into custody, should he reappear. But I have a feeling that he won't, for some time. In the meanwhile, I am to manage Hilltop.'

'You, Mr Anthony? But, I did hear . . .'

'Rumours spread by the blacks, James. You'll not believe nigger rumours, now will you? Of course, there will have to be certain changes. I doubt I possess my brother's patience with lazy swine. I have also long felt that you have been insufficiently rewarded for all your efforts on our behalf.'

Hardy gazed at him for a moment, and then smiled. 'Rumours, Mr Anthony. I'll get to the bottom of them.'

Tony also smiled. He had been looking past his manager to the verandah, where Joshua Merriman was hurrying up the steps; behind him were Absolom and several of the drivers. 'Then I suggest you begin.'

'Mr Anthony?' Merriman stood in the hall, his hat in his hands. 'But what is this I hearing, Mr Anthony?'

Tony went outside. 'Nothing that need concern you, Josh. Save that I shall be in charge of Hilltop for the next few years.'

'You, Mr Anthony? But the master done say . . .'

'I am the master, Josh. You'd do well to remember that.'

Josh frowned at him. 'I got for hear that from the master, Mr Anthony.'

'Another opinion I have long held, Mr Hardy,' Tony said, 'is that this fellow is unsuited to the authority my brother saw fit to give him. From this moment he will take his place in the field.'

'You can't do that, Mr Anthony,' Joshua declared. 'I going talk with Mr Reynolds about this.'

'You can talk to the sky,' Tony said. 'Mr Hardy, that man is at the bottom of all the rumours spread about my brother and me. I want him punished. Fifty lashes, Mr Hardy.'

'Yes, sir,' Hardy cried.

'You can't do this,' Merriman insisted. 'The master done say . . .'

Hardy was at the balustrade, looking down at Absolom. 'Take him down, Absolom. Strip him and have him on the triangle.'

Absolom glanced at his fellow drivers.

'When Mr Reynolds hears about this . . .' Josh said.

But he was not a Hilltop slave. He was Dick Hilton's man, not theirs.

'You coming, man?' Absolom asked. 'Or we carrying you?'

'Thank you, Mr Hardy,' Tony said, and went inside. Things to be done. Mama. She must be told. He must write her a letter, explaining Dick's crimes. And then, Ellen Taggart? She looked like a horse. But a very handsome horse. And a strong, purposeful

146

woman, of whom Dick was very obviously terrified. Why, the poor woman must be absolutely distraught at what had happened.

Besides, he had no idea what arrangements Dick might have made, either with her or concerning her.

'You'll fetch the port, Boscawen.' Anthony Hilton leaned back in his chair, smiled down the sweep of the huge dining table. Ellen Taggart smiled back. She sat immediately on his right. Her mother sat on his left, and James Hardy sat beside Mrs Taggart. The table continued to look utterly empty, save for this corner. But it was an expanse Tony enjoyed. 'So there it is,' he said. 'Perhaps it is difficult to explain, and yet, you know, all my sympathy, all my heart, goes out to poor Dick. Living here, in all this splendour, absolute master of everyone and everything, one loses all sense of perspective, all sense of reality. The same thing apparently happened to Uncle Robert. Isn't that so, Mr Hardy?'

'Oh, indeed, Mr Hilton,' Hardy agreed. 'The former Mr Hilton was renowned for his eccentricity, and his arrogance.'

'And you think my appearance may have pricked Dick's little bubble?' Ellen inquired, softly. She wore a white evening gown decorated with pink lace flowers at the hem, and pink lace gloves. Her bodice was square, but low. Her hair was up; and also decorated with flowers. She was a quite superb horse. And a woman of character. A woman who would never be mastered? Who would never wish to be mastered? What a splendid thought.

'Oh, undoubtedly. Looked at objectively, of course, it was the best thing that could happen to him. There is yet time. But then, to rape that poor child . . . I do beg your pardon, Mrs Taggart.'

'A spade may as well be called a spade, Mr Hilton,' Mrs Taggart said. 'I never did like that young man, if you'll excuse my opinion. I always found him odd.'

'Oh, Mother, you hardly knew Dick.' Ellen frowned at Tony. 'But then, it seems, neither did I.'

Boscawen had placed the decanter of port beside Tony; now he filled Ellen's crystal goblet before passing it to her mother. 'We shall, of course, endeavour to find him, and to be honest with you, Ellen . . . you don't mind if I call you Ellen, I hope . . . I shall endeavour to keep him safe away from Jamaica and the law. Blood is thicker than water, what?'

Ellen sighed, and sipped, and sighed again. 'I could forgive him anything,' she said. 'Even assaulting that poor child. But those lies he wrote in his letters, year after year after year.'

'Unforgivable,' Mrs Taggart boomed.

'Incredible,' Tony said, having discovered the opening he had been seeking. 'One can hardly think of a more peaceful place than Jamaica, and in Jamaica a more peaceful place than this plantation. I'd enjoy showing it to you, Ellen.'

'I'd love to see it,' she said. 'I've only glanced at it from the windows of the coach, as we came in, and the first time, well . . .' a pretty flush scorched her cheeks, 'I was so angry . . .'

'With reason. With reason. Shall we retire?' Tony stood up, pulled out Ellen's chair; Hardy did the same for Mrs Taggart. 'If you ladies would like to see the bedrooms . . .' He smiled. 'I am afraid I don't have such a thing as a housekeeper.'

'And very wise, too,' Mrs Taggart said. 'Will you accompany me, Ellen?'

Ellen had caught Tony's eye. 'I think a little later, Mother. But you go ahead. I'd like some air.' She walked towards the verandah. 'That was a superb meal, Mr Hilton.'

Tony nodded to Hardy, who withdrew into the drawing room. Mrs Taggart was already half way up the stairs.

He joined Ellen on the verandah. 'I think you could try calling me Tony.'

She glanced at him, moved to the rail, looked down at the night, at the twinkling lights in the houses of the town, and at the torches burning in the slave village. 'It is magnificent,' she said. 'So quiet . . . and yet, not so quiet, surely. There was a man, suspended from some posts, when we came in. He had been whipped I think.'

'Oh, indeed, an utter scoundrel named Merriman. Do you know, I have had to flog him every day this past week? The fact is, it was another of Dick's aberrations that these people did not require discipline. But I should have had him taken down before you came. I do apologize.'

Her fingers rested on the rail. 'I am glad you didn't. A plantation should look like a plantation. Besides . . .' She gave him another sidelong glance, and her tongue showed, for just a moment.

He stood beside her, his heart pounding. He suddenly realized he could love this woman. And surely a woman like Ellen Taggart could never really have loved Dick. 'What will you do now?'

'Oh.' She gazed into the darkness. 'I seem to have made a complete fool of myself. Mama and I will have to take ship back to England.'

'Why?'

'Well . . .' Another quick glance. 'We cannot remain here, Mr Hilton. Tony. Quite apart from the scandal . . .'

'There would have been scandal, or at best gossip, even had you found nothing with which to reproach Dick, and married him. Our very name accumulates it.'

'But the name protects as well, Tony. I do not have it. Ouch.'

'A mosquito. We do suffer from them, occasionally. Did it sting you?'

She pulled off her left glove. 'It seemed to get into the top.'

'Don't scratch it.' He took her hand, raised it to his lips, gently sucked the sweet-smelling flesh. 'The name will protect you also, Ellen, if you remain as my guest.'

'Your guest?'

'This house is full of empty bedrooms. You are welcome to stay for as long as you wish. At least until we obtain some word of Dick. Besides, it is already all but December. You'd not get home before Christmas. Christmas on Hilltop. There's an occasion you'll not want to miss.'

'And will my staying here not increase the gossip?'

'I don't see how it can. Your reputation will be safe enough, as your mother will be here with you.' He was still holding her hand. Now he kissed it again. 'Besides, you said you wanted to see a plantation as a plantation. In January we commence grinding. And when that is done, why, then you'll really see Hilltop as it should be. I promise you.'

She smiled at him, pulled on her glove. 'You make it sound quite marvellous. And when people say that I have become your housekeeper?'

Her breathing had quickened, just a little. Tony returned her smile, held both her hands. 'You may spit in their eye. You have the permission of Anthony Hilton of Hilltop. Should you wish to, of course, Miss Taggart.'

'It's fantastic.' Ellen Taggart stood on the floor of the factory, gazed up at the throbbing machinery, the swarming figures. She

149

wore a green muslin gown with a matching bonnet, riding boots, and carried a whip, but presently her gloved hands were pressed to her ears to resist at least some of the noise. And she sweated, and looked quite entrancing, Tony Hilton decided; her sleeves stuck to her arms and shoulders, her skirts seemed to cling to her thighs, little beads of perspiration gathered on her forehead and upper lip, rolled down her neck. 'But the noise.'

'Leaves me deaf for days,' he bawled. 'Will you go up?'

She seemed not to listen, continued to stare above her. And he realized that she was watching the tumbling rollers, the seething cane, the hideous belts, the reverberating drums, less than the black men, naked save for their breechclouts and dribbling sweat, who paraded the catwalks. Her mouth was faintly open. He remembered the night she had come to dinner, and seen Joshua Merriman, hanging from the triangle. He had not even been wearing a breechclout.

Tony's excitement grew. But then, it had been growing with every day she had remained on Hilltop. To belong to Ellen, to be at her mercy . . . and be sure his secret would be kept. Because with Ellen there could be no risk. She wanted the power that went with being mistress of Hilltop; she would never betray the man who could give her that power.

He held her arm. 'Then I think I'd better get you out in the fresh air.'

She seemed to awaken from a trance. 'Oh, I am sorry. It is the noise. I really have never known anything like it.'

'Ah, but it's worth it,' Tony said. 'Every rumble is worth a hundred pounds.' They had nearly gained the doors, and the sunlight. 'And how is your mother this morning?'

Ellen shrugged. 'The heat really does prostrate her. I'm afraid she will not be able to manage summer here. We shall have to think of returning to England.'

'Or she will,' he suggested. 'It will be another five weeks before we can learn anything of Dick.'

She gave him one of her sidelong glances, then arranged her features into a smile as Hardy hurried towards them; the manager was stripped to the waist, as usual when grinding, and wore a bandanna round his neck to absorb some of the sweat. But Ellen Taggart's eyes, Tony noted, remained politely uninterested.

'Well, James,' he shouted. 'How goes it? Another record crop?'

'No doubt, Mr Hilton, no doubt,' Hardy agreed. 'But 'tis another matter concerns me. The big buck, Merriman. He's gone.'

'Gone?' Tony echoed.

'Him and two others. Well, I took him from confinement for the grinding. We need all hands. And runaways, really, they've no place to go. I'll fetch him back, but I may be gone a couple of days.'

Tony shook his head. 'You're needed here, James. I'll do the fetching.'

Hardy frowned at him. 'You'll be careful, Mr Anthony. He'll be making north, for the Cockpit Country. That's bad land. And he's a bad black, or will be, to you. You'll take Absolom.'

'Aye. I'll need a tracker.'

'And food. You won't find any up there. Water, too. And you'll not forget pistols, Mr Anthony.'

Tony punched him on the shoulder. 'I'll fetch him back, James. You just grind the crop.' He held Ellen's arm. 'We'd best get up to the house to prepare. You'll excuse me for a day or so? Anything you wish, just tell Hardy.'

She allowed him to give her a leg up into the saddle. 'I'll not miss you, Tony. It's my intention to accompany you.'

He frowned at her, even as his heart leapt into his throat with joy. 'That's impossible. Apart from the danger, there's the impropriety. You'd be compromised. And the discomfort. We'll be sleeping rough. Anyway, your mother would never agree.'

'I shall tell mother I am going into town to do some shopping, and shall be staying with Clarissa Laidlaw,' Ellen said. 'As for the rest, this is Hilltop, is it not? Did you not tell me that on Hilltop our laws are our own, social or legal?'

'They come this way, all right.' Absolom knelt by the side of the track, peered at the faint marks, seemed almost to sniff the earth. He was acting. They followed the dogs, and the mastiffs were already casting farther on. But in fact, Tony reasoned, there was no other way they could have come. It was late afternoon, and the sun had already disappeared behind the mountains which surrounded them, leaving the air suddenly cool, and lacking the glare which left eyes tired and heads throbbing on normal days. But of course, they were considerably higher up than Hilltop, which was itself several hundred feet above sea level.

They had climbed all day, through trees, dipping down into sudden sodden valleys, before climbing again. Now the trees continued to cling to the slopes to either side, but the slopes themselves were steep and nothing but boulder and outcrop; to climb there would be exhausting and lead nowhere. Only by the valleys could man journey.

And woman? She had tied a bandanna round her neck, as she had opened the collar of her blouse; now she used the tail of the red kerchief to dab at her mouth and eyes. But when she saw him looking at her, she smiled. 'Are they far away?'

She was exhausted. And no doubt as uncomfortable, with sweat and heat and saddleweariness, as he. But she'd not show it.

'Absolom?'

'Well, I ain't thinking so, Mr Hilton, sir. But it only got an hour of daylight left.'

The other two drivers fidgeted, and caused their mules to fidget as well. They were plantation slaves, and the mountains were a place to fear.

'We'll keep going for another hour,' Tony decided. 'I'm sorry, Ellen, but it seems as if we will have to spend a night out, after all.'

'I had anticipated nothing less. It is an adventure. An adventure is good for the spirit, from time to time.' She walked her mule past him. 'But all Jamaica is an adventure, is it not?'

Her head was turned, and she continued on her way. Proving herself a worthy Hilton woman, no doubt. He smiled at her back, and followed, Absolom and the drivers ahead now, picking their way over the stones and through the sudden soft patches. And without warning there came a breeze, damp and thus amazingly chill to their heated skins, soughing through the mountain passes. The dogs came back to them, whining their discontent.

'Eh-eh.' Absolom pulled on his rein.

'What is the matter?' Tony called.

'That is rain, man, Mr Hilton, sir.'

His head jerked. He had not noticed before, but the afternoon had grown dark. There were clouds everywhere, sweeping in from the Atlantic, perhaps, and being pushed upwards by the high land.

'Much rain?'

152

'It going be heavy,' Absolom said, sadly. 'We best stop now.'

Tony looked around him. Trees apart, there was a complete absence of shelter, although perhaps the mountains themselves would provide something in the nature of a windbreak. He pointed. 'Over there.' And urged his mule beside Ellen's. 'I had hoped to find some water to stop by. But it seems it is coming to us.'

'Why all the excitement?' she asked. 'A little rain?'

'There is no such thing as a *little* rain, in this country.' He dismounted, held her stirrup for her to slip to the ground beside him, inhaled the scent of her perspiration, which quite drowned the last traces of her perfume. And felt again excited. He wanted so much, from this woman.

'I have brought a pelisse. And wondered why, at the time.' She looked up. They stood beneath a fringe of trees, heavy above their heads, branches drooping; beyond and above the trees the rock face rose steeply, to other thrusting shrubs, some protruding at right angles. But here the breeze was muted.

'You'd best prepare some food,' Tony told Absolom. 'Will a fire alert Merriman?'

'Oh, they knowing we is here, Mr Hilton, sir. But I thinking the rain going put the fire out.'

'It isn't raining yet,' Tony pointed out. 'And I am sure Miss Taggart would like a hot meal. Christalmighty.'

It seemed the entire sky immediately above his head had exploded. The lightning was a swathe of pure white which slashed downwards through the valley and struck a tree on the far side; they could hear the crack of the shattering trunk for a split second before the thunder overwhelmed them, doubling its noise as it bounced from hill to hill, a louder noise than he had ever heard in his life, spinning his brain and leaving him bereft of senses.

He discovered himself lying on the ground, noise still crashing in his ears; it was, in fact, a succession of fresh thunderclaps. And being pinned there, by drops of water as big as his thumbnails, which had already soaked him to his drawers, crashed through his straw hat to reduce it to tattered grass, pounded on his head, thrusting the branches of the trees aside as if they were twigs.

The darkness was utter, although it could only be just after six, he reckoned. Then another searing flash of lightning ripped the evening apart, but the sudden brilliance left him even more blind and more bewildered than before.

He made a tremendous effort, pushed himself to his hands and knees, heard the whinny of the mules as they huddled close, the howling of the dogs, realized they were all in extreme danger from the lightning shafts striking the trees beneath which they stood. But he could not make himself take the decision to move away from even this perilous shelter, much less order his people to do so. He wished to find only the woman, and crawled forward, knees sinking into the suddenly soft earth, rain pounding on his back and shoulders.

'Ellen,' he shouted. 'Ellen?'

She whimpered, like a frightened animal. She lay on her side, on the earth, her blouse discoloured with mud, her knees drawn up, as if she were attempting to re-enter the womb. He lay beside her, belly against the curve of her back, her buttocks in his groin. He put his arms round her, held her against him; her hair was lank, plastering her head and his face. The pouring water, the crashing thunder, the darting shafts of terrible light, seemed to isolate them, away from their companions, away from the mules, away from the mountains, away even from Jamaica. They might be floating in a timeless cloud, he thought. A wet cloud, he thought, with grim humour. He held her closer and closer, hands seeping under her arms to find her blouse, which seemed no more than a second skin. She wore no corset. Well, that made sense in view of the journey she had undertaken. The adventure, she had called it. He wondered if she would still call it an adventure.

He found her nipples, thrusting through the soaked linen, chilled into hardness. She made no protest, no move either, save to huddle her back closer to him. He could stroke and caress to his heart's content, and in doing so, shelter his own mind from the holocaust around him. And from her, perhaps, draw strength for himself.

A whisper, through the night. But it was no longer night. It was dawn. There was lightness, in the valley, silhouetting the peaks which reached for the sky on every side. There was an absence of sound, save for the whisper of the wind. And only the peaks were visible; the valley itself was shrouded in a white mist, as the moisture coagulated, as the humans sat up, and looked around them. The rain had stopped; the parched earth had hardened again. The grass remained wet, the trees continued to drip water on their heads and shoulders, but a single day's sunlight would soon dry that. By this evening there would be not a trace of last night's storm, save perhaps that the river farther down would be running a little harder. Why, Tony thought, slowly standing up and stretching his cramped muscles, even their clothes would be dry. Although that would be difficult to accept at this moment; water still ran out of his boots.

But what of the humans themselves, he wondered? He looked at the drivers, who peered into the mist as if expecting a return of the thunder and the lightning. He looked at the mules, who had stayed close together, where horses would have galloped into the darkness, driven by the noise. But the dogs were already casting, grunting their hunger.

And he looked at the woman, sitting at his feet. As a woman, she seemed almost destroyed. Her hat was a sodden mass, her hair remained stuck to her head and shoulders as if someone had poured glue over her; her shirt was no less wet, and he could see her flesh, and when she stood up, the nipples he had held through the night. Had she been aware of that? Did she remember?

Oh, yes, she remembered. She glanced at him, and then looked away again, colour flooding upwards from her neck.

'Think anything will burn, Absolom?' he asked, and was surprised at the evenness of his own voice. 'I'd like a cup of coffee.'

Absolom turned over a stone with his bare toe; water bubbled out of the earth. 'No, sir, Mr Hilton, sir. Not for a while. Man, that was some rain, eh?'

'Some rain,' Tony agreed. 'Will it have wiped out the trail?'

'Well, sir . . .' Absolom scratched his head; water ran down over his ears. 'I thinking so, Mr Hilton, sir.'

'And we could all do with a change of clothes,' Tony decided. 'We'd better call it a day.'

'I would like to go on.' Ellen spoke in a low voice.

'Eh?'

'They must have been forced to stop, as we were. They cannot be far away.'

Her face was composed. But there was no questioning the firmness of that mouth, that chin.

'There is no trail. No scent.'

'There is only one way through the mountains,' she insisted. 'If they were following this valley yesterday, if you are sure that they were, then they can only be following this valley this morning.'

Tony looked at Absolom, who scratched his head again.

'So let us have something to eat,' Ellen said. 'And then go on.'

'Man, sir . . .' Absolom began, and then turned, to look into the mist. 'But what is that?'

'Is a *jumbi*, man, is a *jumbi*,' Jeremiah bawled, running for his mule.

'Stop there,' Tony commanded. But the unearthly wail, coming from an invisible source although obviously very close, had goose pimples running up and down his own flesh.

'It is a man,' Ellen said.

They peered into the mist, and saw the black man approaching. He wore nothing but drawers, and they were wet and filthy. He staggered and trembled. The dogs snarled and bared their teeth.

'Man but it is that boy Henry Twelve,' Absolom declared.

'Hold those beasts,' Tony commanded.

Henry Twelve stopped, and stared at them. He shook, like a leaf in a breeze. 'Man,' he said. 'You hear that thunder? Oh, man, you hear that thunder?'

'Where is Merriman?' Tony asked. 'And John Nineteen?'

Henry Twelve turned his stare on his master. 'Merriman gone,' he said. 'He ain't stopping, even in the rain. He gone. He gone.'

Even in the rain. 'And John Nineteen?'

'He done dead, master. He done drown. He lying there, and he head in a puddle. He done drown.'

There was a moment's silence. The mist began to rise in the valley, the first warmth seemed to enter the air. Henry Twelve continued to tremble.

'We got this one, Mr Hilton, sir,' Absolom said. 'We ain't going get Merriman now. Not if he go through the rain. And maybe he done drown, too. We got this one.'

Tony nodded. 'Aye. We'll get on back. Absolom is right, Ellen. There is no point in flogging ourselves to death over a man who may be already dead. We'll eat later, Absolom. Tie this man to the back of your mule, and let's move out.'

'No,' Ellen said. Her eyes gloomed at the shivering slave. 'He must be punished.'

'He will be punished,' Tony said. 'When we get back to Hilltop.'

'No,' she said. 'Here. Bring my mule, Absolom.'

Absolom looked at his master, then went and fetched the mules.

'Send them away, Tony,' she said. 'Send them down the trail. We can catch them up. Afterwards.'

'After what?'

She gripped his arm; her face was only inches from his ear. 'I want to whip him. I have wanted to whip someone, anyone, since I came to Hilltop. I could not say so to you, before last night. I could not do it, on Hilltop, with everyone there, with Hardy there. With Mother there.'

She panted, and colour flared in her cheeks. Her hair was just beginning to dry, and flutter in the morning breeze. She was a stranger, and she knew she was a stranger, to herself. She would not know herself, when she regained civilization. But perhaps the rain, and the fear, had stripped away her last covering of humanity, left only the animal.

And perhaps his fingers had helped, as well. He felt as if he had been dreaming, all of his life, the most wonderful dream a man could have, and had suddenly awakened, to find his dream was continuing, and would continue, forever.

'Let me whip him, Tony,' she said. 'Now. And I will do anything you wish. Anything.'

'You'll have to sound the gong, Boscawen,' Tony Hilton said. 'We'll not be heard, otherwise.'

The butler nodded, and hurried down the room, threading his way in and out of the red-jacketed footmen, the white-gowned maids, who thronged each side of the huge dining room; there was one attendant to each cover, and there were sixty covers.

Tony leaned back in his chair, his glass in his hand, sipped his wine. He wanted to belch. Instead he smiled, at Mrs Taggart, on his right, a perspiring mass of pink flesh and pale blue taffeta, and at Mrs Kendrick on his left, a slim, dark woman, who had eaten little and drunk less, had watched her fellow guests like a predatory bird, storing their idiosyncrasies, their appearances, their mistakes in her mind. But even she returned Tony Hilton's smile.

And if Mrs Kendrick had eaten little, she was the only one. The huge dining table looked like a battlefield, after the conflict. Plates of scattered nuts and sweatmeats lay every which way;

priceless crystal glasses rested on their sides, swept over by a careless gesture, a flailing cuff; knives and forks and spoons soaked in the spilt gravy, some guests still gnawed at their ribs of best beef, others worried their ices and slurped their wine; breasts heaved and shoulders shuddered; moustaches drooped; coats were unbuttoned and stays were clearly straining. The air was heavy with wine and perfume and the stench of beef, and brilliant with the conversation which flitted about the chairs and the chandeliers like a flight of sparrows. Here was gossip, malicious and friendly, stories, droll and dirty, flirtations, light and serious, bubbling away. Here was Sunday lunch on Hilltop.

'It warms the heart, Mr Hilton, indeed it does,' Phyllis Kendrick said. 'Your uncle used to give enterainments of this nature. But that was a long time ago. I remember them, when I was a girl. But truly, of recent years, and of course, when your brother and that detestable Gale person were living here, one could suppose Hilltop to be dead. Now it lives again.' She leaned her elbow on the table, rested her chin on one finger. 'I did not know you were acquainted with so many people.'

'I am not, dear lady,' Tony said. 'I merely had a list made out, and despatched it.'

Phyllis Kendrick continued to regard him as if he were a rare specimen — but then, he thought, I am a rare specimen. 'But at such short notice? Supposing no one had come? All of this food?'

'It could have fed the pigs, Mrs Kendrick.'

Her eyebrows arched, and she receded, her hand flopping on the table.

'But then,' Tony smiled, 'they all did come. Even you came, Phyllis.'

The sound of the gong, booming across the conversation, drowned her reply. Had she been going to make one. Tony rather doubted that she had. He wondered how old she was. Thirty? Thirty-five? Married to a typical planter, unimaginative and entirely physical. So, was she unimaginative and purely physical? A thought for the future. He was concerned with the present. He looked down the long sweep of littered, stained linen tablecloth, past the upturned bottles, the smiling, reddened faces, the fluttering fingers, the scattered napkins. Ellen was hardly visible, seated at the far end of the table. But she was, entirely visible. She wore pale green, and looked cool. Her chestnut hair was gathered loosely, in a ribbon. She talked animatedly, to the men on either side of her, and yet, she seemed to sense that he was looking at her, and turned her head, to send her smile up the table like a message.

What did they share, so far? Not their bodies, as yet. That would come later. On *the* day, she had been exhausted, her passion spent. And there had been a dead man. And Tony Hilton? Why Tony Hilton had been afraid. Of her. That could be admitted, to himself. And perhaps even to the woman.

And since then, they had both been content to wait, to know, what was on the way, to anticipate, confident in the enormous intimacy they already shared. The memory, of a woman on a mule, wet hair tumbling about her shoulders, wet blouse clinging to those shoulders, wet skirt wrapping itself around wet legs, galloping to and fro within the confines of a narrow valley, flailing her whip while a black man had to run before her. The memory of her tumbling breath and gasping cries of pleasure, of her teeming laughter. The memory of her pulling her mount to a standstill, when the black man had finally fallen, and dismounting, to flog again. The memory of the black man realizing that his tormentor was no longer protected, rising to his knees, of himself hurrying forward to save her, and stopping, as he realized she did not require saving. The memory of that booted foot thudding into the black man's face, of the woman standing above him, and using the whip again, with an expertise born of a long dream — because surely she could have no experience — to reduce a man to nothing.

And the memory of the ride back, slowly, in the boiling sun. Her clothes had dried by then, and her hair. Their mules had rode close together, and occasionally his knee had brushed hers.

He had said, 'I must have you.' It had been plain surrender. And Ellen Taggart had merely smiled.

'When you can, Mr Hilton,' she had replied. 'When you can.'

So, now. He rose, and the faces turned to look at him. 'Ladies,' he said, 'and gentlemen. How good of you to come. How good of you to grace Hilltop once again with your presence. How good of you to make this old house live again. I am informed, ladies and gentlemen, that it did live, thirty years ago. I make you my solemn promise, it will live, from this moment on.'

He paused, to smile, and they applauded, and called for more wine. And Ellen returned his smile.

159

'We have eaten well,' Tony said. 'And we have drunk well. This afternoon we shall talk. The ladies about, well, whatever ladies talk about.' That raised a shout of laughter. 'We men shall talk politics. Because I have not invited you here today, gentlemen, neighbours, fellow planters, merely to sample my cuisine. I have invited you here today, gentlemen, to inform you that Hilltop is now back in the hands of a Hilton, not a decrepit old man, not a dreaming boy. But a Hilton, gentlemen. I am aware of what is going on, gentlemen. I read the newspapers. I know how the British Government seeks to coerce us, gentlemen. Financial aid, trading advantages, such as are being offered the new Crown Colonies of Guiana and Trinidad, on condition we accept their "advice" on the treatment of our slaves. No aid at all, should we prefer to go our own way. That, gentlemen, to my way of thinking, is not government, but blackmail.'

He paused, to smile at the nods of agreement, the murmurs which went round the table.

'So you may expect to see me in the Hilton seat, gentlemen, as from the next Session. And you may expect me to give my voice and my vote to opposing all British interference in our affairs. Times may be hard, gentlemen, but they have been harder. We in Jamaica, my family more than most, gentlemen, have prospered these hundred years and more with no British help. By God, we shall do so for another hundred years, or my name is not Anthony Hilton.'

This time the murmurs became shouts of applause, and hands were clapped.

Tony waved for quiet. 'But that is for the next Session, as I say. Before then, ladies and gentlemen, a far more important, and a far more felicitous event is to take place. It is my great honour to tell you that Miss Ellen Taggart has consented to become my wife.'

This time the room rang to the cheers. Ellen smiled at them all.

'Think of it, gentlemen,' Tony said. 'It is near fifty years since Hilltop had a mistress. Since Hilltop was a home, gentlemen, instead of just a plantation. Ladies and gentlemen, that void is now filled. I ask you to rise with me and drink the health of the mistress of Hilltop. Ladies and gentlemen, Miss Ellen Taggart.'

They rose together, glasses held high. 'Ellen Taggart.' And then dissolved in a mass, to accumulate around the end of the table to

160

congratulate the bride to be, to look for her smile and her kiss.

Tony used his napkin to wipe his lips and brow, gave Mrs Taggart a kiss on the cheek, and then followed Boscawen's gaze into the hall.

'Is Mr Reynolds, Mr Hilton, sir,' the butler said. 'He just come.'

'You'll excuse me, Mrs Taggart.' Tony left the table, seized the lawyer's hands. 'Reynolds. How good to see you. 'Tis a warm day for a long ride.'

'Mr Hilton.' The lawyer looked distinctly hot and bothered. 'Terrible news, sir. Terrible news.'

'Not here.' Tony ushered him along the hall, past the stairs and into the study. 'Bonaparte? I had heard. But he will make no progress this time.'

'Not Bonaparte, sir.' Reynolds sat down, mopped his brow. The *Green Knight* anchored two days ago, sir. You'll remember she cleared here but three days after the *Cormorant*. I had specifically asked Captain Morrison to obtain what information he could. I'd have come sooner, Mr Hilton, but the news of Bonaparte's return to France has had all Kingston in a tizzy, and I could not get away.'

'And Morrison has more news yet?'

'Of the very worst, sir.' Reynolds glanced out of the open door at the hall; the sounds of revelry could clearly be heard. 'The *Cormorant* never made Bristol. But Morrison put in at Cap Haitien, on his way back here. The Negroes say wreckage came ashore. You'll remember there was that gale, two days after she left.'

'So we must presume the worst,' Tony said.

Reynolds sighed. 'Sad. Sad. You'll want to send those people home.'

Tony frowned at him. 'Why? They are celebrating my engagement, amongst other things.'

'But with Mr Richard very probably dead . . .' Reynolds' turn to frown. 'Your engagement, Mr Hilton?'

'To Miss Taggart.'

'To . . . Good God.'

'As I endeavoured to tell you just now, I have heard the news. All the news. I have maintained an agent in town these last few weeks, to bring me the first available word from England on the whereabouts of the *Coromorant*. I knew the night before last.

161

Awakened I was, from a deep sleep, at two o'clock in the morning. But it was worth it. As you know, I have long supposed my brother to be dead. But of course I could not invite his fiancée to marry me until I was sure.'

Reynolds gazed at him for some seconds. Then he stood up. 'Your brother is not dead, Mr Hilton. Legally. He cannot be dead until his body is identified, or until seven years have elapsed.'

Tony smiled at him. 'Legally. Yet you will not deny it was his wish that I manage Hilltop in his absence.'

Reynolds chewed his lip.

'And you can hardly suppose it would have been his wish that Miss Taggart linger for seven years, which is a lifetime in the consideration of a young woman, waiting to be sure, when we are both, in our hearts, sure.'

Reynolds sighed. 'I suspect you are very much of a scoundrel, Mr Hilton.'

'And I suspect that the next time you use such words to me, Mr Reynolds, I will have my drivers throw you off this plantation.'

'Your drivers? Aye, no doubt they are *your* drivers. 'Twas your brother's wish, may God rest his soul. No doubt he was too good a man. I cannot interfere with your present prerogatives, Mr Hilton. But I am still the executor of your brother's estate. You'll do well to remember that. The plantation is Mr Richard Hilton's.'

'For seven years.' Tony got up. 'I am a patient man, Mr Reynolds. I have formed a philosophy, which I believe has been expressed before. Everything comes to he who waits. I'll bid you good day, sir. My guests, and my fiancée, are waiting.'

9

The Castaway

Judith's body moved against his, her arms tight round his neck. She squirmed, and seemed able to bounce, even under his weight. And she moved from side to side as well. Lying on her was like being on a ship at sea.

Dick Hilton rolled on to his back, stared at the deck beams immediately above his head, sweat breaking out on his face and shoulders as he realized that he was on a ship at sea.

He attempted to sit up, and banged his head. As if it had been a signal, waves of thudding pain were loosed, to go reverberating through his mind, to crash against his ears, to seep down his neck into his stomach and bring green sickness back into his throat. His chin seemed one enormous bruise.

He discovered himself on his hands and knees, clutching the bunk on which he had lain, bracing himself against the roll of the vessel. And being suddenly bathed in a draught of cool air, seeping around his head.

'Praying, are you?'

He attempted to turn, lost his balance, and fell over. He looked at shoes, and somewhat dirty cotton stockings. The clothes above were hardly cleaner but the face, if unshaven and pockmarked, was not unpleasant.

'John Gibson, at your service.'

Dick licked his lips, slowly, closed his eyes to attempt to shut out the pain. 'What ship?' His voice seemed to come from very far away.

'The *Cormorant*, bound for Bristol, Mr Hilton.'

'Bristol?' Dick seized the bunk once again, pulled himself to his feet. 'I can't go to Bristol.'

'What you need is something to eat, Mr Hilton,' Gibson

decided. 'You'll feel better after something to eat. Boy,' he shouted, sending fresh reverberations crashing into Dick's mind.

He sat on the bunk. 'How came I here?'

'Why, sir, you came out with my boatswain, last night. Insisted, you did. Said you had to get away. Food, boy. Food for the passenger.'

'Had to . . .' Dick scratched his head. Another painful operation. 'I was drunk. Christ, I was drunk.'

'You were that, Mr Hilton,' Gibson agreed. 'Mind you, sir, for a man that drunk, you were wonderfully possessed, you were. Wrote a steady hand and all.' He jerked his head. 'You'd best eat.'

'Eat?' Dick seized the captain's sleeve. 'Listen. You must put back. I was drunk.'

'You booked passage to England,' Gibson pointed out. 'Signed a note, you did.'

'You can keep it,' Dick said. 'I'll sign another. But put me back.'

The captain gazed at him for some seconds, then went into the main cabin and sat down. 'You'll want to think about that.'

'When you've worn ship.'

'Now, sir, that's not going to be easy. You won't believe this, sir, but we've a stern wind. Due west, in the Caribbean, in November. There's chance. Why, sir, do you know, I reckon we've done a hundred miles in the past twelve hours. There's speed for you. But she's a clean hull, *Cormorant*.'

Dick staggered across the cabin, up the companionway, and into the waist of the ship. And was immediately thankful for the cooling breeze which swept over him, cleared some of the cobwebs from his mind. He stood at the starboard gunwale, looked at the mountains on the southern horizon.

'Hispaniola,' Captain Gibson said. 'What the niggers who infest it call Haiti. Like I said, damn near a hundred miles in twelve hours.'

Dick climbed the ladder, crossed the poop, grasped the taffrail to steady himself. But astern the sea was empty, save for the occasional whitecap. It was in fact a peculiar afternoon; the sky was almost yellow, rather than blue, and the wind was hot. And his brain continued to tumble. Memory. But he did not want memory. There were too many unthinkable thoughts banging on the edges of his consciousness. He only knew he must get home.

164

And quickly.

'As a matter of fact,' Captain Gibson remarked, having followed him, 'the sooner we're through the Windward Passage the happier I'll be. There's wind about.'

'Then seek shelter,' Dick said. 'Set me ashore in Haiti.'

Gibson frowned at him. 'Now, I'll not be doing that, Mr Hilton. Why, you'd go to your death. We'd all go to our deaths. Those niggers don't take to strangers. They'd rather slaughter us than slaughter each other, and by all accounts they spend most of their time doing that.'

'Then put about,' Dick begged. 'So it'll take a week to beat back to Jamaica. But it won't. The wind won't stay west.'

'A westerly is just what we need, for the Windward Passage,' Gibson explained. 'We'll be through this time tomorrow. Otherwise it's beating up the Florida Channel, and adding weeks to the voyage. As for putting back . . . it'll cost me all my profit.'

'I'll be your profit,' Dick said. 'I'll buy your ship.'

'Eh?'

'I'm Richard Hilton of Plantation Hilltop. Name your price. I'll sign a note, now. I didn't know what I was doing, last night. I must get back to Jamaica. Name your price, Gibson. Name your price.'

The captain stroked his chin. 'You don't know what you're doing now, either, Mr Hilton. You want to think about that for a while.'

'While you get us out into the Atlantic? Now, Captain. Now. Put about now, and you have my note.'

Gibson stroked his chin some more. 'Well,' he said at last. 'If you're serious, Mr Hilton. There'll be witnesses, mind.'

'Assemble the whole crew,' Dick said. 'But do it now.'

'Aye. Well . . .' Gibson turned, to look forward, and checked, and looked up instead. Without warning the wind had dropped right away, and the sails did no more than flap against their stays.

'You'd best batten those hatches.' Captain Gibson stood at the rail and looked down on his ship. 'And strike those topsails. Quick, now.'

'It'll shift, Captain,' Dick said. 'You've no reason to hold on. And my offer stands.'

'Oh, aye, Mr Hilton,' Gibson sighed. 'You'll go back to

Kingston. When we've weathered whatever's coming.' He pointed at the blackness which was spreading out of the south, overshadowing the distant mountains of Haiti, threatening the drooping sun. 'That's a late hurricane. And we're in narrow waters.'

Dick gazed at the sky. In the four years he had lived on Jamaica they had had sufficient warnings of a tropical storm, but never a full blow. 'What will you do?'

'What can I do, man?' Gibson asked. 'If it comes east, we'll run back. If it stays west, we'll run for the Passage and the open sea. I've no choice, Mr Hilton.'

'And if it is north or south?'

Again the captain sighed. 'North is Cuba, south is Haiti. We'll have to heave to and try not to drift.' He gave a short laugh. 'There's a problem, eh?'

Dick left him, went to the taffrail. Hurricane winds always shifted, and through a hundred and eighty degrees, as the eye of the storm passed. He looked down at the slow bubble of wake. The ship still moved, drifting with the current, propelled by the almost unplaceable breeze, and eastward. He was sailing away from Jamaica. Christ, how memory came back to him. It seemed as if every mistake he had made, every crime he had committed, had suddenly rolled themselves up into a thundercloud as big as the approaching storm, and delivered themselves against his head. Harriet had been a gigantic dream. He had known from the start that she could never be anything more than that. Had known too, that she was in many ways a nightmare. And yet had remained sucked into the warm sensuality of that embrace, long after he had ceased to love, or even to like, the woman herself.

And yet, was Ellen anything less of a mistake? Had she been anything less of a mistake from the very beginning? Was he doomed to know only women who would seek to dominate, to rule? Or was the fault entirely his, in being too submissive, too uncertain of his own temper, his own purpose, to oppose successfully?

And in any event, could marriage to Ellen, now, be anything less than a total disaster? The events of the last four years, and more particularly of the last two days, were there to be hurled in his face whenever they had the slightest difference of opinion.

So, then, why did he hurry back, spend a fortune on

166

commandeering this ship to return? He had never enjoyed planting. His entire being rebelled against the necessities of the business; the brutalities and the injustices; the certainty that someone like Josh Merriman, and God knew how many others, were better men·than he, in every sense of the word, but yet were forced to crawl, should he so desire, merely because his skin was white, and his uncle had been wealthy.

Even more did he rebel against the concept that he could never be one of them, and equally, never be óne of the plantocracy, sitting in the House of Assembly in Spanish Town and waving their fists at the British Government even as they waved their whips at their employees. Theirs was a transitory world. It had to be, no more than that. That it had lasted over a hundred years, that it had provided the Hiltons with wealth and power and omnipotence for so long, was the fault of humanity, not the design of God.

And yet, return he must. To make amends to Judith? How could he make amends to Judith, save by marrying her? There would be the final chapter in the catalogue of disasters. Or would it? Judith was a lovely child. She would no doubt soon become a lovely woman. So she was totally lacking in either education or breeding. That could be provided, and would be a pleasure to provide. But did he love her? He did not know. He had never considered the matter. It was beginning to dawn on him that he had never actually considered loving anyone. Even Ellen had been an achievement, a prize to be won, in the face of opposition, rather than a woman to be loved.

And even more important, did Judith love him? Could she love him, after Harriet, and after an upbringing such as hers, and after he had raped her?

A drop of rain landed on his hand, large and stinging. The afternoon had grown quite dark, and the sun was lost behind the cloud. And the drop had been only the advance guard. He could see the rain approaching him in a solid ˙sheet, like a quick travelling mist. Haiti had already disappeared.

And with the rain, the first of the wind, soughing over the water. Gibson was at the break of the poop, bawling his orders, and the yards were being trimmed; they had already been stripped of most of their sails. Now the helm was put up to take the coming squall on the bow. The *Cormorant* rose and dipped again, a violent movement. Yet the sea remained surprisingly calm, flattened by the deadening rain, which swept across the ship, smothered the deck and poured into the scuppers as if it had been a wave, flowed through the fairleads and cascaded down the sides.

Dick discovered he was wet through, and the water continued to pound on his hair, flood down his neck. He staggered across the deck, grasped a stay close by the wheel, where two men were on duty, waiting for the real wind, with the captain close at hand.

'You'd best below, Mr Hilton,' Gibson bawled. 'No sense in staying up here. Helm. Helm. Up.'

The two sailors leaned on the wheel, and the *Comorant*'s bows came up again. Now the wind was fresh, and now the ship was moving, slicing into the suddenly large, and growing waves, tossing spray aft, taking green combers over the bow to flood the forecastle and come pouring down the ladders into the waist. And now too, she heeled, port scuppers well down, making the already slippery deck the harder to stand on.

'Due west,' Gibson shouted in Dick's ear. 'It'll veer, but slowly. We'll make the passage, if it lasts. Then we'll be safe enough.'

The open Atlantic. Would he ever turn back then? But no man could be asked to risk his ship for the sake of an unwanted passenger.

Dick found the top of the ladder, made his way down, slowly, being thrown against the rail by each lurch of the ship, staring in fascination as the bows went up, up, as she climbed the ever increasing swell, to hang there for a moment, seeming to be pointing at the sky and attempting to launch herself into space, and then plunging down, down, with a stomach-tumbling force, bowsprit now pointing only at surging green water, and apparently intent on hitting the very bottom of the ocean. Then the seas broke, or the bowsprit plunged in, he could not be sure which, and tons of water landed on the foredeck, with a crash which seemed about to stave the timbers, before roaring aft, bursting into the waist, whipping at the canvas covers for the longboat, flooding the deck, crashing against the foot of the ladder like a wave on a shore, filling his boots and splashing up his breeches to join the rain damp already there.

But the *Cormorant* was lifting her bows again, the bowsprit, undamaged, slicing through the heaving sea to aim once more at

168

the sky, the sea itself tumbling over the sides to leave the deck momentarily clear, while all the while the wind increased, from a sough to a whine, from a whine to a scream, and then suddenly to a gigantic roar, a noise which even drowned out memories of the factory, which took away the powers of the mind even as its very force seemed to take away the powers of the body, ripping at the buttons of his coat to send the tails flying, making him gasp for breath, his muscles discovering the ache of a long wrestling match.

He reached the door to the cabin in the midst of a wave, hung there for a moment with water surging at his thighs, wrenched it open and half fell down the ladder to the floor of the cabin.

'Aaagh,' screamed the boy. 'Aaagh. We're sinking.'

'Only a wave,' Dick gasped, grasping the table to pull himself up, and being struck on the side of the head by the lantern swinging from the low deck beams.

'Oh, God,' said the boy, falling to his knees beside Dick. 'Oh, God. Lost, we are, sir. Lost.'

'You've not been in a storm before?'

'A gale, sir. Aye. Nothing like this. We're too close to land. Too close, sir. Too close.'

'Lie down,' Dick recommended, and did so himself, not entirely by design; the *Cormorant* entered a trough sideways and skidded down before bringing up short. There was a crack which seemed to tear the entire ship from top to bottom, and this was followed by a boom which cut across even the wind, and brought another terrified screech from the boy.

Dick found himself lying on one of the berths which walled the cabin, pushed himself up again. But his head continued to swing, and now his stomach was threatening to rebel as well. With fear? Certainly he was sweating.

'What was that noise?' he bawled.

The boy grovelled on the deck, moaning.

And now the *Cormorant* was behaving very oddly, no longer surging to the waves, but rather being slapped, from side to side, each blow shaking the timbers and sending the table creaking, and being followed by water seeping through the deck above his head.

The door was thrown open, and Captain Gibson fell in, accompanied by half the ocean; water cascaded down the steps and swirled over the cabin floor, hurled back the door to the galley and put out the fire with a gigantic hiss of steam.

'God,' screamed the boy. 'Help me, oh God.'

'Shut your trap,' shouted the captain. 'The foremast has gone, Mr Hilton.'

Dick sat up. 'Will she sink?'

'I've men cutting it away. We can run. But there'll be no beating. 'Tis a question of how far the wind will go; she's veering all the time.'

'And how much of this pounding your ship will stand,' Dick said.

'Aye, well, she's stout enough. I've sent Chips down to sound the well. But you'd best come up again. Lash yourself to the mizzen, sir. There's your best chance.'

Dick seized the boy under the armpits, pulled him up. 'Come on deck,' he shouted in his ear.

'Oh, God,' howled the boy. 'Oh, God. Help me, oh, God.'

'On deck,' Dick screamed, and climbed the companion ladder. The captain had already gone, but the door swung open as he reached the top and another wave burst in, pounding on his chest, clouding on his face, splashing on the floor behind him, and draining into the bilges. Sound or not, he thought, she'll not take much of that.

'Please God, help me,' whimpered the boy as he was pushed through the doorway.

Dick closed the door behind him, stood against it to gasp for breath and to look at the sea. Where it had been big before, now it was huge. The swell seemed taller than the masts, and each swell was topped by a rolling, ten-foot-high wall of flying foam. Presumably it was night. The ship carried no lights, but the sky was quite vanished, the clouds seeming to rest almost on the top of the waves themselves, and the rain fell ceaselessly. And then the thunder roared right above him, and the entire universe seemed to split open in searing light which left him blinded, even as the crack of the lightning striking the sea drove the senses from his head. He discovered himself in the starboard scupper, looking up and up and up and up at a towering green monster, and realized that the *Cormorant* would not, indeed, survive. And that he was about to die.

But not immediately. Water poured over the deck, and the

Cormorant seemed to sag, to be struck by another huge wave before she had recovered from the first. For some seconds Dick was submerged, and he lost his breath and inhaled water, which left him spluttering and gasping, and eventually vomiting, in the intervals between waves. Hands seized his shoulders and dragged him back into the comparative safety of the hatchway, where several more of the crew were huddled. By now the lightning was continuous, the thunder merging with the howl of the wind and the roar of the seas to make a blanket of sound across the night, across their senses. But he could look up, at the two remaining masts, now quite bare of canvas. They were driving on, carried in the direction of the wind and the current. And the wind had veered. Gibson had said so, how long ago? But no doubt it had veered even more. With luck they might yet make the Windward Passage. With luck.

And a sound ship. A banging on the hatch informed them that the carpenter was on his way out. They banged back to tell him to wait, chose their moment themselves, and released one of the battens. The three men collapsed into their midst. 'There's five feet down there,' gasped one.

'And gaining,' said another.

'She's just opening up,' said the third. 'She weren't made to take this pounding.'

'There ain't no ship made to take this pounding,' muttered the boatswain.

The *Cormorant* agreed with a gigantic shudder, and speech was lost in another foaming maelstrom of water.

They looked at the captain, clinging to the rail of the poop, gazing down at them. Even through the noise and his own preoccupations, Gibson had noticed that the pumps had ceased.

'Ahoy there,' he bawled. 'What's amiss?'

The carpenter raised himself to his feet, holding on to a stay. 'She's making water too fast, captain,' he shouted. 'She's sinking.'

The men around Dick stirred. The fact they had known for some time had at last been put into words.

Gibson stared at them for a moment, rocking with his ship. But the *Cormorant* had no life left. Even Dick, who knew little enough about the sea, could tell that. She was a dead creature, in the water, and every blow struck by the sea killed her a little more.

'Prepare the boat,' Gibson called. 'Careful now.'

'Careful,' grumbled the boatswain. 'You'd best help me, lads.'

Dick rose with them. He felt as if he had known them all his life, as if he and they were intimates of a thousand bottles, a thousand adventures, perhaps a thousand storms. Shoulder to shoulder with them, he tore at the canvas cover for the longboat—amazingly still in place—and helped them secure the slings. And like them, he looked back at the poop for the orders to launch. And thought that they were a good and faithful crew, who stood no chance at all, so far as he could see. So what chance did any crew stand?

'Now,' Gibson shouted. The wheel had been lashed, to keep the ship as much as possible before the wind, and the captain and his helmsmen came swarming down the ladders to assist them. The boat was raised on the slings, several men hauling on each rope, and pushed by the remainder towards the gunwale. And as if intent to assist them, the *Cormorant* listed to port as well, causing the boat to swing ever faster. The six men pushing slid across the deck, the boat hung clear of the gunwale . . . but instead of the order to release the falls, Gibson gave a strangled scream.

'Get her back.'

Dick's head jerked, and he looked over the boat at another towering wall of green, rearing like a striking snake, its top curling white, hovering some thirty feet above them.

'Get her back.' Gibson's words trailed away into nothing as the sea broke. Dick heard the snap of the parting falls. He realized that, water apart, he was liable to be crushed beneath the falling longboat. But the thought was an abstract. All thoughts were abstract. He was aware only of being in the middle of the water; of striking something solid with his left leg, a jarring blow which left him paralysed; of aching pain and breathless lungs; of water filling his nose, his eyes, his ears, his mouth; of sudden air, which had him choking and gasping; of putting his good leg down to the deck and finding nothing; of rolling over and flailing his arms in desperation; of a sudden, tremendous fear spreading outwards from his belly.

And of anger. He could think of no reason to die. His crimes had been inadvertent, crimes of weakness rather than determined vice. So then, no doubt, God abhorred weakness. He would sooner settle for a man of determination, even if that determination was wholly evil, rather than a man who drifted with the tide, unable ever to do good because he could not make up his mind where the ultimate goodness lay.

Something struck him on his face. The abstract thoughts which kept booming around the back of his mind suggested that he was being rescued. Oh, how he wanted to be rescued. How, on a sudden, he loved Captain Gibson and all his crew. So, then, a rope? Thrown to regain him from the water?

Another surge of pure terror. It was the first time his mind had accepted the fact that he was in the water, that he had lost contact with the ship. Or had he? His arms closed on something solid. They threatened to slip, but by reaching even farther he found he could grasp his own wrist. He thrust feet down to find the deck, find anything, and still could not. So, he was hanging on to the side of the ship, no doubt. He must stay here until someone pulled him back on board.

Why? Did he have the courage to go back? He had begged, implored, and finally bribed Gibson to take him back. Then he had been suffering from the after-effects of drink. But that had only been yesterday afternoon. Had it been yesterday afternoon? Oh, horrible thought, had it only been this afternoon? But surely it was past midnight.

The thought made him raise his head; it had been resting on the wood he was clutching, with water breaking over him. But he had his breathing trained, by now. Breathe, submerge, breathe, submerge, breathe, submerge. He could do that forever, if his strength would last forever. The lightning was gone. Never had he known such darkness. Only the loom of the whitecaps as they surged around him, plucked at his legs, slapped him in the face, dropped on his head. And the whine of the wind. Still the wind. Always the wind.

His head banged the wood, and he realized that his fingers were sliding free of his wrist. He had fallen asleep. How remarkable. And how dangerous. He seized himself again, clutched the rounded wood harder against his chest.

Think, or die. There was a simple choice. Think, or die. Supposing one wanted to live.

But oh, how he wanted to live. There was so much he wanted to do with his life, so much he thought he could do with his life. Then this was the time. It occurred to him that always in the past he had been waiting for something to happen, for his brain to make a decision of its own, when it would assume command, not only of him, but of his entire situation, of all those around him. It would be a cool, a calculated decision, not one taken in anger, as nearly all his decisions had been in the past. That was the only way to rise above the pitfalls which littered life, the only way to survive people like Ellen Taggart, Harriet Gale, James Hardy, Harriet's companion . . . even Tony. The only way. Think, and survive. Always.

But for the moment, only think. Of something which would hold his brain. Of a woman. There was the answer. Of . . . he found himself thinking of Ellen. There was a surprise. But she remained his betrothed. And she possessed the strength he now sought. Had that been the impulse behind that so secret, so confident laugh of hers? Had she known that she was one of the few capable of thought as he now wished to be? Ellen, tall and strong and determined.

He thought of Ellen. He remembered everything he and Harriet had ever done together, throughout the past four years, and replaced Harriet's squirming heat in his arms with Ellen's cool strength. There was a dream to sustain a man.

Then what of Judith? The very thought of her name left an ache in his heart. What of Judith? Oh, my God, what of Judith?

The jar took all his wind away, and was followed by another before he could catch his breath. That had been his belly, pounding on the wood he held. But now his knees jarred as well, and the next wave contained less water than liquid sand, which clogged his nostrils even more thoroughly. He rose to his knees. His knees? He stared up the beach, at the trees, fell forward again as the next gust of wind battered on his shoulders, rose again, holding himself clear of the surf, and stared at the men who came from the trees towards him.

Black men.

Dick made another effort, once again reached his feet, was once again knocked over by the surf which pounded into his back. The water rolled him farther up the beach, and he dug his fingers into the sand to stop himself being dragged back by the undertow.

The men remained standing, before the trees, watching him, but making no effort to help him. It was almost light now, and he could see that they were armed with machetes and rusty muskets, while one had a pistol stuck into his belt. They wore drawers, once

174

white, perhaps, now stained a dirty brown, but no other clothes that he could see, and were barefoot.

He tried to speak, but found his jaws so tightly clamped together he could make no sound. The next wave broke over him with less force, and he was able to regain his knees, and sit down, half turning to look back at the sea. Had he survived that? It was nearly impossible to see the blue, so constant were the whitecaps, racing across the morning. He appeared to have entered some sort of a bay, for the trees curved round to his right. The water in the bay was not quite so tormented, but beyond the sea raged, and there was no sign of the *Cormorant*, or of any other life. Only the spar to which he had clung for so many hours continued to surge in the surf a few feet away.

And the wind still whined, bending the trees, snatching at what breath he retained, drying his face and hair.

Feet, crunching on the sand. He rose to his knees, gazed at them. 'Water.' It was no more than a whisper, but he had spoken.

One of the men grinned at him, he could see the flash of his teeth.

Another spoke, but Dick could not understand what they said, although it sounded vaguely familiar.

Another replied, and this time Dick caught the word '*eau*', although pronounced, 'yo'. French, after a fashion. Therefore he was on Haiti, the French colony known as St Domingue before the Negro revolt.

'*L'eau*,' he begged. '*S'il vous plait. L'eau.*'

They laughed, and one of them spat.

Dick moaned again, '*Eau.*'

The man who grinned came closer, put his bare foot in the centre of Dick's face, and pushed. He rolled over, into the shallow water, his belly twisting. Oh, my God, he thought. Oh, my God. Every tale he had ever heard of Haiti, of the hatred felt by every black man for every white man, clouded his memory. Of the hideous practice of *obeah*, the black witchcraft, of the Voodoo religion, of blood sacrifices and unspeakable rites. He had been to Haiti before. He had visited the Corbeau Plantation, with Mama, to see Aunt Georgiana after she had married Louis Corbeau. And while he had been here the Negroes had risen in revolt, led by Toussaint, and Dessalines, and the young giant of a military genius, the English slave, Henry Christophe. And Aunt Georgiana

175

had been torn to pieces before his eyes. They had gouged out her eyes and cut off her breasts while she had yet lived, and screamed. He could hear her scream now, echoing across the morning, riding the wind.

Mama they had spared, with her two sons. She had supposed for rape and torture, but it had been because her name had been Hilton, and with the blacks had marched the priestess, who in England had been known as Gislane Nicholson, who had loved Matt Hilton, and for the sake of that love had been returned to the slavery from which she had escaped. Gislane Nicholson had personally directed the mutilation of Georgiana, but Suzanne, the sister who had married her lover, she had saved, out of some quirk of humanity, perhaps. Out of delight at being able to play the deity, perhaps, where a godlike omnipotence had been practised so often upon her.

Did these men know anything of that? They looked hardly older than himself, so could have taken no part in those events, a quarter of a century in the past. Except that they might have tugged at Aunt Georgiana's naked body, and screamed their childish delight, and added to the horror of her death.

The men were kneeling. One fingered the material of his coat. Miraculous, that he should still be wearing a coat. Another looked at his pants. His feet were bare; his boots had come off during the night, and his stockings were in ruins.

'He has nothing,' said one of them, as near as Dick could understand.

'He is from the sea,' said the man who smiled. 'There will be a wreck. Other men, perhaps. We will follow the bay.'

'And this one?' asked the third man.

'He has nothing,' said the first one. 'Leave him. He will soon die.'

'He will not die,' said the man who smiled. 'He is plump, and healthy. This cloth is that of a massa. I remember such cloth. I will drink his blood. It will give me strength.'

Oh, God, Dick thought. Oh, God. I am about to be murdered. To have survived so much. To have survived a hurricane. And now to be murdered.

'Perhaps he will scream when we cut his flesh,' said the third man.

'He will scream,' said the smiling man, and Dick saw the flash of his machete blade in the morning sunlight.

So lie here, he thought, and it will be over. Soon. You will even make them happy, by screaming. But I wish to live, he protested. I did not find the strength to last the hurricane, and survive the waves, to be murdered like a pig.

Then find the energy again, and quickly. His fingers were still dug into the sand. He raised both hands, threw the first fistful at the man with the drawn machete, the second at the man by his feet. They gave shouts, of alarm and pain and anger, and fell backwards. Dick rolled on his side, and the man kneeling on his left drew his machete. But Dick was moving his arms again, clasping them together, sweeping them over the sand like a flail, catching the black man at the ankles as he attempted to rise, and when his balance was already insecure. The man gave a gasp of exasperation and fell over, scattering across the beach, and Dick was on his feet.

Why had he not reacted like that to the man who had felled him, Harriet's friend? Had he done so, he would not be here. None of this nightmare would be happening. But he had been drunk, and had supposed himself the guilty one. Before he had even committed a crime.

The man who smiled was scraping sand from his eyes, and he still held his machete. There could be no opposing three men while he was alone and unarmed. Dick jumped over the man whom he had knocked down, and ran up the beach. As he left the water's edge the sand dried, and became soft; his feet sank to their ankles and he almost fell, as much out of despair as from loss of balance. But as his knees touched the ground he reflected that they could travel no faster; he could see their own footprints in front of him, deep, slowly filling with subsiding sand.

He regained his feet and ran, lungs bursting, nostrils and mouth gasping for breath. He heard shouts behind him, but did not look back. He reached crab grass, growing through the sand crystals, and his feet began to grip. He stumbled into the trees, trod on a thorny branch, and screamed in pain. But kept on running, the thorns driving deeper into his instep with every movement, the pain seeping up from his legs and into his calves and thighs, into his very belly. He sobbed, and moaned, and ran, and tripped, and fell through some bushes, down an incline, to land in a hollow, half sand and half earth and half bush. He lay there, panting and trying to control his panting, as he heard the crackle of bushes behind him, the sound of voices. The noise was very close. They were stopped, and arguing about where he might have gone. They were deciding to divide, to fan out, to be sure of finding him. They would not be robbed of their sport. They wanted him to scream. He held his breath, for several seconds, as the feet crackled above and to either side, as the pain seethed upwards from his own feet, and then the noise receded, and he allowed breath to explode from his lungs, and sat up to pant, and stared once again at the smiling black man.

For a moment they looked at each other. Then the black man smiled, and the machete came up, and he slowly began to descend the side of the pit.

Dick rose to his hands and knees, his chest still heaving. With fear? He had been frightened, just now. And this time there was going to be no more surprising them and running away. This time he was going to die. Unless the black man died first.

But the black man held the machete. It darted forward now, in front of the grin. This was sport. He knew the white man was unarmed, and he could see the fear.

Dick fell backwards, stumbled and sat down. The black man's grin widened, and he thrust again. Dick rolled to one side, reached his knees, and then his feet, kicking sand to make some sort of a cloud. And feeling, strangely, an anger bubbling through his veins. He had felt it before and mistrusted it. But now, if he did not trust it, he would be killed.

Sand scattered across the black man's face, and he brushed it away with his right hand. But the smile had gone. Perhaps the white man was not sufficiently afraid. The knife came again, snaking out at the end of the long right arm. Desperately Dick swayed to one side, and the arm brushed him as the black man came close, left hand now seeking to close on Dick's body. But that had to be ignored. Dick grasped the arm holding the knife with both hands, one at wrist and one at shoulder, fingers digging into the taut flesh, forced the arm down, with all his strength, brought his own knee up, with all his strength, heard the gasp of pain, saw the knife drop to the sand, and in the same instant felt a surge of pain himself as teeth closed on his shoulder.

He turned, inside the black man's arms, drumming his fists

against the black belly. But this was hard, ridged with muscle, and he seemed to make no effect. And fingers were closing on his own body, hurting where they bit into his own flesh. And the man was again smiling. But realizing that he was not going to destroy this castaway so easily on his own. The mouth was opening. He was going to call for his friends to come back.

Their bodies were tight against each other, the black man hugging, Dick's arms trapped against the black man's chest. Their faces were only inches apart, and the mouth was opening. That had to be stopped. That was priority number one. Dick made a tremendous effort, forced his arms upwards, closed his fingers on the black throat. The mouth snapped shut, and the smile was gone. Dick squeezed.

The arms left his back, pummelled his shoulders. The eyes so close to his rolled, and showed their whites. The fingers scraped flesh from his back, having already destroyed the remnants of his coat and shirt. The black toes hacked at his ankles, twined themselves round his legs. They fell together, on their sides, and for just a moment Dick's fingers relaxed. Then he squeezed again. To let go was to die.

He was forced on his back. Black fingers searched his breeches, found his genitals, twisted and squeezed. Rivers of pain flowed up each groin into his belly, left him faint. Stars spun before his eyes. But he still squeezed with all his strength.

He found his eyes open, staring at the sky. The sun was already high, although it was still early in the morning. He could not see it, but beyond the fringe of leaves and branches he could see the clear blue of the sky, the occasional fleecy white clouds. Up there was escape from the pain, from the misery of being on this earth. If he could keep his mind up there, he might survive.

Dimly he became aware that the pain was receding from his belly, that the constant motion against him had ceased. Still he squeezed, suspecting it might be a trap. Now he forced himself once again to look at the black face so close to his own, the staring eyes, the opened mouth. There was horror.

There was cramp in his fingers. He doubted he'd be able to maintain the pressure much longer. He felt his muscles already relaxing.

So then, lying here placed him at a disadvantage. He freed his fingers, having to tear them away from the black throat, so deeply were they embedded, rolled away from his opponent in the one movement, rose to his knees and turned, saw the machete lying on the sand and picked it up, turned once more to face the man on the ground.

But the man was still on the ground, lying as Dick had left him. He listened to his own breathing, could feel his own chest heave as it sought air, and wondered why the black man did not also seek air. He dropped to his hands and knees, the knife forgotten, peered at the body. I have killed a man, he thought. Oh, my God, I have killed a man. He turned his hands over, stared at them. They had not changed. They were lean hands, strong, slightly calloused. They were destroyers.

He rose to his feet, still staring at his victim. It had been kill or be killed. But he had not intended to kill. He had wanted to silence, and then perhaps to defeat. Not to kill. As if the two could be separated, in this animal world.

He turned away from the dead man, blundered across the pit in which they had fought, scrabbled up the other side, and realized that he had forgotten the machete. He turned his head to look over his shoulder, saw the man, and the knife. From this distance he looked asleep in the morning sunlight. But he was dead. There was enough cause for horror. And he had friends, who would soon come back to look for him.

Dick plunged into the bush. Branches tore at his flesh, his hair, even his eyes. Fallen tree trunks clawed at his feet. He fell, and got up again, and fell again, and got up again. He staggered onwards.

He found a stream, bubbling downwards, and only then saw that he had been climbing. The sun was overhead now, and very hot. And he had never been so thirsty in his life. He lay on his face and lapped the water like a dog. And lapped and lapped and lapped. And then lay on his back, and panted, while water ran out of his mouth.

And awoke again, to find the heat receding, although it was still light. How long had he lain there? He did not know. But the men who would be following him would know. It was a stupid thing, to lie still when he should be running, and running.

He regained his feet, splashed across the stream, climbed. The earth ceased to claw at his feet and instead became a series of boulders and loose stones, over which he stumbled, often falling, bruising his knees. Hunger began to bite at his belly, and he tore some berries from a tree and crammed them into his mouth, chewed as he continued to climb. Soon it would be dark, and then perhaps he could stop, and rest. If he could rest, he felt he could think, and decide what must be done. If anything could be done. But it was silly to attempt to think until he had rested.

He stepped into space. Desperately he twisted his head, flailed his arms. He had climbed, and the path he had been following had suddenly ended. For the longest moment of his life he seemed to be floating, and the strange thought crossed his mind that he had died, from exertion, and was flying up to heaven. Or perhaps the black man had killed him after all, and it had not been the other way round.

Pain. He had felt pain before, but nothing like this. Where the other pains had begun with his feet or his belly, this began in his face and head. Nothing but pain. Flying through the air? He must have hit a bird. He wanted to laugh. There was absurdity.

It was dark. He must have slept again. Or perhaps fainted. He could feel nothing but pain. His head crashed, but sharper thrusts seemed to enter his cheeks and mouth and chin, making the duller pains of his body hardly interesting. He could not still be flying. Yet he could feel nothing underneath him. No doubt he was dreaming. He put his hand down to push, and gave a scream of pure agony. Or he would have screamed, he realized. Nothing seemed to come out. Nothing which could compare with the drumming in his ears. But that was because he couldn't move his jaw. There was a silly confession.

He fell over, on to his side, gazed at the stars, filling the empty darkness of the sky. And it was cool. But he must get his jaw moving. Why, he might wish to speak to someone.

He tried his other arm, and to his delight it came up. Slowly. If he could straighten his jaw . . . his fingers touched bone. Oh, God, he thought. Oh, Christ. I am going to die, lying here in the darkness.

But that was absurd. He had fought the sea, for a whole night, to live. He had killed a man, with his bare hands, to live. To lie here and die would be a crime, after having done so much to keep alive.

His left hand was the one which had moved. He put it down beside him, waited for the thrill of agony which still coursed up and down his right hand. And felt only stone, hard and brittle, under his fingers. He pushed, cautiously, and then with increasing confidence, found himself sitting up, while the night, the ravine into which he had fallen, spun around him. His mouth filled with ghastly liquid, but to his horror he found he could not move his tongue, either to taste it or to spit it out. He could only hang his head and let it flow through his lips, and realized that it was his own blood.

Come daylight, there would be insects, seeking that blood. What a horrible thought, to lie here, and slowly be eaten alive by insects. Or would they wait until he was dead? He did not know.

And he was not going to die. He had already decided that. He was going to move. If he had to crawl, then he would crawl. Away from here. So the insects would be able to follow the trail of blood. But they would know he was alive, if he moved.

He dug the fingers of his left hand into the stones, used his legs, felt more pain, and had to separate one from the other. So, then, he had one arm and one leg, ready for use. Why, he was still half a man.

He crawled and prodded, and moved, and fell on his face, and crawled, and prodded, and moved, and fell on his face, and crawled, and prodded, and moved, and fell on his face. Sometimes it was dark, then suddenly it was light. Then he thought it was dark again, but he could not be sure. He was sure only of the pain, which seemed to grow and grow until it shrouded his entire body, his mind, his very being. He moved, in a miasma of pain, amazed that he could move at all, determined to keep on moving, to keep ahead of the insects.

But he was losing the race. When it was light, the insects were there, settling on his face and shoulders, buzzing in his ears. Drinking his blood. He was, after all, going to be eaten alive by insects.

Then he might as well surrender. He lay, on his face, and then rolled on his back. He had been afraid to doze, before, in case his mouth filled with blood again and he lacked the strength to turn over. But this time his throat remained dry, so dry he thought he would give all of Hilltop for a cup of water.

All of Hilltop. The thought brought tears to his eyes. But tears were liquid. Perhaps he could drink them. He discovered his eyes were shut, forced them open, and stared once again at men. Black men.

182

10

The Mamaloi

The breeze was cool. He had felt it before. It carried with it a delicious perfume, the scent of the sea filtered by the bloom of a million flowers.

He had smelt it before, as well. It occurred to him that he had been inhaling that magnificent scent for a very long time, without being aware of it.

He moved his shoulders, nestled them in the softness of the bed. Another sensation he remembered, without being sure of how long ago it had commenced. Perhaps he had lain here, forever. His eyes were open, gazing above him at the snowy tent of the bed. Hilltop's linen had never been that clean. But he had never supposed he was on Hilltop. Hilltop was a nightmare, and now he was awake.

To movement. A rustling from around him, a faint whisper. He turned his head, or made the necessary decision to turn his head. And remained staring at the tent. Yet he felt no fear, no sense of panic. He could not turn his head. But as he had lain here, inhaling that breeze, feeling the softness of this mattress, enjoying the cleanliness of these sheets, for so very long, it could be no serious matter.

A face replaced the tent. A black face, serious and concerned, bareheaded but ending in a high military collar, in blue and gold, as his jacket was blue, smothered in gold braid. He said something, but it was in French, and Dick could not immediately translate. Then the man was gone, to be replaced by the gentle rustle he had heard earlier. Once again he attempted to turn his head, and this time discovered that he could. He looked to his right, at two young women, both black, both dressed in white gowns, their heads shrouded in white bandannas, who were busily preparing a bowl of warm water, with which they now proceeded to shave him. Their fingers were light as feathers, their touch delightful; they exuded the entrancing fragrance of the breeze. And yet their touch filled him with a sense of foreboding. He could feel the razor, scraping gently over his chin, and yet it did not seem to be his chin. He wanted to cry out, in sudden terror, but he could form no words, and they were so quick, they were finished before he could even form a thought. Then they busied themselves with his body, rolling back the sheet, and, now joined by another half-dozen young women who presumably had been present all the while, raising him from the mattress to insert towels beneath him, before bathing him, as gently and as carefully as they might have handled a babe. And this time he could feel more; there was no sense of catastrophe as they touched his body. Touched his body. He attempted to move, and was gently restrained. Their faces remained serious, their brows furrowed with concentration. And now one was drying him, patting leg and arm, stroking chest. The sheet was returned, and they disappeared, although clearly remaining in the room, from the whisper, and leaving him utterly refreshed.

And aware of a consuming thirst. 'Water,' he whispered. And discovered again the sense of terror. That had not been Richard Hilton's voice.

He was surrounded by faces, watching him anxiously, willing him to make them understand.

'*L'eau*,' he whispered. Or someone whispered, inside his brain.

They smiled, together, a combination of pleasure and relief. Soft arms went round his head, to raise it from the pillow; his cheek lay against a gently pounding heart. A cup was held to his lips, and the liquid trickled down his throat. It was the most magnificent thing he had ever tasted, clear, cool water.

Then the cup was taken away, suddenly. It was the first abrupt movement he had experienced. His cheek left the comfort of the breast, his head was replaced on its pillow. The girls disappeared, and this time they did not whisper. And a new smell entered the room, a scent of leather, of man. And a new atmosphere. He could feel the sudden power with which he was surrounded, and turned his head again, with an enormous effort, to gaze at the cluster of officers, each dressed in a magnificent uniform, red jackets, blue jackets, pale green jackets, every one a mass of gold braid with a high military collar, worn over tight breeches of white buckskin, every one with a jewel-hilted sword hanging at his side, every one with high black boots and jingling spurs.

And every one with a black face. Then was he dreaming all over again?

'Richard Hilton,' said a voice, amazingly in English. 'You are Richard Hilton?'

He turned his head once again, and discovered that one of the officers had reached the side of his bed. One of the officers? That could not be. This man carried no sword. But then, he did not need a sword. He was several inches taller than six feet, and bareheaded; again unlike the others, he did not carry his hat beneath his arm. His forehead was high, his eyes widespaced; they were sombre eyes, hard, and even arrogant, and yet also containing a remarkably wistful expression. His nose was big, his chin thrusting. His mouth was wide, and as interesting as the eyes. When closed, it suggested no more than a brutal gash; when smiling, as now, it revealed a delightful humour, an almost childish delight in the business of being alive.

'Has he spoken?' he asked, in French.

'He asked for water, Your Majesty,' said one of the girls.

Your Majesty, Dick thought. My God.

The man sat beside him on the bed. 'You may say what you wish, to me, in English,' he said, speaking English. 'My people understand little of it. Do you know who you are?'

Dick concentrated, made an immense effort. 'I am Richard Hilton,' he whispered. 'Of Plantation Hilltop, in Jamaica.'

He was bathed in the tremendous smile. 'I hoped you would say that. Do you know how you came here?'

Dick attempted to shake his head, and found he could not. 'There was a storm. My ship was sunk. And when I reached shore, I was attacked.'

'My country is beset by outlaws,' the man said. 'It is too large, we are too few. But they will be destroyed. I give you my word. And you escaped from them, sorely wounded. Do you know how badly wounded?'

'I fell,' Dick said. 'From a hillside. That is the last I remember.'

'Ah,' said the man. 'We wondered how you came by such terrible injuries. Your leg was broken and your arm. Your ribs were broken. But you would not die. You crawled, in that

185

condition, for a very long way. My surgeons tell me you must have been in that condition for three days, still crawling. And at last you crawled into an encampment of my soldiers. They perhaps would have left you to die, but it so happened that I visited them, on a tour of inspection, that very day, and saw you, and was told how you had crawled. I thought then, here is a man of remarkable courage, remarkable stamina, remarkable determination. Such a man should not die. That was before you spoke.'

Dick frowned at him. 'I spoke?'

'You were delirious. And . . .' For the first time the black man lost some of his confidence. 'You had other injuries, which made it difficult for you to articulate. Yet sometimes you whispered, and sometimes you screamed. You screamed your name. Do you know me?'

He waited, saw the uncertainty in Dick's eyes, and smiled. 'I am Christophe. The Emperor, Henri the First, of all Haiti. But to you, Christophe.'

'To me?'

'I knew your parents. Your mother was a woman of rare beauty, rare courage, rare determination. A fitting mother for such a son. And your father sought to help the black man. Does he still do so?'

'Yes.'

'Ah. Fate is a strange business, Richard Hilton. That I should be able to save their son.'

'Why?' Dick asked. 'I am a planter, not an Abolitionist. And you destroyed my aunt.'

The smile faded, the face became hard, for just a moment. But even a moment was long enough for Dick to know that this man would be the most implacable, the most ruthless enemy he would ever have, were he ever to become an enemy. Then the smile returned. 'I would have you regain your strength, and get well. You and I have much to discuss. Much to remember, perhaps.' The smile went again, but this time the face was sad. 'I do not hide the truth. Your injuries were terrible, Richard Hilton. You were near to death for weeks. And you have lain in a fever, unable to move, for weeks more. My people have fed you and cared for you, and you will be well again, and as strong as ever before in your life, should you choose to be. But even a broken arm, a broken leg, three broken ribs, were not the full extent of your injuries.' He snapped his fingers, and one of the girls hurried

186

forward, carrying a looking-glass in a gilt frame, handed it to the Emperor.

'Now, Richard Hilton,' Christophe said. 'As you are the son of Suzanne Hilton and Matthew Hilton, and as you are a man of courage and determination, as you have proved, look on yourself.'

The glass was held immediately above him, and he stared into the reflection. Because it was a reflection. Christophe had said so, and indeed, he could see the cambric pillow case spreading away from him on either side, and also the fair hair, which had grown to an inordinate length, and scattered to either side as well. But the face between. His heart seemed to slow, and a wild desire to scream filled his brain.

But perhaps it was merely the glass, which was distorted, and thus made him distorted. Because those were his eyes. When he blinked, they blinked. He could stare at himself, in his eyes. So, then, no doubt he was wearing a mask, with slits through which his eyes could peer. And the mask was carelessly made, and perhaps trodden upon by that careless maker. The forehead was high. He had always had a high forehead. But never one split by a deep, jagged groove, ridged with scar tissue. The chin thrust. He had always had a thrusting chin. But it had thrust forward, not to one side in a lopsided lurch, which carried his mouth with it, elongating the lips, making the mouth seem twice as wide as it really was. And he had once possessed a nose. The Hilton nose, the feature above all others which had made Mama beautiful and her sons handsome, small and exquisitely shaped. This face lacked a nose. Rather it possessed two nostrils in the centre of an unspeakable gash, which gave the other grotesque features an appearance of anxious horror.

Christophe snapped his fingers again, and the glass was removed.

'A man should count, first of all, his blessings,' the Emperor said. 'When you fell, from your hillside, you landed on your face. On your nose, I suspect. So you are disfigured. But your brain, I think, is undamaged. And you have lost only a few of your teeth. And you are alive.'

'I am a monster,' Dick whispered.

Christophe smiled, and stood up. 'You are a man, Richard Hilton. Get well, and strong. I have known handsome men, whose beauty disguised hearts of hell, and I have known lovely women, whose beauty sheltered the most vicious of desires. A man is what he is, Richard Hilton. Not what he appears to be. Get well, and we will talk.'

He left the room, his entourage at his heels, and Dick was surrounded by the girls. Now he gazed at them with horror, waiting for the disgust which must animate their faces. But they remained seriously composed, adjusted his covers, raised his head again to offer him another drink. And this time it was rum suitably diluted with lemon juice, but strong enough to send his weakened brain whirling through shadowed corridors. Christophe would take no risks with his sanity.

His sanity. Well, then, what was sanity? He doubted he would ever be sane again. Sanity was, first and foremost, an understanding of oneself and one's surroundings. But his surroundings were unimaginable. Black people, in his experience had been slaves, or, if free, paupers, wearing nothing more than a pair of drawers or a chemise, barefooted, uneducated, amoral. They had lived in one-room logies, and been allowed to die as they became useless, to give birth as they had become pregnant. They had been humble, and they had been afraid. Without, indeed, the fabric of fear which was inextricably woven into the very heart of West Indian society, slavery could not exist.

So then, there was no sanity, in Sans Souci. Because that was the name of the palace in which he now found himself. And it was a palace. Ellen Taggart had called Hilltop a palace. But compared with this endless edifice it was a hut. No doubt Christophe, with his background of slavery, intended it so. Quite unashamedly he had borrowed the design, no less than the name, from Frederick of Prussia. Of all the white men he admired, indeed, and there was a surprising number, Frederick the Great ranked highest. Dick had never been to Prussia. Nor could he see the need, now. In Prussia it was occasionally cold, often damp; the sun did not always shine. At Christophe's Sans Souci there was no natural impediment to endless splendour, endless pleasure, endless delight. Sometimes the trade wind, booming in from the Atlantic, had skirts fluttering, chandeliers swinging, but this same trade wind dissipated the heat, kept the palace cool, kept its inmates smiling.

These were numberless, men and women, treading parquet

188

floors or soft carpets, high heels or spurred boots clicking, silks rustling, swords clinking; and their faces were black. Nor were they overawed by their surroundings. Dick was. When first he left his bed, some weeks after his initial reawakening, he was escorted along endless corridors, decorated in royal colours of brilliant blue, gleaming red, gentle green, imperial purple, hung with paintings of the magnificent country into which he had so strangely strayed. The corridors had ended in galleries, which looked over even more splendid parquet floors, sentried by red-coated guardsmen, armed with musket and bayonet and even bearksin, with ceilings decorated in the classical Italian style, and rising thirty feet above the floor beneath them. To reach the floor he must descend a slowly curving staircase, marble-stepped, gilt-balustraded, down which an endless sweep of superbly dressed, superbly poised, men and women paraded. And they were black.

And beyond the hallways, the reception rooms, with grand piano and upholstered chaise longue, monogrammed silk drapes, twenty-foot-high glass doors leading to the gardens. In here often enough music tinkled and the Haitian nobility indulged in the newest Viennese waltz, a panorama of bare breasts and shoulders, of gleaming uniforms, of witty conversation and whispered flirtation. But the gleaming shoulders and shining faces were black.

And beyond the glass doors, the miles of garden, the shell-strewn walks between the packed flowerbeds, where white-stockinged ministers strolled, gloved hands behind their backs, listening to the pronunciamentos of the Emperor. Where the sea breeze reached its fullest strength, and murmured in the pine trees with which the gardens were surrounded. Where plumed guardsmen, dismounted for their sentry duty, stood to attention with drawn sabres resting on their cuirassed shoulders. And the guardsmen, and the ministers, were black.

Much about them, about the palace, was no doubt ridiculous. At least to European eyes. Most ridiculous of all was the conscious aping of Europeanism, and within that, of Napoleonism. Christophe was the Emperor, and ruled with all the trappings of Paris or Vienna, reviewing his magnificently uniformed guard every morning, conferring far into the night with his ministers, issuing directives, sentencing offenders, making plans, while in the evening he invariably attended the ball which took place in the great hall, accompanied by his queen, middle-aged and soft-voiced, but imperial of presence, with diamonds sparkling in her hair and round her neck, with the train of her white lace gown sweeping the floor. Perhaps it was ridiculous for powdered black people to dance the waltz. Certainly it was ridiculous for the nobility Christophe had created around him to sport names like the Duke of Marmalade, the Count of Sunshine. But there was nothing ridiculous about the gravity, the conscious determination, with which each minister, each belle, each servant and each guardsman went about his duties. Dick took a great deal of persuading to leave his bedchamber, even when he was strong enough once more to walk; he feared that his ghastly face would be an object of ridicule. But no doubt they had been prepared, and indeed, no sooner had he left his room than he encountered the Empress, obviously waiting to insist upon lending him her own arm to descend the stairs, and receive the bows of her people, and never a smile at the disfigured white man.

So then, perhaps it was ridiculous to sit for dinner at a table twice the size of that at Hilltop, with other tables leading off, so that some hundred and fifty people sat down for the meal, to sip French wine and eat breast of chicken fried in butter, to finish with iced sorbet delicately flavoured with soursop, the most sensual of fruits.

But why, he found himself wondering, was it ridiculous? For people consciously to raise their status, from the lowest to the highest, in a single generation? There was achievement, not absurdity. No doubt, to his eyes, incongruous was the more accurate word. And what was incongruous, but a synonym for surprise, for the unusual.

And then, he was forced to reflect, as he strolled the gardens, attended always by his bevy of white-gowned girls, and now supported by two armed guardsmen always at his call, and listened to the bustle of empire just beyond the walls, nothing could even be incongruous, where so much had been achieved. In Jamaica, they had supposed Haiti to be a savage jungle peopled by wild Africans no doubt given to cannibalism, and surviving in the depths of poverty and degradation, at the mercy of the wild superstition they called Voodoo. If the palace of Sans Souci was representative of the culture Henry Christophe had created, then was Jamaica the uncivilized poorhouse.

But was it truly representative? He could not help but remember the empty beach, the sullen forest, the bestial trio who had sought to murder him, when first he had landed. How far then, did Christophe's magnificence stretch? Dick found himself remarkably anxious to find out.

But leaving Sans Souci demanded the same essential as remaining within its magnificent cloisters; the will of the Emperor Henry Christophe. He had said, on the morning Dick first awoke, that he wished to talk. And this was true. As Dick regained his strength, the Emperor set aside an hour a day, first of all to visit his guest in his bedchamber, and then, when Dick began to be able to move around the palace, to entertain him in one of the private rooms, or to walk with him in the gardens. But less to talk, than to listen. He asked questions, concerning Jamaica, concerning Europe, concerning the present state of the Hilton family. As he regularly received embassies, or at least envoys, from various European nations, and as he certainly received overseas news from his own agents, judging by the constant stream of couriers which visited the palace, he was certainly not ill-informed of events outside his own country. Of which he never spoke. Any questions Dick might offer in reply were politely turned aside. It became increasingly difficult for Dick to decide, as he regained his full health and strength, and his brain became correspondingly more alert, exactly what motive Christophe had, in lavishing such care, such attention, on him. He even began to wonder if the repeated questions concerning Suzanne—even if these were equally mingled with questions concerning Matt and the prospects of Abolition in the British colonies—might not be the main reason. Mama had never discussed her months of imprisonment by the Negro army. In circumstances so horrible no one had been disposed to argue about that. But had the circumstances been so horrible?

The thought was itself horrible. But was the thought itself horrible? Or was it just the instinctive reaction of generations of prejudice? What had Mama herself said? The fact of slavery is all the white man has, if he is wealthy, to justify his crime, if he is poor, to justify his pretence at superiority. And every black man in the entire continent of America was a slave, a freed slave, or the son of a slave. And was thus to be doomed to perpetual inferiority?

191

Why, he had recognized the falseness of that in Jamaica, and long before he had known Christophe. Knowing Christophe, seeing what he had achieved, made it even more of a nonsense.

Nor could the idea of love, between white and black, be dismissed out of hand as obscene. He had known the attraction of a black woman, in Jamaica, and rejected it instinctively. Tony had not. And had not Tony, as ever, been right? There came the night, not very long after he was able to take his first steps in the garden, when the door to his bedchamber was opened, and a girl entered. She carried a candle, and wore a deep green negligée, and nothing else. He gazed at her in alarm and she smiled at him.

'I am come to make you happy,' she said, in English.

'I am happy,' he answered, again instinctively. 'You must not stay.'

The girl crossed the room, placed the candle in the holder. She was tall, and slender. She glided rather than moved, and even through the negligée her black flesh seemed to gleam. 'I must stay,' she said. 'It is the will of the Emperor.'

'The Emperor? He has not spoken of it to me.'

'The Emperor knows his own mind,' she removed her negligée. 'My name is Aimée.'

No doubt she had been created especially to be loved. Her slimness was the result of training and exercise, not immaturity. Her breasts filled his hand, and lacked the slightest sag. Her belly was ridged with the muscles of a man. And most remarkable of all to his eyes, her pubes had been shaved, to make her womanhood the more imperious, the more demanding, the more anxious. And now he discovered the reason for the gleam which had surrounded her. She was oiled, from her neck to her toes, with a pleasantly scented unguent, which made her slide over him like a cool breeze. He was inside her before he had properly touched her, his fingers slipping down the powerful arch of her back. And he was spent, it seemed but a single spasm later. No doubt he had wanted a woman, very badly, without even being aware of it.

Aimée kissed him on the nose. 'The Emperor will be pleased. It is a sign of health.'

She made to roll away from him, and he caught her wrist. 'And having done your duty, you will now leave me?'

Her face was expressionless. 'If I remain, Mr Hilton, you will wish to enter me again. And perhaps again.'

'And having done your duty, you no longer wish me inside you.'

'My feelings are of no concern,' she said. 'I am concerned with your strength. It is not yet full.'

'The Emperor's command?'

'The Emperor knows all things.'

'And so he commanded you to love a monster.'

She had been pulling at her wrist, gently. Now her movements relaxed, and she frowned. 'Are you a monster?'

'Have you no eyes in your head, Aimée?'

'You are a man, monsieur.' Almost she smiled. 'A woman should judge a man, not by his appearances, but by his touch. Your fingers are gentle. They seek to give, rather than to take. Your lips are gentle. Your passion is a gentle passion. You are a man to love, because you are a man who seeks to give love.'

No doubt her father had been a slave, and perhaps had torn the flesh from Aunt Georgiana's body while she had screamed and he had laughed. 'Did the Emperor command you to say that?'

'No, monsieur. The Emperor would be displeased with me did he know I was still here. He would have me whipped.'

'But you will come again?'

'Tomorrow night.'

'Then stay this night, Aimée, or do not come tomorrow. I would have you stay, and return, because of me, not because of duty. And if it is because of me, I must be worth at least a whipping.'

She hesitated, and was then in his arms again, and consuming him again, within seconds. And herself? He could swear beads of sweat had appeared on her shoulders, even beneath the oil. And she had sighed.

'And you will not be whipped,' he said. 'I give you my word.'

She smiled. 'I will not be whipped in any event, Mr Hilton. The Emperor left this night, and will not return for at least a month.'

'Left?' He sat up in dismay.

'He campaigns, monsieur. Against Pétion.'

The name was familiar enough. 'I had supposed they shared the same dream. Did not Pétion fight with Christophe, under Toussaint, against the French?'

'Indeed, monsieur. But he is not black like us. His father was a white man. He is what we call a mulatto. And if he wished to be free of the French, he did not wish to be ruled by a black man. He has declared the south independent, and would make himself master of all Haiti. So the Emperor must defeat him, and this is difficult, where there are so many forests, so many mountains.'

'But the Emperor will defeat him?'

'Of course,' Aimée said.

It was as simple as that, to the residents of Sans Souci.

'You are well, Richard Hilton.' The Emperor stood before his desk, hands clasped behind his back. He wore uniform, and looked tired. As well he might, Dick supposed. He had campaigned for some two months, and had apparently only returned to his palace the previous day. And immediately summoned his guest. Or was it his prisoner?

'I am as well as ever in my life, sire. Or perhaps, better than ever before in my life. No man could have been cared for as I have been these last nine months.' Could it really be nine months? It was July. The sea breeze had warmed, and rain clouds were gathering above the mountains.

'That pleases me,' Christophe said. He walked round the desk, and one of his secretaries hastily pulled back his chair for him. 'Sit.'

Another secretary held a chair for Dick. He sat, carefully, adjusting his white breeches as he felt the shoulders of his blue coat brushing the back of the chair. He wore uniform, for the simple reason that everyone in Sans Souci wore uniform; Christophe's tailors apparently did not know how to cut civilian clothes.

'And do you now look in the mirror without a shudder?'

'No, sire. I doubt I will ever be able to do that.'

Christophe gazed at him for some seconds. And then nodded. 'There is news, from Europe. The French emperor, Napoleon, has escaped from Elba and returned to France.'

'My God,' Dick said. 'It will mean a resumption of the war.'

'And a resumption, perhaps, of Bonaparte's power,' Christophe said, thoughtfully. 'The same ship which brought me that news brought inquiries after Richard Hilton. We have had several such inquiries.'

Dick frowned. 'You never said so.'

'You had sufficient cause for distress, in regaining your health,' Christophe said.

194

'Then my family know I am here?'

Christophe smiled. 'I have told no one you are here.'

'But . . .'

'I supposed it was your wish, Richard Hilton. You have never asked to have your family informed. That is strange. But my agents also tell me that you are disgraced in Jamaica, sought for a crime, perhaps.'

'A crime?'

'An assault upon a young girl. A white man's crime, Richard. I do not inquire. Perhaps it was the cause of your leaving Jamaica, perhaps not. I will inform your family that you are alive and well, should you wish it.'

Dick hesitated. Judith had told her mother, and Harriet, in her anger, had brought a charge. No doubt Richard Hilton, of Hilltop in Jamaica, would survive such a scandal, and even a court case, by payment of a fine. But did he wish to be Richard Hilton of Hilltop? Could he ever be Richard Hilton of Hilltop again? Ellen would never forgive him. Poor Ellen. She had travelled four thousand miles to meet disaster, and must travel four thousand miles back again.

Well, then, what of the plantation? No doubt it would be sold. Or managed by Tony. There was the answer. It would be managed by Tony. But he had ordered Tony from the plantation. Only Josh, and Boscawen knew that. No doubt Tony would be able to come to some arrangement with both Josh and Boscawen. And Tony was much more of a planter, in spirit, than himself.

Because he had never wanted to rule, and even less wanted to rule now. Was even less able to rule, now. Having seen what his slaves could become, were they given the chance.

Christophe was smiling. 'You do not choose to inform them.'

'I have been happy here, these last few months,' Dick confessed. 'Happier than I can recall. I was never happy as a planter. Or even before.'

'Why is that?'

Dick hesitated. 'I think I have always been too aware of my name. I have always felt I was not acting the part. Here, I cannot act the part, and therefore I am not perpetually worried about it.'

'Honestly said,' Christophe remarked. 'But I have no doubt that you are a Hilton. What of your mother? Do you not wish to inform her that you are still alive?'

'Yes. But not now. I would like to wait a while.'

Christophe nodded. 'Yet will there be inquiries about this white man who is my friend, once the fact is widely known. They will ask who you are. What will I tell them?'

'Whatever you like. So long as they do not learn my name.'

'Ah. Yet they will want a name.' Christophe leaned back and gave a bellow of laughter. 'I will tell them you are an English soldier of fortune, by name Matthew Warner. There is a name, Richard Hilton.'

'You know of the Warners?'

'I know a great deal. And you will tell me more.' He got up, and the humour faded from his face. 'But I said the truth, when I described you as a Warner, an English soldier of fortune come to fight at my side. We are going on a journey, you and I. You are well enough to travel, my surgeons tell me. You are as well, or better, than ever in your life.'

'Except for my face.' But his heart was pounding. How long had he waited, to leave Sans Souci?

'Where no one knows you with any other face, Matthew Warner — for your name comes into being as of now — no one will find anything to remark on. Come. Our escort is waiting.'

Dick wondered if he should ask permission to say goodbye to Aimée. The girl had become part of him during the past few weeks. But he did not suppose Christophe would be interested, or appreciative, of such a tender emotion. The Emperor did not delay to say farewell to *his* wife, was already striding through the halls and down the stairs, huge cocked hat on his head, sword slapping his thigh, with all his tremendous energy.

And Richard Hilton, alias Matthew Warner, followed, a sword slapping his thigh. A sword he did not know how to use. What would Christophe say when he discovered that?

But it was a good alias.

Their horses waited in the courtyard of the palace, and with them an escort of fifty dragoons, in blue jackets with yellow facings and dusty white breeches, blue tricornes, and armed with muskets and cutlasses. Dick realized for the first time that he was dressed as an officer in the Imperial Guard, and therefore had presumably been granted that rank.

The gates were swinging open, and he looked outside the palace. Beyond was a beaten earth roadway, typical of any in

Jamaica, although he would have expected paving stones, thus close to the palace itself, and in such a kingdom. Christophe cantered through, Dick at his heels, the guards behind. And Dick all but drew rein. For beyond the palace there was a town. If it could be so called. A scattered accumulation of wooden lean-tos—they could not even be described as slave logies—amidst which naked children, thin and emaciated, and almost naked women, hastily and wearily rose to their feet to stand to attention as the imperial entourage went by, kicking dust into their faces. And the faces did not smile.

Christophe had glanced at him. It was necessary to say something.

'There are no men.'

'Those of fighting age are in my armies,' Christophe explained. 'The old men and the boys must till the fields. We are a nation of workers, Matt.'

A slave nation, slaving, Dick thought, and wondered why. Perhaps these people were being punished. Perhaps they were just lazy. He could see the houses of a city ahead.

'Cap Haitien,' Christophe explained. 'The French called it Cap François, but we renamed it.'

Cap François. 'I have been here, with my mother,' Dick said.

'Of course.' But Christophe was preoccupied, returning the salutes of the people who lined the street. Because this was a street. Or perhaps, Dick thought, it would be more accurate to say, this had been a street. Now grass grew through the cracked paving stones; the giant trees had not been pruned in ten years, he calculated, and their branches dropped low and had to be pushed aside as the cavalcade rode by. And beyond the trees were the palaces. He remembered the houses of Cap François, not because they were imprinted on his mind, but because Mama had told him so much about them. But she had not told him about these. She had spoken of turrets and porticoes, of brilliant colours and sheltered gardens, of massed flowers and smiling, beautiful women. Well, there were still turrets, windows gaping holes in the masonry. And there were still porticoes, in which naked decrepit old men squatted to pass the time of day, being pushed and prodded by military boots and gun butts to stand and do obeisance to their emperor. There were no flowers, there were no beautiful women, and there was no scent, but rather a stench, of unwashed bodies and untreated sewage.

And once again, there were no smiles. The streets were lined with soldiers, and these stood to attention, muskets at the present. They would not have been expected to smile. But the women and old men and children behind them did not smile either. They stared at their emperor, some with apathy, more with hatred, Dick thought.

They passed the cathedral. The doors had been wrenched, or had fallen, from their hinges, the great bell tower was cracked. Inside he could see overturned, rotting pews, a derelict altar. So no doubt few of these people were Christians. But he was glad to be out of the city, and taking the road through deserted canefields, with the forest looming in the distance.

'It is not as you remember,' Christophe remarked.

'I do not remember it at all,' Dick said. 'It is not as my mother described it.'

'Ah. Then it was the capital of the French culture in the West Indies.'

'And now it is not your capital?'

Christophe glanced at him, and then looked ahead. 'You know the history of my people?'

'A little.'

'It can be briefly told,' Christophe said. 'As elsewhere in the West Indies, we were brought here as slaves. I was brought here from St Kitts. The Warners' island, Matt. There is a remarkable quirk of fate. And once here, we were ill-treated, on a scale and in a detail that even you cannot consider. Yet, being a supine people, and being too, composed of so many nationalities, we might have suffered for centuries, had not there been a revolution in France. Even then we were not the first to act. It was the mulattoes, who were free, but without social or political power, who sought their rights. In their revolt the authorities became preoccupied, and we saw our chance and rose. Oh, we murdered and we burned and we looted and we raped. We had much to avenge. We have still, much to avenge on the French. And we found ourselves a great man to be our leader.'

'Toussaint.'

They had passed through the canefields now, and were entering the cool of the trees.

'Aye,' Christophe said. 'Toussaint. He beat the French, and he

198

beat the English who would help them as well. I was proud to be one of his men. But then the English and the French signed a peace treaty, thirteen years ago, and Bonaparte was able to send an army against us. An army which had conquered Europe, Matt. They could not conquer *us*. In the field. But they tricked Toussaint into attending a parley, and sent him captive to France, to die in a prison cell. They thought that without our leader we would surrender. But we found ourselves another leader, in Jean-Jacques Dessalines, and we beat the French again. So what was left of them sailed away, evacuated by your British fleet, Matt. And we were a nation. On paper. For the mulattoes, who had fought with us, now sought power of their own. They murdered the emperor, and Pétion declared his independence. I was chosen to take Jean-Jacques's place. I have ruled this country for eight years, and throughout that time I have fought Pétion, and I have fought the dissident elements in my own nation, and I have tried to make my people work, and I have tried to make a nation. So sometimes I am very tired. It is difficult to see the end.'

'Yes,' Dick said.

Another glance. The trees had grown thicker, and their path was climbing.

'You do not approve of my methods? They must be driven, Matt. When people have been slaves, and then are suddenly given their freedom, all they wish to do is enjoy that freedom. They do not understand that freedom carries with it the responsibility to work harder than a slave, to protect it.'

'I was thinking that they are poorer now, than when they were slaves.'

'Haiti is a poor country.'

Dick spoke without thinking. 'Perhaps they wonder how much Sans Souci cost to build, costs to maintain.'

'Are there no palaces in England?'

'Yes, but . . .'

'You would bow to your king did he live in a cottage in Suffolk?'

'A cottage in Suffolk is closer to Buckingham Palace, than are these people's huts to Sans Souci.'

'The huts of the Saxons were not closer to William the Conqueror's Tower of London,' Christophe pointed out. 'A ruler must not merely rule, or he is a tyrant. And a transient tyrant, at best. A ruler must be surrounded not only by the evidence of his power, but by the evidence of the permanence of his power. Sans Souci will stand forever. And my people know that, therefore my authority will stand forever. And more. Sans Souci is an achievement for them to seek, for them to dream of. It cost a fortune, money the nation could ill afford. But had I handed that money to these people, they would have squandered it in seconds. Now it is standing for all to see. For ambassadors to see, to admire, to understand that here is no casual, savage community of outlaws, but a nation of men, determined to last. They need to know that, Matt. We are surrounded by dangers. Not only from Pétion. He is nothing. But from Europe. From Bonaparte, now that he has returned. The first thing he will do, once he has again defeated the allied powers, is despatch an expeditionary force to Haiti.' Another sidelong glance. 'You do not agree with me?'

'I would say Bonaparte abandoned his ambitions in the Western Hemisphere when he sold Louisiana to the Americans.'

'I do not think so. And if not Bonaparte, then some other European ruler. Perhaps your own English, Matt. The Europeans cannot tolerate the existence of Haiti. We are a scar across their ordered, white, slave-supported world. Oh, they will come. In greater force than ever before, because they know how difficult we are to conquer. But when they come, Matt, they will find us impossible to conquer.' He rode out of the trees and into the brightness of the afternoon sunlight, pointed up the hills that stretched in front of them, reaching all the way to the mountains. 'La Ferrière.'

Dick followed the direction of the pointing finger, up and up, through valleys and above escarpments, rising ever higher into the tree-shrouded mountains, to discover what at first sight appeared to be the prow of a battleship, peering out from a rocky crag five hundred feet farther up. And even at this distance he could tell that the stone buttress rose some hundred feet above the rock at its base.

'Come,' Christophe said. 'It is still distant.'

And indeed it was. They camped for that night in a valley, and listened to the wind soughing in the trees. And sat around the camp fire, while Dick listened to the Emperor.

'We shall fight the invader every inch of the way, of course,' Christophe said. 'Ours is a difficult country to traverse, especially for a white man's army. Your English, as well as the French, discovered that during the war. Yet I will never make the mistake of Toussaint, and underestimate the white man's genius, any more than I would ever trust his word. It is possible, with their ability at warfare, their experience and their skill and their superior weapons, that they may defeat us, and capture our cities, and force us back. But this time, Matt, we shall not merely retreat to the forest, and dissipate our numbers along trackless paths. This time we shall retreat to La Ferrière. There is no force in the world can follow us up here, and assault that bastion. It is not just a fortress, Matt. It is the heart of a nation. It is a military city, within the jungle. It is at all times armed and provisioned to enable a thousand men to withstand a siege of a hundred days, and that, Matt, is far longer than any army could maintain a siege, with the guns of the citadel playing upon them, day and night, with my jungle fighters preying on their skirmishers, with my jungle itself bringing fever into their tents. La Ferrière is a dream I have long held. It surely is a dream that every military commander, every emperor, must always have held, the unassailable fortress, the ultimate retreat. But only I have managed to achieve the dream, here in the mountains of Haiti.' His eyes glowed in the firelight. 'You know of another?'

'I was wondering,' Dick said, 'how much *that* cost. Forgive me, sire, and remember that I spent seven years of my life in a bank.'

'You think too much in terms of money,' Christophe remarked. 'La Ferrière cost more than Sans Souci, to be sure. But if I consider Sans Souci, which is only for show, important, try to calculate how much more important I consider La Ferrière.'

'And suppose the European invaders never come?'

'They will come, eventually,' Christophe said. 'They came before. They will come again. It does not matter when. La Ferrière will stand forever. And who knows, as a last retreat for an emperor, it may not need to wait for invaders of my country.'

Saying which he wrapped himself in his blanket and went to sleep, for when on the march he lived like the soldier he had been for so long, slept on the ground, disdained the use of a tent. It was a wholly admirable characteristic, Dick thought, in a wholly admirable man. Well, down to two days ago, he would have said wholly admirable. And indeed, where did he discover the right to criticize? Christophe knew only extremes; that most of his people should starve that the other few might impress, would not seem out of the ordinary to him. And he knew only the dominant, aggressive will of the white man. That he should retain an everlasting fear of them, an everlasting determination never to be conquered again, was entirely natural.

Only the last, unguarded remark, that the Citadel of La Ferrière might possibly have been built as a last refuge, not of an heroic defender rallying the remnants of his people around him, but for a tyrant to retreat from the rightful wrath of his subjects, was less than wholly admirable.

Besides, whatever the motive, the mere fact of the creation of such a fortress in so impregnable a natural bastion, was wholly admirable. Except perhaps for the lives it must have cost.

Dick appreciated this more the following day, when they completed the climb. Christophe told him that every block of masonry, not to mention every cannon, every ball, every sack of corn, had been carried up these slopes on the back of a man; and often enough *they* had to dismount, in order to be sure of not being thrown by their mounts as the horses slipped and tripped on the bare rock.

And always the enormous buttress loomed above them, coming steadily closer, growing in size as it did so, while soon they could make out the mouths of the cannon protruding through the embrasures, and the heads of the men looking down. Certainly it was indisputable that had those men decided to refuse them entry, they could not have proceeded.

But even the buttress soon lost its importance, as they at last gained the plateau, and entered the huge wooden gateway, crossing the drawbridge over a rushing mountain stream. From the outside Dick had gaped at the walls, twelve feet thick at their bases, rising fifty and more feet above the rock into which they had been embedded, every embrasure boasting a cannon. Inside he could only gape again, at the sweep of the parade ground, at the stretch of barracks, at the presidential quarters, a small palace in itself, at the hoists for the munitions, the sheltered wells sunk deep in to the rock. Here was engineering on a scale Europe had never even sought to approach. It made him think of what he had read of the Pyramids.

But there was yet more gaping to be done. Without being told by his host, he dismounted, and ran for the steps leading to the great bastion, hurried to the embrasures, and looked out, at Haiti. The mountains rose in the east behind him, the highest peaks in the entire Caribbean, stretching upwards even beyond the tree-line, to become empty, jagged rock; it was possible to suppose they occasionally knew the kiss of snow. Immediately beneath him commenced the forest through which they had climbed, stretching far, far to the south and west, green, thick, a defensive bastion in itself. To the north he could make out Cap Haitien, and even, he supposed the magnificent scar on the green that was Sans Souci. And beyond even them, the beach, and the endless Atlantic rollers, blue topped with white, which pounded ceaselessly on the sand.

And then the ocean itself. In that direction there was nothing between Haiti and Europe. From here Christophe would gaze upon the sails of the invading fleet, long before his country was more than a heavy cloud on the horizon to them. Supposing the fleet ever came.

'You are impressed,' the Emperor said, at his shoulder. 'That pleases me.'

'I have been impressed, sire,' Dick protested, 'by everything I have seen on Haiti.'

'Even the poverty in which too many of my people live?' Perhaps there was humour in that deep voice, a twinkle in those black eyes. Dick could not be sure.

'Even that, sire. But this surpasses them all. Our historians claim that in all history there have been only seven true wonders created by man. They would have to add this as their eighth.'

'Well said,' Christophe agreed. 'It is my monument. As I said, it will stand forever. And with it, my name, my memory. But I have another wonder to show you yet, Matt. Or, I think, for this occasion, I shall call you Dick. Come.'

The guards stood to attention. Christophe led Dick down the stone steps to the courtyard, and across the yard to the Emperor's house. Here again guards presented arms and remained at attention, and white-gowned girls hastened forward with cups of sangaree, and to relieve them of their weapons. Christophe waved them aside. 'I would speak with the *mamaloi.*'

A girl bowed, and hurried before them, to a curtained doorway leading away from the main withdrawing room. A moment later she returned.

203

'The *mamaloi* will receive you, sire.'

Christophe nodded, raised the curtain, led Dick into a darkened corridor, at the end of which was another heavy drape. This too was removed, and they found themselves in a small room, dark save for the glow of a charcoal fire, and heavy with scent, of the burning wood, to be sure, but with other odours as well, some delicious, and others strangely repellent. The room appeared to be empty of furniture, save for a single high-backed chair against the far wall. And in the chair there sat a woman. In the gloom Dick could only blink, unable to make out more than long dark hair and equally dark gown, with the face no more than a pale glimmer between. A *pale* glimmer.

'The true source of my strength, Richard Hilton,' Christophe said. 'I would have you meet the *mamaloi* of La Ferrière. In English, she was called Gislane Nicholson.'

Dick became aware that Christophe was no longer beside him. He was alone, with the priestess. And she was content to wait for some seconds. Her face remained a blur. But perhaps she could see in the dark.

'Richard Hilton,' she said, at last. 'Light this.' Her English was perfect. Dick moved forward, held out his hand, took the candle; her fingers were cool to his touch.

He knelt in front of the fire, lit the wick.

'Tell me of your father,' she said.

He straightened. 'I have not seen him for five years.'

'But you have heard more recently than that.'

'He is ageing, and therefore weak.'

'And your mother? Is she as beautiful as ever?'

'As ever.' He held the candle above his head, moved closer.

'But she is also ageing. As am I.'

Her face came into the light. And here *was* beauty, he realized. The high forehead, the wideset green eyes, the perfect nose, the wide mouth, the pointed chin. Could she really be more than fifty?

'She also ages.'

She gazed at him for some seconds, then held out her hand. 'Give me the candle. And kneel, here beside me.' He obeyed, and she placed the candle in a holder beside her chair, then thrust her fingers into his hair, tilted his head back. 'You have suffered a

204

terrible injury.'

He flushed. 'I had forgot.'

'And I have reminded you. It is my duty, to remind men, of themselves. Do you know of me?'

'Yes.'

'All?'

'I think so.'

'Told by your mother, or your father?'

'My father does not speak of you.'

Again her gaze shrouded him. 'Does your mother still hate me?'

'I do not think so.'

'Perhaps age has brought her understanding,' the *mamaloi* said. Do you understand, Richard Hilton?'

'That you were taken from your home, and sold as a slave? I think so.'

'Do you? Do you know what it is like for a girl—I was no more—educated as an English lady, to be taken from her home, and made the plaything of every man who wished her? Can you understand that, Richard Hilton? Because of a minute drop of Negro blood in her veins? Can you understand such a world?'

'No,' Dick said. Presumably it was the answer she wanted.

Gislane Nicholson smiled. 'You will understand it. As I have done. When I was a slave, at first, I wished for my heart to cease beating, very often. But then I found myself, and I found my gods, and I wished only to live. So I live, and I am powerful. Your father, who loved me, and sought to right the wrong that had been done me, is as you say, ageing and frustrated. I have all that I could desire. Henry gives me all that I could desire, has always given me all that I desire. Do you admire him?'

Dick realized that only honesty would pay here. 'In many ways.'

'But not all?'

'I do not think all his values are true.'

'You could say that of any man. But he will fight for his values and, if need be, die for them. He wears a silver bullet around his neck, with which he will destroy himself should he ever be defeated. He has told me of you, Richard. *You* are running. Away from being a Hilton?'

'He understands that?'

She smiled. 'I do not think so. *I* understand that. But I do not admire it. No man can run away from what he is.'

205

'I find myself a planter,' he said. 'And yet I respect the intentions of my father. The two are irreconcilable.'

'Nothing is irreconcilable, to a man of courage.'

'Ah, but you see . . .'

'You are a coward? This has been proved?'

'Well, let us say I lack determination. My brother has determination. He is the true Hilton.'

'But you can say that. You must think about it, a great deal.'

'Yes.'

Gislane Nicholson stood up. Her blood-red gown rustled, as she moved round him. He wanted to turn, but dared not move his head. She stood immediately behind him. 'Do you know why you are here? Why Henry wishes you at his side?'

'I have thought about that, too. I wondered perhaps . . .'

'If he loved your mother?' Gislane knelt beside him. Her shoulder touched his. He inhaled her scent. 'No. But he admired her, as he admired your father. As he even admired Robert Hilton. He sought such courage, such determination, such arrogance, if you like, amongst his own people. Without success. His life is a hard one. Perhaps you have not realized that. Perhaps you have seen only Sans Souci. But he must rule, and he must lead, and he must fight. With only his own prowess to support him. His father was not a king, not even a wealthy planter. His father was a slave, and so were the fathers of all his generals, all his soldiers, all his people. Their right to power is as good as his, were they able to prove themselves men as good as he. And there are always some, who have no hope of proving themselves thus capable, who will seek to strike down their leader, to make room for lesser men.'

'I understand that,' Dick said, and at last turned his head. Her face was only inches away from him. He felt quite drunk with the nearness of her.

'It is on his mind, constantly, like a headache. It prevents him doing much that he would wish to do. I am his only source of strength. But I am naught but a woman. He seeks a man. And Fate brought him one.'

'Me? There is a joke.'

'A white man, dependent only upon Christophe himself. There is someone to trust. And when that white man is also a Hilton, he is the person Christophe seeks. Do you not think Fate brought you to Haiti?'

'Well, I suppose, in a manner of speaking.'

'I do not use the word Fate. My prayers, my powers, brought you to Haiti, Richard. I reached out across the sea, and I found you, and I summoned you hither.'

Her voice was so intense, her face was so close, her scent was so overpowering, he almost believed her. Voodoo. But he was a Christian.

He forced a smile. 'You chose the wrong brother, Miss Nicholson. I know nothing of weapons. I can scarce protect myself with my fists.'

If he had sought to break her spell, he had failed. 'You are a Hilton,' she said. 'Violence, power, is in your blood. Are you afraid of blood?'

He licked his lips. 'I . . . I have never spilt any.'

'Nor had yours spilt?' She seized his wrist with her left hand, so quickly and so tightly he could do nothing about it for a moment, and in that moment her right hand had come out from beneath the folds of her gown, and a sharp-bladed knife had been drawn across the back of his forearm. He stared at the welling blood in total horror, felt her breath on his face as she smiled. 'You will not die of it.' She lowered her head, pressed her lips to the cut, sucked it for a moment, raised her head again. 'Good blood.'

It continued to dribble slowly down his arm.

'I will cure the bleeding in a moment. But first, come.' She held his hand, stood up, and he stood with her. She led him across the room to the far corner, turned suddenly. 'Point, at the candle.'

His brain whirling, his arm came up. Blood fell to the floor with a gentle plop. Gislane held his shoulder, stared along his arm. 'Point,' she said. 'Do not wave at it. Point.' He felt an excruciating pain, and realized she had bitten his ear. 'Point.'

His hand settled.

'That is better. But not good. You are indeed nervous, Richard Hilton. Do I make you nervous?'

He stared at her, in the gloom of the corner, at the flash of her smiling teeth.

She held his wrists, brought up his hands. He discovered that her robe was opened. His hands were placed on her breasts, and she inhaled; her nipples seemed to be driving holes in his palms. She released his wrists, and put her arms round his neck, bringing herself even closer. She kissed his mouth, parted the lips, sought his tongue. A woman old enough to be his mother, several times over. The ground seemed to be heaving beneath his feet. His entire being was filled with the feel of her, the scent of her, with the desire for her.

But she was gone again, slipped quietly away, and he could not find her for a moment. Then she was back, at his side. 'Do you desire me, Richard Hilton?'

He turned, reaching for her, and found only the cold butt of a pistol pressed into his hand.

'Douse the candle,' she said. 'Douse the candle.'

He turned, without thinking, save of the woman, brought up his hand, and pointed at the flickering flame. The explosion took him by surprise, filled his nostrils with smoke and the acrid burn of powder, sent his senses reeling. Because the room was utterly dark.

11

The Soldier

'They are taking the lower road.' Henry Christophe prodded the map held for him by his aide; the board rested on his horse's neck. 'There. How many?'

His head came up, and the courier, still panting, heat sweat still rising from his mount, straightened to attention. 'Four thousand, sire. With cannon.'

'Cannon will do them no good here,' Christophe said. 'General Warner.'

It still took Dick a few moments to realize he was being addressed. 'Sire?'

'You will take your regiment down this path. Captain La Chat will show you. He knows the country. You will proceed at a walk. There is time. Soon the drums will begin. When you reach the bottom, you will see the track. The enemy may not yet be in sight. You will maintain your men there until the drumbeat quickens, then you will debouch on to the road and charge along it until you encounter the enemy. Understood?'

No, Dick wanted to shout. No, I do not understand. No, I am not able to carry out your command. I have never led men into battle before. I have never been under fire before. I shall be afraid. I shall likely run away.

But instead he thought of the *mamaloi*, of her scent, of her feel; his right arm pained where her knife had cut his flesh, although, miraculously, uncannily, she had sealed the cut itself with some unguent of hers. He had been bewitched. Oh, undoubtedly. But for this purpose. To fight with the Emperor.

'Understood, sire.'

Christophe continued to look at him. 'There will be no quarter, Matt,' he said, in English. 'It would do you no good to grant quarter, in any event, as your men would merely torture their prisoners to death. This is a war of survival. Understood?'

'Understood, sire.'

Christophe smiled. 'And by the same token, Matt, do not be taken. If you must die, die fighting.'

'Yes, sire.' Dick wheeled his horse, Captain La Chat at his side; the aide was a small black man, dressed in the blue uniform with the yellow facings of the Imperial Guard, like Dick, but wearing a tricorne instead of the cocked hat which marked a commander. They entered the trees, the four hundred dragoons jingling at their heels, commenced the descent, for the moment shaded from the sun, as it was early afternoon, siesta time, and the forest was hot and dry. For the moment. Yesterday it had rained, and perhaps later this afternoon it would rain again; in these mountains, coated with these forests, the clouds accumulated almost without warning. But for the moment it was dry. Only blood would flow, this afternoon.

His blood? Somehow he did not feel that. But blood, to be sure. So then, Richard Hilton, how far have you come, from a stool in Bridle's Bank in Lombard Street, from being the son of Matthew Hilton, Member of Parliament, pacifist, Abolitionist? What would Mama say? Supposing she ever learned of it; he had not been able to bring himself to write her, although Christophe would certainly have despatched the letter. But would Mama wish a monster as a son? And was Christophe not right? Was not Father the man who had travelled far, and away from his own heritage? He did not know, for certain. But this afternoon he would find out, for certain.

'There.' Captain La Chat pointed a gauntleted finger. The trees were thinning, and the road was in front of them, and slightly beneath them. A dusty road, empty of people. And now he could hear the drums, murmuring across the hills, booming in the valleys. They were rada drums, used for Voodoo ceremonies.. They touched a chord in his memory, for he had heard them as a child, as he had heard them often, here in Haiti. They were compelling, compulsive, frightening to a stranger. They spoke of blood, and sex, and lust, and possession. But they could not frighten those who followed Henry Christophe, because they belonged to him.

There was no sound above the drums save for the occasional

whinny of a horse, the occasional stamped hoof, the occasional jangle of harness. The dragoons waited. Did they have confidence in their new general? He dared not look round at them, in case someone might remark on the sweat which clouded his cheeks, the paleness of the cheeks themselves. La Chat was also sweating. But La Chat was merely hot.

The drumbeat quickened. Dick drew his sword, and felt his heart begin to pound. What would happen? What would he feel like, when the first bullet tore its way into his body? What would be his last thoughts, as he plunged from his saddle to the ground, and saw the hooves of his own dragoons, looming about his head?

He pointed his sword at the road, and urged his horse forward. He emerged from the tree screen, and the sunlight made him blink. He listened to the enormous jangle from behind him as his men also debouched into the open. No other sound. They followed him, and would make a noise when the time came.

The noise came from in front of him. A ripple of musketry, a chorus of shouts and screams. He pointed his sword again, kicked his horse again. He rose in his stirrups, to wave his sword round his head. 'Charge,' he screamed. 'Charge.'

The drumbeat was very fast, and was merged in the thunder of the horses' hooves, in the immense scream which rose from four hundred throats. He swept round the bend in the road, with the trees thick to his right, saw the enemy column, arrested by the musketry, hastily forming their ranks to face back and to either side, while the wagons were brought round to form a defensive line, and the cannon was unlimbered. They were not four hundred yards away. His horse's hooves kicked dust, his chest pounded, his sweat clouded his eyes. He could see only the blade of his sword, pointing, and the wagons. And a man, seeing the approaching cavalry, himself pointing and screaming orders, bringing men round to face this new enemy, lining them up, muskets levelled.

Dick sank lower over his horse's head, felt a hot wind embracing him, saw the black powder smoke rising into the air, realized to his surprise that he was unhurt. That indeed the men had scarce taken aim, so frightened they were, and they were already backing away, running for the shelter of the wagons.

The officer stood his ground. He was a brave man, a light-skinned mulatto. He levelled his right hand, and it held a pistol. At this range he could not miss, Dick thought, for he was already upon him. Already upon him. His sword point struck the man in the centre of his green jacket, and blood spurted over the yellow braid, shot into the air and landed on Dick's white gauntlet. The pistol was never fired. It too soared into the air, to fall to the ground. The scream of the charging men rose around him like a paean, and he realized that his own voice was the loudest.

He was in the midst of the running soldiers, cutting and slashing, sending men scattering in every direction. He rode between the wagons, and someone fired a musket at him. But he heard the report, and knew he was not hit, and a moment later the wagon itself crashed onto its side, hurled over by the impact of the galloping cavalry. Men crawled out, weapons discarded, hands raised high in the air. 'Mercy,' they shouted. 'Mercy.'

Dick pulled his panting horse to a halt, stared at the men. At two in particular. Mulattoes? Impossible, with that sun-pink-ened white skin, that fair hair.

As they saw that he was no Negro. One of them ran forward, and the dragoons let him come, gazing at their general for orders.

'Mercy,' shouted the Frenchman. 'As you are a white man, monsieur, mercy.'

Dick glanced at La Chat, who had reined next to him, clouded in sweat and blood. Exhilaration still pumped through his veins. Blood lust still clouded his mind. He had killed a man. No doubt he could have killed several men. They were his enemies, and had he not succeeded, they would have killed him. This was, as Christophe had said, a war for survival.

'Cut them down,' he said.

'It is less a town than a village.' Henry Christophe stood in the midst of his officers, the large-scale map at his feet. His sword was drawn, the point resting on the coloured parchment, already dotted with little holes where he had pressed. In the flickering torchlight he looked a demoniac figure. But then, Dick wondered, were they not all demoniac figures, commanding a demoniac army?

'President Pétion refers to it as a frontier post,' Christophe continued. 'He dreams of a frontier.' The sword point cut a line across the map. 'We do not recognize frontiers, eh, gentlemen?'

The officers growled their agreement.

'So we will eradicate this frontier of his. Now, the palisade is

212

composed of wooden stakes. We will place our battery here . . .' The sword dug into the map. 'This is before the main gate. Two salvoes, and it will be open. Beyond the main gate there is another defence, to enable them to throw back our assault, and then make good the damage. This is what they did last year. But this time we shall take their frontier post, gentlemen. How?'

No one replied; his habit of asking rhetorical questions was understood.

'I will command the foot,' Christophe said. 'And when the gate falls, I will lead them, not in an assault on the breach, but in an assault here . . .' The sword dug once more into the paper. 'This is as far away from the gate as is possible. They will suppose at the first it is a feint. Should they continue to treat it as a feint, and we gain a lodgement inside the wall, the cavalry will charge after we have entered. Should they begin to realize that it is not a feint, and move their main force against us, then the cavalry will charge as soon as the gate is undefended. Because after all we shall be a feint, but a feint delivered with the major portion of the army. Understood?'

The generals nodded agreement, and looked at Dick.

'What are your plans, General Warner?' Christophe said.

Dick licked his lips. 'I will hold my men in readiness behind the battery, sire. Once the gates are down, I will prepare to charge the breach. But I will not charge until you have delivered your assault. Should the enemy remain facing me in force, I will hold my men until you appear behind him. Should the enemy remove men from in front of me to stop you, I will charge as soon as his defences are sufficiently thinned.'

'That is good, General Warner,' Christophe said. 'Gentlemen, to your posts.'

But he waited, to clap Dick on the shoulder. 'Take care, Matt. Take care. A man who exposes himself as you do, courts death. Not even Murat led a cavalry charge as recklessly as you. But then, perhaps not even Murat had your talent, your courage. Take care.'

He mounted his waiting horse, and Dick watched him go. There had been more than affection in the farewell, although he thought that Christophe did feel affection for him. But there was also the concern of a commanding officer for his most successful subordinate.

213

So then, did he court death? He walked to his mount, and his attendant held his stirrup. La Chat, now colonel, was already in the saddle, the brigade of horse, eleven hundred men, were patiently waiting. They would wait forever, or they would ride forever, behind the white man. Over the past two years he had led them in a dozen madcap charges, through the greatest hail of fire the enemy could put up, over broken ground and through rushing streams, always in the front, always with his sword pointing forward, always with his heart pumping exhilaration through his arteries, always with the blood lust clouding his brain. Always the first to strike his enemy dead.

The fact was, he did not care whether he lived or died. He was aware of being happy. But what a terrible confession to make, that he was a commanding general in a savage army, fighting in the most brutal of wars, living only for death and destruction . . . and he was happy. He had left the roadway, that first day, and vomited in a bush. Not at the overwhelming excitement. Not even at the blood which had stained his gauntlets, smothered his arms, splashed against his chest. But at the look of pitiful understanding which had crossed the faces of the two Frenchmen, when they had realized that they were about to die, despite the fact of their captor being a European.

But he had not vomited since.

It was nearly dawn. The breeze was chill, and in the distance, perhaps in the town they would attack, a cock crowed and a dog barked.

He drew his sword. It made a hard, blood-tingling rasp in his scabbard. And behind him there came eleven hundred equally blood-tingling rasps. Where was the Richard Hilton who had stammered in Colonel Taggart's parlour? Where was the Richard Hilton who had been unable to face Captain Lanken? Where was the Richard Hilton who had been afraid of Ellen Taggart and her mother, who had lain in the corridor of the Park Hotel in Kingston, while a bully stood above him?

Had that Richard Hilton ever existed? Or had he been no more than a dream?

Or was *this* Richard Hilton a dream? Induced by the incantations of a Voodoo priestess? Because he still saw the *mamaloi* before him as he charged, inhaled her as he gasped for breath, knew the softness of her breast, the pulse of her belly, as he gripped his sword. Gislane Nicholson was sixty years old. She could not be less. But her snake god, her Damballah, kept her as she wished to be.

He had nearly thought the word, young.

The drums rolled across the forest, and with them, the sudden bark of the cannon, which had been placed in position some hours earlier, while it had yet been light. But it was again light. The Caribbean dawn, sudden and stark, was bathing the scene. They could look at the town, or the village, the frontier post, as Christophe would have it, at the rounded wood of the palisades, at the glimmer beyond, the candles glowing in the houses, the fires burning for the cannon which would reply, in due course. And those inside the palisades, the mulattoes and their French allies, could look out, at the flash of the guns, at the myriad forces slowly surrounding them. He wondered what it must feel like to know that one is being surrounded, that there is nothing to be done, but to stand and fight, and conquer or die. He had never been in that position. In all his dozen charges he had done the conquering. So then, his experience was not yet complete, his courage not yet proved to the hilt.

His demoniac courage.

He stood his horse on a mound, above the cannon, and watched them flash, and heard the roar as the balls struck into the palisade, and listened to the crackle of the timbers and to the drumbeat, rolling out of the forest.

The gates were down, the timbers scattered. Beyond, in the first sunlight, and the firelight now, as well, for several buildings were already burning, he saw the enemy battery, four field cannon of light calibre, drawn up to face the anticipated gap. Of light calibre, but sufficient to tear gaps in his brigade, to demolish a man. Even a devil from hell.

His time was not yet. He waited, and listened to the sudden cacophony from away on the right. He levelled his telescope, stared into the distance. Behind the cannon, there was drawn up a regiment of men. The main defences. They were there, and they were staying there. Or were they?

'Look, General,' La Chat said, pointing.

A company was wheeling away from the regiment, then another. From the far side of the village there came a series of explosions, a sudden brightening of the flame light, as

Christophe's soldiers fired the houses immediately within the wall. The houses *within* the wall.

The men in front of him, those that remained, were wavering. Dick rose in his stirrups, his sword swinging round his head. 'Aieeeeee,' he screamed. 'Charge.'

The morning filled with looming sound as eleven hundred horses surged into the trot, then the canter, then the gallop. There would be a crush in the gate mouth. But not for him. He drove his spurs in, and his mount rose, over the batteries, leaving the frightened gunners gaping up at him. The cannon in front of him spoke, once, but was he not protected, as he was inspired, as his arm was guided, by the power of the *mamaloi*? And unharmed, he was in the gateway, his sword thrust forward, to take the first gunner, who ran at him armed with no more than a ramrod, in the chest. Blood flew, spurted into his face. But he had come to anticipate the blood, spurting in his face. Battle, victory, would not be complete without it. He threw back his head, gave another scream of triumphant joy, and sliced into the shoulder of the next man who would oppose him, while behind him his dragoons uttered shrill cries as they spread across the square, crashed through the ranks of men opposed to them.

There was a standard. How incredibly European. Christophe's men did not fight beneath a standard. They wished only the beat of the drums, the sight of the huge figure of the Emperor. But in Pétion's army the standard must mark the position of the commanding general, especially as it flew in front of a house, and the house was guarded by a company of men.

'To me,' he bawled, reining his horse and rising in the stirrups to wave his sword. Someone fired a musket at him; he could feel the hot air of the ball almost slapping his face. But the man was immediately cut down by his dragoons as they reformed their ranks. 'That flag,' he shouted, and urged his own horse forward.

The protecting guardsmen fired, but it was a hasty, ill-aimed volley. Their morale had been shattered by the swift destruction of the gate and the artillery, by the rising roar of victory which rose from the other side of the town, and came closer all the while. Dick leapt from his saddle at the foot of the steps, La Chat at his side. A man presented a musket to which was attached a bayonet, and Dick swept it aside with a single sweep of his sword, then brought the weapon back to drive deep into the man's body. So

216

hardened was his right arm by now he scarce felt the jar; as the guardsman lurched against the wall, he raised his foot, placed it in the expiring belly, and with a tug withdrew his weapon.

The door had already been hurled open, and the dragoons were swarming in, checked for a moment by a volley which had three of them tumbling to the floor. Dick leapt into their midst, coughing as he entered the smoke-filled interior room, where the noises of the explosion were still reverberating, mingling with the shouts of the men, and the screams of the women.

Of the women? He waved his left hand, dissipating some of the powder smoke, peered at a large room, on the far side of which was a staircase. Before the stairs the remnants of the guard, not more than a score of men, were gathered; on the stairs themselves was a French officer, hatless, his hair scattered and his face stained with powder, but still holding his drawn sword. And on the gallery at the top of the stairs were gathered several women, mostly black or mulattoes, but one, now rising to her feet to look down at the invaders, very definitely white.

'Hold,' Dick shouted, without thinking. And then did think. He was not, then, a savage, after all. His blood lust was still subjected to his instincts. Or was there more?

His men, accustomed to obeying his every command, had checked their weapons, stood instead glowering at their enemies, who, equally bemused, slowly lowered their own swords and muskets, unable to believe that they might actually be receiving a chance at life.

'General?' La Chat inquired.

But Dick was still gazing at the balustrade, as the powder smoke continued to drift away and he could see more clearly. The woman had yellow hair, streaked with red; or was it red hair, streaked with yellow? In the gloom of the morning, the dark faces and dark coats which surrounded her, her hair blazed like a torch. She stared at him, as did everyone else in the room. There were powder stains on her cheeks and forehead, but the dark marks if anything enhanced the whiteness of her complexion. There was hair clustering on her forehead, as it scattered on her shoulders and down her back, long and straight. Her eyes were enormous; he could not see their colour. Her nose was short, and a trifle upturned, her mouth small, and presently open as she gasped for breath. Her chin was smoothly rounded. He thought he could not describe her as beautiful; her face was actually a mass of flaws. But taken together the flaws were deliciously attractive.

Her body was shrouded in a white undressing robe, but he could tell it was at once short and slender; a mere wisp of femininity.

My God, he thought. Her body. And these men wait on my command.

'Throw down your arms,' he said, and was surprised at the harshness of his own voice.

The mulatto guardsmen hesitated, glancing from one to the other, and thence over their shoulders at their general. The white man was frowning.

'You offer us quarter?'

'Throw them down,' Dick said again.

The first guardsman dropped his musket with a clatter. The rest followed his example. The general hesitated for a moment longer, then threw his sword down the stairs.

'We are fortunate,' he said. 'And grateful, monsieur.'

'A *coup de main*, Matt,' Christophe said from the doorway. 'Brilliantly executed.'

Dick turned, his knees suddenly weak. How long had he been there? Christophe still wore his hat, but there was a rent in his jacket, and blood on the hilt of his sword.

'The town is ours.' He strode into the room, gazed at the guardsmen, who had huddled together in mutual fear. 'Take them out and hang them.'

The guardsmen stared at him in horror.

'But . . .' Dick said.

'We surrendered on a promise of quarter,' said the white officer.

'You surrendered when commanded to do so,' Christophe said. 'That is at discretion. Take them out.' He was frowning at the white man. 'D'Estaing, as I live and breathe.'

The Frenchman had been looking at his discarded sword. But it was being picked up by one of Dick's dragoons. Now his head jerked.

Christophe's right hand was extended, pointing at him. 'D'Estaing,' he said again.

'Sire,' Dick began.'

228

'That man once had me flogged,' Christophe said.

'He . . . he would make a valuable hostage,' Dick suggested.

'Not him. I will have *him* flogged. Take him outside, La Chat. Strip him and tie him to a triangle. Flog him. Flog him until his bones are laid bare. But slowly, La Chat. One blow every ten seconds. I do not wish him to die quickly.'

D'Estaing licked his lips. His face was pale. But he was a brave man. He looked at Dick. 'I had thought I was surrendering to a man,' he said. 'Not an animal.'

Hands seized his shoulders, and were arrested by a cry from above. 'No. No, you cannot.' The young woman half fell down the stairs. Now she was closer, her resemblance to the Frenchman was easy to see.

'And her mother watched,' Christophe said.

'You cannot be sure,' Dick gasped.

'I remember the hair.'

'You'll not touch her,' d'Estaing said. It was half a command and half a supplication.

'She'll die first,' Christophe said. 'You may watch her being flogged. Strip her, La Chat, and tie her to the triangles. The General will enjoy this. The other women may be given to your men.'

'You are a creature from hell,' d'Estaing said in a low voice.

The girl was staring at Christophe, her mouth slowly sagging open as she understood the enormity of what was about to happen to her.

Christophe smiled at them. 'You placed me in that hell, monsieur. Now remember, La Chat. Slowly. She should be able to take a hundred strokes.'

'No,' Dick said. And once again his voice was harsh.

Christophe turned his head, frowning.

'They surrendered at discretion, as you say, sire; my discretion.'

'You know my orders, Matt. You should have let them be killed, in battle.'

'They are my prisoners, sire.' Involuntarily, the hand holding his sword twitched.

As Christophe saw. His frown deepened, and then cleared in another smile. 'Ah. The girl. Very well, Matt. She is yours.'

'Both,' Dick insisted.

Christophe shook his head. 'You have dared to oppose me in

219

public, Matt,' he said in English. 'I can do no less than have you shot, should you continue. But you are known as my closest friend, and you are a white man, who would understandably wish a white woman as his slave. I give her to you. The man dies. Take your choice. The girl, or they both are flogged to death.'

There was no arguing with the decision in his tone. Dick licked his lips, glanced at the pair, saw the concentration on their faces. They understood English.

'Take her, monsieur. For God's sake,' d'Estaing begged.

'No,' the girl muttered. 'No.' She clung to her father's arm, stared at Dick.

'Well?' Christophe demanded.

'I will take the girl,' Dick said.

Christophe smiled, slapped him on the shoulder. And was then suddenly serious again. 'But you will do it properly. You have this day revealed a weakness I hoped to have suppressed forever. You . . .' He pointed at d'Estaing. 'Is your daughter a virgin?'

'Of course, Christophe. She is my daughter.'

'Of course,' Christophe mimicked. 'Well, then, Matt. I give her to you. Now. Take her into one of those rooms up there. You will not be disturbed for an hour. Then I will have her examined. Should you have failed to penetrate her, I will give her to my men, for an hour, and then she will be flogged to death. La Chat, take that man outside.'

'No,' the girl whispered. 'No,' she cried. 'No,' she shrieked. Her hands were wrenched from her father's arm, and d'Estaing was marched down the stairs.

'Wait,' Dick said.

La Chat halted, and his men also.

'Do you still wish me to take her?'

D'Estaing looked at him, for some seconds. 'You are a monster,' he said. 'In face and in deed. But your skin is white. Will you throw her aside, like a monster? Or will you care for her, like a white man?'

'I will care for her,' Dick said. 'I swear it.'

'Then take her,' d'Estaing said. 'You have my blessing.'

Dick thrust his sword into its sheath, stepped round the dragoons and their captive. The girl scrambled to her feet.

'No,' she shouted, and turned, to run up the stairs.

220

'Stop her,' Dick shouted at the mulatto women, still gathered on the gallery.

These hesitated in turn, and the girl burst through them with the force of her charge. Yet the shock sent her staggering, red-gold hair flying as she stumbled to her knees, grasped the balustrade, and regained her feet.

Christophe gave a bellow of laughter. 'One hour, Dick,' he shouted. 'One hour. You will need all of it.'

Dick had himself pushed through the women, saw the girl entering a chamber farther along the corridor. Before he could reach it, the door had slammed shut, the lock had turned. But the timbers were old. He struck it with his shoulder, and the whole wall seemed to creak. He withdrew against the balustrade, hurled himself forward again. The lock burst with a crack, the tongue tearing its socket right out of the wood, and he fell into the room.

The girl was at the window. She had picked up a chair, and was hammering at the bars, which only caused the chair itself to shatter. At the sound of his entry, she turned, back against the wall, bodice of the undressing robe heaving as she panted. The colour was slowly fading from her face, and she was endeavouring to control her breathing, closing her mouth and then having to open it again to allow the air to escape. With her left hand she pulled hair from her face, an instinctively feminine and yet utterly entrancing gesture. But she was an utterly entrancing sight. He had never in his life looked at any woman, even Ellen at their earliest acquaintance, without some reservations. Until now.

Slowly she slid down the wall, until she was kneeling, and resting on her haunches at the same time. 'Please,' she said, in French. 'As you are a man, monsieur, kill me, I beg of you.'

He pushed the shattered door to behind him. It would be easy to do, to draw his sword and run through that slender body. Nor would Christophe give him more than a slight reproof. And he would be able to look himself in the mirror once again.

But he wanted her. God, how he wanted her. And it was over two years since he had dared look in a mirror, in any event.

'I came to save your life, not take it,' he said.

'Save it?' she demanded. 'Is it worth saving, monsieur? Will it be worth saving, when you are done with it?' Her head half turned at the sound which seeped through the window, the first crack of a whip. 'Oh, God,' she whispered. 'Oh, God.' Her head sank to her breast, her hair trailed on either side of her cheeks.

He stood above her. Do this, and you are damned forever, he thought. But are you not already damned forever? Did this crime count, with executing the two French soldiers, in that first battle? With slaughtering how many men since? With commanding the slaughter of how many thousands more? Did this girl's body count, beside that?

Afterwards perhaps. There was a compromise. Afterwards he might be able to kill them both, send her to heaven and himself to that hell he so richly deserved. But only afterwards.

He stooped, held her shoulders. She remained limp, and he had to drive his fingers into her armpits to raise her to her feet. Her head flopped back, and she stared at him. She could hear the sound of the whip, slowly, regularly, destroying her father. He could hear nothing save his own panting, save the blood drumming in his ears.

He half carried, half dragged her across the room, to the bed. When he released her she fell, on her back, still staring at him, but making no effort to resist. Not even taking her gaze from his face or closing her eyes. But what she thought, what she felt, what she hoped or what she feared, meant nothing now. He was as much beyond his own control as when he had been falling through space, the last memory of Richard Hilton, of Hilltop in Jamaica, before he became Matthew Warner, of La Ferrière, in Haiti.

He put his fingers into the neck of her robe, closed his fist, tore it down. The material offered no opposition to the strength in that right arm, the force in that shoulder, the power in that mind. Pink-white flesh sprang at him; she was again panting. Her breasts were large, and soft; he knew that before touching them. She was a woman of fascinating contrasts, for the huge breasts gave way to the narrowest of waists and slender hips; yet her pubic hair was thick and bushed at him, dominating the thin legs below. But these glories were discovered with nothing more than a glance. He was preoccupied, his sword belt clattering to the floor, his body crashing onto hers, sending breath once again gasping from her opened mouth.

He could not make himself kiss her, lay instead with his mouth against her ear, his breath inhaling wisps of red-gold hair. Now, he thought. Now. As some men have no more fields to conquer, you have no more crimes to commit. Now the devil can die.

'Now,' a voice said, whispering into his ear. 'Now, monsieur, as you are sated, kill me.' The whisper became a wail. 'Kill me.'

He rolled his weight away from her, lay on his side, gazing at her. He waited, for the guilt, for the horror of what he had done, to overwhelm him. Instead he merely wanted to touch her again, to feel the strands of that splendid hair, to stroke the contour of that face, to caress the softness of those breasts, to search the dampness of that groin.

She sat up. There was so much noise from beyond the window now, so much screaming and yelling, so many explosions, so many clatters of falling timbers, it was impossible to tell any one sound, such as the crack of a whip. The entire village might have been on fire, so much smoke swept past the window. Yet he was not afraid of burning. He was not interested in the possibility of burning. His attention was taken by the woman, by the silky splendour of her movements. Even by the tears on her face. But there were few tears.

He held her wrist, attempted to pull her back to him. But this time she exerted her strength to resist him, and he would not use force.

'I wanted you,' he said. 'I want you now. I shall want you forever. I do not apologize for what I have done. I wish only to make you understand my want. And perhaps feel it as well.'

Her head started to turn, and then looked away again. 'You?' She asked. 'Want *you*?'

'Because I fight for Christophe? Because your father was executed? In Christophe's judgement he was a criminal.'

'Then am I not also a criminal?' She still spoke softly, tugged at her wrist, gently.

'Who has been reprieved. Tell me your name.'

She hesitated, gave another gentle tug. 'Cartarette,' she said at last.

'Cartarette. Cartarette d'Estaing.' It sounded marvellous. 'Yours is a famous name.'

'You are thinking of papa's cousin, monsieur. A distant cousin. Papa was no more than a planter. Who became a soldier of fortune. Who became a criminal. As you say. Will you let me go, monsieur.'

He released her wrist, and she stood up. He thought he could lie here forever, and watch her move. He watched her walk across the

223

room, her back half to him; her breasts quivered and her thighs rolled, as she walked. Her hair reached past her shoulder blades. How had he lived, for more than thirty years, without knowing this?

She reached his discarded clothes, and he realized what she intended. He sat up, only a vague alarm as yet plucking at his mind.

Cartarette d'Estaing drew his sword, with a single long sweep, and turned to face him.

'I will make you happy,' he said. 'I swear it.' Still he was not afraid. It was too long since he had known fear; he had forgotten the emotion. Up to a few minutes ago it had been too long since he had cared whether he lived or died. Now he had suddenly come to care again. He did not want her to end this morning.

'You?' she asked. 'Make me happy? You fight for Christophe. A white man, fighting for a black. That makes you a crawling thing, from the gutter. You fight for a man, who would destroy my father. That makes you a murderer. You have assaulted me, destroyed my value as a woman. That makes you a scoundrel.' The blade was up, the point moving slowly through the air, and now she was advancing. And she had held a sword before. Perhaps never in anger. But her grip was firm, and her tears had dried. 'But most of all, monsieur,' she said, 'you are a hideous thing, a monster. You deserve to die, monsieur. You should be happy, dying.' She lunged, and he rolled to one side, and the girl gave a hiss of annoyance and turned, to face the door as it swung back on its shattered hinges.

'Mutiny?' Christophe inquired, smiling at her.

'You as well,' she panted, and lunged once more. But Christophe's blade was also drawn, and with a single sweep it sent the weapon flying from the girl's fingers. She stood still, gazing after it for a moment, and then the tears did begin, rolling slowly down her cheeks, while her shoulders drooped. Dick realized she had sought only her own death.

'I presume you have been successful,' Christophe said. 'We had best evacuate this place. It burns, and smells. You are to be congratulated, Matt. Your charge, as ever, carried the day.'

Dick got up. 'I had expected your anger.'

'You deserve my anger, certainly. But then again, no. A man is what he is. You are my faithful support, my faithful friend, I

224

hope. With a London upbringing you will never be entirely ruthless, alas. I must use your talents where they are most valuable. As of this moment you are relieved of your command.'

Dick nodded. He had expected worse.

'Your new post will be general officer in command of the Citadel of La Ferrière, Matt,' Christophe said. 'You will select an escort of fifty men and leave immediately. La Ferrière is your responsibility, as of now, Matt. It must be prepared at all times, to receive me, to stand a siege. A thousand men must be able to live there, and fight there, in perfect security. You will see to it.'

'I will see to it, sire.'

Christophe turned, smiled at the girl. 'And in La Ferrière, you will have time to teach your little prisoner to love you. Always providing she does not murder you first. You will see to that also.'

'I will see to it, sire.'

Cartarette raised her head. 'I would like to say goodbye to my father.'

'Then I suggest you get dressed, mademoiselle,' Christophe said, and left the room.

Dick got up, picked up his sword, restored it to his scabbard. 'You will like La Ferrière,' he said. 'It is the best place in all Haiti.'

She glanced at him, stooped, picked up her torn robe. 'Yes, monster,' she said, with sudden composure. 'I have clothes, in another room. Will monster allow me to dress?'

12

The Emperor

He wondered he did not beat her. Surely to beat Cartarette d'Estaing, to tie her up and whip her until she begged for mercy, would be a total pleasure. He could still remember the tumultuous emotions which had chased each other through his mind the day Judith Gale had been whipped by her mother. But that had been in a different world, and the emotions had belonged to a different man. Besides, to whip Cartarette would be to give her another weapon to twist in his side.

He stood on the great redoubt, gazed across the morning at the forest. It waited, silent. But not empty. He knew that now. Yet from the battlements of La Ferrière, with the sea breeze stirring his hair, it might as well have been empty.

He had feared, in the beginning, that she would seize the first opportunity to commit suicide. He had commanded one of his men to ride ever at her elbow, and at night, when they had lain together under the same blanket, he had tied her right wrist to his left, to prevent her getting up without waking him. Now he knew that he had a great deal to learn about women. No doubt she had considered suicide. But if so she had very rapidly discarded it. Dead, she was nothing. Living, she was a constant dagger in his side, taunting him, hating him with every muscle in her body, with every thought which passed through her mind. He stood for Christophe, for Christophe's men, perhaps for every black man in the world, and through him she could satisfy her hatred of every black man in the world.

So, to whip her, to flog her to death, would only be to give her additional reason to hate.

Besides, it was what she clearly wanted, so it would be a victory, for her. Suicide was a form of surrender, to the forces which overwhelmed her. But to drive him to such a state of desperation where he would strike her, or murder her, would be a victory, because he would be but compounding his crime.

So why did he not? What more could he seek from her? He had explored every pore of her body, kissed every strand of hair. He had sated, on that utterly white delight, every dream he had ever had of woman, every desire he had ever experienced. For was she not his slave? Oh, indeed, she was his slave, and no man could ask for a more servile bedmate. She lay absolutely still, whenever he would mount her. She said not a word, until he was done, then she would quietly and coolly remove herself from beneath him, and standing by the bed, ask, 'Shall I fetch the monster's wine?'

She served him at table, allowing her hair to brush his cheek as she placed each plate in front of him. 'Pork today, monster. Sweet-tasting, succulent pork, such as any white nigger would appreciate.'

So, did she despair, did she weep, in what privacy she was allowed? As now, when he was on a tour of inspection, and she was left alone in their quarters? He invariably hurried back, still dominated by the lurking terror that one morning he would find her hanging from the rafters, as he still always left one of his servants with her, to prevent such a catastrophe. And did he still hurry back just to hear the lash of her tongue? Because she could only tongue-lash him when she could see him, which meant that he could also see her, could lean back and look at every magnificent movement, every flutter of that glorious hair, every twist of that exquisite mouth.

So perhaps she also felt frustrated, at his continuing love.

'And will the fortress stand forever?'

He turned, sharply, was enveloped in the gust of scent from the blood-red robe.

'You'll excuse me,' he said.

'No,' Gislane said. 'I will not excuse you, General Warner. Richard Hilton. Why do you avoid me?'

'I have my duty. The Emperor entrusted this fortress to my care. I would not fail him.'

'Nor will you, while you retain your strength, Dick. But how will your strength stand up to such continual torment?'

'You are a creature of blood, priestess. You would no doubt have me cut her throat.'

'Would that not be a waste? You act as if you love the girl.'

'What can you know of . . . of love?'

Gislane smiled. 'You were going to say, of white love? Until I was eighteen I thought I was white, Dick. And I loved. I loved your father. I was prepared to give up all for him. And I stayed in love with him, dreaming of him, for a long time after I was returned to the West Indies. It was only when I understood that he would never come for me, that I sought other loves.'

'And you can forgive my family. Well, then, Gislane, you have strength, power, beyond ordinary understanding. Cartarette blames me for the death of her father as much as anything else.'

'For a thoughtful man, you do not think enough. Your woman knows you did not kill her father. She knows that you tried to save him, and certainly that you saved her.'

'But . . .'

'But this is the fact that is unacceptable to her. She knows she should have died, with her father. She reproaches herself, for having lived, for having lacked the courage to take her own life. Yet a human being cannot live, hating himself, or herself. So she takes out her hate on you. But it is herself that she is hating.'

'Aye, well, no doubt you are right,' Dick said. 'But whatever her reasoning, she practises her hate continuously.'

'And you keep assisting her.'

'Eh?'

'By practising rape upon her, daily.'

'I love her. I cannot see her but I wish to take her in my arms.'

'And you see no reason to practise restraint. You see no reason to treat her as a woman, perhaps, instead of a slave.'

Dick frowned at her. 'She will merely insult me more.'

'I doubt that, Dick. I doubt that. Listen to me. I can give you her love.'

'By witchcraft?'

'As I gave you your strength, your power, your ability, with sword and pistol? Was that witchcraft, Dick? Or was that just a cutting away of fear and inhibition, a removal of dead wood, to expose the strength I knew lay beneath? I can strip this girl of her hate for you, and replace it with love. But you will have to help me.'

'Of course I would help you, could I believe it possible.'

'Because of the crimes you have practised on her it will take a long time.'

'I have nothing but time,' Dick pointed out.

'And when it is done,' Gislane said, 'it is done. You must understand that, Dick. When she loves you, she will love you, now and always. And if I do this thing for you, you must swear to me that you will love her, now and always. I do not speak of physical love. I know the frailty of the flesh. I speak of your care for her, of your respect for her, of your admiration for her, of your determination to place her before all else. You must swear that to me.'

'Before life itself.'

'Before life itself,' Gislane said. 'Be sure that Cartarette will make herself the same promise.'

La Chat opened the leather satchel. 'His Majesty is presently in Sans Souci, and sends you this, General.'

The envelope was sealed. Dick tore the edge, took out the single sheet of paper; writing was an accomplishment Christophe had learned late in life, and he did not waste words.

'I long to be with you, Matt. My spirit is weary. Pétion ails, it is said. His armies retreat. But my people murmur. A man fired a musket at me, but a week gone. He was hanged. They do not worship me, any more, Matt. I long to be with you.'

There was no signature. Dick folded the paper, placed it in his pocket. 'You saw him?'

'To receive that message, General.'

'And he is well?'

La Chat hesitated. 'Perhaps he has been too long at war, General.'

'Aye. Well, rest yourself, La Chat.' He went into his house, sheltering beneath the east battlements, and the girls who waited on him bowed their greeting. Cartarette d'Estaing stood in the inner doorway.

'The monster will have his luncheon,' she said. But her voice lacked the brittleness of a year ago, even three months ago. She was a sorely puzzled young woman. Perhaps she had forgotten what it was like to have her own bed, her own chamber, to be allowed the pleasures of solitude. But if she was puzzled, and disturbed, would she not hate him more? Only Gislane knew the answer to that.

'Yes,' he said. 'You may join me, today, Cartarette.'

'I, monster?'

He had reached her by now, and she stepped aside to allow him in. He could smell her, he could almost touch her, without moving his arm. Had she the slightest inkling of what it had cost him, in determined self-discipline, not to touch her for three months?

'You, Cartarette.' He handed his hat to one girl, his sword to another, his gloves to a third, sat at the table. A fourth girl hastily poured him wine, a fifth held the chair for Cartarette, and she lowered herself, slowly, uncertainly. 'And you will take a glass of wine.' Because Gislane had ordered it. Only Gislane could know.

She drank, again hesitantly. And then ate, as they were served. A special meal, today, of oysters, brought up from the coast, packed in ice. At Gislane's command. And of mixed fruits, soursop and golden apples and sappodillas, at the end. What Gislane desired, she simply commanded. As what General Warner commanded, he received. Was he not the closest associate, the right hand man, of the Emperor himself.

'Finish your wine,' he said.

'Whatever the white nigger commands, his slave obeys,' she said, and drained her glass. But the venom remained absent from her voice.

He rose, held her chair for her.

'Are we leaving this prison?' she inquired.

'We are going on a visit,' he said. 'But within the walls.'

She allowed him to escort her to the door. It remained early afternoon, and the sun was hot; the breeze had died, and the only sound was the tramp of the sentries on the battlements. He gave her a wide-brimmed straw hat, and she settled it over her hair. He placed his cocked hat on his own head, opened the door for her.

She hesitated, blinking at the sunlight, glancing at him, before stepping into the heat. He walked at her elbow, across the huge courtyard, to the curtained door on the far side. And again she hesitated.

'This is the house of the *mamaloi*.'

'Who is also my friend.'

'Voodooism is unspeakable,' Cartarette declared.

'Enter,' he commanded.

She pushed the curtain aside, and he realized she had forgotten

230

to taunt him with her obedience to either the white nigger or the monster.

A girl opened the inner curtain for them. Cartarette glanced at Dick. 'She expects us.'

'A priestess of Voodoo knows all things,' he said, enjoying his own humour.

Cartarette stepped into the gloom beyond, paused to inhale, the incense, the scent that always filled this room, to stare at Gislane, seated in her armchair.

'Welcome, mademoiselle,' Gislane said. 'I have long waited for you to visit me.'

'I am not visiting you,' Cartarette said. 'I was brought here by my monster.'

Gislane smiled, and stood up. 'It is still a visit, and you are welcome. Come.'

Yet another curtain, behind the chair, was swept aside, and they followed her into another chamber. Here it was utterly dark, save for the inevitable fire glowing in the centre of the floor, doubling the heat. Dick felt sweat trickling down his face. And he only suspected what was about to happen.

Gislane stooped, a taper in her hand. When it glowed, she straightened, handed it to Dick. 'Light the candles,' she commanded.

He could see them now, set around the wall. He left Cartarette's side, lit each wick in turn. The room glowed, and the candles were scented. He could hear Cartarette breathing. Perhaps she had also supposed this to be a bedchamber. But it was not. It was a love chamber. In the centre of the far wall there was a mattress, laid on the wooden floor, reaching almost as far as the fire. In the wall, above the mattress, were two rings, to which were attached buckskin thongs. At the foot of the mattress, beyond each corner, were two stakes, to which also were attached buckskin thongs.

Cartarette gave a gasp, and turned. But Gislane had remained behind her.

'You practise witchcraft,' Cartarette whispered.

'In this case, white magic, mademoiselle,' Gislane said. 'Undress.'

'I will not.'

'Then will you be stripped.' Gislane stretched out her hand, stroked the material of Cartarette's collar. 'It will be a pity, to destroy a beautiful garment. And you will be humiliated. We may need to call others. Undress, Cartarette. Then your secret will belong to this room alone.'

Her voice seeped around the chamber.

'My secret?'

'You will have a secret, Cartarette. I promise you. What, are you ashamed, to be naked before your master, who is also your lover? Before me? I am an old woman, Cartarette. I have seen many naked women, many naked men. Many more beautiful even than you.'

Her quiet voice filled the chamber, yet seemed to echo. It made thought difficult, when combined with the heat, and the incense. Cartarette's fingers were already at the buttons of her bodice.

'I will not be bewitched,' she insisted.

'I do not seek to bewitch you, child. I seek to help you. To release you from your prison.'

'My prison?' Cartarette's gown slid past her thighs, and to the ground. She wore no stays, here in the informality of La Ferrière. A moment later her shift joined her gown. She wore no stockings, either, in the warmth of this climate. Only slippers.

'The prison of your mind. Lie down.'

Cartarette hesitated, glanced at Dick, and for the first time that he could remember in their acquaintanceship, flushed with embarrassment. Or was it only the firelight, flickering in her cheeks? She lay down.

'Arms above head,' Gislane said, reassuringly, and secured the girl's wrists.

'If you wish me no harm, madame, why bind me?'

Gislane smiled at her. 'To keep you from harm, child.' She secured each ankle in turn, leaving the girl spreadeagled on the mattress. Then she rose, slowly, with the faintest rustle of material. 'You must also undress, Dick, and stand at the foot of the bed,' she said. 'Your woman must gaze upon you, throughout the ceremony.'

Dick obeyed; the heat of the fire scorched his back, made his blood run the more quickly. But no doubt this was as Gislane intended.

Gislane removed her own gown; she wore nothing underneath. It was several years since she had taken him to her bed, made him over in the image she sought, and now he knew she must be past

232

sixty. Yet these firm muscles, these long, slender legs, could still reawaken all his manhood.

She left the bedside, stooped by a chest in the corner, turned and straightened suddenly, and rose at the same time, throwing both arms outwards. Drops of liquid scattered through the flickering light, brushed his cheeks, fell on Cartarette's belly. The scent was at once erotic and intoxicating, sending his mind, and no doubt Cartarette's as well, whirling into space.

Gislane began to dance, a slow movement, of belly and thighs and groin and stomping feet, accompanying herself with clapping hands in time to the tune she sang. She moved around them, and her sex, her song, served to envelop them, to fill the room. Dick felt himself panting, felt he would explode long before he could enter the woman.

Gislane swept round the room, pausing by the chest to seize a bottle. Her movements stopped, and it seemed the entire day stopped with it. The only sound was their breathing.

Gislane knelt before Cartarette's feet. She uncorked the bottle, poured a little of the liquid into the palm of her hand, and commenced to massage the girl's toes, slowly and gently, humming a little tune. The scent, vaguely sweet, the tune, mind-consuming in its erotic cadence, kept his mind swimming, and no doubt Cartarette's as well. She stared at him, her breath, which had been heavy with fear and anticipation when first she had lain down, slowly subsiding until her breasts did no more than flutter.

Slowly Gislane worked, from time to time renewing the liquid. She came up Cartarette's body, from calf to thigh, from thigh to groin. Now Cartarette scarcely breathed at all, and her mouth sagged open; she was so still she might almost have been asleep, but her eyes remained wide, staring at Dick. And as Gislane reached her belly, her breathing began again, slowly, building up, as was his own.

And Gislane's song grew louder, as she worked. Up from the belly, to caress the ribs, to seek the breasts, to leave them and stroke neck and armpit, before returning once again to stimulate the nipples into erection. Now Cartarette panted, and her ankles strained at the buckskin cords as she attempted to bend her knees. And still she stared at Dick, mouth wide, tongue circling her opened lips.

Gislane stopped, sitting astride Cartarette's thighs, and threw

233

back her head, and gave a gigantic shout, and then leapt up, as if she were the girl.

'Now,' she screamed. 'Now, now, now.'

Dick obeyed. Could this be different? Cartarette had never once attempted to resist him. She had always lain beneath him, in perfect submission. She could not possibly be more submissive when secured. Except that she was no longer secured. For even as he reached his own climax her legs came free, to wrap themselves around his body, as a second later her arms came free, the cords loosed by Gislane, to allow her fingers to close on his back, to eat into his flesh. Harriet Gale had screamed her ecstasy. Cartarette d'Estaing reached hers in silence, but her entire body tightened on his, seeming to suck him against her.

And her arms remained tight.

'I love you,' he gasped.

'I hate you,' she whispered in his ear. 'Oh, God, how I hate you.'

Dick raised his head, to gaze at Gislane, kneeling at the head of the bed.

Gislane smiled.

'What news, man? What news?'

Dick Hilton leaned over the wall above the main gate, looked down on the patrol. They lacked the sparkle he had come to associate with black men, exchanged no humorous sallies with the sentries, rather drooped on their horses' necks. The uniforms of which they were so proud were dirty and untidy. So no doubt they were tired. He had not known men that tired.

La Chat made a signal, and Dick left the battlement and ran down the steps to the courtyard. His aide dismounted, heavily, spoke in a low voice.

'We were fired on.'

'You? Imperial troops? Where was this?'

La Chat pointed at the forest beyond the wall. 'Not fifteen miles from here.'

'Fifteen miles? But good God, man . . .'

'Aye, General,' La Chat agreed. 'It is as you feared.'

Dick gazed at him for a moment, chewing his lip. For better than three months now there had been no word from Christophe. His supply column went down to Sans Souci and Cap Haitien every third month. Last time, the Emperor had been away, and they had brought back rumours, grumbles of discontent with the burden Christophe was imposing upon his people, the unending war, the incessant labour, the increasing taxes required to maintain the edifice of empire. Pétion was dead, but his successor, Jean Pierre Boyer, continued the struggle to establish a republic in the south. But there had been rumours ever since he had first landed in Haiti, six years ago; these had not caused Dick any concern. The absence of the quarterly letter from the Emperor had. Yet he had waited, another three months, before despatching La Chat and his patrol.

'And you turned back?'

'They were in great force, General. Black men, not mulattoes.'

Dick pulled his nose, looked out through the gate once again, at the mountains, at the forest. 'Feed and rest your men, La Chat,' he said. 'This evening we had best decide what should be done.'

'Our orders are to hold La Ferrière, General.'

'Aye,' Dick said. 'For the Emperor. It follows that we would not be obeying orders in allowing the Emperor to be destroyed before he can reach us. This evening, La Chat.'

He walked across the courtyard, his sword slapping his thigh. Perhaps life had been too easy, these last two years. He practised his weapons daily; he was proud of the skill Gislane had given him. Because it was Gislane's skill; he still thought of her every time a pistol butt nestled in his palm, every time his fingers wrapped themselves around a sword hilt. But he had not fired a shot in anger since the taking of d'Estaing's village.

And in every other respect, this last year had been nothing but happiness. Cartarette waited for him now, as became his slave and his mistress. She still acted the prisoner. Her pride would let her do no less. She even still pretended to mock him, constantly. 'News from the coast, monster?' she inquired. But there was less hate than affection in her voice. When he put his arm round her shoulders, her head instinctively rested on his chest, her red-gold hair mingled with the braid on his tunic. No doubt her emotion was mainly loneliness. In all this dark world in which they existed, he was her only friend. Without him her life would be too terrible to contemplate.

'No,' he said. 'And there is my cause for concern. The patrol was fired on.' He sat in his armchair, leaned back his head. She

235

knelt before him to drag off his boots. Often, when he sat here, he thought he was dreaming. The room was comfortable, rather than elegant. This was a fortress, not a palace. But he had secured a charcoal drawing of her, done by one of his own troopers who had burned wood in the forests below La Ferrière before Christophe's net had sucked him up. The drawing was framed on the wall opposite him. And the artist had been skilled. He had caught her expression, the eagerness of her half-parted lips, the dart of her wide-eyed gaze, even the sheen of her hair. But in black and white he had not been able to secure the colour, of her hair no less than her complexion, for she seldom risked herself in the sun. Just as he had not been able to catch the scent of her perfume or the tinkle of her laugh. She, and her painting, added lustre to the plain wood of the room, the simple furniture and the lack of carpets or drapes.

'Then your Emperor will have a cause for shedding blood closer to home,' she remarked, removing his right boot.

'My Emperor wishes only to see his people at peace,' Dick said. 'Do you believe that?'

'No,' she said, removing his left boot. 'He is a savage, as his people are savages. When he has no one left to fight, and maim, and kill, he will die of frustration.'

Dick leaned forward, and her head came up. However she had grown to desire, and perhaps even to need, his sex, she had still always an initial revulsion to overcome. And yet, she was not miserable, he was sure of that. Perhaps she waited for better times. Perhaps she looked forward to being rescued from her monster by some knight in shining armour. She had at the least come to terms with her present.

He blew her a kiss. 'I think he may surprise you.'

'I am always willing to be surprised by a nigger,' she remarked, and got to her feet. 'Even a white one.' She frowned, and looked at the doorway, her chin slowly slipping down.

Dick leapt to his feet, turned, reaching for his sword. And was equally surprised. Gislane Nicholson did not go visiting, as a rule. And this day her face was drawn and hard. For the first time in their acquaintance she looked her age. Almost.

'There are drums.'

He nodded. 'My patrol was fired upon, not fifteen miles from the fortress.'

236

'Those tell a different message,' Gislane said.

He frowned at her. 'What message?'

'That the Emperor is no more.'

'Christophe is dead?' Cartarette's voice was sharp.

'I do not know,' Gislane said. 'The drums say the Emperor is no more. Not that he is dead.'

'He would not give up the throne,' Dick muttered. 'My God, what are we to do?'

'You have your orders,' Gislane said.

'To defend La Ferrière. I had anticipated defending it with the Emperor at my side.'

'Yet must you still defend it, Richard Hilton.'

He glanced at Cartarette; her mouth was open.

'What did she call you?'

He sighed. 'Aye, well, that is my true name. Warner is but an alias. We'll talk of it later.'

Her face was totally confounded. Perhaps she had supposed she knew all about him, in two years of endless intimacy.

'Hilton,' she whispered. 'My God. We know of the Hiltons.'

'I said, we'll talk of it later. Gislane. I cannot just sit here, while Christophe may be fighting for his life.'

'The drums will tell us,' she promised. 'Wait for them, at the least. Wait . . .' Her head turned, slowly, towards the opened door. The distant humming had ceased.

And a sentry was calling. 'Men approach,' he shouted. 'The Emperor comes.'

'Thank God for that. My boots, girl, quickly.' Dick sat down, and pulled on his boots, then ran outside. Gislane and Cartarette remained in the doorway, joined now by the other servants. 'Turn out the guard,' he called. 'Turn out the guard. Open the gates.' He ran up the steps on to the battlements, only then realized he was bareheaded in the noonday sun. But it was unlike Christophe to ride in the noonday sun.

And at the embrasure he paused in dismay. This was no imperial entourage. This was scarce fifty men, driving exhausted horses, uniforms torn and soiled. Yet there was no mistaking the huge figure at their head.

He ran down the steps again, into the gateway, helped his friend from the saddle. 'Sire?' There was alarm in his voice. Christophe looked older than ever before. It was time to

237

remember that he too was past fifty.

'I heard firing, earlier.'

Dick gave a sigh of relief. There was no change in the resolution of that voice. 'A patrol, sire. It was fired on by bandits.'

Christophe's eyes gloomed at him. 'It was fired on by revolutionaries, Matt.' He turned to La Chat. 'Feed my men. Water their horses. And close those gates.' He walked across the courtyard. 'I must have food, Matt.'

'Food, for the Emperor,' Dick shouted at Cartarette.

She ran inside, driving her girls before them.

Gislane remained standing in the doorway. 'It has happened, then.'

Christophe glanced from right to left, ducked his head, entered the house. 'I made them what they are,' he said. 'Dukes, princes. Generals. I gave them their power.'

'The Empress?'

He shrugged, sat at the dining table, throwing his hat on the floor. 'Taken. Dead, perhaps. Unless they would use her against me. They have Sans Souci. Have it? It was always theirs, with me away. Their headquarters are in Cap Haitien. They declare me a public enemy, battening upon the blood of my people.' His head raised. 'How many men have you, Matt?'

'Three hundred.'

'And I brought fifty.' For a moment his mouth turned down. Then he smiled. 'But we have La Ferrière, eh? Food.'

The girls were placing platters on the table, wine at his elbow.

'By all the gods in heaven, I am starving. Oh, sit down, Matt. Sit down, madame. I cannot eat alone.' He glanced at Cartarette. 'You should be laughing, mademoiselle. Why are you not laughing?'

'Will you die as bravely as my father, sire?'

Christophe frowned at her, then gave a booming laugh. 'When the time comes, mademoiselle. But I am not going to die. I have been betrayed before. I have been chased into the forest before. But then, then I did not have La Ferrière. And I did not have Matt.'

'Then you had the undying love of your people,' Gislane said, very quietly.

Christophe's head turned. 'Old woman, you have served your purpose. Remember that.'

She would not lower her eyes. 'As you have served yours, Henry Christophe.'

'Eh? Eh? My purpose is to make this pack of lazy niggers into a nation. That is my task. Destiny gave me that task.'

'Destiny commanded you to be a legend, Henry,' Gislane said, still speaking quietly. 'You are that, and in your own lifetime. Destiny required that your people be given an example, a man always to remember. You will always be remembered. La Ferrière will always be remembered. Sans Souci will always be remembered.'

'Bah,' Christophe shouted. 'La Ferrière will stand, forever.'

'As will your memory, Henry. But the girl was right, just now. She said you know only fighting, bloodshed, warfare. Your people want peace. And you cannot give them that. You can only give them your memory, for when next they have to fight.'

He glared at her, then threw down his knife, pushed back his chair. 'You are a stupid old woman. And she . . .' He flung out his hand, pointing at Cartarette. 'She wishes only to avenge herself. I know not how you have put up with them this time, Matt. They should be flogged.' He got up. 'Come with me.'

He left the room, and Dick raised his eyebrows at the women before following. Christophe stalked across the courtyard and into the maproom. 'Out,' he bawled at the clerks waiting there. 'Get out. You are all spies, all revolutionaries. Out.'

The men glanced at each other, at Dick, and then sidled from the room. Dick closed the door.

'They think I am finished,' Christophe said. 'Even the *mamaloi*. There is faith for you. Do you think I am finished, Dick?'

'I will defend La Ferrière for you, sire.'

'That is no answer.' He frowned at the white man. 'Or is it, indeed, your answer?' He smiled. 'A thousand men, for a hundred days. Therefore, as we are less than five hundred men, we should be able to withstand a siege for two hundred days. Am I right?'

'You are right, sire.'

'But even two hundred days will be insufficient, if my enemies are left to conspire against me. No, no. We must use the citadel as a rallying point for the people who remain faithful to me. There will be many thousands of those. We will despatch messengers, to every part of the country. Yes. We will negotiate with Boyer. We will . . .' The frown was back. 'You do not believe the people will rally to me?'

'I do not know, sire.'

Christophe walked to the window to look at the courtyard; his entire body seemed to freeze, until his arm slowly came up. 'But what is that? I told La Chat to rest my men.'

Dick ran to the door. The entire garrison was lined up, under arms. Behind them waited the women and the children. His own serving girls were there. And Cartarette?

She stood in the doorway, watching the preparations. Watching Colonel La Chat marching across the courtyard towards him.

'What is the meaning of this parade, Colonel?' Dick demanded. 'You are under no orders to leave the fortress.'

'The men wish to leave, General.'

'Leave? Where can they be as safe as in La Ferrière?'

'There is no safety here, General. We cannot withstand the nation.'

'The nation?' Christophe bellowed, joining Dick in the doorway. 'A few conspirators, who have turned the heads of the people. We will soon deal with them, Colonel. Then, then, will I remember those who have been faithful to me.'

'My apologies, sire,' La Chat said. 'The *mamaloi* has told us you will not rule again.'

'You'd listen to the ramblings of an old woman?'

'She is the *mamaloi*, sire. You have believed her, long enough.'

'Too long,' Christophe shouted. 'Too long. Where is she?'

'She prays, sire,' La Chat said. 'The men believe her.'

'And you?'

'I believe her also.' La Chat faced Dick. 'You have commanded us, faithfully and well, these past four years, General Warner. We invite you to accompany us. We have been offered a place in the army of General Boyer in the reuniting of Haiti. We would march under your command.'

Dick frowned at him. Here was loyalty. But where was *his* loyalty? 'You'd desert your Emperor?'

'He will rule no more,' La Chat repeated. 'My men will not wait.'

'Go with them, Dick,' Christophe said. 'You have served *me*, faithfully and well, these past six years. I release you from your allegiance.'

240

Dick hesitated, looked across the courtyard at Cartarette. She was looking at him, but he could not tell the expression in her eyes, at this distance. Yet did she still wear nothing more than her housegown. She had never doubted his decision.

'You saved my life, my reason, my dignity, sire,' he said. 'I will serve you while you live.'

'Aye,' Christophe said. 'Would I had but a hundred more like you, Dick. Well, La Chat? What are you waiting for?'

The Colonel hesitated, then turned on his heel and marched back to his men. He mounted, and the dragoons mounted with him; the Colonel raised his arm, and the regiment moved forward; the women and children with their dogs and chickens, walked behind.

Dick felt a thickness in his throat he had never known before. It was all so dignified. They had not turned on Christophe, and murdered him, as true revolutionaries might have done. They had simply marched away from him. He did not dare look at the Emperor.

'A thousand men,' Christophe said. 'For a hundred days. Well then, Dick, two men for fifty thousand days. We shall die of old age.' He was looking at Cartarette. 'But there are also two women.'

He left the doorway, strode across the courtyard. Through the opened gateway, the sound of the horses picking their way down the hillside still rose to them. Dick had heard it often before, coming the other way. Now he wondered at the absence of booted feet, striking the wooden floors surrounding the walls.

He followed Christophe. The Emperor paused before the door to the commandant's house. 'If we are taken,' he said, 'you will be raped, and then murdered. Slowly. Why did you not go with them?'

'I have been raped before, sire,' Cartarette said.

He snorted. 'Where is the *mamaloi*?'

'She returned to her own chambers,' Cartarette said. 'Sire . . .' She flushed. She had never directly addressed him before, since the day he had sent her father to his execution.

'Well?'

'She but spoke the truth as she saw it.'

Christophe stamped through the curtained doorway. Dick ran at his heels, and Cartarette followed him, holding his arm as the curtain was thrown aside.

Gislane sat on her chair, facing them. The room was as gloomy as ever, the candles burned low.

'You have betrayed me,' Christophe shouted, his voice echoing. 'I will have you flogged.'

The woman did not reply.

'Oh, my God,' Cartarette said.

Christophe crossed the floor, slowly. He stretched out his hand, and then withdrew it again.

'Even she,' he said, 'has deserted me.'

'Or she waits for you,' Dick said. 'In her own heaven.'

Christophe glanced at him, and looked back at the woman. Once again his arm extended. This time he took the *mamaloi*'s hand, and raised it to his lips, before letting it fall again. Then he turned on his heel and left the room.

Cartarette went closer. 'She is not marked,' she said.

'Gislane must have had sufficient poisons,' Dick said.

'She told me she had been your father's lover,' Cartarette said. 'That she had been one of the leaders of the revolution here. That she had made you what you are.'

'All true,' Dick said. 'All true.'

'And now she is dead.' Cartarette sighed. 'She must have been very lonely, at the end. Will you bury her?'

'Aye. There are spades in the armoury.' He turned, and checked at the explosion.

'Oh, my God,' Cartarette said again.

Dick ran from the room, thrust the curtain aside, pounded across the courtyard into the commandant's house. He paused in the front room, inhaling the smell of cordite, gazed at the table; the covers were still set, Christophe's half-eaten meal still scattered. But in the centre of the table, there was a canvas sack, and to the sack was attached a note.

He pulled it free, opened it. 'Take your woman and leave this place', Christophe had written. 'The money is for you. And remember me.'

He released the cord securing the bag, looked at the gold coin, heard Cartarette.

'There must be a thousand pounds,' she whispered.

'Ten thousand, more like.' He pulled open the door to the inner room, looked at the Emperor. Christophe lay on his side, the

242

pistol still in his hand, his head a gaping wound. His jacket was open, the snapped cord he had worn around his neck trailed onto his lap, but there was no sign of the silver bullet. No doubt it was still lodged in his brain.

13

The Crisis

The music ballooned the length of the great withdrawing room on
Hilltop, escaped the opened windows to cascade across the
verandahs, flooded down the hill to the town and the slave village
beyond, caressing the logies with its dying cadence. At the bottom
of the hill the triple time was almost restful, lulling many a
piccaninny to sleep.

Inside the Great House it drowned thought, obscured decency,
left manners exposed, without reason, without objective. The
ladies whirled, skirts held high in their right hands, left arms tight
on their partners' waists, bodices sagging as shoulders and breasts
glistened with perspiration, hair rapidly uncoiling itself in the
frenzy of the gyrations. Men were no less abandoned, white-gloved
fingers biting into taffeta waists, or naked arms, seeking every
opportunity to let thigh brush thigh in the frenzy of the dance,
smiling their sexual adoration into the equally smiling faces only
inches away from their own.

The entire room became a vast emotional storm; it
communicated itself even to those not dancing, seated in the
chairs which had been pushed against the walls this night, or
lounging beside them, the women with heads close together, fans
fluttering, destroying reputations with effortless envy, the men,
also mouth to ear, shrouded in tobacco smoke, building hopes
and creating fantasies, exchanging experiences and perpetuating
scandals. Even the servants seemed part of the evening, for the
white-gowned girls waited in a cluster in the arch to the hall, trays
laden with sangaree, ready to dart forward and refresh the
overheated white people the moment the music stopped,
conscious always of being under the disapproving scrutiny of
Boscawen should they falter or slacken their efforts; his cane

waited in the kitchens for any maid who caught his eye, for whatever reason.

'Eighteen thousand pounds?' Phyllis Kendrick gaped at Tony Hilton's smiling face. 'Why, 'tis a fortune.'

'Money, my dear Phyllis.' Tony brought her close to prevent her shoulder cannoning into a fellow dancer, held her there for a moment. 'Money is for spending.'

'But now . . . Toby says cane will never recover.'

'Oh, bah. Prices are affected by the uncertainty. No one knows what that pack of lunatics in Whitehall will do next. But once we have made it perfectly clear that we shall not submit to their blackmail, that we are capable of running our own affairs, that if pushed too far we will seek our own remedies, why, you'll see.'

The music was dying. He had arranged it so that they finished their last rotation in a corner by the doors to the verandah.

'But . . . eighteen thousand pounds,' she said again, allowing herself to be guided into the cool darkness. 'For an old building?'

'Cheaper than *re*building. Most of the stand was still solid. You'll see tomorrow.'

She stood at the verandah rail, looked out at the darkness, and then at the twinkling lights of the town below them. 'A race meeting, on Hilltop. I attended one as a girl.'

'You told me.' He was behind her, leaning slightly forward so that he touched her. His hands rested on her shoulders, gently kneading the flesh.

Her breathing, which had commenced to settle after the exertions of the dance, began to quicken again. He loved to hear her become excited, to feel her become anxious.

'Do I bore you awfully?'

He smiled, into her ear as he kissed it. 'You entrance me, continuously, Phyllis. But I do not wish to be reminded of my uncle's successes, at least until I have had one of my own. I have dreamed of tomorrow since I first came to Hilltop, and that is better than twenty years ago, you know.'

'I remember.' She turned, in his arms, moved her thighs against his. 'The Hilton boys. Oh, you caused quite a stir.' She smiled at him. 'Everyone was so disappointed when you did not immediately spring to the forefront of Jamaican society.'

He kissed her nose. 'That was my brother's doing. Have I disappointed recently?'

She gazed at him, frowning. 'The music is starting again.'

'Then they are less likely to miss us.'

Her lips parted. She became anxious, so very quickly, and so very anxious, as well. Because. he had never actually done anything more than flirt, although he had held her in this very place on the verandah, at least a dozen times in the past. He had always wondered if he would ever do anything more than flirt. She was the elder, if only by a year or two, but age had nothing to do with it. She was not particularly attractive, but looks had very little to do with it either. He enjoyed the sensation of awakening woman, different women, and few of them responded as readily as Phyllis Kendrick. Why, the poor woman must be quite desperate, which was not very surprising, as she was forced to live with that stuffed egg Toby Kendrick, and even worse, was forced to share Rivermouth Great House with Kendrick's mother. A mistake he had not made, once Ellen had agreed to marry him.

Oddly enough, tonight he felt like doing more than flirt. Tonight, this entire weekend, he was celebrating. It had been a dream of his for twenty years to re-establish the Hilltop race meetings. It had taken far longer than he had supposed possible. In the first place, that ghastly prig Reynolds had been against the idea, had successfully resisted the expense as long as there was a legal prospect of Dick still being alive. And even when he had been forced to admit Tony as rightful owner of Hilltop, the work had dragged, while breeding an unbeatable stable—Tony had no intention of not winning his own meetings—had taken even longer. But now, it was done, and tomorrow Hilltop would regain the very last of its former glories. Why even Mama must surely write to congratulate him, and she had written less and less often these past few years. No doubt his name figured in the newspapers too often for either her or Father. They disliked what the missionaries wrote about him, and they disliked his leadership of those planters who would carry their defiance of the British Government even as far as secession. Well, they could dislike whatever they pleased; they accepted their share of the Hilltop profits without argument.

He squeezed Phyllis Kendrick's elbow, gently turned her away from the rail. 'Shall we walk?'

'Walk? But . . .' She was already allowing herself to be guided along the verandah, gulping as they passed close to another couple, half lost in the shadows, leaning against one another. He could feel her tremble, and desperately seek for conversation. 'Your manager, James Hardy. He is not here tonight.'

'James is on holiday. Nevis. Have you been to the Grand Hotel?'

'Toby says it is far too expensive. He says the prices they charge are simply outrageous, and for what? To be smoked in a sulphur bath?'

'Oh, 'tis worth a visit. You meet all the best people.' He turned her in at the side door, and the servants hastily parted. 'Who'd have thought it, eh? Little Nevis, the poorest place you could ever imagine, suddenly becoming wealthy, because of a sulphur spring.'

'Absurd.' Her voice was trembling now, as well. 'Tony . . . Mr Hilton . . .'

'The painting is in my study,' he explained, to anyone who might be listening, and paused, at the second arch to the ballroom, to smile at the dancers. And then to catch Ellen's eye. She dominated the room, as she was the tallest woman present, and the most expensively dressed; the candlelight flickered from the emeralds of her earrings, the diamond necklace which roamed her breast as she spun in her partner's arms. And because she was Ellen. There were prettier women present. But there was no one with that arrogance, that superb panache. And there was no one present, either, with quite that glitter in her eye. Dances affected Ellen. But then, a great many things affected Ellen. She would be at her peak tonight. He doubted she would have the time for him, just as he doubted he would have the strength for her. A fact which was known to them both, and accepted by them both. So she smiled as she saw Phyllis Kendrick on his arm. But it was a contemptuous smile.

The door to the study opened, and closed. The sound of the music was slightly reduced. The study was dark, only a faint lighter darkness forming the window. Phyllis Kendrick's thigh touched the desk, and she turned, into his arms. 'Is the painting very striking?'

'I think so. It is of Ellen.'

'Who else. And you keep it in front of you, while you are working.'

He could feel her breath on his face, although he could hardly see her. He smiled, to be sure *she* felt *his* breath. 'A man should keep his wife always in mind.'

She touched his face with her tongue, tentatively, exploring, waiting. Ellen had smiled, contemptuously. Ellen even felt contempt for Judith. She feared no rival, because she did not really care. She knew his weaknesses, his inabilities, indeed, and she felt sorry for them. No doubt genuinely. But her pity was contempt. She did not love him. Ellen did not love anyone. Ellen did not even love Ellen.

But Ellen loved the mistress of Hilltop. And the mistress of Hilltop was contemptuous of her husband's weaknesses.

Phyllis Kendrick's hands were inside his coat, sliding round his waist, seeking a way into his pantaloons. 'Oh, Tony,' she whispered. 'I have wanted this, for so long. So very long.'

But he could think only of Ellen's smile. God, how he hated her.

But how he also loved the mistress of Hilltop.

'It does a woman good, to want,' he said. 'We'd best get back to the dance.'

Hooves drummed, dust kicked, the earth trembled. The twelve ponies hurtled round the bend, clinging close to the white palings, the multicoloured silk jackets of their black riders staining dark with sweat, the horses themselves foaming and baring their teeth as they reached through the heat and the swirling dust and sweat for the front.

The people in the grandstand rose to their feet as if plucked forward by a gigantic string, all together. Hats were waved, along with parasols and kerchiefs and scarves. Screams of pleasure from the women mingled with the bellows from the men. Another noise to shake the plantation, to crowd through the air of the slave village. But this did not lull. Out in the fields the black people crouched over their cutlasses as they weeded the paths, the fields, performing their interminable, back-breaking tasks, and muttered at each other at the white man's conception of enjoyment. Perhaps they too would have enjoyed it, had they been present. The older men and women recalled that in the days of Master Robert — and how good they seemed in retrospect — a race day had meant a slave holiday, and they had all been permitted to crowd the rails of the track, and even to exchange their own bets, certainly to imbibe some of the pleasurable excitement of watching the ponies matched.

But such a relaxation of effort did not appeal to the latest Hilton. He believed slaves should work, and work, and work. Save where they were required for entertainment.

The noise began to die. The ponies were cantering to a stop, before being returned to the unsaddling enclosure. The grandstand began to subside, ladies remembering their coiffures, men wiping sweat from their faces, those who had won hurrying off to collect their bets.

'A good mare,' said the Reverend Patterson. 'Oh, indeed, a good mare. You must have made a fortune this day, Hilton.'

'It'll pay for her keep.' Tony Hilton was one of the few men who had not risen to see the finish. Yet he wiped his brow as hard as anyone, replaced his grey silk hat. 'If Clay will not accommodate us, then we'll go over his head.'

John Tresling frowned at him. 'Jackson?'

'Why not. He is a statesman. Clay is an ignorant Virginian cotton planter.'

'Um.' Martin Evans, the fourth in the Hilton Box — the ladies were separately accommodated on the upper floor — scratched his nose.

'They say Jackson is a firm upholder of the Monroe Doctrine.'

'Well, then . . .'

'Oh, he accepts that there are colonies, French and British, which have a longer standing than the United States itself. His concept is that there should be no expansion of those colonies, and that there should be no excuse for sending any European armament to the Caribbean, or anywhere else for that matter.'

'So it follows,' Tresling pointed out, 'that he would be averse to any action which might involve the United States and Great Britain in a controversy. There is controversy enough, over the Oregon boundary.'

'Statesmen,' Tony remarked, 'have this habit of assuming that the world will stand still while they form doctrines and make pronunciamentos. Now, then, gentlemen, Jackson, we are told, and I believe, because he is an honest man — my God, an honest politician, there is a contradiction in terms — is utterly opposed to European intervention in American affairs. He will do anything to avoid it, such as not even considering a Jamaican appeal to be included in the United States. Very well, then, what do you think would be his reaction were we to declare independence? But first, what would be the British reaction?'

'You speak treason,' the parson muttered. 'For God's sake keep your voice down.'

'George Washington also spoke treason, until he won,' Tony pointed out.

'He's right, Reverend,' Tresling said. 'Whitehall would never stand for a Jamaica declaration of independence.'

'They'd send a fleet,' Evans said.

'Indeed they would,' Tony agreed. 'And what would your General Jackson do then, do you think?'

The two planters looked at each other, and then both looked at the parson.

'A desperate step,' Patterson said.

'Yet one which will, eventually, have to be taken,' Tony said. 'Better in our own time, than in theirs.'

'You cannot know it is inevitable,' Evans objected.

'You have brains in that head of yours, Marty. Why do you think the Government has pulled back from Abolition? For the very reason that they fear an extreme reaction on our part. But all the while British public opinion is being prepared for the ultimate step. Worse, all the while our own public opinion here in Jamaica is being prepared for such a step. Now, seven, eight years ago when Amelioration was first mentioned, our people dismissed the idea of British interference in our affairs, out of hand. So then Whitehall set to work. There is talk of their being no longer able to support preferential treaties for West Indian sugar. No longer able, by God. It is again, pure blackmail. They will remove the preference, unless we agree to their principles. And *this* is not being rejected out of hand. We three may be able to weather any economic storm. But there are those of us who cannot, who are already suggesting we had best accommodate Whitehall. And all of this, gentlemen, is under a Tory government. But my latest despatch from England says that the King is ailing. What happens when he dies, and there is an election? Suppose the Whigs gain power? The Whigs, gentlemen. The party of Wilberforce. Of my own father, bless his besotted soul. But not a party elected, or desired, by us. They talk of patriotism. Where, I would like to ask, does patriotism begin, if not in Port Royal?'

' 'Tis a difficult matter,' Evans said. 'With the price of sugar falling . . .'

'Is this a confession?' Tresling inquired.

'It is not,' Evans declared. 'I'll back you, if you'll set to it. But it's not a matter can be resolved by secret discussions. We've had enough of those.'

'Well, then, let us stop this one.' Tony smiled at them, and got up. 'I shall be in communication with you. And shortly.' He left the box, making his way through the throng, all calling their congratulations on the prowess of his mare, slapping him on the back, shaking his hand, and waited by the steps for the ladies as they left their boxes. 'Why, good afternoon to you, Phyllis. Did you win?'

Phyllis Kendrick turned her head and ignored him, but her cheeks were pink. She would never forgive him for last night. She thought. She would never come to Hilltop again. She was determined. Until her next invitation. Poor Phyllis.

'I think I am to congratulate us.' Ellen came last, shepherding the last of her guests. She wore her favourite pale green, and looked as cool and self-possessed as Phyllis had been hot and bothered.

'Oh, indeed. Although the odds were not very good. Hilltop Dancer's reputation is growing.'

'None the less, I shall give Peter Eleven my personal congratulations.' She smiled at her husband. 'I even think, as he rides so well, we could grant him the use of a decent name. I shall think of one and let you know.'

He held her arm. 'Shall I come with you?'

A darting look, before she once again studied the stairs they descended. 'I'm sure that will not be necessary, Tony. I was under the impression that blacks bored you. Besides, have you not got dear Phyllis to see to? I trust you spent a pleasant night?'

They had reached the foot of the stairs, and the grooms were lining up as they passed. The slaves feared the mistress more even than the master. No one knew for certain what had happened on that afternoon fifteen years before, but a man had died. While attempting to run away, certainly; that was the official account. But Absolom and Jeremiah had not been able to stop themselves whispering.

Ellen smiled at them, glanced at her husband. Their guests were already strung out across the grass, making their way slowly back towards the house, gossiping and laughing, anticipating another sumptuous meal, another bout of indiscriminate drinking and indiscriminate flirting. Or more. And were Ellen to suspect that he had not bedded Phyllis, last night, her contempt would undoubtedly grow.

'My night was much as I expected,' he said. 'And yours?'

'Oh, the same. The same.'

'His name?'

She stopped, and turned, her fan coming together into a short wand, held with the tips of her fingers, to slap him gently on the chest. 'You would break the rules? And it would merely make you jealous.'

'Of one of those pot-bellied, pasty-faced planters?'

'Your guests,' she gently reproved. 'But then it need not have been one of your guests, need it?' She gave that arch, secret smile he adored.

'I don't believe you. I know you like to look. You'd never stoop so low.'

This time the secret smile became a secret laugh, as she turned away. 'Why do you think Peter Eleven rode so well, today?'

The cavalcade wound its way through the valley. When the first of the carriages was already entering the road through the hills, three miles from the Great House, the last was just rumbling down the slope outside the house itself. Dust hung on the air in a long swathe, travelled with the light breeze, scattered across the town and the village and the factory, coated the cane stalks.

Ellen Hilton held a handkerchief to her lips as she waved. 'Thank God that is over, for another season,' she said. 'Truly, I am ceasing to wonder at your uncle's decision to shut himself away here, and take no part in Jamaican society. It would be difficult to imagine a more boring, a more vulgar and a more uninteresting lot.'

Tony lowered his arm. 'But you enjoy playing the queen of that society.'

'I wonder if it is worth it.' She turned, and went into the comparative cool of the house. 'A light breakfast, Boscawen,' she stretched. 'And then a long, long siesta. Will you be going aback?'

He watched her climb the stairs. 'It hardly seems worthwhile.' He climbed behind her.

At the top she seemed to realize for the first time that he was

252

following her, and hesitated, before continuing on to the gallery. Her hand touched the knob of the door to her bedchamber, and again she hesitated, realizing that he stood at her shoulder.

'I really am quite exhausted,' she said. 'I am going to lie down.'

'That will suit me admirably,' he said.

She turned, frowning at him, and he reached past her to open the door, allowing his body to come against hers. The door opened, and he walked forward, using his right hand to hold her round the waist and half lift, half push her in front of him. Bridget, Ellen's personal maid, stared at them in alarm.

'Out,' Tony said.

'Oh, really, Tony,' Ellen complained. 'You are not going to play the fool, I hope.'

'Out,' he said again. 'Your mistress will manage for herself today.'

Bridget gave Ellen a terrified glance, and received a quick nod. She scurried through the door.

Tony kicked it shut behind him, released his wife. 'I don't believe what you said yesterday,' he remarked. 'If I thought it was true, I'd set the dogs on him.'

'Oh, pfft,' she said, and sat at her dressing table. It was huge, with three mirrors, and made out of best Honduras mahogany to her own design.

'So, tell me it is not true.' He sat on the bed.

She watched him in the mirrors. 'We made a bargain, you and I. As mistress of Hilltop, you promised me, I could do what I liked, when I liked, and with whom I liked.'

'As long as you were also my wife.'

She smiled, at herself, and at him, in the mirror. 'I am quite prepared to be your wife, whenever you wish me, Tony. I had supposed you were well suited.'

He sat up. 'You'll not pretend you are jealous of Judith?'

'That creature? No, no. I suspect she can attend to your needs better than I. She was trained to it, by her poor, unlamented mother. I was, unhappily, educated to be a lady.'

'You are a bitch.'

She turned, and stood up. And continued to smile. 'I am speaking with my husband, in the privacy of my bedchamber. Will you assist me?' She crossed the room, stood in front of him, turned her back. She waited, for his fingers to touch the buttons on the neck of her gown. 'We are both perverted, you and I,

Tony. In the oddest of ways, I suppose. People imagine us to be far worse than we are. They respect us for it. They would be utterly contemptuous, did they know the truth of us.'

The gown was loose, she shrugged it from her shoulders, past her thighs, stepped out of it. She left it lying on the floor, herself took off her petticoats, but returned to the bedside, and again presented her back to him.

'You are talking rubbish.' His fingers plucked at the ties for her stays. Although she wore a cotton shift under the whalebone, the garment was still soaked with sweat, and the bows rapidly turned into knots.

'Oh, indeed. But look at yourself, Tony. Tony Hilton. *The* Hilton. You are the wealthiest man in Jamaica, and possibly the most handsome. You have other assets, such as your name and even an understanding wife. You could take your pick, over and over again, of every woman in this island. Of every woman in the West Indies, I would say, should you choose to travel. Yet you find all your comfort at the hands, quite literally, of a little whore whose mother was a whore and whose grandmother, I have no doubt at all, was also a whore.' She spoke perfectly quietly and evenly, allowed herself a faint sigh of relief as her lungs and belly were at last released, reached over her shoulder to take the garment.

'I have always felt responsible for Judith,' Tony pointed out, and lay down again, his hands behind his head. 'You know that. What with her childhood, and then, being raped by Dick . . .'

'Do you really believe that?' Ellen stood in front of her mirror to remove her shift. She did it slowly, raising the garment first of all to her thighs, to expose her legs, long and strong and powerful, and then higher, to allow him to inspect her wide thighs, her pouted belly, and then over her head, slowly, inhaling at the same time to push her somewhat low slung breasts away from her chest.

'And with her mother dead,' Tony muttered. But he was watching her, as she could see in the mirror.

The shift joined the rest of her clothes on the floor. Only her hair remained. Slowly she unfastened the bows, keeping her breathing carefully under control. 'A man should try to be honest with himself,' she said, quietly. 'Judith is the only woman you dare approach. You only lie about the others. As you lied about the night before last.'

He sat up. 'Lie? Me? Why . . .'

'I had Charmian keeping an eye on you.' The chestnut hair fell past her ears, rested on her shoulders.

'Then she saw us go into the study.'

'She also saw dear Phyllis leave again, very briefly, and very angry. And she also saw you sleep in there, later on. All by yourself. My God, how absolutely childish, to be quarrelling about whether you did or whether you did not sleep with that detestable woman.' She crossed the room, slowly, sat on the bed, close enough for him to touch her, if he chose.

His face was red and angry. When he was angry, only the coarseness showed through. The Hilton grandeur quite disappeared.

'Well, then,' he demanded. 'What of you?'

'Ah.' She lay down, beside him, rested her head on his shoulder, placed her left leg carefully across both of his. From where he lay he would look down a long sweep of very white, faintly freckled flesh. 'I am more honest than you.' She exerted all her strength to keep him flat. 'I did try a buck, once.'

'You . . .' He attempted to get up, was held still. She rolled on to his stomach, straddling him with her legs, placing her hands one on each side of his face. She shook her head to tickle him with her hair.

And smiled at him. 'You always knew I wanted to.'

His hands rested on her back, but lightly. 'I knew you wanted to whip a man.'

She nestled her head against his neck. 'It is merely a form of sexual attraction, to wish to whip a man. But as I say, I only tried it once. Oh, it was magnificent. But I felt ashamed afterwards.'

'And where is he now?'

She gave her secret laugh. 'I'll not tell you that, Tony dear. And it was not Peter Eleven, if that is what you are thinking.' She raised her head, smiled at him. 'Does that knowledge repel you, or make you want me?'

'I ought to whip *you*.'

She shook her head. 'I would not enjoy being whipped. But you could make love to me. The amusing thing is, you could have made love to me, last night. I also slept alone.'

His eyes were watchful. 'You?'

'Why not?' She smiled at him. 'I entertain your friends. I do not accommodate them. When I wish to share my bed I seek a more positive approach. And at this moment that positive approach is absent.'

His brows slowly drew together as a terrible suspicion crystallized in his mind. 'You are lying.'

Ellen kissed him on the nose.

'I'll kill him.'

'You won't. Firstly because I would not let you, secondly because without him you are nothing. And you know that.'

Once again he strained, once again she pressed him flat.

'And anyway, your jealousy is quite absurd. I am not jealous of Judith. And I am your wife, wherever I find my pleasures. I think you ought to make me pregnant.'

'Eh?'

'Well, really, Tony dear, have you no thought of the future? I am thirty-seven years old. I shall shortly be too old for motherhood. I have shared your bed for fifteen years. And we have no children. Worse, there are no Hilton children anywhere. At least, no legitimate ones. You do not even have any distant cousins to inherit. What will happen to the Hilton wealth, the Hilton name? 'Tis a most serious matter.'

Her voice mocked him, her smile mocked him, the faint movements of her body mocked him. She was angry, because she had so deliberately gone about seducing him, and he remained unseduced.

And did he not want to be seduced, by his own wife? Had he not dreamed, for so long, of having this so self-possessed woman in his arms, surrendering to his passion? Or having him surrender to her. But there was the entire cause of the estrangement. She enjoyed mastering men, but not her own husband. His confession, on only the fifth night of their honeymoon, that his secret desire was to be tormented into orgasm had brought contempt, not understanding. The mistake had been his. He had sought more than was perhaps possible from a marriage. Than was perhaps possible from anyone, save Judith.

Then what did she find in Hardy?

Her face twisted. 'Or can you not manage such a thing, Tony dear?' she whispered softly.

'Aaaah,' she gasped. 'Aaagh.' Her body writhed to and fro, but he'd not let her go. His fingers dug deeper and deeper into the taut brown flesh, squeezing tighter and tighter. She had small

256

buttocks, and he had large hands. She lay on her face, on his belly, and tears mingled with the sweat on her cheeks, distorting the handsome, almost beautiful features, making the huge dark eyes expand, the whites show, while that splendid mouth sagged open, to reveal her teeth and her tongue, and saliva dribbled over her lips. She was the most beautiful creature he had ever known, and to turn that beauty into a mask of despair was the greatest pleasure he had ever known.

But today, there was no pleasure. He released her, violently, threw her away from him, watched her scatter across the bed, got up himself, with equal violence, went to the dresser, poured himself a glass of rum.

Judith Gale lay on her side, her head on her arm, and watched him. He had not climaxed, was in fact, still totally aroused, his naked body a quiver of blood-filled veins and arteries. Therefore he was still dangerous. Only she knew how dangerous. On the rare occasions he would play the master and not the victim, his whole being seemed consumed with hate, because it was hate which inspired the passion in the first place.

And she could only wait, for the pain in her back to subside, for a new pain to start. When he was ready.

Waves of apprehension drifted up her legs, into her belly. They were thin legs, as it was a thin belly. As they were narrow shoulders and small breasts. She worried about her thinness, but Tony told her it was what he liked about her. When he was in a good mood. He liked to trace the lines of muscle beneath the skin, and he liked to trace the arteries on her neck, and he liked to be able to take an entire breast in his hand, just as he would never permit her to wear her long dark hair other than loose on her back. Whatever her age, she must remain always the child he had first known, and wanted.

A child to be beaten, when he so desired. And what did the child feel about her tormentor, she wondered? It was not a luxury she usually permitted herself, to wonder about her situation, about her love, about her future. Her present was secure, in a purely material sense. Tony Hilton had paid for this house, and he had bought her slaves, and he paid for her clothes and her food. All he wanted in return was her utter obedience to his whims. So sometimes she thought other men would pay as much for Judith Gale. And demand much less. But would other men arouse *her*

257

passion? Because in a strange, perhaps a horrible, way, this man did.

He turned, his cup in his hand. 'Did I hurt you?' He was beginning to subside.

'Yes,' she said.

'So have a drink.' He held out the cup, and she hesitated, because if he was in one of his moods he would just as readily empty the liquid over her and the bed. Then she sat up, slowly, took the cup, sipped, felt her chest burn, some of the fear leave her mind.

'Why are you angry?'

He took back the cup, sat on the bed. 'I am angry. There is all that need concern you.'

She lay down again, rolling on her belly, propped her chin on her hands, allowed her eyes to gloom at him. She knew her assets. Her eyes counted higher than her hair. 'I thought, if I knew the reason, I could help you.'

'Aye,' he said. 'You will have to. Just now.'

'But what has so upset you?' she asked.

'I am a married man,' he said.

'Ah,' she said. 'Was your entertainment not a success?'

'It was a great success. Too successful, perhaps. She wants a child. Does she want a child? Or does she merely seek to humiliate me?'

'Why do you put up with her at all?'

His head turned, and she realized she had made a mistake. His eyes could also gloom, and when his eyes gloomed, it meant pain. But not for him.

'Would you replace her?'

'No, I . . .'

He turned, quickly and violently, seized her hair as she attempted to roll off the bed. He brought her back, while her eyes seemed to be forced from their sockets, rolled on top of her, bit her shoulder and tore at her flesh, and collapsed in a flood of sudden tears.

Judith lay still, afraid to move. She had known his moods before, but this was more than she remembered.

'You would replace her,' he whispered. 'You would be a superb mistress of Hilltop, Judith. You would be a superb wife to me. Wouldn't you, Judith?'

258

She gazed at the ceiling, felt his teeth on her ear. If only she could tell when he was baiting her, and when he was serious. She had never been able to tell that.

He raised his head. Tears still stained his cheeks. 'Well?'

She licked her lips. 'I . . . I would try, Tony. Would you let go of my hair?'

His fingers relaxed, slowly. 'And you would give me a child.' His frown returned, gathering that high forehead, that slightly receding hairline. 'You have not given me a child.'

She breathed, cautiously, inflating her chest against his. 'I did not know you wished any. I had supposed it would make you angry.'

The frown deepened. 'You can choose, whether or not you have a child?'

'I can make it likely or unlikely.'

'By using a douche? By counting days? None of those are certain.'

'I did not claim they were. I cannot breathe.'

'So, you could have become pregnant. Were I able.'

'I do not know, Tony. Please.'

For reply he gripped the bed and pressed his body even harder on hers. She gasped, and tried to push against him. 'Ellen has never taken any precautions.'

She gasped again. 'You do not sleep with her very often.'

His weight was gone. Cautiously she opened her eyes. He had rolled away, was sitting up.

'Ellen,' he said. 'If I could treat her as I treat you, just once.'

Judith drew up her knees, slowly and cautiously. 'Is she stronger than you?'

His head turned.

'It is just a matter of will,' she said. 'If it is that important to you.'

'But after,' he said. 'Would she love me, or hate me?'

'I do not know.'

'Do you love me, Judith?'

It was the first time he had ever asked her that question. 'I . . .'

'The truth.'

'I desire you. Even when you hurt me.'

He stared at her for some seconds, then turned away, got up, went back to the table.

259

'But you love her,' Judith said. 'After all this time, you love her, and you fear her.'

'How perceptive you are,' Tony remarked. 'She regards me with contempt. She regards you with contempt also.'

'She is entitled to do that.'

He drank, facing the wall. 'To hurt her,' he said. 'To make her beg . . . what the devil is that?'

Feet, clattering on the steps. Fingers, rattling on the door.

'Mis' Judith. Mis' Judith.'

'I shall certainly beat *her*.' Tony reached for his pants.

'It must be very important.' Judith got up, pulled on her undressing robe, turned the key. 'What is it, Melinda? You know I'm not to be disturbed when Mr Hilton is here.'

'Is Mr Hilton he does want, Mis' Judith.'

'He?'

'Who wants me?' Tony went to the door, fastening his belt.

'Is a man from the lawyer, sir. He saying it is very urgent.'

Tony pushed Judith to one side, went down the stairs. He glared at the clerk. 'Hanson? What the devil do you want?'

'There's a ship in, Mr Hilton,' Hanson panted and had lost his hat. 'The passengers came ashore an hour gone. And two of them went straight to Lawyer Reynolds.'

'Eh? What has that got to do with me?'

Hanson licked his lips, ran his fingers through his hair. ' 'Tis the name he claims, Mr Hilton. He says he is Richard Hilton, sir. Come home.'

14

The Claimant

'Way for the general. Way for the general.' The dragoons rode
their horses wide, on either side of the dusty street, scattering
passersby. 'Way for the general.'

Dick came next, sword slapping his thigh, pistols clinging to his
horse's neck. Behind him was another file of dragoons. The
general, returning from his tour of inspection.

To his city. There was a remarkable thought. Cap Haitien had
scarcely changed in appearance in the ten years since Christophe
had taken his own life; the country was poor, and money was
endlessly needed for the war against those black men who
continued to resist the unification of the nation, deep in the
mountains of the interior. But the people had changed. No doubt
they were even more poor than under their legendary emperor.
But they were also more happy. President Boyer might lack the
personality of his predecessor, but he was a sensible man who
understood the strengths as well as the weaknesses of his people.
The strengths he had used to conquer the island, to create a
nation. The weaknesses he had indulged to the extent of letting
them starve in their own way, if they chose. Which left the armed
forces the more attractive to any young man with a belly to fill.

The gates of the barracks swung open, the blue-coated guards
presented arms. There were no smarter soldiers in the entire
army, and they were General Warner's. Another stroke of Boyer's
genius for common sense. He had amnestied all of Christophe's
generals, providing they brought their men with them. And in
Matt Warner's dragoons he had found an elite. They had been the
van of the 1822 campaign which had finally conquered the old
Spanish half of the island.

He returned the salute, and his groom held his bridle. He

dismounted, strode up the steps to the commandant's quarters, and again the guards presented arms.

La Chat waited in the doorway. 'There are cases, sir.' For Cap Haitien, as indeed all of Haiti, remained under martial law.

Dick nodded. 'I will be with you in a moment, La Chat.' The door was being opened by one of the housemaids, and he went inside, and was surrounded by shouting children. Richard was eight, Anne was six, Thomas was four. Perfectly spaced. All healthy, bubbling Hiltons, except where they possessed the softer contours of their mother. He stooped to hug them each, looking all the while to the inner door, where Cartarette waited.

He sometimes supposed he lived his life in a long dream, firstly that the Dick Hilton he had been, and remembered, and still was deep in his heart, should have turned into this big, gaunt, ruthless soldier of fortune, and secondly that he should continue to share his bed with so gorgeous a creature. She had been seventeen years old that terrible day in 1817 when her father had been flogged to death. Now she was thirty, and four times a mother; her first daughter had died within two months of her birth. Yet was she hardly changed. She greeted him with a smile, put up her face to be kissed. She stood by his shoulder now, as she had stood by his shoulder for most of those thirteen years. Gislane's magic had made her his, physically. It had not been able to do more, to his knowledge. She stayed by his side because she had no choice. Her mother had died when she was a girl, her father had died beneath Christophe's whip. Her cousins had returned to France since the Restoration, but she was a poor relation, and she would rather be a general's woman than a case for charity.

Besides, he thought, she would not know how to live without him now—he had offered her freedom more than once. So they worked together, and talked together, and on occasion even laughed together.

But was she happy? He thought of her as he remembered thinking of his mother, years ago. She was his woman—they had never even been legally married—and so she was his support. She slept with her head on his shoulder, when he was in Cap Haitien. And did she weep herself to sleep when he was gone? He had stopped asking. It was a stupid, immature question. She was his. She could belong to no one else, now. Their lives were inextricably bound.

But she had never said that she loved him.

She held him close for a moment. 'Every time you leave,' she whispered, 'I suppose you will not come back.'

He kissed her forehead. 'There is no guerilla left within fifty miles of Cap Haitien.'

At last she released him. 'You have killed them all.'

'Aye.' He rubbed Richard's head; the boy still clung to his left arm. 'And what have you been up to?'

'I have built a fort, Papa. Well, Anne helped me. You must see it.'

'I shall, in a moment. La Chat has some villains for me to judge.'

'And hang?' Cartarette asked.

He sighed. 'If they require hanging, my sweet. I'll not be long. And then, this afternoon, I shall holiday. And look at your fort, Richie.'

He walked along the corridor, boots dull on the wood. Guards presented arms, and he was in his office. General Matthew Warner, military governor of Cap Haitien, taking court. It was the aspect of his life he liked least. But then, he was growing increasingly restless, year by year. There were no more fields to conquer, here in Haiti, and he was forty-five years old. Would he spend the rest of his life being nothing more than a policeman? 'Yes?'

The adjutant stood to attention; Colonel La Chat took his seat on the far side of the room. As provost marshal it was his duty to carry out the sentences.

'Antoine Dugalle, charged with the murder of his wife.'

Dick frowned at the big, sweating black man. 'Are you guilty?'

'Me, General? Man, General, we did fight, and I hit she on the head with she bottle. No more than that, General.'

'Witnesses?'

'Pierre Clousot.'

The other man came forward. 'Is true that she strike he first, General.'

'Whose bottle?'

'Well, she did be the last to drink, General. Is a fact.'

'Acquitted. Next.'

Johann Misère, charged with stealing one boat.'

This was a small man, paler in complexion than the others. But

263

also sweating.

'Are you guilty?'

'Is me crabs, General, sir. Me own boat get holed in that storm last month. Man, General, if I ain't taking in me pots we going starve.'

'So you took someone else's boat.'

'Well, man, General, sir, he ain't going to lend it to me.'

'Twenty lashes. Colonel La Chat, advance this man two pieces of gold to have his own boat repaired. Next case.'

'I thanking you, General, man, sir,' Misère said. 'I thanking you.'

'Aye,' Dick said. 'Next time I'll hang you. Next.'

'James Morrison, charged with smuggling.'

Dick raised his head. 'Guilty?' And frowned.

The white man badly needed a shave, and his face had collapsed in jowls, while his hair was almost entirely white.

'I didn't know I was smuggling, General. 'Tis the truth,' he gabbled. And he also sweated. 'This fellow asked me to bring the wine in, General, last time I was here.'

'When was that?'

'Last year, General. I didn't know there was a duty. And he collected it on board, sir. I didn't bring it ashore.'

Dick leaned back, stared at the man. How memory flooded back. Of everything he had considered, everything he had attempted, everything he had once been. And would be again? That was impossible. Dick Hilton was dead. Dead, dead, dead. He had never even been able to bring himself to write his mother, in fifteen years. Better that for her, too, he was dead. What, a son who fought for the murderers of her sister? And who had, in any event, changed into a monster.

But Morrison, God, what a memory. And what sudden temptation. Or had the temptation been there, all the time, and Morrison no more than a catalyst?

'Do you come here every year, Captain?'

'Well, sir, General, most years.'

Dick stood up. 'Court is finished for today. I would speak with this man, privately, La Chat.'

'General?'

'He may have news of my home, my people. You understand me, La Chat?'

'Of course, General.' La Chat came to attention, and the guards did likewise. Morrison gaped at them.

'Through that door, Captain Morrison,' Dick said.

The captain glanced around himself fearfully, then walked along the corridor. The children had returned to their fort in the yard. Cartarette stood by the front door, looking pensively at the courtyard, at Misère being placed between the uprights. She turned in surprise.

'Begging your pardon, mistress.' Morrison twisted his hat between his hands.

Cartarette looked at Dick, her eyebrows arched.

'An English sea captain,' Dick said. 'You'll take a glass of wine, Morrison.'

'Eh? Oh, aye, I'd take that very kindly, General Warner, sir.' He continued to stare at Cartarette in total bemusement.

'Accused of smuggling,' Dick said, and filled three glasses. 'Sit down, Captain.'

Morrison licked his lips, sank sideways into a straight chair. 'All I do is trade, General Warner. I'm no smuggler.'

Dick sat opposite him, Cartarette remained standing, but she moved closer to Dick. 'You have heard of me?'

'Everyone has heard of General Warner.'

'Then drink to General Warner. And tell me what they say of me.'

Morrison sipped cautiously. He could not stop his eyes drifting towards the woman. But Cartarette's face was expressionless.

'They say you are a great soldier.'

'I would like the truth, not flattery.'

Morrison shook his head violently. 'That is the truth, General. They say there is no cavalry commander like you. They say you served Christophe, faithfully and well. Now they say you command Cap Haitien.'

'Where do they say these things?'

'Everywhere, sir.'

'In England?'

'Oh, yes sir.'

'In Jamaica?'

'Oh yes, sir.'

'You trade with Jamaica?'

'I am on my way there now, sir.'

'Indeed? And what are things like, in Jamaica, at this moment?'

'Ah, sir,' Morrison said. 'Bad.'

'Bad? What do you mean?'

'Well, sir, there is friction, friction, sir, with the British Government. Over slavery, you'll understand, sir. What happened was, you see, the British gained some colonies from the French, as a result of the war. And these colonies, sir, were organized as possessions of the Crown, rather than as proprietary affairs, as were the old West Indies. Thus in the new colonies, the word of Whitehall is what counts, and Whitehall is for ameliorating the lot of the slaves. Some say they lean towards abolition of slavery, but that I cannot myself believe, sir. Well, as I say, what the British Government decrees is law in Guiana and Trinidad. But in Jamaica and the Leewards, why, sir, the Houses of Assembly there have long had total internal autonomy, and they resent any interference in their affairs from outside. So there is friction, sir, increased because, as you may know, sugar is in decline, sir, and the planters need all the help they can get in the way of tariff relief and open markets. 'Tis not only the state of the world, sir, 'tis also the growth of the beet industry in Europe. Bonaparte's doing.'

'The devil,' Dick said.

'Well, sir, the British Government has offered the colonies, the old colonies that is, all the assistance they require, providing they will adopt the new slave laws. And the colonies, sir, refuse, claiming blackmail.'

'And leading the colonies, as ever, will be Jamaica,' Dick said.

'Oh, indeed. There is talk of secession, sir. Of asking to become a state of the Union.'

'Planter's talk?' Dick asked. 'Who is involved?'

'Well, sir, the leader of the planters, in Jamaica, and indeed in all the West Indies, as he has property in Antigua, is Hilton of Hilltop.'

'Hilton,' Cartarette said. 'Of Hilltop.'

'Oh, a terrible man, mistress. He was a passenger on my ship, once. A long time ago. But even then he was a terrible man. Picked a duel, he did. Oh, a terrible man. A man who, it is said, treats his slaves like animals, and is totally opposed to any amelioration. That name, sir, you have heard it?'

Dick gazed at him, frowning, unimaginable ideas whipping

through his mind.

As Cartarette understood. 'You said you would never again deal with a black man, other than as an equal,' she said.

'Nor will I,' he said. 'But those people on Hilltop, they are my responsibility.'

'*Your* responsibility? After sixteen years?'

He finished his wine. 'I wonder why I stay here. I accomplish nothing now.'

'You are bored, because there is no war left to fight.'

'Have you no wish, ever, to return to a white society?'

She flushed. 'I doubt I would know how to set about it. Besides . . .' She hesitated.

'It will be difficult? Oh, indeed. But interesting. And if there is conflict . . .'

'Ah,' she said. 'Now it comes out.'

'Begging your pardon, sir,' Morrison said.

Dick glanced at him. 'This man who fought the duel on your ship, his name was Anthony Hilton.'

'The very man of whom I speak, sir. *The* Hilton.'

'But he had a brother, did he not? The real cause of the duel? The real Hilton, in point of fact.'

'Well, yes, sir. There was a brother. But he was lost at sea. Back in 1815.'

'So it is said,' Dick agreed. 'Have you ever met me before, Morrison?'

Morrison frowned at him, glanced at the woman. 'Met you, sir? Why . . .' He flushed.

'You would remember so hideous a countenance? But you will observe that my face is disfigured, so once it must have looked different. What of my voice? Do you remember nothing of my voice?'

Morrison's frown deepened. He finished his wine. 'Truly, sir . . .'

'Because that too has changed,' Dick said. 'Well, then, what of my memory. That duel on your ship. Was it not fought over a lady, called Joan Lanken?'

'You never mentioned her before,' Cartarette remarked.

'It was a botched affair. But I have no doubt the captain remembers it.'

'My God.' Morrison peered even closer. 'My God. It cannot be.'

'You'll remain in Cap Haitien, Morrison, while I write a letter to General Boyer. Then you'll give me passage to Jamaica,' Dick said. 'And on the way I shall refresh your memory.'

'Ratchet,' Morrison said. 'Ah, Harry Ratchet. A good man, Ratchet. You remember Ratchet, Mr Hilton?'

'I remember Ratchet.' Dick leaned back against the bulkhead, watching the wine swaying to and fro in his glass. What memories the movement of the ship brought back. And over the same water, too. But the weather was fine, the wind was where it should be, north east. It was impossible to suppose that brilliantly blue sky ever turning black, this gentle zephyr ever howling, this calm blue water ever rearing above the ship like a snake.

'Who was Ratchet?' Cartarette asked. The children had already been put to bed, and she sat beside him; their shoulders touched. Did she suppose this to be just a holiday, as he had told the President? Or did Boyer also know the truth of his intention. But did *he* know his intention? Haiti was perhaps the only place he had known happiness. His dragoons were the first men he had ever loved, could ever love. And he had turned his back on them. Because his name was Hilton.

'Mate of this ship, when last I sailed on her,' he said.

'A good man, Ratchet.' Morrison poured more wine. 'He got his own ship, soon after that voyage, Mr Hilton. Did well at it too. But was lost, sir. On the Atlantic crossing, and with all hands. There is sadness.' He smiled at them. 'But not the conversation for a return from the dead, I'll be bound. There'll be some surprised faces when we make Kingston. That Lanken, eh, Mr Hilton? I'll wager you have many a chuckle over that. Only a lad, then, Mistress Hilton. Only a lad. With no knowledge of weapons. I wonder what Lanken would say were he opposed to you now?'

'And this duel was over a woman, you say?' Cartarette inquired.

''Tis all in the past, Mistress Hilton. All in the past. We'll be in Port Royal harbour tomorrow morning.' He leaned forward, placed his elbows on the table. 'Oh, there'll be a to-do when you reappear, Mr Hilton. Oh, yes. They'll not believe it.'

'You believe it.'

'Well, you remember things only Richard Hilton could, and there's a fact. Seeing you now . . .' He shook his head. 'There'll be a to-do.'

268

'Aye.' Dick got up, braced himself against the bulkhead with his hand. 'I am for bed. Cartarette?'

She rose without a word, went into the cabin. Morrison's own cabin, as being the largest and the best. Only the best, for Richard Hilton. How long was it since he had thought that?

Cartarette avoided the swinging lantern, sat on the narrow bunk.

'Thirteen years,' he said. 'I would like to marry you, as Richard Hilton. Will you?'

She stared at him, tears forming behind her frown.

'Well?'

'It would be best, for the children.'

'But not for you?'

Again the long stare.

'Or have you not yet forgiven me for my sins?'

She moved back against the bulkhead. He could not clearly see her eyes in the gloom. 'I would know what you mean to do.'

He sat beside her. 'Why, reclaim my plantations. My name. My place in society.'

'Why?'

He frowned at her.

'Have you not wealth enough?'

'I do not pursue wealth,' he said.

'Would you avenge yourself on your brother?'

'I have nothing to avenge. I disappeared, he assumed my place. That is logical.'

'Well, then, I do not understand. You wish to leave Haiti? I can understand that. In Jamaica we have but to remain on board this ship, and within a week we will be bound for Europe. No one will recognize you, unless you choose to reveal your memory. Morrison will say nothing, should you require him to be close. And the alternative is strife. You do realize that, Mr Hilton? You may feel no animosity towards your brother, but he, if he has enjoyed your prerogatives for this long, will have to be a perfect paragon to welcome you back. Is your brother a paragon?'

Dick smiled at her. 'No, I cannot honestly say that he is. Oh, Tony will not be pleased, I can promise you that. But he is a minor matter. There will hardly be a white face in Jamaica smiling at my return.'

'Yet you wish to return. Is it that you do not know what to do with yourself, now you no longer have a war to fight? So you would oppose an entire country?'

'It is a difficult matter.'

'Beyond my understanding, certainly.'

'Well, try. I have spoken of my father.'

'He is an Abolitionist.'

Dick nodded. 'And brought me up in his beliefs. He was also a pacifist. Then I found myself pitchforked into the ownership of a plantation. Always I felt in a false position, but I was nevertheless happy to enjoy that position. Until all my . . . they were not truly sins. All my weaknesses, perhaps, crept up on me, and I fled, like a frightened child. To a world which made my fears, my uncertainties, truly seem childlike.'

'A world you conquered,' she said. 'You can have no fears of Jamaica, now.'

'I do not have any fears of Jamaica,' he said. 'But it seems to me that fate has been leading me on, perhaps all of my life. I have thought a good deal about it, this past year. I am the heir to a great crime. I was not allowed to survive so much, experience so much, become what I am, to continue condoning that crime.'

'Abolition is best left to missionaries,' she said.

'I do not think missionaries have the strength. I have had little to do with God, these past fifteen years. But I do remember He is a God of wrath. And it must have been His choice that I survived, and became strong.'

'You are starting to talk like a Biblical prophet,' she said. But her tone was soft.

'I will free my slaves, Cartarette,' he said. 'It is something I have always wanted to do, and lacked the courage.'

'And will they thank you? Can black people organize their lives, to survive, to prosper? Can you really say that, after living in Haiti? After what happened to Christophe?'

'His failure is the proof of his ineptitude.'

'His . . . he was your friend.'

'That does not alter the fact of the man. He had vision, and ability. But he knew nothing but slave, and master. When he drove out the white masters, he could think of nothing better than to replace them with black.'

'There must always be, masters, and men,' she said.

'There must always be leaders,' he said. 'And followers. You do

270

not lead, with a whip. You inspire men to follow you.'

She began to unfasten her gown. 'I doubt the world is yet ready for such a philosophy.'

'I have thought of that. So perhaps you are right, after all, and I only know how to fight, now, and so I wish to continue fighting. Cartarette . . .' He caught her hands. 'You have fought too long. I would not have you involved in this business.'

'I am your woman.'

'Hardly by choice. Nor do I expect you to defend a black cause. If you would like to remain on board this ship, and take passage to England, I will make sure you are forever wealthy, and respected.' He smiled. 'I may even be able to join you, one day, supposing you wish it.'

'I am your woman,' she said again. 'No doubt I too would be bored to cease fighting. I will stay with you.'

'And support me?'

'Of course.'

'Whether or not you agree with me?'

'Of course,' she said again.

'And will you be happy?'

She gazed at him for some seconds, then gently freed her hands. 'I was made the slave of a man I hated, and whom I came to . . .' her tongue touched her lips thoughtfully, 'to respect. Now it seems that man no longer exists. So now I belong to, and am asked to marry, a stranger. You must give me time to get to know this new man.'

'And when you do get to know him?'

'Then I will know whether or not I am happy, Mr Hilton.'

'My word,' Reynolds said. 'What a to-do. What a to-do, eh?' He leaned across his desk, frowning. 'Richard Hilton, back from the dead? I cannot believe it.'

Dick sighed. Twenty years had passed since the first time he had sat in this chair—it could very well be the same chair—and nothing had changed at all. The harbour had not changed; there were fewer ships than usual riding to anchor, but the bending palm trees on Los Palisadoes, the rise of mountains behind the town, were the same. The waterfront had not changed, unless the docks had become even more rickety; there had been the same crowd of touts, white and black, to greet Cartarette and himself

271

and the children, as they had stepped ashore. Harbour Street had not changed; the brown paint still peeled from the walls, dust still gathered in the corners of the verandahs, dogs and poultry still scratched in the alleys. And Reynolds had not changed, save perhaps to become even more shrivelled and precise in appearance.

Only one aspect of the situation had changed. The man who now claimed to be Richard Hilton.

'You remember nothing about me?'

Reynolds leaned back, looked at Cartarette, then at Morrison. 'Well, sir, yours is an unusual face, if I may say so. One a man would remember.'

'It is the result of an accident,' Dick said, patiently.

'And he is Mr Richard, Mr Reynolds,' Morrison said. 'Why, he can remember events on the voyage out here, like if they was yesterday.'

'Richard Hilton,' Reynolds said, and suddenly beamed. 'If you knew, sir, how I have dreamed of your return, how I have longed for your return.' He rose, came round the desk, seized Dick's hands. 'Oh, happy, happy, day.' Then his face fell as if someone had jerked a string to take the pleasure away. 'I have sent my boy along to Mr Tony Hilton, to request him to visit me here . . .'

'You have sent to Hilltop?'

'Why, no, sir. This day, Mr Hilton happens to be in town . . . why that must be him now.'

Booted feet clattered on the outside staircase. Dick stood up, turning to face the door. Cartarette also turned, still seated, her face seeming to close with tension.

The door opened. 'Reynolds? What farce is this?'

Reynolds mopped his brow. 'No farce, Mr Hilton. Why here is your brother, returned from the grave.'

Tony had not put on his coat, and was bareheaded. He stood in front of the doorway and gazed at Dick for some seconds. Then he burst into laughter.

'*That*? Is my brother? I have never credited you with so much humour, Reynolds.'

'Why, sir . . .' Reynolds gave Dick an imploring look.

Dick held out his hand. 'You could at least say welcome.'

'To you, sir? Who are these people?'

Reynolds sat down again, heavily. 'Why, sir . . .'

272

"'Tis Mr Richard, all right, Mr Hilton, sir,' Morrison said.

'And this is my wife, Cartarette,' Dick said. 'My brother, Tony Hilton.'

Cartarette held out her hand. 'Indeed sir, I am so happy to make your acquaintance. To gain some idea of what my husband may once have looked like.'

Tony looked from the woman to the man, frowning. 'The joke grows tiresome. Once looked like, you say? That monster?'

'But it is Mr Richard, sir,' Morrison insisted again. 'Why, Mr Hilton, he can remember all the events of that voyage from England, back in 1810. Mistress Lanken, the duel . . . everything.'

Tony gave him a glance. 'Indeed? Do you still drink, Morrison? There is rum on your breath now. How much did this fellow vouchsafe, and how much did you tell him, in your drunken gibbering?'

'Why, sir . . .' Morrison protested. But he took a step backwards at the same time.

'Your own brother, Mr Hilton,' Reynolds said. 'I'd have thought you'd recognize your own brother, Mr Hilton. His voice . . .'

'Is like the croak of a corpse,' Tony declared, and came closer, carelessly brushing against Cartarette to dislodge her hat. 'I do not know your little game, sir. But I will tell you this. I am Anthony Hilton. *The* Hilton, of Hilltop. I had a brother once, who died at sea, may God rest his soul. I loved him dearly, sir, and will not have him used as a plaything in some attempt at fraud. I tell you this, sir. I will give you twenty-four hours to leave Jamaica, and take your woman with you, or by God I will have you thrown into gaol.'

All of Dick's bubbling anger seemed to well up through his chest to explode in his brain. His two hands, as powerful as steel claws from his long years of campaigning, came up together, to seize the front of Tony's shirt and half lift him from the floor as he brought him close.

Tony gasped in amazement, and for the moment, sheer fright.

'Mr Hilton,' protested Reynolds. It was impossible to decide whom he was addressing.

Morrison clapped his hands in delight. But Cartarette merely moved herself out of the way. She knew no other Richard Hilton.

'You . . . you . . .' Tony gasped, attempting to swing his own fists, but finding himself unable to move, as Dick held him close.

'You, listen to me,' Dick said. 'And look at me, very carefully. My face is changed. My voice has changed. But my eyes have not changed. Look carefully, brother, and you will recognize me.'

'You . . .' Tony continued to struggle to free himself, but from the expression on his face it was clear that he was realizing he had no chance against his strength.

'And then you will understand, brother,' Dick said, still speaking quietly, 'that it is you would practise fraud, and you who will likely wind up in gaol. Think about that.'

He released the shirt front so suddenly that Tony lost his balance, and almost fell over. He braced himself on the desk.

Dick wiped his hands on his kerchief. 'So, I will inform you, brother, that I propose to take up residence on Hilltop, and within the week. I will give you that long to prepare yourself.'

Tony pulled his clothes straight, glanced at Cartarette. His face glowed with anger.

'By God, sir,' he said. 'Did I suppose you to be even half of a gentleman, I'd call you out, sir. Then we'd have you singing a different tune.'

'One week,' Dick repeated.

Tony looked at Reynolds. 'And you, sir, beware you do not yourself fall victim to fraud. My brother? Dick Hilton? You remember Dick Hilton, Reynolds. Can you really suppose this . . . this bully has anything in common with so gentle a soul?' He backed to the door, opened it. 'Be sure the law will attend to you, sir. Be sure of it.' He closed the door and ran down the stairs.

The horse wheezed to a halt before the steps. It had been galloped too far. Foam settled around its lips, and its legs quivered; it could barely stand.

The grooms held the bridle, and exchanged glances. But the master was a law unto himself, and he looked in scarce better shape than the horse.

Tony Hilton stamped up the steps, sat in one of the cane chairs on the verandah. 'Boscawen,' he bawled. 'Boscawen. Bring me a drink. Quickly, man.'

'Yes, sir, Mr Hilton. Sangaree?'

'Rum.' Tony leaned back, looked out across the plantation,

down at the town and the slave village, at the factory and the trembling cane stalks. His plantation. It was his. He had made it what it was.

Boscawen set the tray with the bottle and the glasses beside him, straightened in a hurry as Ellen swept through the front door. She wore pale green as usual, a sun bonnet, and carried a parasol.

'Tony? You're back early.'

He frowned at her, drank, frowned some more. 'Where are you going?'

'For a walk. I walk most afternoons, when it gets cool.' Her turn to frown. 'Are you all right? You look as if you've seen a ghost.'

His head jerked. 'A ghost? My God.' He drank some more. His hand shook, and some of the liquid dribbled down his chin.

Ellen's frown deepened. She laid her parasol on the table, sat in the chair next to his. 'You've quarrelled with Judith?'

'Oh, be sensible.' He refilled his glass.

'You are the one who will soon be *in*sensible. Whatever is the matter?'

He glanced at her, peered into the glass. 'We must leave.' He drank, and made an attempt to square his shoulders. 'Aye. There is a ship in the harbour. We must leave. You'll pack, and we'll go into town tonight.'

'Are you utterly mad?' Ellen inquired, her voice assuming that brittle texture he knew, and feared, so well.

'Suppose . . .' He licked his lips. 'Suppose I told you I *had* seen a ghost?'

'I would repeat, you have gone mad. Or that is not your first bottle.'

'But this ghost,' Tony went on, half to himself, 'lives and breathes and speaks. And acts. Dick.'

Ellen's frown returned. 'Whatever are you talking about?'

'Dick. He is in Kingston. I think.'

'Dick? Dick is dead. You told me he was dead. He was drowned.'

'He is in Kingston, I tell you.'

'You saw him?'

'I . . .' He drank some more rum. 'I think so.'

She gazed at him for some moments, then got up. 'You had best come with me.'

'Where?'

'Somewhere that scoundrel Boscawen cannot overhear us.' She

walked down the steps, waited.

Tony finished his glass, looked at the bottle reluctantly, then rose and followed her. She walked in front of him, away from the house, into the cemetery. Here they would see anyone approaching them long before they could be heard.

'Now try,' she said, 'to talk some sense.'

'Reynolds sent for me.'

'Reynolds *sent* for *you*?'

'Well . . .' Tony flushed. 'He sent a message that the matter was urgent. So I went to his office, and this . . . this man was there.'

'This man? Just now you said it was Dick.'

'Well . . . he claimed to be Dick.'

'Oh, for God's sake,' she cried, at last revealing her own anxiety. 'Don't you know your own brother?'

'Ah,' he said. 'There's the point. This man has had some sort of an accident. You really should see him. His face is quite disfigured. Hideous.'

'Dick's face?' she asked in a lower tone.

'It could be anyone's face.'

'He spoke to you?'

Tony shrugged. 'It could be anyone's voice.'

'Oh, you really are a *fool*,' she declared. 'Why did you not just have the scoundrel arrested?'

'Well, he remembers things . . . he had Morrison with him, and a woman. A Frenchwoman, who seems to be his wife.'

'His wife?' Ellen inquired, her voice becoming softer still.

'Aye. A pretty woman. Well, striking more than pretty. Aye. But the fact is, Morrison thinks he is Dick.'

'And who,' Ellen asked, with great patience, 'is Morrison?'

'Oh, I'd forgotten . . . the captain of the *Green Knight*. The ship which brought us out here.'

'Twenty years ago?'

'Aye. There is the point. This man remembers much of what happened on that voyage.'

'He remembers the duel, I have no doubt at all,' Ellen said. 'And the name of the woman involved. Joan Lanken. Am I not right?'

'Indeed you are. But . . .'

'I remember them too, you see. And I was not there. But you

276

have told me about it. Once. I think.'

'That thought occured to me also,' Tony said, 'But . . .'

'Where did this man come from?'

'Well, from Haiti.'

'Haiti?' she cried.

'Cap Haitien, in point of fact.'

'A white man?'

'Well, it seems he has been fighting with the blacks. Oh, he is a right soldier of fortune. Big, and strong, and violent of temper. His manners are as terrible as his looks.'

'And you suppose such a man to be Dick?'

'Aye, well, it is incredible. But yet, the ship was supposed to go down off Haiti.'

'And this proves it did. It may even prove that Dick reached the shore, and may have lived for some time. And no doubt confided much of his past to this fellow. Thus he has waited this long to begin his charade. For as he *has* begun his charade, you may be sure that Dick is certainly dead.'

'But,' Tony said again.

'And you'd run away from a fraud,' she said scornfully. 'Are you so afraid of your own deception? I supposed I had married a man, not a coward. Or are you afraid of the man himself? Big, you say. Terrible. Strong. And you the most feared duellist in all Jamaica. You must be suffering from the heat. Have the man arrested, and put an end to it.'

Tony chewed his lip. He walked to Robert Hilton's grave, stood above it, looking at the headstone, fists opening and shutting.

Ellen watched him for some moments. 'Or is there something you haven't told me?'

Tony inflated his lungs, let them collapse again. It could hardly be called a sigh; more it was a gesture of despair. 'He assaulted me,' he muttered.

'Assaulted you? This creature dared lay a finger on you? You broke his head, I hope.'

'Just for a moment,' Tony said. 'He held me close. He made me stare into his eyes. My God, Ellen. Those eyes. They belonged to Dick. I swear it. The man had Dick's eyes.'

The dining room of the Park Hotel in Kingston was a quiet place. John Mortlake liked it so. For too long the establishment had been

277

little better than a brothel, but since the end of the war he had worked hard on improving his reputation along with its cuisine and decor. The decor remained a trifle garish; Mr Mortlake had a weakness for red, on walls and ceiling, to which he added gold-coloured curtains. But the waitresses, slave girls dressed in white and with red sashes and caps, were carefully taught to move as silently as their bare feet would permit, and woe betide any young woman who rattled a cup or clattered a fork.

Conversation, too, was encouraged in whispers. Mr Mortlake himself sat at a table in the corner of the room, and was liable to gaze with a forbidding frown at anyone who raised his or her voice so that it could be heard at even the next table. The Park Hotel's reputation *had* improved. Not only was it the place in town to stay — the number of the rooms having been doubled by the addition of an annexe — but it had also become a place to dine. And on a Saturday night it was invariably full, every table displaying a couple in evening gown and dark broadcloth sack coat, regardless of the heat, and laden with the best food and the best wine Kingston could provide, while in the corner an orchestra, consisting mainly of fiddles, scraped away to make each conversation even more private. Saturday night was an occasion to gladden any hotelier's heart, especially as on this most special night in the week Mr Mortlake felt entirely justified in doubling his prices.

Yet he was not a happy man, this Saturday night. He occupied his usual place in the corner, and looked across the tables and his customers, watched his girls scurrying about their duties, and attempted to listen to as little of the poorly played Mozart as possible. And watched the couple on the far side of the room, aware that every other person in the room was doing the same, equally surreptitiously, but with equal interest.

He had no reason to complain about them, certainly. The man might be as disfigured as a nightmare, but his clothes were good, and he had paid for his room, as he would pay for his dinner, in gold coin. And he was a quiet-spoken, reserved fellow. The woman was quite charming, her colouring a delight to the eye as the candlelight sparkled in her titian hair, her gown, in royal blue silk, the most expensive in the room. She wore no jewellery, not even a wedding ring, but that was her choice, surely her choice. No one could doubt she could afford it if she wished. Her children were noisy, but by eight o'clock on a Saturday night were already in bed.

Looked at in a purely commercial sense, they were the most promising customers the Park Hotel had entertained for some time. But Mr Mortlake worried. Rumours were sweeping the town. They had certainly reached the ears of all of his other guests. As they had reached him. He did not know whether to believe them or not. He only knew, as he dipped his spoon into the soft green flesh of his avocado pear, the most delicate and digestible of vegetables, that his stomach seemed filled with a leaden sense of foreboding.

What did they discuss? For the first time in his life he wished to overhear a customer's conversation. The man smiled, and the woman smiled in return. When she smiled she was beautiful. When he smiled he was the most terrible thing Mortlake had ever seen. But not, apparently, to his wife. And they seemed happy. And confident. Yet they could not be unaware of the rumours, having started them.

He scraped the last of his avocado, raised his head with the spoon, and swallowed before the food actually reached his mouth. The lead in his stomach redoubled its weight, so that he felt quite incapable of rising.

He looked through the opened doors of the dining salon into the hotel lobby, and thus could see anyone who entered the hotel from the street. As Mr and Mrs Anthony Hilton had just done. And as now one, and then another, of his guests, had also just noticed. Heads were beginning to turn, and the whisper of conversation was beginning to become a murmur, rising above even the scrape of the fiddle bows.

Mr and Mrs Hilton had dined elsewhere, it seemed. Mrs Hilton wore a crimson gown beneath a white cape; her hair was up, and there were diamonds at her throat and hanging from her ears. Mr Hilton wore black. Nor were they alone. Two other couples entered the lobby behind them, both also planters, the Treslings of Orange Lodge, and the Evans of Green Acre. They also wore evening dress.

Mortlake put down his spoon, hastily rose to his feet. 'Play,' he growled, as he passed the orchestra. 'Play, damn it.'

The fiddles recommenced their wail. Mortlake reached the doorway. 'Mrs Hilton,' he said. 'What an honour. Mr Hilton, welcome, sir, welcome. Harvey. Harvey. Prepare a table for Mr Hilton and his guests. Why, Mrs Tresling, how good to see you. Mr Tresling, sir, you are looking well. Mrs Evans . . .'

'I would see the monster,' Ellen Hilton said, speaking in her loudest voice.

'Eh?' Mortlake realized to his horror that the fiddles had again stopped.

Gwynneth Evans gave a high pitched giggle. 'We've come especially, Mortlake. To see the monster.'

'The monster,' Grace Tresling cried. 'The monster.'

Mortlake scrabbled for his handkerchief. Three of the leading planters' wives in all Jamaica, and every one drunk. Well, at least, two were drunk. He did not feel Ellen Hilton was anything less than deadly sober.

'It will be entertainment,' she declared, and swept into the dining room, her husband at her elbow, her friends spreading out to form a flanking movement. The other diners stared at her. Mortlake dared not look across the room, but even from the corner of his eye he observed that the man with the disfigured face had risen.

'My God.' Ellen Hilton pointed, her fan forming an extension of her fingers. 'It *is* a monster.'

'A monster, a monster,' chanted Gwynneth Evans.

'Gad,' John Tresling remarked. 'What a horrible looking fellow.'

Ellen crossed the room, her skirts swinging, causing the other diners hastily to pull their chairs closer to their tables. One couple got up and left the room. Mortlake wished he could do the same.

'Ellen,' Dick said. 'My God, Ellen Taggart. How simply splendid to see you. Why did not someone tell me you were still in Jamaica?'

'My God,' Ellen said, coming to a halt before them. 'It *is* a monster.' She glanced at Cartarette. 'Are you the creature's minder?'

Cartarette watched Dick.

'Tony?' he asked. 'What farce is this? When did Ellen return?'

'I'll trouble you to mind your tongue, fellow,' Tony said, also speaking very loudly. 'You are addressing Mistress Hilton, of Hilltop.'

Dick gazed at Ellen for a moment, and then could not stop

280

himself laughing. Once, he remembered, he had feared she would look like her mother, as time went by. He had been pessimistic. Her face had hardened, and become more gaunt, her teeth were prominent. But her wealth, her arrogance, shrouded her in splendour.

'Mistress Hilton, of Hilltop? Well, well. So you achieved your ambition after all. And I must say, my dear Ellen, the position does suit you. What a pity you will have to give it up.'

The forced humour had left her face. The pink spots he remembered so well were gathering in her cheeks. And now she swung her hand.

But he caught her wrist without difficulty. The force of her blow carried her onwards, so that she half fell against him.

'Mr Hilton,' she cried. 'The beast is assaulting me.'

The hubbub became uproar. Women screamed, men scrambled to their feet with a scraping of chairs and a scattering of crystal and crockery. Mr Mortlake stood in the doorway and tore his hair.

'Scoundrel,' Tony bawled, starting forward, supported by Evans and Tresling. 'Wretch, I'll have you whipped, by God. I'll . . .' He gave a gasp and fell to his hands and knees, Cartarette having allowed one of her feet to creep out from under the table and catch his ankle.

'By God, madame,' he spluttered.

Dick had by now completely turned Ellen round, so that her back was to him, while he retained his grip on her wrist.

'I see you, at the least, have not changed at all, Ellen,' he said. 'How is your dear mother?'

'You . . . you . . .' She wriggled and tried to kick backwards, and only succeeded in dislodging her hair, which fell forwards down her face, fluttering as she tried to breathe.

'Why, Ellen,' Gwynneth Evans remarked. 'You are coming undone.'

Tony held on to the table to pull himself to his feet. Cartarette prudently rose as well, backing against the wall.

'John,' Tony bawled, waving at Tresling, who had stopped and seemed uncertain what next to do. 'Arrest that man.'

'Who, me?'

'You are Chief Custo,' Tony bawled. 'Arrest him. Throw him in gaol.'

'On what charge, would you say?'

'Why, common assault. Look at the way he is manhandling my wife.'

'You may have her back,' Dick said, giving Ellen a gentle push which sent her into the arms of her husband.

'You must call him out,' Evans said. 'Oh, yes. He has insulted you, Tony.'

Tony gazed into his brother's eyes. 'Call him out? Call that . . . that monstrosity out? I fight with gentlemen, Evans. Not renegade nigger lovers.'

'And perhaps not with your brother,' Cartarette said, speaking for the first time.

Tony glared at her, then turned back to his friend. By now the other diners had retreated to the far side of the room, where they clustered around Mortlake as if protecting him, or seeking his protection themselves.

'Arrest him,' he said again. 'I'll prefer the charges. Fraud. Perjury. Oh, I'll prefer the charges.'

Tresling took an uncertain step forward.

'If you come one step closer without a warrant,' Dick said, speaking quietly, 'I shall break your head.'

'My word,' Tresling said. 'My word.'

'Oh, Ellen,' Gwynneth whispered, loudly. 'You do look a mess.'

'Am I to take it,' Dick remarked, 'that you intend to persist in denying that I am Richard Hilton, that you intend to attempt to hold on to your possession of Hilltop, illegally?'

'Why, you . .. .' Tony's face was dark with blood.

Ellen finally gave up trying to blow her hair away and used her hands, scraping it to either side of her face. 'We intend to charge you with attempted fraud, with perjury, and with assault,' she said, also keeping her voice under control. 'We are going to see that you go to prison for the rest of your life. Mr Tresling will obtain a warrant in the morning.'

Dick gave her a slight bow. 'And tomorrow morning, Mr Hilton, I shall file formal claim to Hilltop and Green Grove, as Richard Hilton. I look forward to seeing you ladies and gentlemen again, in court.'

15

The Witness

'His Excellency will see you now, Mr . . . ah, Hilton.' The secretary was a small, precise man, with a pince-nez. 'And . . . ah, Mistress Hilton, of course.'

Dick rose, gave his arm to Cartarette. He had abandoned his uniform in favour of a severe black broadcloth coat over white buckskin breeches, to look the perfect picture of a planter. As Cartarette, in dark blue, was also most soberly dressed. There could be no questioning her utter support, her utter loyalty. As if he had ever questioned that.

But it was amazing to consider that this was the first time he had ever set foot in Government House since leaving his card, twenty years before.

The double doors were opened, the long sweep of the Governor's office stretched in front of them; at the rear french windows led to the garden, an expanse of lawn. It was a large, pleasant, cool room. But the floor needed polish as the walls needed paint.

The Earl of Belmore stood behind his desk. He looked tired, and his heavy features had dissolved into jowls. He wore a black band on his arm, as the flag on the staff beyond his window drooped at half mast, as some of the shops on Harbour Street were draped in black crepe. But the news of the King's death had had little impact on Jamaica; George IV had not been the most popular of men. People hoped for more from his brother, who at least had a personal acquaintance with the West Indies.

'Mr Hilton,' he said. 'Madame. You would prefer me to use Hilton?'

'It is my name, your Excellency.'

'Of course. Of course.' Belmore peered at Dick's features. 'Of course,' he said a third time. 'Please be seated. Lomas. Chairs.'

The secretary had already placed two straight chairs before the desk; now he held one for Cartarette.

The earl lowered himself, slowly. His hand flapped on the desk. 'A warrant, for your arrest.'

'I understood there was to be one, your Excellency.'

The earl sighed. His hand flapped on another piece of parchment. 'An affidavit, attested by Mr Reynolds, claiming that you are Richard Hilton, the rightful owner of Hilltop. The warrant alleges intent to defraud, conspiracy, assault. To prove your innocence of that charge, you will have to prove the validity of the affidavit.'

'I intend to do so, your Excellency.'

'Exactly. There have been representations. By the planters, to ignore the affidavit until the criminal charges have been proven.'

Dick waited. He would not have been invited here had the Governor intended to take notice of the planters.

'That of course, would be a grave injustice, if you *are* Richard Hilton,' Belmore said. 'So I will hold the warrant, for the time being. Or perhaps I should say, I am inclined to do so.' He sighed again, and looked at Cartarette. His features relaxed just a little before once more tightening. 'If I am persuaded.'

'By my proof?'

The Governor's head turned, slowly, back towards Dick.

'That in a moment. Are you familiar with events in Jamaica? Present events?'

'I am rapidly becoming so.'

'Matters are rushing to a crisis,' Belmore said. 'Between Great Britain and the planters here. Depending upon what happens in the general election in England, now King William is on the throne, the crisis may already be upon us. There is a spirit of rebellion abroad. And the planters' leader is Hilton of Hilltop.'

'So I have heard.'

'I never knew Richard Hilton,' Belmore said, half to himself. 'I have heard he became involved in scandal, and social ostracism, almost immediately upon his arrival in Jamaica. But I have also heard his reputation, as a man who looked after his people, brooked no unnecessary ill-treatment. I have heard that he dismissed his entire bookkeeping staff for brutality, within twenty-

284

four hours of his arrival on Hilltop.'

'That is incorrect, your Excellency. The bookkeeping staff left Hilltop because of that very scandal you have just mentioned.'

The Governor gazed at him for some seconds. 'Do you know,' he said at last, 'I am beginning to believe in you, Mr Hilton.' He picked up the warrant, folded it into two halves, and then tore it across, dropping the pieces daintily into the wastepaper basket beside his desk. 'I am assuming you have not changed your point of view.'

'I have not, your Excellency.'

'Yet you will understand my personal belief in your ability to recall one or two things which Richard Hilton may be expected to remember will not win you your suit. When I sit in judgment, I must be entirely impartial. Have you any plan of offence, or defence for that matter?'

'I have written to my mother,' Dick said.

'A good beginning. She knows your handwriting, no doubt?'

'Unfortunately, that too has changed,' Dick said. 'Slightly, but enough to remove the difference between the real thing and a skilful forgery. At least according to Mr Reynolds.'

'Hm,' said the Governor. 'Hm.'

'I must also tell you that this is the first letter I have written my mother for sixteen years.'

'Why?'

'Well . . .' Dick bit his lip. 'I was very ill, following my shipwreck, and when I recovered my senses, it was to discover myself as you see me now. I doubt my own mother would have recognized me then. And I was myself upset by my appearance. I put off writing to my family, until I felt more familiar with my new self, but then I became enrolled as an officer in Christophe's army, and in the midst of that brutal war I could no longer bring myself to believe in Richard Hilton, or that my mother would wish to recognize me.'

'Hm,' the Governor said again. And looked at Cartarette. 'But you know the truth, madame?'

She flushed. 'I know nothing that will be of value to a court, your Excellency. I met my husband as Matthew Warner. But I believe in the truth of what he says, as I know the man.'

'As you say, hardly proof,' the Governor mused. 'What do you hope of your mother, Mr Hilton?'

'That she will write back and acknowledge me,' Dick said. 'I have listed in my letter certain events which happened in my youth, which she should remember.'

The Governor sighed. 'I should say that in the application for your arrest as a fraud, Mr Hilton, your . . . ah . . . brother dismisses your claim to remember certain events on board the *Green Knight* twenty years ago, as being possibly told to you by the real Richard Hilton, his words, before his decease. The same stricture could be made with regard to boyhood incidents. Nonetheless, I agree that acknowledgement by Mistress Hilton of you as her son, would be of the greatest value to your case. Obviously we must put back the court hearing until such word is received. And just as obviously your opponents will wish it held as soon as possible. You may leave that in my charge. It is a civil case, and these matters always take a great deal of time. However, I do feel that you would be well to attempt to obtain some additional proof of your identity.'

Dick frowned at him. Then slapped his hand on the desk. 'There are a great many people who knew me when I lived here sixteen years ago. My manager, James Hardy . . .'

'Hm,' said the Governor. 'Hardy is very much an adherent of his employer, *the* Hilton. He is indeed a rabid anti-Abolitionist.'

'Well, then, my slaves. What of Joshua Merriman, my field manager?'

'Ah. When I realized that this case was coming before me, I looked up the files on that event. Joshua Merriman ran away from Hilltop, about a year after Richard Hilton's disappearance. Frankly, there were disquieting suggestions about the whole affair. As you say, Richard Hilton had employed him as a field manager, whereas Anthony Hilton promptly demoted him to being a field slave, and I believe inflicted a merciless flogging as well. Alas, whatever the truth of the matter, Merriman certainly ran away, and was never heard of again. Nor did he seek refuge in the Cockpit Country, for we had the matter investigated. I am afraid he very likely died, from exposure or starvation.'

'My God,' Dick said. 'Josh? He was my truest friend.'

'An honourable sentiment, Mr Hilton. But one which cannot help your case.'

'Mr Boscawen?'

'Anthony Hilton's butler? I would remind you that he has been the butler on Hilltop for the last sixteen years, at the least. What does that suggest to you?'

'I would not have expected my brother to do less than reinforce his position to the utmost.'

'In every way,' the Governor pointed out. 'Marrying your erstwhile fiancée, for example. Were Ellen Hilton to identify you, and who better? You must have been . . . ah . . . intimate with her during your betrothal, so presumably she would be capable of identifying you. But she has added her denunciation to that of your brother.'

'For an obvious reason,' Dick said. 'As she has tied her fortune to his.'

'Oh, quite,' said the Governor. 'Yet the fact is there.'

'You spoke of Harriet Gale,' Cartarette said, quietly.

'My God,' Dick cried. 'Fool that I am. Harriet Gale. She will certainly be able to identify me.'

'Harriet Gale?' The Governor frowned. 'Mistress Gale died, three years ago.'

'Died? She was not very old.'

'She drank, Mr Hilton. As you no doubt remember. And she lived a most scandalous life, as you also no doubt recall. My apologies, Mistress Hilton. But you seem to be aware of the woman's part in your husband's life.' Again the heavy sigh. 'The situation is not so easy as might be supposed. But at least now you know the odds which oppose you. Be sure you take steps to counter them, Mr Hilton. I have torn up your warrant, which will not please the plantocracy. Yet must they abide by my decision, until I have been proved to have erred in my judgement. They cannot harm *me*. But they will certainly wish to harm you. Your suit against your brother will be to all intents and purposes a criminal trial, and should you fail to make good your claim in law, there will be another warrant which I will not be able to destroy, and concerning which the evidence will have already been heard, and the judgement already given, at least as regards any jury you may discover in this island. Bear that in mind, for God's sake, Mr Hilton.' He rose. 'I bid you good day. Madame, this has been a very great pleasure. I would hope when next we meet it may be in happier circumstances.'

'Do you suppose,' Dick mused, 'that the good Governor was

attempting to hint that it would be best for me to drop my case, and leave Jamaica?'

They walked down the street, arm in arm, Cartarette's right hand holding her parasol. And were the principal source of interest in Kingston, clearly. Passersby gave them a hasty nod, and then stopped to look back, curtains were surreptitiously moved aside to permit them to be overlooked from the houses. The fracas in the Park Hotel was common knowledge by now.

'He was certainly making sure you understood at once the dangers and difficulties of your position.' Cartarette ignored the searching glances, the stifled whispers which swirled around her, proceeded on her way with a serene determination. In his more confident moments he presumed that she possessed a serene trust in her husband. But was she happy? She loved him physically, with a desperation which precluded doubt. But was that mere witchcraft, Gislane's powers stretching out from beyond the grave to suggest to her that only his touch, his body could ever drive her to ecstasy? Or even worse, was it merely, as he was the only man she had ever known, that she was by now used to him?

But for the rest, did she hate him?

'I am aware of them,' he said. They had reached the Park Hotel, and Harvey the waiter was opening the door for them. 'What will you do, if I fail, and am sent to prison?'

'Visit you,' she said. 'But you will not fail. Merriman has disappeared, no doubt dead. Your old mistress has drunk herself to death. Your domestics have been suborned. Your mother may not reply. But you lived in Jamaica for four years, Mr Hilton. Surely there is *someone* who can make a positive identification of you, who would know you even wearing a mask and disguising your voice, because that is all it amounts to.'

'My God,' he said. 'Of course. Judith.'

'Judith?'

'Judith Gale. Harriet's daughter. She was only fourteen when I left Jamaica, but . . .'

'But she knew you as well as her mother?'

He flushed. 'She lived in my house for four years, and . . . she will know me. Presuming she is still in Jamaica. Will you excuse me?'

She inclined her head. 'I will expect you for luncheon, Mr Hilton. And good fortune.'

288

He squeezed her hand, hurried round the corner to Harbour Street. Harriet dead. His last memory of her was a bitter one, of a naked woman rising from her bed in angry contempt. Yet had she made him happy, for four years. Had she been fortunate enough to know Christophe's general instead of Robert Hilton's heir — but Christophe's general would have known *her*, immediately, for what she really was.

And Josh. He had not properly considered Josh, not properly considered his grief, and his guilt. Because Josh would have died from loyalty to him. No question about that.

And now Judith. Why, Judith would be . . . past thirty certainly. He wondered what she looked like, and felt his heart beat pleasantly at the thought; she had been a quite lovely child. Whom he had raped. His stride slowed. How long ago that seemed. But would it be long ago to her? It would have changed her entire life. She would hate him, now, as she must have hated him then.

But she was his only hope.

He climbed the stairs to the lawyer's office. 'Reynolds?' He pushed open the door.

The clerk sprang to his feet. 'Mr Reynolds has a client, sir.'

'I will not take a moment of his time.' Dick pushed open the inner door. 'My apologies, Reynolds. The matter is urgent.'

Reynolds stood up. 'Really, Mr . . . ah . . . Hilton, you cannot burst in on a man so.' He flushed. 'You'll not have met Mr Kendrick.'

Dick gazed at the short, stout planter in delight.

'Toby Kendrick, as I live and breathe.' He thrust out his hand. 'How are you?'

Kendrick ignored the hand. 'I am very well, sir. But I have not had the pleasure of meeting you.'

'Meeting me? I am Dick Hilton.'

'Ah.' Kendrick got up. 'I remember Richard Hilton, sir. I do not remember you.' He glanced at Reynolds. 'I'll take my leave, Reynolds. You'll consider the points I raised. Good day to you, sir.' He left the room.

Reynolds pulled out a handkerchief to wipe his forehead and neck, sat down again.

'A friend of Tony's, eh?' Dick also sat down. 'That is to be expected. He was certainly no friend of mine. Well, it is of little consequence.'

'I do assure you, sir, it is of great consequence,' Reynolds protested. 'The plantocracy are closing their ranks against you. There is no more powerful body in the island. The Governor himself can scarce oppose them.'

'Except where they are proved legally wrong, my dear Reynolds. So stop worrying. I have thought of an absolutely positive identification which will prove my case once and for all. Judith Gale.'

'Proving the plantocracy legally wrong is a difficult matter, Mr . . . ah . . . Hilton. They make the laws in Jamaica. And I am sorry to have to tell you . . . *who* did you say?'

'Judith Gale. Harriet's daughter. Does she still live in Jamaica?'

'Judith Gale? My word. She lives in Kingston.'

'Give me her address.'

'Mr . . . ah . . . Hilton, that is quite impossible. Why, Judith Gale . . . if you are Mr Richard Hilton, you'll remember there was a charge of rape against you, with regard to Miss Gale.'

'Was there now? Well, I deserve it. And if anyone is going to charge me with a crime committed by Richard Hilton, they have to admit I *am* Richard Hilton, surely.'

'Good heavens,' Reynolds said. 'I never thought of that. Judith Gale.'

'Her address, man.'

'Mr . . . ah . . . Hilton. I'm afraid there is something else of which you are unaware.'

'Her address,' Dick said again.

Reynolds rested his elbows on his desk, placed his fingertips together. 'Miss Gale has an . . . ah . . . position.'

'Oh, yes?'

Reynolds began to flush. 'She is . . . ah . . . Mr Hilton's . . . ah . . . housekeeper. Mr Anthony Hilton.'

Dick leaned back to stare at him. 'Judith? And Tony? You're not serious.'

'Of course I am serious.'

'On Hilltop? Ellen would never stand for it.'

'Miss Gale does not live on Hilltop. She has an establishment here in town. And it is not my part to discuss the relations which may exist between a man and his wife.' He cleared his throat. 'But you do understand that Miss Gale would be reluctant to do or say

290

anything which might jeopardize her position with Mr Hilton.'

'Aye. Tony seems to have this entire community sewn up into a bag.' He leaned forward again. 'Yet I will see her, Reynolds. Give me her address.'

'It can do no good, sir.'

'Reynolds, you are going to make me angry in a moment. Her address.'

'She occupies a house in King Street, sir. Number six.'

'Thank you.' Dick got up. 'I'll go along there now. I'll probably be back immediately after lunch, Reynolds. And you be ready to see Miss Gale, and make out a sworn statement and an affidavit.'

Reynolds cleared his throat again. 'I'm afraid that will not be possible, Mr . . . ah . . . Hilton.' He stared in front of him at the opposite wall.

'What do you mean?'

'I . . . ah . . . I find I can no longer act as your attorney, Mr . . . ah . . . Hilton.'

'Why not?'

'Well, sir, I am afraid I must advise you, as a lawyer, that I consider you entirely lack sufficient proof to substantiate your claim. Even should you, ah, secure the testimony of Miss Gale, I still do not think your case will stand up in court, and so . . .'

'Balderdash,' Dick said.

'Mr . . . ah . . . Hilton, I have given you my opinion . . .'

'You have relayed a message just conveyed to you by Toby Kendrick, you mean, on behalf of the plantocracy.'

'Why, sir . . .'

Dick placed his hands on the desk, leaned forward. 'Try the truth.'

Reynolds met his gaze, for just a moment, and then looked away again. 'I have a wife and children. My prosperity depends upon the amount of business given me. I dare not, sir.'

'And what of Hilltop's business, when I am reinstated?'

'You will not be reinstated, sir. I am assured of that. And Mr . . . ah . . . Hilton, I already have Hilltop's business.'

Dick walked up the steps, across the verandah, knocked on the door. The house was set somewhat back from the street, and was reached by a path between what presumably were intended as flower-beds; they seemed mostly crab grass. The curtains of the houses to either side were drawn.

But the house itself was freshly painted, and now the door was being opened by a white-gowned girl.

'Yes'm?' She peered at him, and her frown became a gape.

'I'd like to see Miss Gale.'

'Eh? Miss Gale ain't in, sir.' She started to close the door.

Dick placed his hand on it, and pushed, very gently. The door went the other way, carrying the girl with it. 'Miss Gale,' he said. 'You tell her that either she comes down, or I will come up.'

The girl released the door and retreated towards the stairs. Dick closed the door behind him. The house smelt cool, and pleasant. Judith Gale, following in her mother's footsteps, but perhaps even more successfully than Harriet. He couldn't blame her for that. But there was the trouble. He couldn't blame any of these people. Not Reynolds, for being afraid, not Judith, for accepting the best possible position. In his heart he could not even blame Ellen for marrying Tony, or Tony for grasping the plantation.

So, then, why did he not just steal away, as the Earl of Belmore had suggested? He needed only Cartarette to be happy, and he retained enough of Christophe's bag of gold to set them up wherever they chose to live.

And then he could forget people like Josh Merriman, who had trusted him, and who had paid for that trust with his life. And he could blame Tony for that. He could even hate Tony for that, could reawaken the anger which was always bubbling deep in his belly.

He looked up the stairs. Judith stood at the top, wearing a pink undressing robe. She even aped her mother's colours. But where Harriet had been handsome, Judith was superb. The features were at once flawless and calm; even the watchfulness of the dark eyes did not reach the calmness of her expression. And when she descended the stairs her long dark hair did no more than flutter, very gently. But how that gentle flutter brought back memory.

'You should not have come here.' She reached the bottom of the stairs, halted. She did not offer her hand.

'Will he beat you?'

Her eyes gloomed at him. 'I would like you to leave.'

'But you know who I am?'

'I recognize your face, by what I have heard of it.'

'Is it as hideous as they say?'

292

She hesitated, and then nodded. 'It is as hideous as they say.'

'But you know who I really am, Judith.'

Once again the long stare. 'What am I supposed to remember about you, sir? Your penis? It was dark, in that room.'

The words seemed strange, coming from those perfect lips. He took a step forward. 'But you know it is I, Judith.'

She did not move, allowed him to take her hand. 'If it is not you, Mr Hilton, then it is a total fool, to challenge the plantocracy. To challenge a man like Tony.'

'But it is me, Judith.'

Her head turned, her fingers tightened. 'Oh, my God,' she whispered. 'Dick. Dick Hilton.' Her whole body turned, and she was in his arms. 'Oh, Dick. Why did you leave? Why did you run away?'

He kissed the top of her head. 'Did I not have cause, Judith?'

'Because of me? Don't you think I wanted it?'

'It made you what you are.'

'Tony's mistress,' she said. 'I would have been yours.'

'But I ran away.'

'And now you have come back,' she said. 'You have stopped running.'

'Oh, aye.' He held her away from him, smiled at her. 'No more running. But it seems I need help.'

There were tears in her eyes, starting slowly to dribble down her cheeks.

'Will you, Judith?'

'*I* will need help, Dick.'

'My right arm, until I am re-established. And any money you may require. After I am again *the* Hilton, you have but to ask.'

Her eyes were enormous, even through the tears. 'They say you have a wife.'

'Whom I love.'

'Ah,' she said.

'Will that make a difference?'

She hesitated, then shook her head. 'I would wish to be loved, like that. What must I do?'

'Make a deposition, to begin with. But you cannot stay here.'

'Oh, nonsense,' she said. 'This house is all I possess.' She kissed him on the chin. 'Anyway, who's to know?'

'This is Kingston, Judith. Everyone will know, the very moment you sign the paper.'

She smiled. 'Very well then, Dick. I will move out, and into your protection, the moment I sign the paper. But you must at least give me time to pack.'

'You'll have that. I've just remembered I still have to find someone to draw up the affidavit.' He kissed her forehead. 'But that is a detail. You have just guaranteed the success of my claim. I'll be back this afternoon, with my attorney.'

Her fingers released him, reluctantly. 'Does your wife know of me?'

'No. Not as you mean. But in any event, she is for me, for us, totally. You have nothing to fear from her.'

She smiled, but it was a sad smile. 'I am under your protection, Dick. Until this afternoon.'

He closed the door behind him, stood on the verandah, breathing the still midday air. Clouds were gathering above the Blue Mountains, and it would rain this afternoon. He was back in Jamaica. But it would be good rain. His instincts had not let him down.

He went down the steps, checked at the sound of movement, turned. From the side of the house a man emerged. He was a white man, but roughly dressed, and surprisingly, was armed, with a hanger as well as a cudgel.

Or was it so surprising? For now a second man emerged, from the other side of the house, also armed. Dick turned, to look at the street. At the gate there was a third man, and he too was armed. And the curtains on the houses to either side remained drawn; the cul de sac of Judith's garden was isolated, in the middle of a Jamaican morning.

Judith's garden. Presumably he could run up the steps and into her house. But they would follow him, and that might involve her in the coming fight. Presumably he could also shout for help, supposing anyone passing on the street would dare go to the assistance of the man who would oppose the plantocracy.

But why do any of those things? They were the instinctive reaction of Dick Hilton, because he was once again in Kingston, and Kingston, and Jamaica, had always been too much for him. For *that* Richard Hilton. Not for Christophe's general. Presumably Tony was making the same mistake, in assuming that the Richard Hilton he remembered would not survive a beating.

294

He was not even angry, merely happy that, after so many long months, he was going to be fighting again. He smiled at them, and the sight of that ghastly face breaking into a grin made even the three hired thugs pause, within feet of him, cudgels already swinging to and fro.

'Gentlemen,' he said, and stepped forward. They did not lack courage. One swung his club, and Dick had to throw up his left hand to take the blow, feel the pain shooting up his arm and into his shoulder. To awake the anger.

'Aieeeeee,' he screamed, as if his eleven hundred dragoons were at his back. He turned, suddenly, reached for the man. Another club struck him on the shoulder, but he was beyond feeling pain. The spirit of the *mamaloi* was rising inside him, sending vicious strength bubbling through his muscles. He swept the first club to one side, seized the man by the front of his shirt and the slack of his trousers, swept him from the ground while his victim gave a startled squawk of fear, swung him round, and used his body to send the other two tumbling. The first man he dropped at his own feet, stooped to drag the hanger from his belt, straightened, uttered another terrifying whoop of excited joy, and ran through the belly of the second clubman as he regained his balance and attempted to use his weapon.

The man dropped to his knees, blood bubbling around his hands as they closed on the blade. But the blade was already being withdrawn, leaving its victim dead before he ever hit the ground, to come up and sweep sideways and sever the third man's right arm at the wrist, crashing through flesh and bone and blood to slice into the thigh beyond. The club struck the ground with a dull thud, and the man looked down at his still quivering hand, bleeding into the grass.

The first man, remaining on the ground, held his head in his hands and screamed his fear.

'You'd best get up,' Dick recommended, his anger fading into compassion. 'You, give me your wrist.'

The stricken man was slowly sinking to his knees. Now he held out the shattered arm, and Dick whipped out his own kerchief to make a tourniquet. 'Tell the surgeon it is Richard Hilton's charge. And you.' He stooped, seized the unharmed man by the collar, dragged him to his feet. 'See to your friend. And tell my brother, next time to come himself.'

*

'Oh, my God.' Cartarette stood up as Dick entered the lobby of the hotel. 'Oh, my God.'

'You are bleeding, Mr Hilton. Bleeding.' Mortlake hurried forward. His side was taken, or it had been taken for him, as Ellen Hilton's last words before leaving the hotel the previous week had been to the effect that she would never demean herself by entering these doors again. From Mortlake's point of view, either Richard Hilton proved his claim, or the Park Hotel went bankrupt.

'Not my own, Mortlake.' Dick put his arm round Cartarette's waist. 'Three men attempted to discourage me.'

'Oh, my God,' she said again. 'Your brother?'

'I have no idea. Either him or someone interested in his support. Mr Mortlake, I have killed a man.'

'Killed . . .' Mortlake swabbed his brow.

'And grievously wounded another. The wounded man I have sent to a surgeon. The dead man must be removed from Miss Gale's garden, and the Governor must be informed. It was self defence. I have ample witnesses to the fact that I do not carry weapons. I had to remove the fellow's sword before running him through.'

'Oh, my God,' Cartarette said. 'Will they arrest you?'

'Not if the facts are true, Mistress Hilton,' said a deep, slow voice, and Dick turned in surprise to look at the mulatto, dark-skinned but well dressed in coat and breeches who stood at the side of the room.

'Oh, Mr Harris,' she said. 'Mr Hilton, this is Mr Harris.'

'Indeed?' Dick shook hands.

'Attorney-at-law, Mr Hilton,' Harris said.

'But . . .' Dick frowned at him.

'Oh, indeed, sir.' Harris smiled. 'My father sent me to England to school, and later to the Inns.'

'Well, then, Mr Harris. Welcome. How did you know of my problem?'

Harris lowered his voice. 'A message from Mr Reynolds, sir. But he would rather the matter were kept private. He does not usually send me business.' Again the quick smile. 'Nor is the business always happy to come.'

'I shall be happy, Mr Harris. You know the facts?'

'Some. We must have a talk.'

'This afternoon. I must wash this blood and change my clothes. Then I would like you to accompany me back to Miss Gale's house, to take a sworn statement.'

'She will identify you?' Cartarette squeezed his arm.

'She will. And now I have an attorney as well. The cards are starting to turn in our favour at last.'

'I'll see to that other matter, Mr Hilton,' Harris said. 'And meet you at Miss Gale's in an hour.'

'Good man.' Dick slapped him on the shoulder. 'Mr Mortlake, will you send some luncheon up to our room? There will be gossip.'

'Oh, aye, I'll see to it right away.' Mortlake scurried for the kitchen.

Dick left his arm round Cartarette's waist, slowly escorted her up the stairs. Her head rested on his shoulder.

'Are you really unhurt?' she whispered.

'I have a couple of bruises about my shoulders, which are painful. But there is nothing broken. I did not mean to kill that fellow, Cartarette. I lost my temper.'

'And thought yourself back alongside Christophe. Perhaps it was necessary, to teach these people you will not be frightened away.'

'Aye, well, it will do that. It will also give them something more to hang me with, should my claim fail. Where are the children?'

'They have already eaten. I have sent them into the garden. Thank God they did not see you like this.'

She closed the bedroom door, eased his coat from his shoulders—his arm was becoming slowly more and more stiff and difficult to move—then unbuttoned his shirt, her face creased with concentration.

'You are not beginning to have doubts?' She pulled his shirt free. 'Oh, my God. You have turned blue.'

He looked over his shoulder at himself in the mirror. 'Better it comes out. No doubts. Save that I fear to involve you in violence.'

She kissed his flesh. 'You took me, with violence, and I have known little else since. You'd not expect me to be bored in my old age, would you? There is a letter for you.'

'A letter? From my mother?'

Cartarette shook her head, began making wet compresses from her linen and pressing them to the shoulder. 'A local letter. Not paid for, but delivered by hand.'

He saw the envelope lying on the table, reached for it with his free hand. It was sealed, but he tore it with his teeth, extracted the sheet of paper.

'If the claimant to Hilltop is truly Richard Hilton, he will find it to his advantage to talk with the Reverend Joseph Strong. A boy will call for your answer.'

There was no signature.

'When did this come?' How good her fingers felt, pressing gently into the tortured flesh. And how tired he was, on a sudden.

'Within minutes of your leaving. The boy said he would return this afternoon.'

'Joseph Strong. I have never heard of that fellow. Well, I see no harm in it. He may have some information of value. I must get up and dress, sweetheart. There is Judith's statement to be taken, and . . .'

'You lie there and rest,' she said firmly. 'There is our luncheon, in any event. Come,' she called.

The door opened, to admit Harvey the waiter with a laden tray, which he placed on the table. 'There is also the coloured gentleman,' he said. 'Wishing to see you.'

'Harris?' Dick rolled over and sat up. 'Come in. That was quick.'

'The body had already been removed, Mr Hilton.' Harris held his hat in his hands. 'Quite a crowd had gathered. They are calling it the Massacre of King Street.'

'Oh, really? Mobs will find a source of amusement in anything.' He frowned. 'You do not look amused.'

'As I was there, Mr Hilton, I called at the house, to inform Miss Gale when we would be attending her for her affidavit.'

'And?'

'The door was opened by Mr James Hardy.'

'Eh? He wasn't there when I spoke with Miss Gale.'

'Indeed not, sir. Yet he must have been close. He asked my business, and when I said I wished to speak with Miss Gale, he laughed, and said he knew who had sent me, and to tell you that Miss Gale will not be receiving you again. He said, tell that upstart that she is Mr Hilton's witness, not his.'

'He must have set his men on you, and watched the whole affair,' Cartarette said. 'Oh the scoundrel.'

'Aye,' Dick mused. 'And the moment I left, he visited Judith.

That poor child. What can he have done to her?'

'I did not see the young lady, sir,' Harris explained. 'But Mr Hardy's words seemed strange. I visited Lawyer Reynolds on the way here. You'll know Reynolds has been retained by *the* Hilton?'

'I didn't know. But it seems likely.'

'Aye, sir. Well, I told him what had happened, suggested we would be within our rights to bring a charge of assault on Mr Hardy . . .'

'Supposing it could ever be proved,' Dick muttered. He could not get the thought of Judith from his mind. Will he beat you, he had asked. And she had not replied. Except to accept his protection. And what good had that done her? 'I must get round there right away.'

'No,' Cartarette said. 'You may not be so fortunate the next time.'

'Your good lady is right, sir,' Harris said. 'Miss Gale is widely known to be under Mr Hilton's protection. You would have no rights were you to attempt to force an entry. Anyway, the damage has been done. She has signed a deposition against you.'

'Against me? What can she say, against me?'

'Simply this, sir. Miss Gale has testified in writing how she was raped by the real Richard Hilton, as she puts it. She has sworn that she would also have known the man who so cruelly assaulted her — I am quoting — and she is prepared to swear under oath, as she has written under oath, that you are not that man.'

16

The Trial

The sun, huge and round and glowing, dipped in the calm waters of the Caribbean Sea, and in that moment it was dark. Instantly the fireflies commenced their activity, lighting the way for their more noisy fellows the mosquitoes, who came buzzing out of the undergrowth, to follow the sandflies in their quest for blood.

How memory came back to Richard Hilton, of his very first ride into the Jamaican hinterland, how long ago. Then, as now, the thought had crossed his mind that he might be being lured by his guide to some lonely spot, there to be murdered. But then he had been unarmed, and had had no idea of how to cope with the violence, should it come. And for that reason, perhaps, had not known how to be truly afraid.

This night he was not afraid either. He wore a sword, and there were two loaded pistols attached to his saddle, and another in his coat pocket. He was ready for a fight, and this night he would welcome one. So if the message from this Reverend Strong was nothing more than another of Tony's attempts to save himself by violence, he could count on being accommodated.

He smiled at the back of the Negro youth who rode in front of him, but it was a savage smile. Last week, he remembered, he had realized he felt no animosity towards Tony, or any of Tony's friends. He had not even really felt animosity towards the three men who had intended to beat him. This evening he was angry. He had returned to Judith's house, against the advice of both Cartarette and Harris, and been met by armed men who had refused him admittance, in the name of Judith Gale. He had been prepared to brush them aside, and Judith had herself called from the upper window, telling him to leave as she did not wish to speak with him. Had it been Judith? Oh, indeed, the voice had belonged to Judith, even if the face itself had been veiled and invisible. But it had been a voice trembling with fear, and perhaps pain, just as each word had been uttered through swollen lips.

And he had offered her his protection. Now he could only offer her his vengeance. When he won his case. If he won his case, now.

And if she would wish his vengeance, after she had been dragged into court to recount the events of that night, sixteen years ago, to be humiliated.

'How much farther?'

The boy turned his head. 'The chapel does be not far now, master.'

'Chapel?'

'Is Mr Strong own chapel, master.'

They threaded through the trees, reached a cleared space, could see the low wooden building, the scattered huts beyond. They must have ridden twenty miles from Kingston, Dick estimated, in the main following the coast, and here was a sheltered bay, a few banana trees, some fishing boats drawn up on the beach, and beyond, the sea.

The boy had stopped his donkey, and was waiting, as black men emerged from the trees on either side.

'Who you got there?' one called.

'Is the white man,' the boy called. 'Come for to see the reverend.'

Dick dismounted. These men were not armed, and they kept their distance. His boots crunched on the sand.

'You had best come close,' said a man, and Dick frowned, his heart giving a sudden leap as he realized he knew the voice. But that was impossible.

He hurried forward, into the light of the fire, gazed at the black man who stood there. The Reverend Strong wore a white shirt and white breeches, black boots. The neck of his shirt was unbuttoned, his sleeves rolled up. But his face had not changed.

'Josh,' Dick cried. 'They said you were dead.'

Joshua peered at him. 'They said the same of you, Mr Richard.'

Dick squeezed the black fingers. 'But you know me.'

The hand returned his squeeze. 'No. But *you* know *me*.' He turned, went into the hut. Dick followed.

'There is some explaining to do.'

'Yes, sir, Mr Richard. You'll take a drink?'

It was a mug of rum. Dick sipped, watched Josh do the same. The hut was filled with black men, waiting, quietly.

'I ran away,' Josh said. 'I had to do that, Mr Richard. You understand?'

'Aye,' Dick said.

'My companions died. One drowned, in a rainstorm. The other was beaten to death.'

'By my brother?'

'By his woman, Mr Richard.'

'Ellen? That's clearly rumour.'

'I watched her, Mr Richard. From up the hill. She rode her mule, behind him, up and down, up and down, flogging. And when he dropped, she dismounted and kept on flogging.'

Dick frowned at him. 'Who else was there?'

'Your brother. He had a gun.' Merriman sighed. 'And I was tired, and frightened. My people are always frightened.'

'You are not frightened now, old friend, or you would not have sent for me.'

'I am a Christian, Mr Richard. I have learned how to pray. Alone, in these mountains, starving, afraid, I couldn't do anything else but pray. And my prayer was answered. People helped me, did not ask who I was, or where I came from. I could hide, for years, until I realized I had a duty to my people. So I took a new name, pretended I was from the United States, come to pray for them all. These people believe in me, now. In my prayers. I have prayed for help and understanding, from the missionaries. But I do not believe they understand us. And as for help, they speak loudly when they address us alone, and curl up and crawl away when the planters come close. So I have prayed for help and understanding, from England. And I have heard now they would help and understand. But then we are told how the planters will not obey them, would rather declare independence than obey them. So I despaired, and prayed for a strong right arm. And this prayer has been answered.'

'You would consider Richard Hilton a strong right arm?'

Josh smiled. 'Richard Hilton was a boy. But who in Jamaica has not heard of General Warner, who fought for Christophe? And who in Jamaica has not heard of Richard Hilton, who destroyed three men with a wave of his arm, but a week ago?'

'You would have me lead you into battle?'

'We would have you lead us, Mr Richard. You must say where.'

Dick looked at the black men, waiting in the gloom. Free men, certainly. But they had been slaves, and they had earned their freedom by labour, or gained it through a quirk of white generosity. No man here had fought for it. Besides, the idea was impossible.

'Even generals need armies, Josh,' he said. 'I have no army. Your people's freedom must be an act of law.'

'Jamaican law?' someone growled.

'It will be Jamaican law,' Dick said. 'When the planters show sense.'

'Prayer will not accomplish that,' Josh said.

'I think you are right. But they can still be shown, by example. By *the* Hilton. They will follow his lead. Indeed, they have been following his lead these past fifteen years, which is why things have reached this state.'

'Will you win your claim?' Josh asked. 'I have heard it said there is no one will vouch for you.'

'No white person,' Dick agreed. 'They know I am their enemy, or they are afraid of my brother.'

'And I should not be afraid of your brother?' Josh asked. 'I am a runaway, from Hilltop.'

'It would mean two hundred lashes,' said one of the men.

'If your identification should make me once again *the* Hilton,' Dick said, 'then you have nothing to fear.'

'Would they take the word of a black man?' asked another voice.

'He is a reverend,' said another.

'But a runaway,' said a third.

'They would take the word of a man who risked two hundred lashes,' Dick said.

'And if they do not?' asked a fourth voice.

Dick hesitated. But of course the risk was enormous. He could promise nothing. He had promised Judith his protection, but that had not saved *her*. He looked at Josh, and sighed. 'They are right, Josh. I cannot ask you to do this. The risk *is* too great.'

Josh's turn to hesitate. And then to sigh, in turn. And then to smile. 'I prayed for you to come back, Mr Richard. If you don't get Hilltop back, then none of us ever going to be really free. You send for me, man, when you are ready.'

303

The tap on the door had him instantly awake, instinctively reaching for the sword which lay by his bed. It was hardly dawn.

Cartarette sighed, and rolled over, her hand on his arm. The tap came again.

Gently he eased himself from the bed, dragged on his breeches, tiptoed to the door, his sword in his hand. He released the bolt, allowed the door to swing in.

'Mr Hilton?' John Mortlake whispered.

'What's amiss?'

'Why, sir, perhaps nothing. There is someone to see you.'

'At this hour? And on this day? Court sits at ten.'

'Aye, sir. There's the mystery, and perhaps the hope. 'Tis Mistress Hilton.'

Dick frowned into the half-light.

'True, sir,' Mortlake insisted.

'You've an empty room?'

'Next door, sir.'

'Then show her up.' Dick stepped into the corridor, went into the room beside his own, opened the jalousie; light was just reaching along the street. He listened to footsteps in the corridor, watched the door open. He preferred not to anticipate, not to wonder, even. He laid the sword on top of the dressing table.

Ellen stepped inside, closed the door behind herself. She wore a poke bonnet over a black pelisse, and a veil. But there could be no doubting the identity of that tall figure. She hesitated, looking from him around the room, seeing the sword.

'How splendid you look,' she said.

'Even disguised as a monster?'

'Monsters can be splendid.' She released the ribbon under her chin, took off her bonnet, shook out her hair. 'Today is the day. Are you excited?'

'No.' He remained on the far side of the room, watching her.

She placed the bonnet on a chair, glanced at the bed, slowly released her pelisse. 'Are you confident?'

'I am a confident man.'

'Ah.' She laid the pelisse beside the bonnet. Her gown was pale green. 'You were not always so.'

'I have changed.'

She sat on the bed. 'Indeed you have. I am to give evidence

304

against you.'

'So I believe.'

'My evidence will destroy you, when taken in conjunction with that of Judith Gale.'

'Perhaps.'

She frowned at him. 'You do not believe me? You should. And if you lose your case, you will be imprisoned. At the very least.'

'Did Tony send you here to threaten me?'

'Tony does not know I am here. Neither does James.'

'James?' Dick's turn to frown. 'Hardy? Would it matter if he did?'

She smiled. 'It would matter. Have you never wondered how two brothers could be so different in character? That puzzled me even in England. Now I know the answer. Two brothers cannot be so different in character. Tony has the ability to project himself as a dominating man. He has not got the strength of character to *be* a dominating man.'

Dick nodded, slowly. 'I am beginning to understand.'

'Without James at his shoulder, he would be nothing. James, and me, of course.'

'Oh, quite.'

'But it is you we are discussing. I would not have you go to gaol, Dick. However badly you treated me, I would not wish that on you. You have a pretty little wife, and three charming children. You have never wished to be a planter. You have no friends, here in Jamaica, thus you have no reason to remain. There is a ship in the harbour clearing for England at ten o'clock. At the very moment the court sits. With a little haste you, and your wife, and your children, could be safely on board her, free as the wind. And waiting for you at your very own Bridle's Bank in London would be an order on the Hilltop crop. Shall we say ten thousand pounds a year?'

'All this, to save me going to gaol?'

'All that. And perhaps because I did, once, love you.'

'Does it not occur to you that you have just ruined yourself as an adverse witness?'

'I have not admitted your identity. At least, not *before* a witness.'

'You are here. Suppose I made you stay?'

'Then would you be adding kidnapping to the other crimes of

305

which you will certainly be accused. I will merely say that I came here to offer you a settlement out of court, presuming that an imposter such as you is really only in search of money. People will say I was foolish to do so, but no one will condemn me for it. I am Ellen Hilton.' She got up, crossed the room, stood beside him. 'Why do you not make me stay, Dick? I would rather enjoy being manhandled by a monster such as you are become.'

He inhaled her perfume. If she had come out of fear, she concealed it well. And how much did he want to seize her, but not from love. If Josh's tale was true, he at last knew all her secrets, all the lurking desire behind that secret smile, all the cesspool that was her mind. To touch her would be to break her neck. And she dared remind him of *her* love.

Yet in removing her from the arrogant pleasure of being Mistress Hilton of Hilltop, he would be doing her a far greater injury than any physical punishment he could bestow. As she knew, or she had not come this morning.

'I am touched by your solicitude, Ellen. Thus you have my promise that when I regain Hilltop, I shall give *you* an income of ten thousand a year, also.'

Her smile died, her lips became a steel trap. 'Do not be a fool, Dick. I am offering you your only chance of surviving this day a free man.'

'And I am refusing your offer, Ellen.'

She stared at him for a moment, then turned to the bed. She put on her pelisse, looked in the mirror to adjust her bonnet. She walked to the door, and there turned. 'I do not know what you hope to achieve,' she said. 'But I promise you this, Dick Hilton. I will destroy you, no matter what the outcome of this case. And as you have rejected me, I will destroy your wife as well. Think about that, Dick. Appear in that court, and you have signed your own death warrant.' She stepped outside, closed the door behind herself.

'At last.' Cartarette adjusted his cravat, stood back to look at him. 'Confident?'

He kissed her on the nose. 'I'd be more confident if you were coming.'

'It will be a long day, and a hard one, for your supporters. We will wait to hear the outcome from your own lips.' She turned away, sat down.

'Cartarette . . .' He knelt beside her, arms round her waist to hug himself against her breast, quite upsetting the cravat again; he had told her nothing of his strange dawn visitor, had been back in bed before she awoke. She had enough to worry about. 'Cartarette. How I love you.' He waited, for a moment, could hear nothing but the beat of her heart. And sighed. 'You have inspired me to fight again, and again, for our rights.'

She kissed him on the forehead. 'And be sure you win, dear Mr Hilton.'

He gazed at her for a moment. But time, after all these months, was at last pressing. And she had used the word dear for the very first time. It might be unwise to press his fortune further.

He stood up. 'Oh, aye,' he said. 'I'll win.' He closed the door behind him, gently. She was right about remaining here. Why, she should not have risked going abroad these past two months. And now, after Ellen's threat . . . the planters would find an easier target in the Claimant's wife and children, than the Claimant himself. His reputation had gone abroad. Black people smiled at him, the little boys and girls ran behind on the street, as they were preparing to do now, shouting and cheering. The white people, if they had anything at all to do with planting, crossed the street to walk on the farther side when they saw him coming. The opposing sides had solidified.

And yet, he thought, as he went down the stairs, the end was in sight. It had been a long wait, but one intended by the Governor to be entirely in his favour. An unsuccessful wait, alas. Ships had come and gone. His letter had travelled with Morrison on the *Green Knight*, and Morrison had assured him it had been delivered. But Morrison had brought no reply. And now that he was here again, why, the case had to come to court; Morrison was one of his only two witnesses.

Harris waited in the lobby, looking suitably grave. With him was a black man, carefully dressed in black, with a white cravat.

Dick shook their hands. 'Well, Mr Barker. Confident?'

The barrister smiled at him. 'Oh, aye, Mr Hilton. *I* have nothing to lose. And an entire reputation to gain should we win.'

Presumably his honesty was an asset, Dick thought. They walked up the street together, stared at from behind curtains and from the far side of the street, cheered by the rabble who followed them, waved at most ostentatiously by John Mortlake, standing on the verandah of his hotel.

'Any word from Strong?'

'He is in Kingston, Mr Hilton, and waiting. He will be there this morning. But he feels it best to remain concealed until the court is called to order.'

'Aye. I wish I could feel more secure in his safety. More secure in anything. Do we have a case, Harris?'

The mulatto gazed at the ground in front of him as he walked. 'Strong is a powerful witness, Mr Hilton. Had Miss Gale also adhered to us there would be no risk at all.'

'And with her evidence against me?'

Barker sighed. 'I will have to destroy her in cross examination.'

Dick turned his head to look at him. 'You said you risk nothing. Yet she is white, you are black. Will you not also destroy yourself?'

Barker smiled, but the smile was sad. 'Mr Hilton, have you not sat back and thought, some time during these past few months, how many lives are hanging on this case. I do not think my *life* is at risk. And I possess nothing else, save my certificate.'

'My God,' Dick said. Because he hadn't really thought of anyone save himself.

The courtroom was packed. It was necessary for Reynolds and Harris to sit almost alongside each other, as it was equally necessary for Dick to sit almost alongside Tony, immediately behind the two lawyers. Tony merely glanced at him, then stared straight ahead. Ellen was not in court; she would be in the witness room, beside Judith. Her friends were certainly here, Gwynneth Evans and Grace Tresling, and a half a dozen other women, but most of them were veiled.

And time for speculation was past, as the jury filed in. All planters there, and therefore all hostile. His hope must be in the Governor, here acting as Chief Justice, as this was a civil case. The earl's face was impartially severe.

Barker had been given the signal by the clerk, and was clearing his throat. Dick could see the beads of sweat standing out on his forehead.

But his voice was firm, and deep. 'May it please the court,' he said. 'I represent Mr Richard Hilton . . .'

He was interrupted by a chorus of boos and hisses from the galleries.

The earl gazed over the room. 'This court can easily be cleared,' he remarked. 'Indeed, it will be somewhat cooler. Proceed, Mr Barker.'

'Mr Richard Hilton,' Barker said, even more firmly. 'Who is here today presenting suit to regain rightful title in the plantation known as Hilltop.' He paused, as if expecting another barrage of sound, but this time the court remained quiet. 'My learned friend Mr Calthorpe appears for the present occupant of Hilltop, Mr Anthony Hilton.' He paused again, to bow towards Calthorpe, who gave a brief nod of acknowledgement.

'The plantation, Hilltop,' Barker said, 'was left to Mr Richard Hilton by his uncle, Mr Robert Hilton. This fact is not disputed. Mr Hilton, accompanied by his brother, Mr Anthony Hilton, came to Jamaica in 1810, and took up residence on the plantation. Four years later Mr Richard Hilton left Jamaica suddenly. We need not go into the reasons for his departure . . .'

Calthorpe cleared his throat, very loudly, but did not interrupt.

'Except to say,' Barker went on, slightly raising his voice, 'that in leaving the island, Mr Hilton had no intention of abandoning his possession of his plantation. Indeed, he intended to return as soon as possible. However, the ship on which he travelled, the *Cormorant*, was never heard of again. It was, in fact, wrecked on the coast of Haiti. But as no word was heard from Mr Richard Hilton, he was, in the course of time, assumed to be dead, and after the lapse of the term demanded by law, seven years, Mr Anthony Hilton was granted ownership. He had already been in possession, operating the plantation in his brother's name, for those seven years.'

Barker paused, and looked around the courtroom with the air of a magician about to pull a rabbit from a hat. 'However, Mr Richard Hilton was not dead. He had, in fact, gained the island of Haiti, the sole survivor from the wreck of the *Cormorant*. And on Haiti he remained, for the next sixteen years. Now it is pertinent to ask why.'

The jurymen were nodding their agreement.

'The fact is, Mr Hilton suffered some serious and terrible injuries soon after reaching the land. He fell from a great height, and so disfigured his face that he could scarce recognize himself. This accident was also a severe shock to his system. He lay ill for more than a year, and then he found himself able to take such a part in the life of the community in which he found himself, he wished to remain there for a time. It was in this period that he assumed a false name, that of Matthew Warner. But indeed, my lord, his very choice of this name is an indication of his identity, for the Hilton and Warner families were in the past closely connected, and Anthony Hilton the First and Sir Thomas Warner were the two very first Englishmen to settle in the West Indies.

'And then, my lord, in the course of time, Mr Hilton regained sufficient health, and sufficient confidence in himself, to return to Jamaica. He anticipated being welcomed by his brother. But on the contrary, my lord, he was rejected. Mr Anthony Hilton professed not to recognize him, and indeed attempted to institute criminal proceedings against him, for fraud. Mr Richard Hilton therefore appears here today, my lord, as a supplicant for a restoration of his legal rights, and it will be my responsibility, and my pleasure, to prove beyond any reasonable doubt that my client is indeed Richard Hilton, the Hilton of Hilltop.'

He paused, and sat down. The Earl of Belmore glanced at Calthorpe, who was already on his feet.

'You do not have to say anything at this stage, Mr Calthorpe.'

'I understand that, my lord. But my point is a simple one. My client counterclaims that the entire case is based upon a fraud, and requests your lordship to dismiss it. The whole list of circumstances related by my . . .' he gave Barker a glance of total contempt, '. . . learned friend is so obviously a tissue of lies that it is difficult to understand his temerity in presenting it. The *Cormorant* was lost at sea. That is an indisputable fact. It is possible that Richard Hilton may have survived the wreck. But is it likely that this man, the wealthiest planter in the entire West Indies, would prefer to live in a Negro, a savage, an anarchistic community for sixteen years, when he had but to return to the comfort and security of his Jamaica home? This man, this Claimant, bears absolutely no resemblance to the late Richard Hilton. His case is based upon certain events from Richard Hilton's past, which he appears to remember. Sheer common sense must suggest to this court that these events are hearsay, perhaps related to the Claimant before Richard Hilton's death, perhaps, and more likely, gleaned by his inquiries over the past sixteen years, which indeed informs us why he has waited this long to present his claim. He had to build up his own, false, background, and he had to wait for memories in Jamaica to fade. My lord, it is as plain as a pikestaff that this man is an imposter, and I request this court to dismiss his claim, and to permit the counterclaim, of attempt to defraud, which is accompanied by other charges of criminal nature, to be heard.'

Calthorpe sat down. The jury was whispering, but Belmore ignored them entirely, and looked straight ahead of him.

'I trust, Mr Calthorpe, that you are not suggesting this court lacks common sense. However, it seems to me that as Mr Richard Hilton, or General Matthew Warner, whichever he really is, has brought this case, and as his advocate is prepared to substantiate his claim, the least we can do is hear the evidence. Are you prepared to call your witnesses, Mr Barker?'

'I am, your lordship. I call Captain James Morrison.'

The call was sent out to the witnesses' room. Morrison came in, slowly and uncertainly, blinked at the sea of faces, gave a nervous smile, and was shown to the stairs leading up to the witness box by the clerk. He took the oath in a low mumble.

'Your name is Captain James Morrison, and you are master of the brig *Green Knight*,' Barker remarked.

'Aye.'

'What did the witness say?' inquired the earl.

'He said yes, my lord, in a nautical fashion,' Barker explained.

'Ah,' said the earl, and made a note.

'And for how many years have you traded between England and the West Indies, Captain Morrison?'

'Longer than I can remember.'

'Well, sir, try to remember.'

'Oh, aye, well, thirty years for sure.'

'Thank you, Captain Morrison. Now, can you remember a voyage you made, in June and July of the year 1810?'

'Oh, aye, that I can.'

'Why can you remember it? We are speaking of some twenty years ago.'

'Ah, but it were what happened, you see.'

'Tell us.'

'Well, there were these two young fellows on board. Hilton, their name was. Anthony Hilton, and his brother Richard. Heirs to the Hilton estates, they were. And there was this quarrel, you see, with a gentleman named Lanken.' Morrison paused and

311

looked around the crowded room.

'What was this quarrel about?'

'Ah, well, it were over a woman, to be sure. And Captain Lanken challenged Mr Richard Hilton to a duel. Well, then it were discovered that Mr Richard had malaria, so his brother fought in his place. Oh, no blood was shed. But a duel, on my ship. Why, it weren't something a man forgets.'

'Indeed not,' Barker agreed. 'And when did you see Mr Richard Hilton again?'

'Aye, well, not for a long time. He was a big planter, and me just a trading skipper. I heard of him, though. Then I heard how he had been lost at sea, and I was mighty sorry. He was a good man, that.'

'But when did you see him again?'

'Aye, well, Jamaica ain't the only West Indian island I trade with. I calls at Cap Haitien, that which used to be Cap François, from time to time. Risky it is. Them niggers are unpredictable. But a man must try to earn himself a profit.'

'Go on, Captain Morrison.'

'Well, last year it was. I called at Cap Haitien, as usual, and the ship was invaded by these black fellows. Soldiers they was. Arrested me they did, on a false charge of smuggling, and hauled me before their general. Well, I can tell you, I thought I was for it. But this turned out to be a white man, General Warner.'

'You knew him?'

'Oh, no. Not me. But I'd heard of him. Well, who hadn't heard of Christophe's cavalry commander? Well, I went along. I didn't have no choice. And you could have knocked me over with a feather when this general claps me on the shoulder and says captain, don't you remember me?'

'And did you?'

'Well, not at first. But when he started to speak, why, I knew it had to be Richard Hilton.'

'Why?'

'Well, he remembered things that only Richard Hilton could.'

'Things about the voyage?'

'Oh, aye. Names, and what happened.'

'Captain Morrison, is Mr Richard Hilton, of Hilltop, the man you carried to Jamaica in 1810, seated in this court?'

Morrison affected to peer into the room. 'Oh, aye, there he is.'

'Where?'

Morrison pointed at Dick.

'You have no doubts at all about it, Captain Morrison?'

'Doubts? Why should I have doubts? That's Richard Hilton.'

'Thank you, Captain Morrison,' Barker said, and sat down.

Calthorpe took some minutes to stand up. He consulted his notes, rustled his papers, and only when Belmore had cleared his throat did he actually rise to his feet.

'Morrison,' he asked. 'Do you drink?'

'Eh?'

'I asked, do you drink?'

'I take a sip, from time to time.'

'Thank you. Do you tell tales?'

'Eh?'

'You are a seafaring man, who drinks. When you are . . . happy, in a bar of an evening, home from the sea, do you ever regale your companions with tales, of the sea?'

'Why . . . I suppose I do.'

'Have you ever told anyone of the events of that voyage in 1810, that voyage which was so eventful you can remember it today as if it was your last?'

'Why . . .' Morrison glanced at Dick. 'Maybe,'

Calthorpe appeared to consult his notes. 'You have testified that on landing in Cap Haitien, on the occasion of your last visit there, you were boarded by Negro soldiers and commanded to appear before the general. You thought you were for it. I quote. Would I be correct in interpreting that to mean you were afraid?'

'Afraid? Well, yes, I was afraid. Them niggers . . .'

'You have told us about them niggers, Morrison. Did you take a drink, before going ashore?'

'Eh? Well . . .'

'You are under oath, Morrison.'

'Well, yes, I did.'

'And on being taken ashore, under armed escort, you were confronted with a white man, a general, a very powerful man in that community, who greeted you by name, and when you showed surprise, this man recounted some events which you felt were of significance.'

'Aye. So he did. Eventually.'

Calthorpe frowned, for the first time. 'What do you mean?'

'Well, sir, when first we met, Mr Hilton didn't *want* me to recognize him. Or so it seemed to me. He wanted to know about Jamaica. It was only after I started telling him that he asked if I remembered him.'

'He *asked* if you remembered him.' Calthorpe smiled. 'And you were happy enough to do so.' He held up his hand as Morrison would have spoken again. 'I have only two more questions to ask of you, Morrison. And I recommend you answer them very carefully, lest a charge of perjury be brought against you. You have related that on that so well remembered voyage, there was to be a duel, between Richard Hilton and a Captain Lanken. But Richard Hilton could not fight, because of an attack of malaria, and his place was taken by his brother, Anthony. Now, Captain Morrison, is it not true to say that there *was* no attack of malaria? That the illness was a subterfuge to save Richard Hilton, because he had no knowledge of weapons, and because he was afraid of Captain Lanken?'

'Well, now,' Morrison said. 'Afraid? Well, now . . .'

'You are under oath, Morrison.'

'Well . . .' Morrison gave an apologetic glance at Dick. 'There was some talk, about how it might be a subterfuge.'

'Then tell us this, Morrison. Can you conceive of the man standing over there, the Claimant to the Hilton estates, being physically afraid of anyone? Or being ignorant of the use of weapons? This man, who fought with Christophe, and obtained a reputation as a most formidable soldier, this man, who came to Kingston, and upon being attacked by some ruffians, killed one, maimed another, and disarmed a third, all in a matter of seconds? Can you really suppose the shrinking coward of the *Green Knight* and the notorious Matthew Warner of Haiti can be one and the same man?'

'A man can change,' Morrison said. 'A man can be taught the use of weapons.'

'No man can change that much, Morrison. Now, my last question. Did Matthew Warner, when reminding you of your mutual past, tell you anything that he could not have learned, from hearsay, perhaps from Richard Hilton himself?'

Morrison frowned at his inquisitor. 'Why, of course not. He remembered what there was to be remembered, and there is an end to it.'

'Thank you, Morrison.' Calthorpe sat down, took a drink of water.

'You may step down, Captain Morrison,' the Earl of Belmore said. 'Mr Barker?'

Barker stood up, half started to turn to look at Dick, and then checked himself. But it needed no glance to convey the information that Morrison had been destroyed, as a witness. It was all or nothing now.

'I call the Reverend Joseph Strong,' Barker said.

Josh entered the courtroom, severely dressed in a black suit, wearing a dog-collar. He looked neither to left nor right, as he climbed the stairs to the box and took the oath. Calthorpe was consulting his notes; Tony leaned back and considered the ceiling. Obviously he would have forgotten what Josh looked like. He would not have forgotten the name, however.

Barker was on his feet. 'May it please your lordship, I would like to introduce this witness.'

'We know of the Reverend Strong,' Belmore pointed out.

Barker cleared his throat. 'Indeed, your lordship, the Reverend Strong is well known, and greatly respected, throughout the island. Yet he comes here today under a handicap, and I would beg the court's indulgence.'

'Handicap? Can the man not speak?'

'He can speak, your lordship. The nature of his handicap will become apparent when I commence examining the witness. Have I the court's indulgence?'

'Yes, yes, man, get on with it,' Belmore barked. He was also unhappy with the way the cross examination of Morrison had turned out.

'Thank you, my lord,' Barker said, and turned towards the witness box. 'Your name is Joseph Strong, and you are a parson of the Baptist Church?'

'That is correct,' Josh said, his voice slow and deep.

'And are you acquainted with the Claimant?'

'I am.'

'In what way?'

'I have known Mr Richard Hilton for twenty years. Since the day of his arrival in Jamaica.'

'And you have no doubt that the man you see behind me is Mr

315

Richard Hilton?'

'None.'

'How can you be sure?'

'I am sure because when we first met, on his return to the island, although I did not identify myself, he recognized me immediately.'

'Thank you, Mr Strong.' The court was silent, and once again Barker half turned as if he would look at Dick, and then changed his mind. Clearly he was sorely tempted to leave matters as they were, and see if Calthorpe would press matters in his cross examination. But the risk was too great of alienating Belmore. Any confession had to come from this side. 'Now, Mr Strong, my learned friend will no doubt wish to point out, in cross examination, that when Mr Hilton first came to Jamaica there was no Reverend Strong preaching, and indeed that it is only in the last five years that your reputation as a man of God has become widespread.'

Calthorpe stood up. 'My lord, I would prefer to ask my own questions.'

'Mr Barker is supposing, Mr Calthorpe,' Belmore said.

'Thank you, your lordship,' Barker said. 'I would therefore like you to tell this court what you were doing when Mr Hilton arrived in Jamaica, in 1810, and how you came to know him so well.'

Josh hesitated for just a moment, then continued speaking in his slow, clear tone. 'I was a slave, in 1810, and worked for Mr Reynolds the lawyer.'

'Bless my soul,' Reynolds remarked, completely forgetting himself.

A rustle spread through the court, and Belmore banged his gavel before leaning forward. 'You were a slave, you say, Mr Strong? Of Mr Reynolds?'

'Yes, my lord.'

'And were manumitted?'

'No, my lord. I was sold, to Mr Richard Hilton, at his request.'

Tony sat up, and the murmur grew.

'Ah,' said the earl. 'And it was Mr Richard Hilton gave you your freedom. Yes, indeed, I understand. You would remember that.'

Josh took a deep breath. 'No, sir, your Excellency. Mr Richard made me his head man. That is why I remember him. He treated me as a friend. But when he disappeared, and Mr Anthony Hilton

316

took over the plantation, he treated me too bad, your Excellency. So I ran away.'

'Ran away?' The earl seemed unable to believe his ears.

'By God.' Tony was on his feet. 'Josh Merriman. Arrest that man.'

'Quiet. Order. Order in this court,' the earl bellowed, banging his gavel.

The noise slowly subsided.

'I demand my rights, your Grace,' Tony said, still standing. 'That man is a runaway from Hilltop.'

Dick also stood up. 'You have no rights at all, Tony. As you say, Josh is a runaway from Hilltop. The matter is my concern.'

'Your concern? You upstart fraud . . .'

'Gentlemen,' the earl said. 'It may be irregular to hear a case of this nature while both the principals are confined in a cell, but I assure you it can be done.' He turned back to Josh. 'What is your real name?'

'Joshua Merriman, your Excellency.'

The earl loooked at Reynolds. 'You recognize this man, Mr Reynolds?'

The lawyer peered at the witness box. 'It is a long time, my lord, but certainly I owned a slave by that name whom I sold to Mr Richard Hilton.'

'And who has been masquerading as a Baptist minister,' the earl mused. 'Mr Barker?'

'I knew of the risk Merriman was taking, my lord. But the fact that he has taken this risk surely establishes the truth of his evidence.'

The earl sighed. 'That is for the jury to decide. I would but remind you, and your principals, that aiding and abetting an absconded slave is a felony. Mr Hilton?' He looked at Dick.

'I was under the impression that I could do as I wished with regard to my own slaves,' Dick said. 'I have already granted Merriman his freedom, so that he may continue his excellent work as a preacher.'

'My lord,' Calthorpe said, entering the debate for the first time, having been handed a scribbled message from Tony. 'This case has not yet been proven. It may never be proven. In my opinion, which has been but hardened by what I have seen and heard here today, it can never be proven. The Claimant may assume what he pleases, surely the fact is that in law this witness is the property of my client until it is otherwise proved.'

'Hm,' said the earl. 'Hm. It will have to be considered. I will adjourn the court until tomorrow while I consider the matter.'

'And in the meanwhile, my lord?' Calthorpe inquired.

The earl looked at Dick, and then at the jury, and then at Josh. 'The slave will have to be confined, of course.'

'In my client's custody, my lord,' Calthorpe said.

Barker got up. 'I must protest, my lord. This man is a witness against the defence. To place him in the care of the defence is to transgress all rules of justice.' ́

'On the contrary,' Calthorpe said. 'It is you, my learned friend, who have broken the rules. My client merely wishes his rights under the law.' He turned back to the bench. 'My lord, you *are* the law in this island. Surely you cannot be seen to do anything other than uphold the law.'

The earl frowned at him. 'I do not need you to remind me of my duty or my responsibilities, Mr Calthorpe. Merriman, I am returning you to the custody of your legal owner. Leave the box.'

'My lord,' Dick cried.

'Quiet,' the earl said. 'I will have quiet in this courtroom. Mr Hilton . . . Mr Anthony Hilton . . . you will produce the man Merriman, in this court, well and able to give evidence, whenever I so order. Is that understood? Bailiffs.'

They already waited at the foot of the steps. Merriman gazed at Dick for a moment, then descended.

'And now . . .' the earl began.

'And now, my lord,' Calthorpe said. 'I would like to make a further protest against these affairs. Hear me out, my lord, in order that you may consider my point during the adjournment. This case is the clearest attempted fraud I have ever seen, and not a very clever one, at that. Where is the Claimant's proof of identity? It rests in the testimony of a drunken sea captain and a runaway slave. Your lordship will have seen for himself how simple a matter it would be to convince the sea captain, Morrison. And your lordship may well imagine how easy it would be to secure the favourable testimony of a slave, by promising him his freedom if the case is. won. As the Claimant confesses he has already done. My lord, these are not witnesses. But my lord, the defence has witnesses to prove that the Claimant cannot be

318

Richard Hilton.'

'Is this an opening speech, Mr Calthorpe?' the earl inquired. 'I do not believe Mr Barker has closed his case as yet.'

'I am endeavouring to save the time of this court,' Calthorpe said. 'It is a well known fact, my lord, that the real Richard Hilton was betrothed to be married before his disappearance, to a Miss Ellen Taggart. That lady is now the wife of Mr Anthony Hilton. Now, my lord, who should better know a man, whatever his present appearance, than a woman to whom he was for four years engaged to be married? I am prepared to produce Mrs Hilton in this court to testify that that man is not Richard Hilton. And further, my lord, it is also a well known fact that the late Richard Hilton perpetrated a criminal assault upon a young lady in Kingston, the night before his disappearance. Now my lord, surely that young lady would be able to remember the identity of her assailant, a man who locked her in a hotel bedroom and brutally raped her. My lord, I am prepared to produce that young lady in this court, also to swear that the Claimant is not Richard Hilton. My lord, I most earnestly entreat that unless my learned friend can offer evidence as conclusive in character as this, that this civil case be dismissed immediately, and that criminal proceedings be instituted against the Claimant.'

The earl stared at him for some seconds, and then at Dick. But clearly his faith in him had suffered considerably. Particularly was he obviously thinking that no matter what view he might have, the jury would certainly find for Tony. And there was nothing to be done, now. He had gambled and lost. It would only have worked had the earl been determined enough to ride over the legal objections in his determination to discover the truth. And there was nothing he could do. He had not felt so helpless for a very long time.

'Hm,' said the earl. 'Hm. Mr Barker?'

Barker stood up, licked his lips. He also knew the case was lost.

'My lord . . .'

'My lord,' said a quiet voice from the very rear of the room. 'The Claimant may well possess a witness of superior value to those listed by Mr Calthorpe.'

'Eh? Eh?' Belmore peered at the speaker.

Dick turned, as did Tony, both as if plucked by a long rope. Alone of everyone in the court, they had equally recognized the voice. Previously seated amidst the veiled women at the back of the room, the speaker had now thrown back the gauze covering her face to reveal herself as Suzanne Hilton.

17

The Incendiary

'Mother?' Dick exclaimed, in total consternation.

'Mother?' Tony cried, no less astounded.

'What? What?' cried the earl.

'You do not know me, my lord.' Suzanne wore black, and stood with the aid of a stick. Dick realized she was seventy years old. But her voice had not changed. 'My husband and I left Jamaica some forty years ago. But I am Suzanne Hilton, wife of Matthew Hilton, sister of Robert Hilton, and mother of Anthony and Richard Hilton.'

'My God,' the earl cried. The court burst into noise, and people scrambled on their chairs the better to see. Suzanne smiled at them all. Her hair was now entirely white, and there were lines on her face and neck. But that marvellous bone structure was also unchanged.

'Mother.' Tony left his seat and ran to the back of the court to take her hand. 'Why did you not inform me you were coming?'

Suzanne freed herself. 'I thought it best.'

'But . . . how long have you been in the island?'

'Two days.'

'Two days? And not a word?'

'Again, I thought it best.' She had reached the front rows, stood beside Dick. 'Well, sir, have you nothing to say?'

Dick could only stare at her; dimly he heard the earl's gavel calling for order. 'I supposed you had rejected me,' he said at last. 'Did you not receive my letter?'

'Had I not, I would not be here now.' She walked past them, into the well of the court.

The earl continued to bang with his gavel. 'Order. Order. I will have the court cleared.' He leaned over his desk. 'Suzanne Hilton?

By God. Madam, I hope you will allow me to entertain you, at a more suitable moment. But you see us here . . .' He remembered why she was there at all. 'Will you identify that man as your son?'

'If you will allow me a few minutes alone with him, my lord, I will either identify him or swear that he is not my son.'

'Aye, well, there it is. Court will adjourn for fifteen minutes.' He glared at the jury, only now subsiding into quiet. 'You'll accompany me, Mrs Hilton. And you as well, Mr Hilton.'

He was addressing Dick, but Tony hurried forward. 'Am I not entitled to speak with my mother?'

'By all means accompany us, Tony,' Suzanne said.

'Mr Hilton.' Barker leaned out of his seat. 'This is make or break.'

'Aye,' Dick said. 'But she is my mother, Mr Barker.' He followed the earl into the judge's chamber at the rear of the court.

'I will leave you now, madam,' Belmore said. 'To speak with these gentlemen.'

He went outside, and the door closed.

'Well,' Tony said, loudly, 'thank God you are here, Mama, to put an end to this farce. The man's an imposter, some white nigger who fought with Christophe, took the name of Warner, and now has the effrontery . . .'

'Be quiet, Tony,' Suzanne said, softly. She held Dick's arm, peered into his face. 'My God,' she said. 'What did they do to you?'

'It was a fall from a cliff, Mama. But you . . .'

'Mama?' she asked. 'Have you the right to use that word to me?'

'But . . . my letter? The handwriting . . .'

'Bore very little resemblance to the last letter I had from Richard Hilton, a long time ago.'

'The events I described . . .'

'Could easily have been learned.'

'I cannot imagine why you troubled to undertake such a long and dangerous journey,' Tony remarked.

'Perhaps a mother never actually believes her son can be dead,' Suzanne said. 'Perhaps she must dream, always, that he will come back to her.'

'Aye,' Tony said. 'I can understand that, Mama. And I can understand how deep must be the disappointment at the end. But this blackguard shall pay for it, you have my word.'

322

Suzanne continued to look at Dick. 'Are you a blackguard?'

'Mama, I . . .' He took a step forward, checked himself. She waited, for some sign to convince her, and he could think of nothing, to do or to say.

'Yes?' she asked, her voice soft.

He stared into her eyes, as she stared into his. His hands closed on her shoulders, and she was in his arms, fingers tight on his back, cheek pressed against his.

'Blackguard,' Tony bellowed. 'By God, I'll . . .'

'Be quiet, Tony,' Suzanne said. 'Oh, Dick, Dick, if you knew how long I have waited to hold you in my arms, with what hopes and with what fears I landed from that ship.'

'If only you had told us you were here.'

'Why?' She removed her hat, and sat down. 'To be badgered, or bullied, or worse.'

'Mama . . .' Tony began.

'I have been receiving letters from Tony, for the past sixteen years,' she said. 'Relating his successes, and your failures, Dick. I supposed you dead, on his hearsay. Why did you not write?'

'With a face like this? Oh, I got used to it. But by then I had become caught up in Christophe's dreams of empire, his perpetual war. I was indeed no longer Matt Hilton's son, Mama.'

'But always Suzanne Hilton's son,' she said. 'Robert Hilton's nephew. I never doubted that when you found your way, you would be a Hilton.'

'You mean you accept his story?' Tony demanded.

'I said, I would end this farce. I travelled with Morrison on the *Green Knight*, swore him to secrecy. I have lodged, privily, and watched and listened, and heard, how you attempted to have your brother murdered, Tony.'

'Murdered? My brother? Why . . .'

'Because he *is* your brother. I have watched him and his wife, from the window of my room. He may not look like Dick, he may not talk like Dick, but he most certainly walks like Dick, as his gestures are Dick's.' She smiled at him. 'As he married the woman Dick would have married. She is very beautiful, Dick. I look forward to meeting her.' She got up again.

'You . . . you will betray me,' Tony cried.

'Betray *you*, Tony. I have come to rescue you from the consequences of your own iniquity. It is now my duty to intercede

323

with Dick on your behalf.'

'Intercede?' he shouted.

'You'll have an annuity,' Dick said. 'Provided you leave Jamaica.'

'Annuity? Leave Jamaica? You think this business will be as simply settled as that?'

'It can be, if you are sensible,' Suzanne said. 'Dick is being more than generous.'

'You'll not have Hilltop,' Tony said.

'I shall come out tomorrow,' Dick said. 'You'll have time to pack.'

'You?' Tony demanded. 'The planters will not stand for it.'

'They'll obey the law.'

'Damn the law. That law was made in England. You are an Abolitionist, a nigger lover. Well, we have finished with those. We are on the verge of declaring our independence. Aye, then we'll make our own laws. You attempt to set foot on Hilltop, and you'll spark a revolution.'

'Why, you . . .' Dick reached for him, and Tony reached for the door.

'Dick.' Suzanne's voice was sharp. 'I'll not have you fighting, when I am seeing you for the first time in twenty years. I had hoped this matter could be happily resolved. I still hope it will be. Tony is upset. That is entirely reasonable. You'll pack your things, Tony, and prepare to leave Hilltop. But when Dick and his wife, and I, come out tomorrow, we will lunch together, and be friends.'

Tony stared at her for a moment, glanced at Dick, then turned and left the room, banging the door behind him.

'We must . . .' Dick attempted to follow, but his mother held his arm.

'Dick. Let him go. And let me hold you, just for a moment. Your letter . . .' She clung to him, her head on his chest. 'I had always supposed you alive, and known that it was nothing more than a mother's prayer.' Her head went back, to allow her to look at him. 'Your letter all but gave us both a seizure.'

'Papa?'

'Is better than for years. The election has rejuvenated him. Even if he could not take part himself, he knows a Whig victory is

324

his victory. Grey is dedicated to reform, and a reformed House of Commons means Abolition. He is proud of you, Dick.'

'For becoming a soldier?'

'For being his son. For returning to Jamaica. You said in your letter it was to emancipate your slaves. Do you mean that, Dick?'

'Aye. But it will not be an easy matter.'

'Nothing worthwhile is ever easy. And you will have me to help you. If you knew how I have longed to help you, Dick, how I have longed to make myself known to you, as I watched you walking yesterday afternoon, with that lovely woman, and those splendid children. My grandchildren, Dick.'

He kissed her forehead. 'And you shall see them in minutes. But we had best return.'

For noise was again bubbling out of the courtroom. He opened the door for her, and the shouts slowly died as they re-entered the room. The earl was already there, waiting at his desk. The jury looked thunderstruck. Calthorpe and Reynolds looked as if they had seen a ghost. Barker and Harris were plainly delighted.

The earl banged his gavel. 'Order. Order. This is but a formality, Mistress Hilton, as Mr Anthony Hilton has seen fit to leave the court. Will you take the box?'

Suzanne climbed the curved staircase, took the oath in a quiet, clear voice. The courtroom had fallen so silent it was possible to hear people breathing.

'Mr Barker?' the earl invited.

Barker rose. 'Will you state your name, please.'

'Suzanne Hilton.'

'Have you ever seen the Claimant before in your life, Mrs Hilton?'

Suzanne smiled at Dick. 'He is my son.'

A great sigh swept through the court room.

'Thank you, Mrs Hilton. Your witness, Mr Calthorpe.'

Calthorpe stood up. 'I have no questions, my lord.' He licked his lips. 'My client accepts that he was mistaken, and that the Claimant is indeed his brother, the rightful owner of Plantation Hilltop.'

Now the noise burst forth. No one had expected it to be set out in quite those terms.

'Blackguard,' shouted one of the jury at Calthorpe.

'You were not so instructed,' cried another.

325

'Mr Hilton.' Harris shook hands.

'My thanks,' Dick said. 'And to you, Barker. You may be sure of my gratitude.'

'Mr Hilton.' Reynolds hesitated. 'I did what I had to do. I sent you Harris.'

'Indeed you did, Mr Reynolds. I'll not bear a grudge.' He descended into the well to meet his mother as she came down the stairs. The earl also descended.

'Congratulations, Mr Hilton. You'll dine with me. Indeed you will. I have long wanted to meet your charming wife again. She is not in court?'

'She is at the hotel with our children. We thought it best. My lord, I would like to see the Reverend Strong.'

'Good heavens, I had quite forgot the fellow. Oh, indeed. You must set him free, if only to legalize his position.' The earl waved at his provost marshal. 'You'll descend to the cells and get the reverend up here.'

The marshal nodded, and hurried for the stairs.

'Just look at them go,' Suzanne said, watching the planters file out. The jury had not waited to be dismissed, but were also leaving, muttering at each other.

'A stiff-necked lot,' Belmore grumbled. 'And you may depend upon it, they will be putting their heads together to see what can be done. Oh, there is more than a spark of treason hidden in that gang. But we shall be ready for them, eh? And now, Mrs Hilton, Mr Hilton, if you'll excuse me . . .' He frowned at the provost marshal, reappearing in the room.

'Well?'

'He is gone, my lord.'

'Gone?' Dick shouted.

'Well, sir, he was sent out to Hilltop.'

'By whose orders?'

'By Mr Hilton's orders, sir. Mr Anthony Hilton. You'll understand, sir, when it was done Mr Hilton was still *the* Hilton, and well, I'm afraid Connor the cell-man is a follower of the plantocracy.'

'The devil,' Dick said. 'I must get a horse.'

'No,' Suzanne said. 'You will fight. I did not come out here to have either of you kill the other. My lord, my son Tony has defied a court order.'

'By God, madam, you are quite right. I'll send the military, indeed I will. You may rest assured, Mr Hilton, the man will be returned here by this very night, or your brother will likely find himself occupying the same cell. Oh, indeed.'

Suzanne squeezed Dick's arm. 'So you may rest easy. And take me to meet your wife and children.'

The Earl of Belmore rose to his feet, raised his glass. 'Ladies and gentlemen. I give you Richard Hilton, of Hilltop.'

The company stood. 'Richard Hilton, of Hilltop.'

Dick felt his eyes fill with tears as he looked at them, at his mother, on his right, at Cartarette on his left, at the earl, at the garrison commander, Colonel Barraclough, at the various other government officials, and their wives, at John Mortlake, and at Mr and Mrs John Harris, and Timothy Barker. He supposed it was a unique occasion, when two black men and a black woman dined at Government House.

'For I tell you this,' Belmore said. 'My interest in this affair is far from being merely that of judge, as Mr Hilton well knows, and understands. Hilltop, I would like to think, has returned to sanity. And where Hilltop leads, the rest of Jamaica must surely follow. Who knows, ladies and gentlemen, an end to the disputes, to the wrangling, and even to the downright treason of the last five years may be in sight.'

He sat down, and Dick rose in turn. 'I thank you all,' he said. 'For your support, for your congratulations. And my lord, you may sleep easy tonight. Hilltop has indeed returned to sanity, and if it is possible to accomplish, Hilltop will now set an example which we hope will be followed by all who have the welfare of Jamaica, and of Jamaicans . . .' He paused to bow to the two black men, 'at heart.'

Suzanne squeezed his hand. 'Matt will be proud of you, Dick, in every way.'

'Aye.' He sat down. 'I wish I could rest as easy as I invite you to.'

'If Hilltop is indeed twenty miles outside of Kingston,' Cartarette pointed out, 'the soldiers cannot possibly return before midnight, supposing they ride like the wind.'

For the colonel had not let them go until three, when the heat had started to leave the sun. But Josh had been sent out at eleven.

'I know that,' Dick agreed. 'Yet it rests heavy on my mind. It is

327

not only Josh. It is Judith Gale as well.'

'Now, Dick,' Suzanne protested. 'By all accounts . . .'

'She is no better than she should be. And that is true enough. Yet did she volunteer to testify for me.'

'And changed her mind,' Cartarette said. 'I am not surprised she chose to ride with your brother, instead of remaining in town.'

He smiled at them. 'I am outnumbered. Yet with Tony in a savage mood, who can tell what may be happening while we dine the night away . . .' He paused to watch the Governor's secretary enter the room.

'Lomas,' said the earl. 'What news?'

Lomas wore a worried frown. 'A rider, from Captain Painter's platoon, your Excellency.'

'From Hilltop, you mean?'

'No, your Excellency. Captain Painter has not gone to Hilltop.'

'What?' Dick was on his feet.

Lomas studied the hastily written note. 'They were halted by a messenger from Plantation Golden Acre, my lord. Mr Reed says his house is being surrounded by a mob of blacks.'

'Eh?' Belmore wore an expression of complete bemusement. 'Surrounded? Blacks?'

'May we have the man in, your Excellency?' asked Colonel Barraclough.

'Oh, indeed. Indeed. As long as he does not frighten the ladies.'

Lomas snapped his fingers. He had apparently been expecting this decision. The trooper's red coat was stained with dust, his face with sweat. He stood to attention.

'At ease, man. At ease,' Barraclough said. 'What took place out there?'

'Well, sir . . .' The soldier inhaled. 'First of all there were conch shells, sir. All about us, but mostly in the north.'

'Conch shells?' Cartarette inquired.

'They use them as the people in Haiti use their drums,' Dick explained. 'For the sending of messages. What messages?'

'Well, sir, we did not know. Then. But at Eastside village, where the mountains begin, we halted, and inquired of the headman. Oh, afraid he was, sir. Afraid.'

'Of what, man?' Belmore shouted.

'Well, sir, your Excellency, it seems the conches started the moment the Reverend Strong was arrested this morning. It seems

328

the people had been afraid this might happen, and had been already agitated. Why, sir, a dozen of the young men at Eastside had already gone north.'

'But those are free blacks,' the Governor protested.

'This man, Strong, has a large congregation there,' Barraclough said.

'My God,' said the Governor. 'My God. Well, go on, man.'

'Yes, sir, your Excellency,' the trooper said. 'Well, the captain decided to continue, but about three miles farther on we were met by this bookkeeper, sir, from Golden Acre. It seems the Reverend Strong had been allowed to preach there, your Excellency. And when the conches started this afternoon the slaves came out of the fields without being bid. Mr Reed sent one of the bookkeepers amongst them, sir, with a whip, and he was dismounted and beaten, sir.'

'My God,' Belmore said. 'My God.'

'Then they set fire to the village,' the trooper said. 'Mr Reed retreated to the Great House, with the rest of his white people, but sent this one man for help. Well, sir; your Excellency, Captain Painter decided he could nothing less than ride out there. But he sent me back to town to inform your Excellency of the situation.'

'But why Golden Acre?' Suzanne asked. 'Was not Strong sent out to Hilltop?'

'Indeed he was, Mrs Hilton,' Barraclough said. 'But he will have no congregation there. As a runaway he would not have dared return. Even had he not been a runaway, I do not suppose Tony Hilton would have given the necessary permission. No, no, Strong's people are to be found in the north and west.' He turned to the Governor. 'Your Excellency, I would like to take a squadron out there. This thing must be nipped in the bud. Or it may very well spread.'

'If it has not already done so,' Harris remarked.

'Well, sir, your Excellency,' said the trooper. 'I saw flames when I was riding back. Far away, they was, but it could have been Plantation Rivermouth.'

'My God,' Belmore said. 'Flames? The house, you mean?'

'Well, no, sir, your Excellency. It looked more like the fields.'

'Aye.' Barraclough was on his feet. 'They'll start with the cane.'

Dick had remained standing. 'Then what of Hilltop?'

Barraclough hesitated. 'Well, sir, Mr Hilton, there is no report of violence on Hilltop, as yet. And we know the people there do not attend Strong's church . . .'

'Yet will the contagion spread to them,' Harris repeated. 'They have no cause to love Tony Hilton.'

'Oh, my God,' Suzanne said.

'He has a large force of bookkeepers, Mrs Hilton,' Belmore said.

'He also has Strong,' Dick said. 'Is not the way to end this trouble to show the blacks that their parson is not under arrest, after all?'

Barraclough hesitated. 'True. I could send some men . . .'

'And what of Kingston, sir?' Belmore demanded. 'Kingston must be defended.'

Barraclough chewed his lip.

'And it must be done quietly, for the time,' Suzanne said. 'If these people hear there is a slave revolt on even one plantation, there will be a panic.'

'Aye,' Barraclough said. 'That is true enough.'

'You must go to Golden Acre,' Cartarette said. 'With what men you can spare. There may be a massacre.'

'A massacre?' Belmore cried. 'My God. In Jamaica?'

'Aye,' Harris said. 'When you tamper with a man's religion you hurt him more than when you take a stick to his back.'

'Take your men, Colonel,' Dick said. 'Ride to Golden Acre. I'll get out to Hilltop, and bring Strong into town.' He glanced down at his mother. 'It is the only way, Mama. Strong is the only way we can stop this business before it becomes a full scale revolution. Even Tony must see that.'

Barraclough looked doubtful. 'I can spare no men, Mr Hilton.'

'I don't need men,' Dick said. 'We have just established that there is no riot at Hilltop, as yet. Nor will there be if I get there in time.'

'Well . . .' Barraclough stroked his chin.

'Of course you are right, Dick,' Suzanne decided. 'I will come with you.'

'You, Mama? But . . .'

'But nothing. It is thirty years since I have visited Hilltop. Too long.'

'A ride in the dark?'

'We will take a carriage. You can provide one, my lord?'

330

'Of course. But really, Mrs Hilton . . .'

'I must be there, don't you see, or my sons will merely fight.'

'Your mother is right, Dick,' Cartarette said. 'And I will come too.'

'You?' he cried. 'But . . .'

'For ten years you have regaled me with tales of the splendour of your home. Do you not suppose I am anxious to see it?'

'But what of the children?'

Cartarette looked at John Mortlake.

'Oh, indeed, Mrs Hilton. They will be taken care of.'

'And we shall be back tomorrow,' Cartarette said. 'Will we not, Mr Hilton?'

'Of course, but . . .' Dick looked at the Governor.

'Ladies, riding out into the country, after dark,' the earl said. 'When there is riot about. Oh, no, no. We cannot tell how far the contagion may have spread . . .'

'My lord,' Suzanne said, getting up. 'We are discussing *my* plantation and *my* family. The contagion has not spread this far, that is plain. If Colonel Barraclough is taking his men to the west, and we are riding north, he will be between us and any rioters. And I do assure you, we are perfectly capable of taking care of ourselves.'

'Yet may you need support,' Harris said. 'I will accompany you.' He glanced at his wife. 'There will be no danger, as Mrs Hilton says. But even less if we are sufficiently strong.'

'He's right, Mr Hilton,' Barker agreed. 'I'll come too, if you'll have me.'

'Why, you are more than welcome,' Dick said. 'But I do not see why you should be involved . . .'

Harris grinned at him. 'Man, Mr Hilton, Hilltop is my principal client.'

'Settled, then,' Suzanne said. 'If you'll provide a carriage, my lord, my daughter-in-law and I will change our clothes.'

'And we'll get some weapons,' Harris said.

'Aye.' Barraclough was already at the door. 'I'll turn out my men and ride for Golden Acre.'

'Bless my soul,' said the earl, still sitting at the head of the table. 'Bless my soul. Who'd have thought it, in Jamaica.'

Dick caught up with Cartarette at the door. 'Are you sure you know what you do? I had supposed we had done with fighting.'

She smiled at him, kissed him on the chin. 'You, finish with fighting? Besides, we are not going to fight, Dick. We are going to stop a fight. And we are going to claim our home. I'll not have it burned before I even see it.'

'You'll take no chances.' Barraclough sat on his horse beside the carriage, his troopers waiting at his back. The air was chill, and the first cock had already begun to crow; it had taken an interminable time to prepare the carriage. 'There are half a dozen muskets and an ample supply of powder. And you have your pistols.'

'We'll take care,' Dick agreed.

'Aye, well, supposing the trouble at Golden Acre is less serious than we suppose, or that we manage to put a stop to it soon enough, we'll come over to Hilltop to see how things are progressing.' He leaned from the saddle to look into the interior of the coach. 'God speed you, ladies.'

'He will, Colonel, as our cause is just,' Suzanne said. She was in a state of high excitement, Dick realized. Partly no doubt from being back in Jamaica at all. But equally because she was adventuring, recapturing some of her youth. Cartarette on the other hand was perfectly composed. She had wrapped herself in a pelisse, and wore a bonnet tied tightly under her chin. She had not awakened the children, but merely kissed each one before leaving them in the care of John Mortlake and the servants at the hotel. As she had said, she would be back tomorrow.

So why did his stomach seem so filled with lead? Because he was not galloping at the head of his dragoons? Because it was so many years since there had been a slave revolt on Jamaica, and he could not help but feel that his court case had precipitated it?

Or because his entire being was out at Hilltop, and not only with Josh. Ellen was out there as well, and Judith Gale. He had no cause to love either of them now, but they were white women, in danger. Perhaps.

Then was he not a fool, and a criminal, to place two more white women in danger? But they would not abandon him now. He would have to use force. Well, he could do that, no doubt. But the truth of the matter was he wanted them to come. He wanted them at his side when he saw Hilltop again, for the first time in sixteen years. And he wanted Suzanne there when he confronted Tony.

Because he did not wish to fight his brother? Or because, when it came down to it, he was still afraid of him?

He had not known doubts such as these for sixteen years.

'Ready, Mr Hilton.' Harris was already up on the top of the coach, with Barker.

'Aye, ready.' Dick closed the door. 'I anticipate no trouble, Mama, Cartarette. But should there be, you'll remain close.'

Suzanne stroked her pistol. 'Oh, aye, Dick. My God, I feel a girl again. Indeed I do.'

It occurred to him that she would welcome trouble. He sighed, and climbed on to the box beside Melchior, the Governor's coachman. 'Let's go.'

The whip cracked, and the equipage rolled out of the courtyard. Colonel Barraclough raised his arm, and the troop of cavalry followed. The town remained quiet, and asleep; there were no lights in any of the houses. Although at least one began to glimmer as the cavalcade rumbled up Harbour Street. Whatever Belmore elected to do, Dick realized the news would be widespread by breakfast. But perhaps by then the business would have been settled, one way or the other.

The houses thinned, the road divided. The carriage turned right, along that so well remembered route. The cavalry rode left, for the sea coast and the plantations to the west. Now the darkness was turning to grey. They should be at Hilltop by noon. How memory clouded back. The first time he had ridden this way had been with Josh. Twenty years ago. How excited he had been. How uncertain he had been. And how confused he had been.

Now? He found it difficult to decide on his emotions. His heart pounded pleasantly at the thought of seeing Hilltop again. Remarkably, he felt no elation at having won his court case. He had never supposed he would lose it, even when it had seemed that he would not be able to secure a witness, of any description. Even more remarkably, he once again felt no animosity towards Tony, who had only tried to be a Hilton. Save for Josh. Were Josh harmed . . . but Tony would not dare harm him.

The sun rose, with West Indian suddenness. Wisps of mist still clung to the hillside, and the grass remained damp. But not for long. The heat became instant, and Cartarette was banging on the roof. 'Will you take breakfast?'

Melchior pulled the horses to a halt, and they got down to

stretch their legs. The road had already risen by over a hundred feet; the hills climbed to their right, the land sloped away in thick woods to their left. Kingston had disappeared, although they would see it from time to time as they climbed the hills, he remembered. The morning was quiet, now the drumming of the hooves had ceased.

'My God, how long it seems.' Suzanne also stepped down. 'How long it is.'

Cartarette spread her cloth on the folding table Melchior had erected. Harris was opening the wine. A picnic, on a Jamaican morning.

'We have a pie here,' Cartarette said. 'And some good bread. At least, they say it is good bread.' She sniffed a slice. 'Why cannot the English make bread, Mother?'

'The French make good bread,' Suzanne explained, 'because they lack the potato.'

Dick sipped a glass of wine. Incredible, that perhaps only thirty miles away a plantation was in flames. He saw Cartarette's frown, and hastily smiled.

'You anticipate,' she said. 'Pie, Mr Harris? If it comes to blows you'll do better on a full stomach.'

'Blows, Mistress Hilton?' Harris held out his plate. 'Why, I do not think that will happen.' But then he frowned, and gazed at Dick.

Who slowly lowered his glass. The sound of the conches was unmistakable, eerily wailing through the valleys.

Suzanne was filling her plate, calmly. 'How far away is that noise?'

'I have no idea,' Dick confessed.

'Not far, sir,' Melchior said. 'Maybe five miles. Is the hills make it echo.'

'Five miles. You'll take some wine, Melchior.'

'That is kind of you, sir.' He held up his glass. 'But what is that?' They faced the path, listening to the drumming hooves.

'Can't be slaves,' Barker said. 'They'd never ride.'

Dust clouded into the morning air, rising almost like smoke, and the riders pulled their horses back. Three white men, armed and anxious.

'A picnic, by God,' cried their leader.

'James Hardy.' Dick stepped forward, right hand resting on the butt of the pistol in his belt. 'Why have you left the plantation?'

Hardy peered at him, and some of the colour faded from his cheeks. He had filled out with age, but still wore his moustaches, and still neglected to shave with any regularity. 'The monster.'

Dick merely smiled at him. 'I asked you a question.'

'They say the country is in arms,' said one of the men behind.

'There is your reason to stay with the estate, not desert it,' Suzanne said. 'Where is my son?'

'Your son?' Hardy frowned at her. 'Well, well, he spoke of you, to be sure. Your son has gone to Orange Lodge.'

'Orange Lodge?'

'Tony has abandoned Hilltop?' Dick demanded.

'What, stay and fight for a plantation which is no longer his?' Hardy inquired. 'There is no sense.'

'But what of my slaves?'

'I know nothing of them,' Hardy said. 'They have not yet joined the revolt, if that is what you mean. But we held no field conference this morning. They are still in their village, so far as I know.'

'My God,' Suzanne said. 'Just to ride away, and leave them . . . is that not an invitation to violence?'

Hardy shrugged. 'You must ask your son that, Mrs Hilton.'

'What of the firearm store?' Dick asked.

'We took sufficient for our own defence.'

'And left the rest? Muskets, with powder and ball?'

'We were in haste. It was Mr Hilton's decision. He took our people across to Orange Lodge, where Mr Tresling will defend himself, and sent us into town for the military.'

'The military are already out,' Dick said. 'And we are now on our way to Hilltop. You'll accompany us.'

'Us?' Hardy cried.

'It is your plantation.'

'Are you offering us employment, Mr Hilton?' asked a voice behind.

'I am giving you a chance to prove that you are worthy of employment,' Dick said.

'Supposing you still have a plantation,' the third man muttered.

'I will have a plantation,' Dick said. 'Whether I have to regain it by force or not.'

'Aye, well, you're welcome to it,' Hardy said. 'I'm for town to

335

raise the populace. You hear those conch shells? Any white man . . .' he peered into the carriage, 'or white woman, who goes abroad with those black devils on the rampage is looking for trouble. As for riding with them . . .' his gaze settled on Harris and Barker.

'You'd best be off then,' Dick recommended. 'Melchior, pack up these things; we'll be moving along. But before you go, Hardy, tell me this. Where is the Reverend Strong confined?'

'The Reverend Strong?' Hardy demanded. 'You mean the runaway, Josh Merriman.'

'His name is immaterial,' Dick said. 'He is known as the Reverend Strong to these people. If they are revolting, it is because they suppose their minister imprisoned and abused .'

'Oh, aye,' Hardy said. 'They are revolting on his behalf all right. No doubt about that. Thus we have treated him as the first of their ringleaders to fall into our hands.'

There was a moment's silence. In the distance the conch shells continued to wail.

'You have done *what*?' Dick asked at last.

'The punishment for revolt is death, as you well know, Mr Hilton,' Hardy declared, and grinned at him. 'So before we left the plantation we strung the devil up.'

Dick's brain seemed to explode. He stepped forward, seized the little man by the thigh and shoulder, and swung him from the saddle.

'Aaaagh,' Hardy screamed. 'Help me!'

The two bookkeepers made a concerted move to dismount, and were brought up by the levelled muskets of Barker and Harris.

'You *hanged* him?' Dick shook Hardy as a dog might shake a rat.

'Let me go,' bawled the manager. 'Let me go.'

'Dick,' Suzanne said. 'Do not harm him.'

'Harm him? I'll break his neck.'

'Aaagh,' Hardy screamed. 'Help me.'

'Dick.' Cartarette's voice was imperative. 'That will not help. You stupid man,' she said. 'Do you not realize the blacks are in arms simply because their minister was arrested?'

Dick slowly unclamped his fingers; Hardy slipped down his legs to kneel on the ground, fingering his throat and gasping for breath.

336

'As for what will happen now,' Suzanne said.

Hardy regained his feet, backing away from Dick. 'Now?' he snarled. 'We'll hang the lot of them. Everyone with a black skin and weapons in his hands. Aye . . .' He flung out his hand, the finger pointing. 'You two as well.' He vaulted into his saddle. 'And those who would give them arms.' He kicked his horse, sent it careering along the road. His companions hesitated but a moment, then chased behind him.

'There is no sanity,' Harris said. 'When it comes to blows.'

Dick looked down on his hands. Then slapped them together. 'We'd best hurry.'

'Where?' Suzanne asked.

'I came out to repossess my plantation, as well as regain Josh's freedom. I have failed in the one. I'll not fail in the other.'

'Three men?' she looked at Melchior.

'And two women,' Cartarette said, softly.

'You'll go back,' Dick decided. 'The moment we reach the plantation. Melchior will drive you back.'

'I thank you very much, sir,' she said. 'I also came to see my new home. I suspect I will be safer there than on the road. Mother?'

Suzanne hesitated. Dick wondered how far the years were rolling away to allow memory to come creeping in. All the way to St Domingue, in August 1791?

'I think your wife is right, Dick.' she said. 'We are best together.' She smiled at him. 'And I also came to look at Hilltop once again.'

'Then let's get there.' He bundled the breakfast things together, while Melchior folded the table, and Barker helped the ladies back into the coach. 'Keep your weapons primed, I beg of you,' he said, and climbed on to the box. The whip cracked, the coach rumbled forwards into the valleys, creeping ever upwards into the mountains, accompanied now by the sun, bringing sweat to their cheeks, scorching the last drop of moisture from the trees and bushes. There was no cloud in the sky, as yet; there would be later, for the daily shower of rain. And there was no sound either, above the rumbling of the wheels. The conch shells had ceased, for the moment.

He checked his pistols, from sheer restlessness. What did he intend? What could he intend? Hilltop was built to withstand a siege. No doubt about that. But only if adequately defended. And

337

in any event, what would he find, on a plantation abandoned by its white population for several hours?

The horses wheezed their way upwards, slowly, topped the last rise. The sun played full down on the valley, gleaming on the rich green cane stalks, on the village and the factory, on the house. There had been no destruction as yet.

Suzanne and Cartarette were leaning out of the windows. 'But it is beautiful,' Cartarette said. 'So big.'

'Do you see anyone, Dick?' Suzanne asked.

He levelled his telescope. 'Aye.' There were people, milling about the slave village. Not yet decided what do do? What to destroy? And there were hideous, bald-headed carrion crows circling before the Great House. 'Make haste, Melchior. Make haste. Ride for the house.'

The whip cracked again, the coach careered down the slope. Within seconds they were in the fields, hidden from view, as a coach, but no doubt signifying their presence far and wide by the dust rising from their wheels. Dick looked round at Barker and Harris, and the lawyers crammed their tall hats the more firmly on their heads and grinned at him. They were mulattoes. But their white blood had earned them nothing but enmity from the planters. So then, why did they risk their lives?

Or was it for Jamaica?

The town came in sight, and beyond it the slave village. And the people there had seen them, had coagulated into a mass in front of the gate, staring, chattering, waving their arms.

'You want me to stop, Mr Hilton?' Melchior asked.

Dick shook his head. 'Make the house.'

They charged up the slope, pulled to a rest before the front steps. The crows gave resentful squawks and fluttered to a safe distance. The doors swung open, the house looked undamaged. But from the central beam over the steps there hung the body of Josh Merriman.

'Oh, God,' Cartarette said. 'Oh, God.'

Dick climbed down. 'Help me,' he said.

Barker and Harris joined him on the verandah. Dick climbed on the rail to cut the rope, and the two mulattoes caught the black man as he fell. He had been dead for about twelve hours, and the sun was noon high. Every wave of the hand scattered a swarm of flies.

'There'll be spades in the stables, Mr Barker,' Dick said. 'Mama, you and Cartarette go inside.'

'We can fight, Dick.'

'And you may have to. But inside. Those people will not have firearms. Melchior, Mr Harris, you'll help me barricade . . .' He paused in surprise as Boscawen came out of the house, fully dressed, even to his wig. 'Mr Boscawen? What has happened here?'

But Boscawen was staring at him in turn.

Dick shook him by the shoulder. 'I am Richard Hilton, old man. Remember me?'

'Mr Dick?' Boscawen peered at him. 'Ow, me Gawd. Mr Dick? They did say you is all mark up.'

'Aye, but it is me. And this is your new mistress.'

Boscawen fell to his knees. 'You got for forgive me, master. You got for forgive me.'

'For working for my brother? Oh, aye, get up, man, and tell me what has happened here.'

Barker was back with a spade. 'You'll help me, Johnny,' he said.

He and Harris lifted Josh's body down the steps.

'Man, Mr Dick,' Boscawen said, rolling his eyes. 'It is bad.'

'Tell me.'

'Well, sir, Mr Tony, he came riding out here with he friends, and they quarrelling, quarrelling, and they seizing Mr Strong there and hanging he, while the mistress did be looking on, and you knowing what, Mr Dick, sir, she spit on he while he hoisting up.'

'And what were our people doing this time?'

'They standing and staring, because them bookkeeper all armed with musket and pistol and thing, and then the master . . . oh, begging your pardon, Mr Dick, is Mr Tony I speaking about, he tell them get the hell out of there and they gone back down to the village, and the master and he people they saddle all the horse and ride out.'

'For Orange Lodge?'

'Well, I hear them saying that. I hear them saying they ain't staying to defend no place what ain't theirs.'

'How long ago?'

Boscawen rolled his eyes. 'Before daylight.'

'And what have our people done since?'

'Well, sir, Mr Dick, they ain't knowing what for do. They come up here one time, and I tell them go, go, and they gone. One or two gone break in the rum store, and they singing, like, and one or two gone up north, I thinking. But most just talking. And look there.'

Dick turned, watched the black people trailing up the hill. Even after sixteen years and at a distance he could make out the giant figure of Absolom.

'Mr Harris,' he shouted. 'Mr Barker. To me.'

The grave was only half dug. The two lawyers dropped their spades and ran back to the house.

'Inside, Cartarette, Mama.' There was no arguing with the bite in his tone. The two women hurried inside. 'Mr Harris, Mr Barker, your muskets, if you please.' He himself stood at the head of the outer steps, watched the men coming towards him. He tucked his thumbs into his belt where the butts of his pistols were close to hand. But he possessed only two bullets. He took a long breath. 'Good morning, Absolom. Remember me?'

They stopped, about thirty yards away. He estimated there were perhaps fifty of them. But the rest, numbering more than a thousand, were watching from a distance.

'You is Mr Dick?' Absolom asked. 'Them boys saying you done change.'

'I am Mr Dick,' Dick said. 'I am come back to live here. I shall not go again. Mr Tony will not be back.'

Absolom and Jeremiah exchanged glances, looked at their fellows.

'And the mistress?' someone asked.

'If you mean Mr Tony's wife, she will not be back either,' Dick said.

Absolom came forward, alone. 'A boy done come,' he said. 'But an hour gone. He saying all Jamaica in arms. He saying the day is here, to kill all the white folk, to burn all the plantation, to make Jamaica a free country for us black people, just like Haiti.' He pointed, at where Josh had swung. 'He saying now the reverend man done dead, there ain't nothing more to be done with the white people.'

He paused for breath.

'Is that man still here?' Dick asked.

'He gone for to raise the next plantation. But he saying them boys marching. He saying there does be thousand and thousand, and they getting musket and thing. He saying they ain't stopping until they taking Kingston itself. He saying we got for join with him. He saying they going be here this afternoon.'

'It is afternoon now,' Dick said.

'They going be here soon.'

'You listen, man, Mr Dick,' Jeremiah said.

The faint howl of the conches could be heard, wailing in the hills. And behind that, a deep roar, like a turbulent sea. Or an army of marching men.

How it made his blood tingle.

'Why are you telling me this?' Dick asked. 'Why are you not already murdering me and my people, and taking our weapons?'

Jeremiah looked embarrassed, glanced at Absolom.

'Man, Mr Dick, sir, we ain't got no grudge with you. You did treat us right when you here,' Absolom said. 'But you must see we got for go with them boys. So what I am saying to you is, mount up and ride back out. Get down to Kingston and take ship, and take them white people with you, or they's all going to get chop up.'

'You want to do this?' Dick asked. 'You want to fight? Be sure a great number of you will be killed. Be sure that your women and children will starve. Be sure that there will be many white soldiers to fight you. I have lived sixteen years in Haiti. I have fought with Christophe and Boyer. I have seen people die, and people starve. In Haiti, it was necessary. Here it is not necessary. Listen to me. There has been an election in England. A new government is in power and that government is dedicated to freeing the slaves. You will be free men, within five years. I promise you that. I promise you more. Remain faithful to me, and you will be free men sooner than that. Go to war with these revolutionaries, and you will be killed. You will be hunted into the mountains, and you will starve. If you are caught you will be hanged.'

Absolom and Jeremiah exchanged glances. 'Man, Mr Dick, we knowing what you say, but we got for . . .'

'Why?'

'Man, Mr Dick, them boys coming. Thousand and thousand.'

'They have to pass here,' Dick said. 'They cannot leave Hilltop in our hands. They must take this house, before they can go down to Kingston.'

'Man, Mr Dick, sir, then they going burn this house, and they going kill everybody what ain't joining up with them.'

'With thirty men I will hold this house against an army,' Dick said.

'Thirty men?' Absolom looked around him as if expecting them to materialize out of the ground.

'You pick them, Absolom. Thirty men, who will be prepared to fight and if need be to die. For their freedom. Because that will be your reward.'

Absolom licked his lips.

'And what about them others?' Jeremiah asked.

'There is no room in here, and I have weapons for only thirty. Send your people into the canefields. Tell them to go far from the village, and hide there. Tell them to take food, and some buckets of water, and to stay there until the battle is over.'

'Man,' Jeremiah said. 'We all going get kill.'

'You are going to get killed for sure, if you rebel,' Dick said. 'I am giving you a chance to live. I am giving you a chance to let your women and your children live, as well.' He pointed at Absolom. 'Thirty men, Absolom. The best you have. I want them here in half an hour. Melchior, get back on your coach and ride for town. Tell the Governor what has happened, and that we are defending the House. Tell him I reckon we can hold for twenty-four hours. Hurry man.'

He went inside.

'Will they fight?' Suzanne asked. 'Against their fellows?'

'They'll fight,' Dick said.

'But those men know nothing of weapons,' Cartarette said.

'Neither do the men who will attack us,' Dick said. 'And we will have firearms. A noise, at the least.' He smiled at her. 'No dragoons, sweetheart. But men with a dream. They'll fight.'

It rained at three o'clock. This was usual for the time of year. The clouds swung low over the Great House, and the steady patter of water cascaded off the roof, trickled along the gutters, filled the fresh water vats which were situated at each corner of the building. The teeming water made a mist which clouded the hills around the valley, obscured even the village, left the factory chimney a shadow. And shut in the Great House behind a wall of

342

sound. The noise of the conch shells died, as did the rumble of people.

There was little conversation inside the house. Boscawen carried round food, and the men ate at their posts. Absolom had picked well, and the thirty slaves were big and strong and eager. And embarrassed, to find themselves actually inside the Great House. The furniture, the piano and the tables and the chairs, had been pushed against the inner walls and covered with dust sheets. The men knelt or sat, two to each window, ten to a side; Harris commanded the south face, Barker the east; Dick himself commanded the north and west faces, from where the insurgents were expected. He had recruited an additional ten of the most alert women, to help Suzanne and Cartarette with the loading. They had rehearsed, and seemed reasonably proficient. As he had sixty muskets, with adequate service he hoped to maintain a fairly consistent fire. So, then, he was defending Hilltop, the first Hilton ever to do so. And against people he wished only to help. But there was no other way. He had discovered much to admire in Haiti. But there had been even more to hate and to fear, forty years after the blacks had taken their freedom by force. If these people could be made to wait, for just a little while, to receive their freedom as a human right, the tragedies might be avoided, the triumphs still achieved.

But how ironic that he must kill, where he wanted only peace.

He walked the verandahs, talking to his men, reminding them of his instructions, of the orders he would give them. Looking over the canefields meant nothing, now. Every moment the insurgents delayed increased the house's chance of survival.

And at dusk, when Boscawen served supper, they still had not come.

'Tell me of 1791,' Cartarette said.

'Why?' Suzanne asked. 'It was terrible.'

'I would like to know.'

Suzanne sighed. 'There were forty men in the house. But the blacks would not be stopped. They swarmed up the patios, broke down the door. It was really very quick. Do you remember anything of it, Dick?'

'I remember Aunt Georgiana screaming,' Dick said, and walked to the window. All the shutters had been closed, save one, facing north. Outside it was already dark.

'This time,' he said, 'if they get inside, you must kill yourselves. I may not be able to get to you.'

'I will not kill myself,' Cartarette said.

'Mama . . .'

'Nor will I permit your mother to murder me, Dick.'

His turn to sigh. 'Aye. Well . . .' he had expected nothing different. Not from Cartarette. He did not even suppose she would scream, when they cut her body. But that thought made him sweat, made him fume with impotent rage. It must not happen. And only he could stop it. Unless the military came. But the troopers had more than enough to do.

The air cooled, the night grew darker, some of the men slept. Dick watched the clock. At midnight he almost made himself believe they had, after all, been bypassed.

Suzanne went upstairs to bed. Cartarette slept in a chair. Dick watched her face in the glimmering candlelight. When she slept she regained her youth, was again the girl who had been his slave. Who Gislane had tied to the lovebed. A woman to love.

His head jerked. There was again sound, seeping through the morning. The wailing of a conch shell, but close at hand.

He closed the shutter, bolted it. Suzanne came down the stairs. Cartarette sat up. 'You'll take to the cellar if the house burns,' he said. 'And make your move the moment you hear a door break. Promise me.'

The women hesitated, looking at each other.

'We promise, Dick.'

'Aye, you've children, Cartarette. Remember them. And you have a husband, Mama. Remember him.' He walked round the walls. 'They are close. Check your priming. No man is to go outside, and no man is to show himself more than enough to fire his weapon. They will not know how many we have inside, what they have to beat. Remember what I have told you. Point the musket at their bellies, and squeeze the trigger. The ladies will load for you.'

The slaves fingered their weapons in bewilderment.

Dick went into the front hall, found Harris. Between them they opened the door.

'What is your plan?' Harris breathed deeply.

'To hold.'

'You have done this before?'

Dick shook his head. 'My family has. Our history is nothing but holding. But we have made mistakes. Our plantation Green Grove in Antigua, was overrun by Caribs, a hundred and fifty years ago. Christopher Hilton made the mistake of trying to gain the maximum fire power. He assembled his men on the front verandah. His first volley halted the Indians, but before he could reload, his men were scattered and the house was taken. My uncle-in-law, Louis Corbeau, made the same mistake in St Domingue, in 1791. We will sit behind our windows, and sit and sit.'

'They will destroy your plantation,' Harris said.

'They will do that anyway.' Dick pointed. Flames flickered in the canefields.

How many? He levelled his telescope; the nearest field was over a mile away. Hundreds? Thousands? He caught the glint of steel. But only machetes.

Flames clouded the sky. Cartarette stood beside him, her fingers tight on his arm. She knew the worst that could happen to a woman, should the house be overrun. Or did she consider him the worst that could happen? He had not raised the question of her happiness since that night on the boat.

People were pouring out of the burning canefields. Many men, dark-skinned and dark-faced. They flooded towards the slave village, and paused there, giving shrill shouts and yells, punctuated with peals of near hysterical laughter. They could not believe what they were doing. In their hearts, they knew they were committing suicide.

'Inside,' he commanded, and they obeyed. Cartarette gave his arm a last squeeze and withdrew to the drawing room. Dick walked up and down behind his men crouching at the loopholed shutters in the dining room, and beyond, in the kitchen. The kitchen, built away from the main building to reduce the risk of fire, formed a salient. It was the most vulnerable part of the house, a relatively small area which could be assailed from three sides at once. Here he had seven men, and here Suzanne would act as loader.

He stooped to a loophole, looked down the hillside. Flames began to issue from the village. They had got over their surprise at discovering it empty. And men were coming up the hill, pausing at the white town, to break down doors and rampage through houses, to destroy the church. They were revolting in the name of a Baptist parson; they regarded the established church as their enemy. The factory would be next. This day's damage would take half of next year's crop to put right; this year there would be no crop at all.

The noise was loud now, shrieking voices, loud laughter, the crashings and bangings of a hundred homes being destroyed. Cartarette's fingers were back on his shoulders. 'Why do they not come?'

He straightened. 'You aren't afraid?'

'Oh, aye. I'm afraid,' she said. 'Yesterday there seemed so much to live for.'

'There is more today. They'll soon be here. Do not let these people see your fear.'

She gave a grimace, and returned to the drawing room. Dick looked through the loophole once again, watched the flames in the factory. They were burning the roof, because they could not burn the machinery. A pall of smoke lay over the town, mingled with the smoke drifting down from the canefields; he could not see it in the dark, but he could smell it. Come dawn, Hilltop would be marked for miles, by the smoke drifting over it. But how many plantations would be similarly marked?

The first man came up the hill. He walked confidently, wearing only cotton drawers, swinging a cutlass, holding a bottle from which he drank from time to time. The village and the town was deserted. No doubt the house was similarly empty, even if the shutters were closed.

Others came behind him, But he was a good way in front. Time. There was the essence. How to make them withdraw for another hour.

Dick stood up. 'No man fires until I tell him to,' he called. 'I will see to that one.'

He walked through the hall, boots dull on the parquet floor. He opened the front door, signalled Boscawen to stand close, to shut it again at a signal.

He took a long breath, stepped on to the verandah. He remembered the morning before he had assaulted the frontier post, and found Cartarette. Then he had wondered what it must feel like, to watch death and destruction approaching, to know there was nowhere to run, nowhere to hide. He had wondered,

346

then, if he would be afraid, if he would truly be a brave man, until he had known that experience.

And here it was. And he was not afraid. Only preoccupied, with all the things that must be done, with the importance of this first shot.

The man stopped, twenty feet from the steps, gazed at the white man.

'Throw down your machete,' Dick called. 'Tell your friends to surrender. Or they will die.'

The slave looked past Dick at the opened door, the darkened hallway. His head turned, left and right. Dick could read the thoughts passing through his brains as if they were printed. No horses, no people that he could see. A white man, but the town was empty. Just one white man.

The slave turned his head to look over his shoulder. His friends were coming closer, and more and more people were moving up the hill. The town burned merrily now; the crash of the factory roof as it fell in boomed across the morning.

'Aiiieeeee,' screamed the slave, and ran at the steps. It occurred to Dick that he must have sounded just like that, when leading his cavalry into the charge. But his thought, and the black man's scream, were already history. His arm was levelled, the pistol was kicking against his fingers, black smoke was eddying into his face. The man had reached the steps when the ball struck him square in the chest, at a range of eight feet. His head went back and both arms went up. The machete arced through the air behind him. His chest exploded into red, and he hit the earth with his shoulder blades.

The crowd moving up the hill checked. But it would only be for an instant. Dick stepped inside, and Boscawen slammed the door. Dick dropped the heavy bolts into place, looked back at the house, the tense faces; Cartarette, standing in the centre of the drawing room, a musket in each hand, Suzanne, looking through from the pantry, Barker and Harris, staring at him. Of them all, only he had ever killed in battle. Only he and Cartarette and Suzanne had ever been under fire.

'Hold,' he said. 'And wait.' He stood by the front door, watched the black army swarming up the hill, spreading out as they ran to cover the house from every angle, forming a gigantic enveloping movement.

347

'Present,' he shouted. 'But hold.'

There was an explosion from the drawing room.

'Hold, God damn you, he yelled. 'Change your weapon. Reload, Cartarette, Reload. Hold.'

The black men reached the top, panting now, waving their cutlasses; they had all been at the rum. A man climbed over the verandah rail, screaming at the wooden shutters, for the first time noticing that every loophole contained a musket barrel. Now he was joined by his fellows. The verandah was full, and creaking. The first man banged at the front door. At this range a blind man could not miss.

'Fire,' Dick screamed. 'Change your weapons.'

The entire house shook. The crash of the explosions whanged around his ears, and he was surrounded in a seemingly solid cloud of powder smoke, turning his face and hands as black as his assailants. Yet even the noise of the explosions was drowned by the unearthly screams from outside.

'Present,' Dick bawled, the noise ringing in his ears. He left the door, and ran round the house. 'Present,' he bawled, slapping men on the shoulders to bring them back to their senses. 'Present.'

The fresh muskets went back through the loopholes. Cartarette and her aides were already gathering the used weapons, cramming ball down the barrels, thudding away with their rods, while her titian hair tumbled about her ears; it too was streaked with black powder.

Dick stooped by a loophole, gazed at a scene of destruction not even his experienced eyes could remember. Men lay dead and dying all over the verandah; blood ran into hollows and dripped under the rail. Those left were still standing, dazed, one or two already edging back.

'Fire,' Dick shouted again.

This time he stayed, looking through the aperture. Noise eddied about his head, accompanied by the endless smoke. He watched men collapse, men fall to their knees, men jump from the verandah and stagger down the hill. There were still hundreds of them, perhaps thousands, gathered at a safe distance from the house. And now was the dangerous moment, when all muskets were emptied, save for the few Cartarette and Suzanne had managed to reload. But the slaves were retreating. They had lost perhaps forty men in those two deadly volleys. But far more than

348

mere numbers, they knew that the next time they charged, the leading forty would die again.

He straightened, slowly. His men were withdrawing their muskets through the loopholes, staring at each other in delight. They had used the white man's weapons, and they had killed.

'Well done,' he said. 'Well done. Mr Boscawen, a ration of rum for every man.' He crossed the room, stood beside Cartarette, watched her work, ramming home ball after ball, priming musket after musket, face and hair and dress blackened with smoke, sweat dribbling down her temples, mouth flat with concentration.

She saw his boots, raised her head. 'Will they come again?'

'Not for a while. They'll have to regain their courage.'

He walked into the hall, unbolted the front door, threw it open. Some of the smoke found its way out, the atmosphere became lighter. He wondered if he would ever get his ceilings clean again.

He stepped outside, looked at the dead men. Soon they would smell, whenever the sun rose. Josh had told him that, on his first night here. How many eternities ago.

Someone moved. A hand came up, holding a cutlass. Dick levelled his pistol, squeezed the trigger. The man gave a little leap, and lay still again.

The noise brought Cartarette running through the hall, to check in the doorway in total horror.

'My God,' she said. 'My God.'

He put his arm round her shoulders, the pistol into his belt, took her back inside. Boscawen waited with a tray of rum. Dick took it from him, and the old man closed the door.

'Them boys done, Mr Richard,' he said.

'Aye.' Dick held a glass to Cartarette's lips, and she drank, and coughed, and drank some more.

Suzanne stood in the inner doorway. 'Are all battles like that?'

'All victories.'

'Listen.' Harris had been upstairs to oversee the blacks. 'They're leaving. Listen.'

They could hear the drumming of hooves. Boscawen was hastily withdrawing bolts again. Dick stepped outside, his arm still round Cartarette. Blood dribbled across the floor to wet their boots. 'Oh, God,' she said. 'I am going to vomit.'

He squeezed her against him, went down the steps. The black men were streaming into the fields, running as hard as they could.

And galloping up the road was a company of horse, accompanied by a score of white men.

'Barraclough?' he said. 'Hardy? I've almost a mind to forgive your sins.'

'When I forgive yours, Hilton,' Hardy said.

The colonel dismounted, peered at the corpses. 'My God. What happened here?'

The soldiers stared at the Negroes, who now came out of the house, muskets in their hands.

'Present,' Hardy screamed. 'Present.'

'Put them down,' Dick snapped. 'They fought for me.'

'You armed slaves?'

'I used what I had. And they fought well.'

'By God,' Hardy said. 'There's a confession, Colonel. A confession. Serve your warrant, man. Serve your warrant.'

'What madness is he spouting?' Dick demanded.

Barraclough shifted from foot to foot, gazed at Cartarette, then at Suzanne, standing on the verandah in the midst of the black men, then back at Dick again.

'Hardy's doing,' he muttered. 'He met me on the road. Brought me back here. But not to rescue you, Mr Hilton.' He unbuttoned his jacket, felt inside, pulled out the rolled parchment. 'There is a warrant for your arrest.'

18

The Day of Retribution

Dick could only gape at the officer, for the moment too taken aback to speak.

'For his arrest?' Cartarette cried. 'You must be out of your mind.'

'Count yourself grateful you are not included,' Hardy said.

'Why, you . . .' Dick reached for his pistol, and was halted by the sight of a score of musket barrels levelled at his chest.

'They won't take you, Dick,' Suzanne called from the verandah. 'We have thirty men in here, Colonel. All armed, and all experienced; they have just repulsed the rebels. Look at the verandah.'

Barraclough licked his lips. He had already looked at the verandah.

'Mr Hilton, I beg of you,' he said. 'Humour me, for the moment. Things are not going well, sir. You may have saved Hilltop, but at least a dozen plantations are in the hands of the insurgents. White people have been killed. More have been insulted. Kingston is in a ferment, and the whole island has been placed under martial law. The militia has been called out. If we exchange shots here, I would not like to say what will happen.'

'Show me the warrant,' Dick said.

Barraclough gave him the parchment, and he looked at the signature.

'John Tresling?'

'Countersigned by the Governor, Mr Hilton. It is legal.'

Dick glanced at the charge. It described him as an incendiary who had roused the blacks to revolt.

'You must know this is utter nonsense, Barraclough.'

'I know it, Mr Hilton, and so does the Governor.'

'Then why did he attest his signature?'

Barraclough sighed. 'Perhaps I would wish he could have shown more spirit, sir. The earl . . . well, his prime concern is the preservation of peace. All soldiers are needed on the plantations, Mr Hilton. Therefore Kingston must be defended by the militia. And the militia refused to mobilize unless all incendiaries are confined. Your name heads the list.'

Dick hesitated, still gazing at the paper.

'And who will guard my husband in the Kingston gaol?' Cartarette asked. 'This same militia?'

'He will be safe, Mrs Hilton. The Governor gives his word. But surrender, sir, and show that you have confidence at once in your own innocence and in our triumph. Those are the earl's own words, sir.'

Cartarette's fingers bit into his arm. 'Defy them, Dick. They'll not take you. They'll not move, if you say the word.'

'Aye,' he agreed. 'And then I would indeed be a revolutionary.'

'Dick, the mob will lynch you.' Her voice was urgent.

He smiled at her. 'I've survived worse than Kingston mobs,' he said. 'Belmore may not be the strongest of characters, but he is an honest man. And there are more lives than just mine at stake. But I leave the children, and indeed my defence, if it comes to that, in your care.'

Her tear-filled eyes were only inches from his face. 'I'll get you back, Dick,' she promised. 'I have grown to love this new man.'

He kissed her forehead. 'Then make it soon.' He released her. 'I'll ride with you, captain. But provide me with a horse.'

'You'll hand over your weapons,' Hardy demanded.

'It would be best, sir,' Barraclough agreed.

Dick nodded, gave the colonel his pistols.

'And you'll command your people to throw down their muskets,' Hardy said.

'And leave my plantation undefended?' Dick inquired.

'I will leave ten of my men here, sir, to see to your plantation,' Barraclough promised. 'I beg of you, sir. I cannot leave any black people with weapons in their hands.'

Dick hesitated, for the last time; but he knew the blacks would not return, and ten soldiers should be sufficient to protect *his* blacks from white revenge. 'So be it. Cartarette, tell Absolom to surrender those muskets.' He swung into the saddle. 'Thank them for me. Tell them that when I return from Kingston, it will be as I promised them.'

He could not look at the house any longer, but turned his horse and led the cavalcade down the drive. He could hear Barraclough giving the necessary orders, the banging of the shutters as they were opened. Sunlight would flood the Great House, and the dead would be buried.

And the plantation? The road led by the white town, and the factory, and the slave village. Piles of smouldering ash, from which the smoke rose to tickle his nostrils. The factory had done best, the great machinery, used to overwhelming heat, merely protruded through the collapsed roof. But he had retained his slaves. They came out of the fields, men, and women, and children, to stare at the destruction, at the soldiers, at their master. And not even all of the cane had burned. There were sufficient green fields to salvage part of a crop, supposing he was there to do it.

But of course he would be there to do it. He was Richard Hilton. He had survived too much in the past to be depressed by mere legal formalities now.

Except that he was tired. Suddenly. And it was not merely exhaustion from a sleepless night.

Hardy rode alongside him. 'You'll hang, Hilton. Oh, aye. Not even the Governor's support will save you now.'

Dick glanced at him, looked ahead again. They were beyond the smoke now, and the morning air was cool.

'You'd best get back to Orange Lodge, Mr Hardy,' Barraclough said. 'Those devils may come again.'

'Oh, aye,' Hardy agreed. 'I'll do that. Mr Hilton will be pleased to learn that the incendiary has been brought to book.' He spurred his horse and made off, his volunteers behind him.

' 'Tis a serious business,' Barraclough said, perhaps to himself. 'Oh, aye, a serious business. These people are frightened. There's naught so frightening as frightened people, when they also hold power.'

Dick ignored him as well. Had he made a mistake? But what else could he do? To have gained a brief victory over the soldiers at Hilltop would have made him an outlaw for ever. He could only hope to stay alive until sanity returned, until the Governor regained his nerve, until the Whigs found out what was happening here.

It was near noon when they entered Kingston, and then *his* nerve nearly failed. The streets were packed, but mostly with white people, who could ignore the martial law. The men carried arms, the women were outraged already, at least in their minds. They clustered round the cavalcade, shouting obscene threats and promises of revenge. Barraclough had to form his men in a moving wall around his prisoner, to protect him as far as the gates of the city gaol.

It was almost a relief to be inside the heated compound. When he gazed at the black faces of the inmates—there were no other white prisoners—he could almost feel himself back in the safety of Cap Haitien. And these did not jeer or threaten.

'You've a cell to yourself,' grunted Owens the gaoler. 'Comfortable, you'll be, Mr Hilton. And no lynching in this gaol.'

He was walking a fence, a government official, but a white man.

'Send for Reynolds,' Dick said.

Owens nodded. 'I've done that, Mr Hilton. He'll be here directly.'

Dick stepped inside, listened to the door clang behind him. The cell was on the top floor. There was a single barred window, high in the wall, but by standing on tiptoe he could reach it. He could not look down sufficiently to see the beach, but he could see the pale green water, and then the ships at anchor. This had been his first glimpse of Jamaica. Why, he could make out the *Green Knight*, riding to her mooring.

He sighed, and inspected the rest of the small room, tried the trestle bed, hastily returned the lid to the slop bucket. The best cell in the prison. He had been in pleasanter stables.

Feet, on the corridor. Owens unlocked the door, And Reynolds stepped inside.

'Mr Hilton. A grim business. Oh, a grim business.'

'Aye. And not one I'll stomach for long, Reynolds. You'll file a writ of habeas corpus and have me out of here.'

Reynolds frowned at him. 'Your own lawyers . . .'

'Are coloured and will not have so speedy a service. You asked for reinstatement. Hilltop's business is enough for all.'

Reynolds sat down on the bed. 'It will not be easy. Kingston, Jamaica, has been placed under martial law. Habeas corpus has

354

been suspended.'

'Then get me an interview with Belmore.'

'Ah, well, that will not be an easy matter.'

'You seem once again unsure whose side you are on,' Dick remarked, mildly.

'Ah, well, 'tis not that, Mr Hilton. Oh, indeed not. But it is a serious matter.'

'A trumped-up charge of incendiarism, which no court would admit for a moment?'

Reynolds shook his head. 'The matter is more grave than that, sir. Think of it. This island is being threatened by a slave revolt. Rumour has it there are twenty thousand blacks under arms. Troops have been sent for from the Leewards, and the Navy has also been summoned from English Harbour. Now, sir, is that not a clear parallel with events in Haiti, but forty years ago? And have you not recently returned from Haiti, having served one of the leaders of that original revolt faithfully and well for sixteen years?'

'Of all the rubbish . . .'

'None the less, sir, they are saying you came to Jamaica to do nothing less than incite a similar revolution here, with a view to making yourself dictator. Then there is the fact of your secret meeting with the Reverend Strong. Strong has already been arrested and brought to justice, I understand.'

'He was murdered, you mean.'

'Aye, well, justice is the word they use in Kingston. But the important fact from your point of view is that there is possible evidence of conspiracy. And then, the revolt happened on the day you regained your plantation, and thus obtained a position of authority. Was that not a signal?'

'By God, Reynolds . . .'

'Not my opinion, sir. I am but quoting. And then, finally, you successfully defended your plantation. Every other plantation attacked by the blacks has fallen or been evacuated.'

'I *defended* it, Reynolds. More than forty were killed.'

'Oh, indeed, sir. I have no doubt of that. But there it is. Why . . .' He sighed. 'The situation is grave, sir. Grave. They are saying it is a hanging matter.'

Feet, along the corridor. Dick raised his head. Woman's feet. He leapt up, hastily tugged his shirt straight, ran his fingers into his hair.

And frowned through the bars. 'Judith? How on earth . . .'

Judith Gale waited while the key turned in the lock.

'Half an hour,' Owens said, and left.

Judith remained standing by the door. 'You do not look pleased to see me.'

'I am pleased to see anyone,' Dick confessed. 'But I had hoped for Cartarette.'

'She has been refused permission to visit you.'

'My own wife? But you . . .'

'I bribed Owens. He is a lecherous man.'

Dick sat down again. 'My God.'

'You would not have your wife stoop so low, I trust.' She sat beside him on the bed.

'She knows you are here?'

'Of course. When I left Orange Lodge, I visited Hilltop, to see if I could be of assistance.'

'When you left Orange Lodge? Forgive me, but my brain seems to spin.'

Judith flushed. 'I would have given evidence for you, Dick. I would have helped you. But to oppose Tony, perhaps it takes more courage than I possess. Than I possessed, then. But when I heard what had happened, I ran away. To Hilltop, and thence to town.'

'He'll not forgive you.'

'No. Thus I will need your protection, after all.'

'My protection?' His laugh was bitter. 'Locked away in here, day after day, week after week. Do you know I have been here a month? Seeing no one. I have asked for Reynolds, and he has not come. I have asked for Harris, and he has not come.'

'Harris and Barker are under arrest. They are in this very building.'

'Under arrest?'

'For carrying arms. It is forbidden for any person of colour. They were lucky they were not hanged on the spot. Over four hundred of the blacks have been hanged.'

Dick nodded. 'I have heard the drumroll. The revolt is over then? I saw the ships arriving, with fresh troops.'

'Oh, that revolt is over, certainly. Not that people will forgive, for a long time.'

'But it is over,' Dick insisted. 'Thus must I be freed or brought to trial. Belmore. I have asked to see Belmore, and he has not come.'

'Very simply because he is no longer here. He resigned his post and left, oh, a fortnight back.'

'Resigned? My God. But who commands the island?'

'The general, Sir Willoughby Cotton. He came from Antigua. The entire colony remains under martial law, pending the arrival of a new Governor. That at least accounts for your survival. Cotton will not permit the planters to try you, and they will not force matters to a head until they discover the political complexion of the new Governor.'

'Cotton,' Dick said. 'Well, then, I must see Cotton.'

'I doubt he will accommodate you.'

'Why not? You say he holds the entire island under military discipline? Surely he cannot be afraid of the planters?'

Judith sighed. 'Perhaps not afraid. Yet does he also tread a tightrope, Dick. He still lacks the men properly to police the entire island. So he relies upon the volunteers for assistance, and they are either planters, or in their pay. Thus he must shut his eyes to their depredations.'

'Depredations? Your tale grows more and more unhappy. What depredations?'

'Well, you see, they claim the entire revolt was inspired by the Baptists and the other missionaries, and was, quite apart from being directed against white people and against slavery, also directed against the overthrow of the Colonial Church. This is how they have succeeded in securing so much support from the more moderate elements in the island, and how, indeed, they hope to obtain eventual support from England. Yet are they impatient for the day of retribution, as they call it. There is a band of them, calling themselves the Colonial Church Union, which rides abroad after dark, their faces masked, burning Baptist or Nonconformist chapels, lynching any man of colour who would oppose them, or who they find at large. It is a fact no decent person will venture out after dark.'

'Cotton condones this?'

She shrugged. 'There is nothing he can do about it. He does not himself know whether or not the Union will eventually find favour in London.'

Dick got up, paced the cell. 'God, to be trapped in here . . . who leads this Union?'

'No one knows. They are masked, as I said.'

'Tony?'

'I do not know, Dick. I personally have not seen them, thank God.'

He smashed his right fist into his left palm. 'But if they ride abroad, what of Hilltop?'

'You have naught to fear there. A platoon of soldiers is maintained on the plantation.' She seized his hand as he passed her. 'That indeed was the main purpose of my visit. Your wife sends her love. So does your mother. Your cause is being fought to the limit of their ability.'

'And my children?'

'Are well. And safe with their mother. Even the plantation prospers. Your mother has recalled her youth, on Hilltop itself, and manages the place for you. Cane is being replanted, buildings are being repaired. You really have nothing to worry about, on that score.'

'On that score.' His shoulders slumped, and he sat down again. 'To be trapped in here . . . and now you have prostituted yourself for me . . .'

'I would do so again. Anyway, all he wanted was to get his hand inside my bodice. He is a simple fellow. Dick . . .' She squeezed his fingers. 'I will come again.'

'Not at that price.'

'But . . .'

He held her close. 'Dear Judith. I am in your debt too far as it is. But for that day, you would not be in this position.'

'But *I* caused that day, Dick.' She raised her head to look at him. 'Therefore it is I who owe you.'

'You will make a good lawyer.' He smiled, kissed her again, listened to Owens' boots on the stone floor. 'Take care.'

She got up. 'I will do that.'

'And come again, only if there is bad news. Promise me.'

She hesitated, then nodded. 'Or when the final good news, of your release, is received. Keep courage, Dick. It will not be long.'

Keep courage. It will not be long. Dick reminded himself that his great ancestor, Christopher Hilton, had once been confined in gaol in Antigua for upwards of a year, on a charge of murder. And had survived. But Kit Hilton had been a figure of legend, even while he lived.

Then was not Richard Hilton, alias Matthew Warner, a figure of legend? It was all the hope he could cling to. The man who had charged at the head of Christophe's dragoons surely could not just be left to dwindle in a Jamaican cell.

And then he remembered that Toussaint l'Ouverture, the man who had led Haiti to independence, had been left to dwindle in a French cell, until he had died, of heartbreak not less than neglect.

He saw no one, save Owens, and the Welshman was not communicative. He was given half an hour's exercise every day, but alone, in the yard. He could look up at the other cells, and see faces, looking down at him. He could identify Harris, and Barker, but he could not speak with them. And presumably they were as much in the dark as regards the true situation as he.

He could look out of his cell window, at the ships, coming and going. They were not easy to identify at this distance. There were trading vessels, from England, and leaving again, for England. There were men-of-war, bringing additional troops. And there was the *Green Knight*, back again. He could recognize her all right. It was only her return gave him an idea of how much time had passed, how many weeks, how many months, he had been locked away in here.

Cartarette sent him some books, but he was not in the mood for reading. He separated each leaf, looking for the message she would also certainly have sent. But someone else had separated the leaves before him; there were dirty finger marks and several of the pages were torn. And Cartarette's message whatever it was, had been removed and destroyed.

Every day he demanded from Owens the right to see his lawyer, and every day he was refused. He had no need of lawyers, Owens said, until he had been charged. 'Well, then, charge me,' he shouted.

'That's up to the authorities,' Owens pointed out.

'I have got to be charged,' Dick insisted, keeping his temper with difficulty. 'Or released. That is English law.'

And Owens smiled. 'But Jamaica is under *martial* law, Mr Hilton. I don't see what you're grumbling at. The longer the delay, the more chance for people to forget their anger at you.'

'Their anger at me?' Dick demanded in amazement.

'Incendiary,' Owens grumbled, and took his leave.

His only straw of hope was the non-return of Judith. Oh, how he longed to see Judith. As the weeks became months he longed to see her almost as much as he longed to see Cartarette, almost as much as he longed to have a hot bath and a decent shave; he was allowed the use of a blunt razor but twice a week, and then under supervision. As if Richard Hilton would ever contemplate suicide, unless driven mad.

But perhaps that was their intention. They did not know of his arrangement with Judith, his arrangement for sanity.

The rain started, in early summer. By then it was so hot in his cell he stripped to his breeches, and lay on his bed, and thought of Cartarette, of riding with her around Hilltop, of sleeping with her in the enormous fourposter, of hearing her laugh and stroking her hair. Of knowing she was there.

Owens' boots, on the stone. He sat up. He had breakfasted some time before.

The key turned in the lock, Owens stepped inside, closed the door again, handed the key to the Negro sub-warder, waiting in the corridor. 'Rain,' he said. 'I like to hear the rain, pattering on the roof. This cell is the best for that. Nearest to heaven, you could say.'

'Is this a social call?' Dick inquired.

'You could say that. Oh, aye. A social call.'

Dick leaned against the wall; the stone was cool, and no doubt Owens would get around to whatever he wanted to say in his own good time.

'It won't be long now, Mr Hilton,' Owens said. 'Do you know, there hasn't been a hanging in a week? All those that need it are dead. Oh, they're licked. They'll not revolt again, not in a hundred years. Oh, we taught them a lesson, we did.'

'I'm sure you did,' Dick agreed.

Owens inspected his fingernails. 'They'll be getting around to people like you soon enough, now.'

'I can hardly wait.'

'You should be happy to wait, Mr Hilton. The planters aren't in a forgiving mood. Oh, no. They'll get to you. They'll get to them all. They'll get even to those they can't put in a court. Oh, yes.'

Dick sat up again.

'What did you say?'

'I said . . . aye?'

For Dick had seized his shirt front. 'What? Who have they got to, that they can't put into court? My wife?'

'No. Now look here, Mr Hilton, you let me go. I'll have you put in solitary, I will.'

'Oh, you're a humorist, Owens,' Dick said.

'Bread and water.'

'Funnier and funnier. You won't be doing anything with a broken neck, and they *will* have cause to hang me. Who, God damn it?'

Owens licked his lips. 'That little bit of yours.'

'Judith? My God, Judith? What happened to her?'

'Took her out, they did. From her own house.'

'Took her out? Who took her out?'

'Why . . . it was the Union, most people say. Who's to know? When those fellows ride abroad people keep their curtains drawn.'

'Oh, my God. Where is Judith?'

'Well, I wouldn't know. People living down King Street say they heard her screaming and fighting. But it weren't no good, against half a dozen men.'

'Half a dozen men? Where was the military?'

'Well, Mr Hilton, the military have enough fighting to do with the blacks. They ain't anxious to start fighting the whites as well. Not when those same whites pay their wages. You letting me go, or I'm shouting for help?'

Dick let him go. Throttling Owens would hardly help either Judith or himself. And he had been congratulating himself because she hadn't come.

Owens stood up, dusted himself off. 'Thought you'd like to know, Mr Hilton. Thought you'd like to know. Boy,' He bawled. 'Come let me out.'

'Owens,' Dick said. 'If you want to avoid being throttled when I am finally released from here, find out what happened to Judith Gale. Find out where she is now. And find out who was responsible. Names, Owens. I wish names.'

The Negro was at the door, and it was swinging in. Owens got on the far side, closed it, and turned the key. Then he smiled at Dick.

'Thought you'd like to know, Mr Hilton. As for finding out, well, it ain't altogether safe to go asking questions about the

Union. But the word is they gave her something to be remembered by. They cut a T on each cheek. T, Mr Hilton, for traitor, you know.'

How he sweated, at the thought of it. Judith Gale. She was perhaps the most beautiful woman he had ever known, and the most tragic. Her tragedy had been being born the daughter of a woman like Harriet. Of being involved with people like the Hiltons. Of knowing him at his worst, instead of at his best.

He tossed on his narrow bed, and dreamed, and heard her laughter, and then with it, her scream of fear. He had never heard Judith Gale scream with fear, in the flesh. But she would have screamed, when exposed to the nightriders of the Union.

And then he heard her feet, in the corridor, crisp, short steps, her heels striking the stone, multiplying as they approached. Closer and closer, they came, Judith Gale, returning to avenge herself on the man responsible for her misery.

He found himself awake, and staring at the ceiling of his cell. And still the feet came. It was only just past dawn. He sat up, turning to look at the cell door, to listen to the scrape of the key in the lock. He stood up, his back against the wall, still uncertain that he was not dreaming, watched the door swing in, gazed at Cartarette.

For a moment he could not speak. The Negro gaoler stood at her shoulder; Owens was not there.

'Mr Hilton?' She spoke hardly more than a whisper. 'Mr Hilton?' She crossed the cell. 'Dick? My God, what have they done to you?'

It was, after all, no dream. He could inhale her scent, he could touch her, if he dared move. His fingers closed on her arms, slipped up them to her shoulders, held her face to kiss her lips.

'Cartarette. Cartarette. They have let you see me?'

'You are free, Dick. Free.' She clung to him for a moment then stepped back. 'Free.'

'Free?' he repeated stupidly. 'But . . .'

'A ship arrived yesterday, dearest Dick,' she said. 'Bringing a new Governor, the Earl of Mulgrave.'

'Harry Phipps? I had supposed him too old for such a post.'

'Sir Henry Phipps died last year,' Cartarette said. 'This is his son, Constantine. A young man, Dick, not yet thirty-five. A man

362

of vigour. A man of the Whigs. Dick.' She clung to his arm again. 'A Bill is being prepared, to emancipate the slaves. It will be law by this time next year.'

'But . . . will they accept such a thing, here?'

'They must. The Colonial Church Union has been outlawed. All surviving insurgents are to be amnestied. And Richard Hilton of Hilltop is to be set free. The Governor himself waits to see you, Dick. But he gave me the privilege of taking you from this place.'

'Free.' He allowed himself to be pulled towards the door. He listened to his own feet on the stone of the corridor. He stood on the top step and gazed at the empty exercise yard, still bathed in shadow, as the sun had not risen far enough to reach it, and at the rows of windows which surrounded it. And seized her arm once more. 'Harris? Barker?'

'They too will be free this day. But the Governor wishes the prisoners released one by one. He will have no more cause for riot.'

He went down the steps, Cartarette holding his arm, crossed the yard, found Owens himself waiting at the main gate.

'Ah, a happy day, Mr Hilton. A happy day.'

Dick gazed at him, and the warder flushed.

'You'll understand much of what I said was jest, Mr Hilton. What? I tried to keep up your spirits, nothing less, sir.'

'Oh, aye,' Dick said. 'You did that. Cartarette. Where is Judith Gale?'

Some of the pleasure left her face. 'At Hilltop.'

'Hilltop? But . . .'

'I could do no less, Dick. She is half out of her mind with fear and shame. I can only pray your release will give her some peace.'

'You are a treasure, Cartarette. You know the truth, of her and me?'

She glanced at him. 'She is a wreck, Dick. I could forgive her anything. I have forgiven her everything. Mama,' she shouted, dragging him across the street to where the phaeton waited. 'Here he is.'

Dick hesitated, glancing from left to right. But at this hour in the morning the street was empty. The Earl of Mulgrave was obviously at once a thoughtful and intelligent man. And there was Suzanne, waiting to take his hands, to hold him close.

'Dick. Oh, Dick. I never doubted. But the news . . . Cartarette has told you the news?'

'She has.'

'It is the seal on your father's life. I must get back to him.' She smiled, as archly as ever in her youth. 'After I have shown you what we have done for Hilltop.'

'Then let's be out there.'

'The Governor . . .'

'Can wait. I'll see him after I have avenged Judith Gale.'

Cartarette picked up the reins, flicked them over the horse's back. The equipage moved down the street. 'No one knows who they were.'

'Judith must.'

'I doubt even she does. It is said they never speak a word on their midnight rides. What they must do is all planned beforehand, every man knowing exactly his task. This silence is part of the terror they spread amongst the blacks.'

'And now the Union is disbanded, will none of them ever be brought to justice?'

'I doubt that, Dick,' Suzanne said. 'Mulgrave's duty is to prepare Jamaica for Emancipation, certainly. But yet must the island remain British, and thus be ruled by white men. He has also to heal old wounds, maintain the peace, restore the island's prosperity. He is hoping you will play your part in that.'

'I mean to. But I also mean to track down the men who destroyed Judith. You must see that, Cartarette.'

She leaned across to squeeze his arm. 'I had expected nothing less. I imagine even the Governor expects nothing less. But it cannot cloud your entire life. You have Hilltop to manage, you have your children to father, you have your slaves to free, and you have me to husband. You have spent all but twenty years in constant conflict. Promise me you will learn to live a little, in the last half of your life.'

He looked down at her, and then across at Suzanne, smiling at him.

'You must forgive me,' he said. 'I am a fool. No doubt my brain supposes itself still in that cell. Freedom is not a commodity one thinks about until it has been taken away.' He squeezed both their hands. 'I shall be a happy husband, a happy son, a happy father, I swear it.' The phaeton was already leaving the town behind, and beginning its climb into the mountains. 'How could a man be less than happy,' he shouted. 'In Jamaica.'

So, once again, that so well remembered road. The last time the three of them had ridden here had been in the dawn, with conch shells whistling, with the certainty of death and destruction awaiting them. And the unknown beyond that.

Now that was in the past. There was so much to be done. There was Judith to be avenged. There was the problem of Emancipation to be faced. There would be an inevitable drop in the plantation profits. The great days of the plantocracy, of buying and selling men, politicians not less than slaves, were finished. But that had been a shadowy, unreal world. The future remained there for the taking, without a troubled conscience, without a constant look over the shoulder, without a constant apprehension of the morrow.

And Father would die happy. His life had hardly contained less turmoil, and he had had to wait much longer to achieve his final triumph. He smiled at his mother, and then leaned back, watched Cartarette's firm hands on the rein as she guided the horse up the steep incline, allowed it to find its own way down into the damp, tree-shrouded valleys, and sat bolt upright as without warning she dragged on the brake, almost rising to her feet with the effort.

The horse pulled to a stop. They were down in a valley, trees to either side obscuring the hills which rose around them, isolated them from the rest of the world. And one of the trees had come down, immediately across the road.

'That's strange,' Suzanne remarked. 'It was not there when we came in yesterday.'

'And there was no wind, last night.' Cartarette climbed down, and Dick followed her. 'Can you move it?'

'I think so.' He parted the branches, bent to lift the trunk, and checked. There was no torn stalk here, but a clean severance.

He turned, heard Cartarette's breath whistle as she too looked round. For the little valley was filled with horsemen, six to either side of the phaeton, walking their horses from the trees. They wore black capes and flat black hats, and black domino masks. And every one carried a pistol.

'Oh, my God,' Cartarette whispered.

Dick stepped in front of her. 'Well, gentlemen,' he said, 'I have long looked forward to making your acquaintance.' For only confidence would pay here. And strangely,he felt no fear at all. Only a bubbling, angry exhilaration.

The horsemen came closer. They ignored the phaeton, Suzanne sitting rigid inside it, her face pale; on a sudden she looked even older than her seventy years.

'What, gentlemen, dumb? And perhaps deaf, as well,' Dick said. 'The law wishes to see you. The law will see you, gentlemen. You had best beware it does not hang you all.' He felt Cartarette's fingers on his arm. She at the least had no doubts of their danger.

'The law,' said one of the mounted men. He spoke in a hoarse whisper to disguise his voice, and certainly Dick did not recognize it. 'We are the law here, Richard Hilton. Those milksops in England may have chosen to release you, but we know you for what you are. And you will pay for it.'

Think, Dick told himself. Think. You will not make them angry. Can you bluff them into supposing there are mounted men behind you? But they would have overseen their approach. And there was no sound in this valley.

He watched ten of the men dismount. The other two remained in their saddles, their pistols pointing at him.

'Richard Hilton,' said the spokesman, one of the two still mounted. 'You are accused of inspiring all the ills that have overtaken this unhappy country, this past twenty years. You are accused of fomenting rebellion amongst the slaves, of serving the black savages of Haiti, of sowing dissension amongst the plantocracy. You have been tried by this court, in respect of these crimes, and have been found guilty. Have you anything to say before sentence is passed?'

The dismounted men stood close around him. Ten of them. No doubt he could survive an encounter with most of them, as they had holstered their pistols. But what of Cartarette, standing at his shoulder, scarce breathing? And what of Mama?

'Then so be it,' said the mounted man. 'Richard Hilton, you are condemned to death, the sentence to be carried out immediately.'

Before he could move, two of the men had seized his arms, throwing Cartarette to one side, and a third was binding his wrists together behind his back, leaving him helpless.

'No,' Cartarette screamed, running forward. 'No.'

One of the men caught her round the waist.

'Your turn is also here, Cartarette Hilton,' said the mounted man. 'You are accused of aiding and abetting the condemned man in all the crimes of which he is guilty. Therefore you are as guilty as he. Therefore will you suffer the same fate.'

Cartarette's arms had already been seized, and now they also were bound. Her hat was knocked off, to allow her hair slowly to cloud about her shoulders. She stared at the mounted men in total disbelief.

Two other of the men were taking ropes from their saddle horns.

'You are mad,' Dick said. 'Do you think you will get away with such a crime?'

'We will defend ourselves, if we need to, Richard Hilton,' said the mounted man.

'Then defend yourselves now,' Dick shouted. 'Like men, instead of animals. Give me a sword, a pistol, and take your places in front of me.'

'Condemned felons have no rights,' said the mounted man. 'We would not demean ourselves. And that you may better appreciate the depths of your iniquity, the consequences of your insensate folly, this court decrees that your wife shall die first. Now.'

Cartarette turned her head to look at Dick, her mouth faintly open. He thought for a moment she might faint, with sheer horror. For the first rope was already being looped over the tree, and now she was pulled back towards it.

'What?' asked the horseman. 'No words of farewell?'

'Dick,' Cartarette begged. 'Help me.'

The cords ate into his wrists. His brain seemed to be consumed with fire. But there was nothing he could do. Nothing he could say, save to utter futile threats of vengeance, and he was all through uttering threats. But allow him to be free, he thought, for one moment. He'd need no weapons. Not now.

The rope was looped around her neck. Her hair trailed on her shoulders, a blaze of colour against the brown and green of the tree, against the black of the cape of the man holding her. Cartarette Hilton. How much had she suffered for him.

'Hold.'

The voice was old, and quavered. And yet cut the morning like a lightning shaft.

Their heads turned, to look at the phaeton, and Suzanne Hilton, leaning slightly forward, a pistol in her hand.

'Release her,' Suzanne said. Her left hand also came up, and it too held a pistol.

The men stared at her in amazement. Then the mounted man gave a brief laugh. 'What, afraid of an old woman scarce able to stand? Beware, old lady, that we do not hoist you beside your son.'

'Drop your weapon,' Suzanne said. 'Or I will blow the teeth from your grinning mouth.' She spoke in an absolutely even tone.

'Why, you . . .'

'She'll do it, you fool,' shouted one of the men on the ground, and Dick's head jerked again.

'Tony?'

'Tony,' Suzanne said, with bitter satisfaction. 'As I supposed. I will do it, John Tresling. It will be a pleasure.'

Still Tresling hesitated, then made a convulsive movement with his right hand.

The explosion of Suzanne's pistol crashed through the valley. The powder smoke rose around her, but her face could still be seen, and the quick movement as she transferred the loaded second pistol to her right hand. But by now they were looking at Tresling, his mask destroyed along with his face, slowly turning as he fell forward, rested for a moment on the horse's neck, and then struck the ground with a thud.

'Pistol shooting,' Suzanne remarked with satisfaction, 'was for many years my favourite sport. Who will be next, you, Ellen?'

'Oh, my God.' Ellen Hilton ran forward, tearing off her mask as she did so, allowing her chestnut hair to float, pausing above Tresling. 'He is dead.'

The other mounted man threw down his weapon.

'How did you know us?' Tony's face was pale.

'I suspected for some time,' Suzanne said. 'And just now I identified one of you as a woman. That made it easy. If not acceptable. You are lower than the gutter to which you belong.'

Ellen continued to stare at the dead man.

'Release my daughter-in-law,' Suzanne said. 'And my son.'

Fingers tore at the ropes holding Dick's wrists. He stooped, picked up Tresling's pistol. Cartarette was also freed. She gained a weapon, turned to face her erstwhile captors. She breathed deeply, and her cheeks were pink, but her face was composed.

'Your prisoners, Dick,' Suzanne said.

'Aye,' Dick said. 'Well, Ellen, Tony, your night riding is over.

Was it you, Tony, who savaged Judith?'

Tony hesitated, glancing at his companions. 'It was us.'

'Your own woman,' Dick said. 'I will see you hang.'

'No,' Suzanne said. 'Not a Hilton, Dick.'

'You'd have him crawl away?'

'No,' she said again. 'I find it hard to believe you are my son, Tony. I find it hard to accept that, but for my interference, in sending you with Dick, this could not have happened. You deserve to die. I would shoot you myself, had I the strength.' Her voice was brittle, at last. 'You'll leave Jamaica, tomorrow. Take that . . . that creature with you.'

'No,' Dick said. 'He would have hanged Cartarette. I'll not let him go, mother. I swear it, I will not let him go.'

'You cannot shoot him down in cold blood, Dick. That would be to lower yourself to his level.'

'Aye,' Dick agreed. 'Then give him a pistol. Cartarette, give him yours.'

Tony Hilton smiled. 'Aye,' he said. 'You'll die like the hero you are, little brother.'

Cartarette glanced from one to the other.

And Suzanne sighed. 'Give him a pistol, Cartarette. I suppose this could end no other way.'

Cartarette took a weapon from one of the saddle holsters, then slowly approached Tony, held it out. He snatched at it, brought it up. Dick watched his hand moving, levelling. How strange he felt. How long had he admired this man's skill, with people no less than with weapons. How long had he feared this man's anger.

And how detached he felt at this moment. Ellen had said her husband lacked determination. What then did he see in that handsome face?

'Dick,' Cartarette screamed, as she saw him accept the shot.

But Tony had already fired, and was staring at his brother in horror, as he realized he had missed.

'Too much haste, Tony,' Dick said. 'Too much haste.'

Tony licked his lips. His gaze seemed attached to the pistol in Dick's hand, as if connected by a string. The sounds of the shot slowly faded away, and the morning was silent, save for the restless movements of the horses.

Tony attempted a smile. 'What, little brother? No stomach for a murder?

Dick gazed at him. Who was, after all, *the* Hilton? They had fought in the past, viciously, with every means at their disposal, to gain, and to hold. Tony had done no less, up to this very morning. So, then, at the end, it was Richard Hilton who was the changeling.

He lowered his weapon. 'Take your woman, and go. Take these gutter rats with you.'

There was a moment's silence. Then Ellen swung round, her hand outflung. 'Now, now, now, Jim!'

Hardy's hand came out from beneath his cloak, a pistol in each. The first was levelled and exploded before anyone could even draw breath. Tony Hilton threw up his arms and fell over backwards without a sound, shot through the chest. Cartarette and Suzanne fired together, but Hardy had already leapt behind a tree, and from there returned his fire, at Dick. Dick was turning and dropping to one knee and also firing. His bullet smashed into the tree trunk.

The noise, the explosions, crashed through the morning. The glade became a smoke-filled hole, and a death-filled hole as well. Hardy darted away from the shelter and ran up the hill, while Dick hastily sought another pistol.

'Oh, my God,' Suzanne said, and half fell from the phaeton. 'Oh, my God.'

She knelt beside her son. Cartarette hastily secured two more pistols from the horses, but the rest of the Union was too shocked to move, just stood, gaping at their dying leader.

Who stared at his wife. 'Ellen?' he whispered. 'Ellen?'

Her lip curled. 'You never were much of a man, Tony Hilton. You could try to die like one.'

'But . . . you, and James? What you hinted was true?'

'Why else should I stay?' she asked. 'To listen to your vapourings? I stayed because James wished it. He wished to see both you and your brother into the grave. He wished to cuckold you to his heart's content.'

'James?' Tony whispered. 'But . . . he was my friend.'

'He hated you,' Ellen said. 'He hated the very name of Hilton. He made your plantation prosperous, while he brooded on how to destroy you, both. And in me he found his weapon. And he has destroyed you, Tony. He will destroy Dick as well. He has sworn it. And I will help him.'

Dick stood at her shoulder, looked down at his brother. Tony's mouth opened and closed, but he could no longer speak.

'But why?' Dick asked. 'We gave him a home, position, money. Tony at the least certainly befriended him.'

'Oh, aye,' she said. 'As your father hanged his father.'

He frowned at her. Suzanne slowly lifted her head. 'James Hardy is Hodge's son?'

'Oh, aye,' she said. 'Do you not find it amusing, dear Mama, that the son of the man your husband murdered should have been the real ruler of Hilltop these past sixteen years? Oh, he enjoyed that. He enjoyed knowing that he could step aside, whenever he chose, and watch all the Hilton wealth, the Hilton power, crumble into dust. He was considering doing just that, when Dick reappeared. Then he could sit back and watch the pair of them destroy each other. There was amusement, Mama. Oh, how we laughed. Hiltons.'

'You foul thing,' Suzanne said, slowly rising from beside her dead son. 'You . . .'

But Dick no longer heard her. He leapt into the saddle of Tresling's horse, kicked its flanks, sent it bursting through the trees. Hardy—or Hodge—could not be far. And the trees were hardly more than a fringe. In a matter of moments he emerged beyond them, once again on the road leading up into the hills. Behind him he heard more hooves. But this was his business. Perhaps in his heart he had always known it would be his business, in the end.

And there in front of him was the little figure, crawling into the mountains. Running for his life. As if any man could escape the anger of Richard Hilton, of Matthew Warner, Christophe's cavalry commander.

He set his horse at the slope, and it scrambled up. Hardy paused to look back, and his face cleared as he realized he was pursued by only one man. He stopped, and panted, waiting for his breath to settle. He once again reached beneath his cloak, whipped out a machete.

'Both,' he said. 'Both.'

Dick reined, dismounted. Here was what he had wanted to do, for all those weeks in prison. To fight. To hurt. To kill.

Hardy grinned. 'Both,' he said again, and thrust the knife forward. And then frowned, as Dick merely continued walking

371

towards him. 'Are you mad?'

Dick was now within five feet. Hardy sucked air into his lungs, rose on the balls of his feet, thrust, with sudden desperate energy. The hillside became a sandpit, the morning became hot and still, and Hodge's face became that of a black man. Only the knife was constant. The knife, and the surging angry exhilaration.

Dick swayed to one side, and the knife scraped through his coat, slicing his flesh as well to bring a sharp thrill of pain. His left hand descended to seize the wrist before it could withdraw, his iron fingers eating into the flesh. Hodge gave a gasp of pain and attempted to bring up his knee, but Dick's fist had already closed and was smashing into the unprotected jaw. Hardy's head jerked and he fell backwards, and the knife slipped from his fingers. Dick released his wrist and hit him again before he could fall, then stooped to twine his fingers in the cape, bring the man back to his feet, and hit him twice more.

Hardy lay on the stony ground, scarce breathing. Dick stooped once more, wrapped his fingers around the sallow, beard-stubbled throat, lifting the inert body from the ground as he squeezed.

'Dick,' Cartarette said.

He hesitated, his fingers still tight.

'Your mother waits alone, holding ten villains at gunpoint,' Cartarette said. 'Besides, there is a law, for such as he. For such as the woman. I would have you, us, done with killing.'

The slaves filed slowly down the hill, away from Hilltop, back to their village. They chattered amongst themselves as they walked. Perhaps they thought themselves dreaming.

Certainly Boscawen thought himself dreaming. He approached Richard Hilton, slowly, uncertainly.

'Man, Mr Dick, sir,' he said. 'Is true what you told them people? That they going to be free?'

'True,' Dick said. 'You as well, old man.'

Boscawen stared at him for some moments. Then he slowly took off his wig to scratch his head. 'Ayayayay,' he remarked, and went towards his pantry.

Dick turned back to look at his plantation. He had worked hard these six months; so had his slaves, for the last time as slaves. The cane was growing again, the town and the village had been rebuilt, the factory re-roofed. Hilltop looked as it had always looked in the past; it was impossible to suppose that a year ago several thousand men had charged up this hill, shouting for blood, and that each one of those loopholes behind him had belched death and destruction. Impossible to believe. That was as it should be.

Judith waited in the doorway, veiled, as always now.

'Cartarette wishes me to stay.'

'So do I.'

She walked to the verandah rail, looked at the plantation. 'I loved Tony, Dick. Do you know that?'

'I suspected it.'

'Even when he was cutting me, I loved him.' She turned. 'Only him.'

'I understand that.'

'But the only happiness I ever knew, was here.'

'Then you'll stay,' he said. 'And be our friend.'

He went inside, climbed the stairs. Suzanne had her trunk in the middle of the floor, was packing, helped and hindered by her grandchildren. Cartarette sat on the bed. 'There was no noise.'

'They listened, in silence, and then went back to their homes, in silence. I suppose they do not really believe it. I cannot really believe it myself.'

He sat beside his wife. 'Must you go in such haste, Mama?'

Suzanne pushed herself to her feet, a grandchild's hand in each of hers, smiled at them. 'Of course. Matt is waiting for me. And besides I can do no more here. I would be nothing more than a nuisance. Just be sure, when I decide to visit you again, Hilltop is ready for me.'

'Hilltop will be ready, Mama,' Cartarette said. 'Hilltop will stand forever, and be Hilton, forever.'